Sister Suffragists

Sister Suffragists

·A NOVEL·
BY
Susan N. Swann

New Voices
BOOKS

New Voices Books

Sister Suffragists is a work of fiction. All incidents and dialogue, and all characters with the exception of historical figures, come from the author's imagination. In all other respects, any resemblance to any actual persons, living or dead, businesses, companies, events, or locales is entirely coincidental. A list of historical figures may be found at the back of this book.

Published by New Voices Books

ISBN: 978-0-9848645-3-9 (paperback)
ISBN: 978-0-9848645-4-6 (ebook)

New Voices Books
Copyright @ 2020 by Susan N. Swann
Cover design by Dana Tolbert
Interior design by Will Robertson

Printed in the United States of America

To my great-grandmother
Louisa L. Haight,
a woman of faith and courage.

In the early, heady days when we won the right to suffrage and expanded our domain as women, we could not foresee how our lives would change as those liberties were stripped from us.

Sister Suffragists

Part One

"The best protection any woman can have is…courage"

Elizabeth Cady Stanton, National Suffragist

One

Katie
1870

I often dreamt of my little brother Adam lying dead beneath sweat-soaked sheets. This time he raised a hand and looked at me, a sense of sadness in his milky white eyes. I awoke with a start, a chill running up my spine, cold frost blanketing the window. I went to the sink in my room and splashed cold water on my face to dispel the images.

Moving to the large brown wardrobe in the corner, I put on a plain gingham dress and walked downstairs to the kitchen. I removed a hard-boiled egg from the ice box and paired it with a generous slice of cornbread, eating slowly. I dreaded the almost certain confrontation that lay ahead. When the grandfather clock in the hall chimed seven, I cleared away the plate, squared my shoulders, and made my way to the parlor.

Aunt Ada was sitting by the window, the morning sun peeking through beveled glass. My mother's sister had lived with our family for as long as I could remember, having never married. When she was seventeen, the boy she had promised herself to died crossing the prairies to Utah. She sometimes spoke wistfully of his strong arms and freckled face.

Ada's now white hair was pulled back in a bun, head bent over her thin frame, single-point knitting needles clicking efficiently across what was to become a scarf. I sat next to her and leaned in so she could hear me better. When I revealed my plans to attend the meeting in Salt Lake City tomorrow, she glared at me over the rims of her large, round glasses.

"Kathryn Leavitt," she said in a stern tone, "I'm surprised at you. No girl fifteen years of age has any business attending such a gathering. It's both unseemly and unladylike."

"But Aunt, they may speak of suffrage."

She reminded me in no uncertain terms that women do not have the right to suffrage and that was the way it was meant to be. "In the world in which we live, many things are not desirable which is why men make several decisions on our behalf."

"The world around us needs to change," I said, lifting my chin.

"That's not up to you to decide, and I forbid you to attend tomorrow's meeting."

"If Father and Mother weren't away in Ogden, they'd permit me to go. Father's cousin Sophia has invited me to accompany her."

"I rather doubt they would, but they're not here, and I'm the one in charge. You're to go to your room and think about the disrespectful way you've spoken to me," she said, returning to her knitting.

I turned on my heel and walked out of the parlor, not surprised at her response. After reaching my room, I removed the note from my desk drawer that I'd composed earlier, reading over the words advising Aunt where I was going and when I'd be back. I placed the message on top of the desk, slipped out of the gingham and selected a dress that was olive green in color with lovely white lace at the neck. *That's better*, I thought, looking in the mirror, placing a smart-looking hat atop my head.

I have my mother's red hair, my father's green eyes, and this dress is perfect for me. I pulled on a heavy wool cloak and went out the back way, shivering against the January cold.

My friend Emma was waiting across the yard, her grandmother's town coach and driver at the ready. The two of us have been friends for as long as I can remember. We've grown up together in the little foothill community of Farmington, Utah, that sits on a narrow bench of land overlooking the Great Salt Lake. She and I share a love of the written word, though I prefer Jane Austen and Emma likes Edgar Allan Poe. She has curious brown eyes, is given to wearing her hair in a braid that drapes over the front of her dress, and is two years older than I am.

I trudged over mud-caked snow to the carriage, gathered my long dress in one hand, and climbed inside with an assist from the driver. I slid across the red plush cushions, sat next to Emma and said, "Very nice rose-colored dress you're wearing. Suits you."

"High praise coming from the fashion authority." She smiled.

I laughed and gave her a hug.

"It's nice you can laugh at yourself, Katie."

"With you, I can."

"That's because we're best friends."

"I'm grateful for that, and I'm delighted to be on this journey together."

"I wouldn't have missed it. Would you care for a blanket?"

"Thank you," I said, burrowing under the heavy warm covering she offered. Then I noticed Anne's absence, Emma's cousin whom she should have picked up on the way to my house. "Did Anne decline to accompany us?"

"She wished to come, but Charles forbade her."

"He exercises such sway over her."

"I fear he's more interested in what the Whitman name may do for him than he is in Anne."

"Sadly, that wouldn't surprise me. I've never trusted him."

"Did Ada object to you attending tomorrow's meeting?"

"She was all horns and rattles and sees no need for women to change their station. I'm grateful your grandmother understands our desire to participate and has provided us the use of her coach," I said as we traveled through the snowy hills.

"Grandmother Phoebe says we live on the frontier of America and believes this is the place where men—and women—may both make new beginnings."

15

"I pray she's right." I drew back the curtain on the small window and peered out at the trees. It was a bone-chilling morning, and the ride from Farmington to Salt Lake City would take almost four hours with a stop to rest and water the horse. Emma was already falling fast asleep to the rhythm of the rocking coach.

I watched the barren trees pass and recalled again that dreary morning three years ago when Adam had lain prostrate for days with a raging fever, vomiting in bed, head aching as if it would burst. He'd been outside playing in the woods and developed a rash. It spread across his body, and we could do nothing to save him. I stood powerless, watching our cherished little man pass from this world to the next.

Alone that night in the dark of my room, tears streaming down my face, I dropped to my knees and prayed to my Heavenly Father. As I rose, it became clear that my life's calling was to relieve the suffering of others, and I determined to dedicate my life to improving public health and saving children—but as a doctor, not a midwife.

The carriage jostled through a hole in the road, returning me to the present. Emma awakened as the coach lurched across a washboard road and we were almost thrown from our seats. We clutched tightly to each other for the remainder of the ride.

It was nearing noon when we reached Cousin Sophia's home in the tree-lined streets in the Avenues above the City. As a widowed artist of forty, she relishes living here among other artists who see the world as she does. When we got out of the carriage, Sophia came down to the street level to greet us. "Come in, come in," she said, smiling.

Her convivial stone and wood home had a large fireplace with a welcoming blaze. A pair of black and white ceramic dogs bookended the mantle, and a floor-to-ceiling bookcase rose in the center of the room, filled with books of all genres.

Emma and I moved into the small dining area and found that lunch was ready. "Please sit down," Sophia said, "and I'll bring the turkey. We have cake and custard for dessert."

"Thank you for inviting us and preparing this delicious meal," I said, enjoying the pickled peaches and preserved cucumbers most of all.

"Yes," Emma said, spooning applesauce into a small bowl. "Your home is lovely."

"It's my pleasure to have you both here. When you've eaten your fill, we'll move to the parlor. Katie, I'm hoping you'll favor us with a few selections on the piano."

After we finished our meal, I sat at the piano and Sophia lit two candles that stood on the lid. I began my musical rendition with Beethoven, ending with the lively selection, 'Flying Trapeze.' Sophia and Emma were delighted and clapped to show their appreciation. We drank hot cocoa and ate johnny cake until we were stuffed.

"Sophia," I asked, blowing on my chocolate to cool it, "is Eliza Snow likely to be present at tomorrow's meeting?"

"I'm quite sure of it. She travels throughout our Church, instructing the sisters and assisting bishops in re-organizing the local Women's Relief Societies, giving women the opportunity to hone their organizational skills and speaking abilities. She also makes certain the ladies are living up to the Relief Society's stated purpose of searching out the poor and suffering."

"Father told me you and Eliza Snow are friends. Would you be willing to introduce us?"

"It would be my pleasure," Sophia said.

"Is it true she has no children?" Emma asked.

"It is, but she's a mother to us all, and many of us younger than she refer to her as Aunt Eliza. She's also a gifted writer and speaks publicly."

I was surprised when she said that because it's rare for women to speak in public, let alone to be articulate enough to do so.

After an enjoyable evening, Sophia suggested we retire early. "Our meeting's in the morning, so a good night's sleep is in order." We collected our shawls and made our way up the stairs to a room with large feather beds where we both slept soundly.

We rose early January 6, anxious to get a look at the women's Society Hall that the Salt Lake Women's Relief Society had built. Sophia told us they called it "our hall," with the upper story dedicated to art and science, and the lower level to commerce and trade. The meeting room was almost full when the three of us arrived.

President Sarah Kimball began the discussion by declaring, "We would be unworthy of the names we bear or the blood in our veins should we longer remain silent."

Sophia whispered. "You'll find Sarah a strong advocate with a warm heart."

Later in the meeting, Eliza Snow spoke of the Relief Societies and urged the sisters to take a wider sphere of action. "We are not inferior to the ladies of the world," she said, "and we do not want to appear so."

The room was abuzz with women's voices at her declaration.

Bathsheba Smith, another ardent suffragist, issued a call to action, saying, "I move that we demand of the Governor the right of franchise." Many agreed with her, though some did not. But when all the women voted on her motion, the vote carried.

I knew the territorial legislature of Wyoming had granted women suffrage the year prior, and they were the first in the country to do so, making it a landmark decision.

Lucy Smith moved that women be represented in Washington, and Eliza Snow and Sarah Kimball were elected. I looked around the room and thought, *This is where I want to live—among vocal women such as these*, and my mind came alive with possibilities. Why not attend the University of Deseret and study chemistry? I couldn't wait to share my ideas with Father and Mother.

Before we left the hall, Sophia introduced us to Eliza Snow. She was a fashionable looking woman with a large pocket watch on a gold chain that draped down her lovely black dress. In addition to being over all the local Relief Society organizations, she was a gifted poet. As we conversed, she said, "Winning the ballot is an important aspect in expanding our domain as women. Entering the professions is another."

"Such as going to medical school?" I asked.

"Do you wish to make medicine an occupation?"

"It's more than a wish. I'm called to be a doctor, Sister Snow."

"Then your time will come, and when it does, you'll have my support. We're all sisters in the gospel, Katie, and sisters in winning the ballot; one doesn't preclude the other. I hope to see you again soon," she said, shaking my hand.

"Thank you," I said, grateful that the beliefs of our faith allowed us to be both dedicated wives and mothers and self-reliant, educated women.

When our coach pulled into the yard the following evening, I noticed Father's carriage had returned. My twelve-year old brother, Joseph, was removing a bit from the horse's mouth, preparing to move him into the barn. Joseph turned to me with a look of disapproval and I scowled back at him. *Perhaps he's forgotten that I'm the oldest child in this family?* Bidding Emma good-bye, I walked over to speak with him.

"You've home, I see," he said, steadying the horse.

"Then your eyes do not deceive you."

"Why did you go to Salt Lake when Aunt Ada forbade it?"

"It was a crucial meeting, and I'm glad I attended. How's Mother?"

"She still suffers pains throughout her body, and the doctor in Ogden knew no more than the others," he said, shoulders drooping.

I embraced him, my heart breaking, tears standing out on my cheeks.

He reached into his pocket and offered a handkerchief.

"Thank you, Joseph," I said, dabbing my eyes. "I'm sorry I was short with you a moment ago."

"It's all right. The meeting must have been important."

"It was, and I'll tell you more about it later."

My gentle mother, Elizabeth, suffers from severe aches and pains, which some days are more tolerable than others. Generally, the pain is in her legs, so she doesn't move them much, and sleeping for her has become almost impossible. I have a stack of medical

19

books in my room, most of which I've read, but I can find nothing to explain her symptoms.

Mother was languishing on the couch when I walked into the house and sat next to her. Ada prickled at my very presence but said nothing.

"Katie, is that you?" Mother asked, suffering one of her occasional bouts with brain fog, a result of her mysterious illness.

"It is," I said kneeling before her and clasping her hands in mine.

"I'm so glad. Ada said you've been away."

"I've been in Salt Lake with Cousin Sophia."

"Well, isn't that nice."

Ada bit her tongue when she saw Father walk into the room. He's a tall man and cuts an imposing figure, and he's always been my greatest support. I rose and embraced him. "I have so much to tell you, Father."

"I'm certain you do. Why don't you begin with why you disobeyed Ada?"

"I went to a women's meeting in Salt Lake and met Eliza Snow."

"Did you now?" he said. "I know her brother Lorenzo, and the two of them are quite close."

"Sophia introduced us, and she allowed me to address her as Aunt Eliza, encouraging me when I told her I wished to become a doctor."

Ada said, "If you must practice medicine, be a midwife. Much more practical."

"One day I will be accepted as a doctor, I assure you, Aunt."

A smile broke at the corner of my father's lips. "I believe you will yet be what you wish to be. My sister May, God rest her soul, set the working tradition for women in this family when she nursed soldiers on the battlefields of the Civil War."

"I wish I'd known her, Father."

"I remind you that May was a nurse and not a doctor," Ada said, raising her eyebrows.

"I need no reminding of that, my dear Ada," Father said. "See, it looks as if Elizabeth's glass is empty; she could use more water."

Ada went into the kitchen as I whispered, "Why is she so difficult, Father?"

"Perhaps because she's had a difficult life, Katie. Let's not judge her."

When Ada came back into the parlor, she handed the water to my mother, kissing the top of her head. "Come, my own," she said tenderly, offering her hand. "You need to rest now."

With the obedience reminiscent of a small child, my mother walked with her, and I found myself grateful for the love Ada had for her sister.

Emma

Emma was nearing the end of Wilkie Collin's book, *The Moonstone*, and was about to ascertain which character had stolen the cursed diamond when a rap came at the door.

"Oh, bother," she said aloud, rising and putting her book down, just as her father walked into the room.

"I'll answer that," he said, striding across the floor.

As he opened the door, Emma heard a woman's voice she did not recognize. "Good morning," the voice said. "Sheriff Gregory, I presume?"

"Yes, Mrs. Shaw, do come in."

Emma saw a woman of about thirty, simply dressed in brown skirts and bodice, her rather short hair pulled back from her face. She was plain but attractive and there was something about the raise of her eyebrows that conveyed a smart, no-nonsense look. Emma waited to be introduced.

"Mrs. Shaw," Father said, "this is my daughter. Emma, Mrs. Rosemary Shaw."

Emma was shocked to see a badge pinned to Mrs. Shaw's cloak that read 'Pinkerton National Detective Agency.' Noting her surprise, Mrs. Shaw smiled. "Yes, my dear, women are agents as well as men. They call us The Pinks."

Emma's eyes widened. "I had no idea, and I'm so pleased to meet you." Emma's heart was drumming in her chest, and all she could think of to say was, "I've been reading *The Moonstone*. It's a detective story."

"An excellent choice. Take care not to catch detective fever." Mrs. Shaw smiled.

"I fear it may be too late," Emma replied in earnest.

"This way, please," Emma's father said, escorting Mrs. Shaw into his office and closing the door behind them.

Something was clearly afoot, and Emma counted herself fortunate that she was the only one at home besides her father. Her stepmother had taken Emma's older stepsister, Christina, and younger half-brother, David, to the general store for supplies. Emma was nine years old when David was born and had practically raised him.

She removed a glass from the kitchen and placed it against the wall to the office so she could better hear their conversation, recalling that Miss Clack in *Moonstone* had done the same thing when she intended to eavesdrop. Emma had never done such a thing before and was a bit ashamed, but curiosity quite got the better of her. A female Pinkerton detective was in the house, and Emma simply had to know why.

Their words were faint but intelligible through the glass. As they spoke, Emma learned that an inmate had escaped from the Utah Territorial Penitentiary, and the U.S. Marshals in charge had contacted the Pinkerton Detective Agency in Chicago. Alan Pinkerton himself had sent Mrs. Shaw do some undercover sleuthing. She was telling Father they had not yet apprehended the inmate, and her sources had informed her he was headed their way.

Farmington? Nothing ever happens here.

"He's coming for a man by the name of John Leavitt," Mrs. Shaw said.

What?! Katie's father? Emma sucked in a quick breath and pressed a hand against her chest.

Mrs. Shaw continued, "I understand he's the Davis County prosecutor and the one who sent the convict to the penitentiary. The prisoner is seeking revenge."

"What's his name?" Father asked.

"Fred Grimes."

"I remember him. Shot and killed his own wife in a nearby town."

"He's a malicious character who will stop at nothing."

"We must warn John," Emma's father said, his chair scraping as he stood. "Let's proceed to the courthouse."

Emma moved away from the wall and took a seat on the sofa, placing the empty glass on the table. They barely noticed her as they walked out the door. *What to do now?* Katie needed to know what Emma had just learned. What if Grimes went to her home instead of her father's office at the courthouse?

Pulling on cloak and gloves, Emma plodded through the snow for several blocks, looking over her shoulder as she neared the Leavitt domicile. Breathless, she knocked on the door, and Katie answered. "Emma, come in, you'll catch your death of cold. Here, warm yourself by the fire," she said, taking her cloak and hanging it on a hook in the hall.

Emma was only too happy to oblige, stretching her chilled hands toward the flame and greeting Katie's mother. "May we speak in your room?" Emma whispered. "And will you lock the front door behind us, please?" she pleaded under her breath.

Katie looked puzzled but did as Emma asked.

"Why are you locking the door, Katie?" her mother asked.

"One never knows who might be lurking about," Emma offered.

She smiled. "You girls enjoy your visit."

Katie led the way upstairs. "You appear shaken, Emma," she said, as they sat. "What is it?"

"I know something I'm not supposed to know, and it's a matter of much importance that I heard while listening to a conversation through the wall of Father's office." Her words tumbled over themselves.

"You listened to a conversation through the wall?" Katie sounded surprised. "How did you do that?"

"I pressed a glass against it."

"Clever. Tell me more," she said, leaning in.

"I overheard Father talking to a Pinkerton detective."

"What's a Pinkerton doing way out here?"

"She's been assisting the U.S. marshals to locate an escaped prisoner."

"Did you say, 'she'?"

"Yes. I was just as surprised as you are. Isn't it wonderful?"

"It is indeed. I knew women were expanding into the professions, most particularly in the West, but detectives?"

"Her name is Rosemary Shaw, and she sports a badge when not undercover."

"I'm astonished."

"So was I." She paused. "Katie, the news I have is upsetting," Emma said, catching her eye, "and it involves your father."

Katie was taken aback. "What is it?"

"An escaped inmate your father sent to prison for murder is coming for him."

"Are you sure?" she said, folding her arms over her stomach, looking as if she might be ill.

"Quite certain, I'm afraid." Emma clasped her hand. "I feared something might happen here before my father got to yours at the county courthouse, so I came right away. And I brought my gun," Emma said, lifting her skirts and pulling the weapon from a small holster strapped to her leg.

Katie blanched. "You're very brave, Emma, and the best friend in all the world."

Just then they heard Katie's father's voice. "Come down here, children," he called up the stairs.

"You'd best put your gun away," Katie said, taking Emma's hand. "And don't worry; I won't let on that you told me anything, but it helps to know what we may be up against."

Emma and Katie walked downstairs behind her brothers. Emma's father was in the room as well. *Does he suspect that I overheard his conversation?* Emma wondered. *I don't think so. He knows I spend much of my time at Katie's house.* He nodded at her, acknowledging her presence.

"Sit down, please, children," Katie's father said, sitting next to his wife and holding her hand. Katie sat between her younger brothers Andrew and Jacob. "Sheriff Gregory has some distressing news for us," Mr. Leavitt told his family. "But fear not, we will be well protected. Sheriff, please proceed."

As Emma's father described the escaped convict and his intent to come after Mr. Leavitt, Katie took Andrew's and Jacob's hands in hers, and they moved closer to her. Fear stood out in their eyes.

"All will be well, boys," Sheriff Gregory said seeing their reaction. "I've posted a new deputy from Salt Lake outside the house, and he'll stand watch. Wesley Hatch is a good man, very experienced. Nothing gets past him. I assure you I won't allow anything to happen to any of you." No sooner had Emma's father finished his sentence when a shot rang out.

"Get down!" he ordered, drawing his six-shooter, and they all dropped to the floor. He moved to the door, peered through the glass, and edged outside as everyone lay shivering next to each other. Emma touched her hand to the gun under her skirt, and after several more shots were fired, she could sit still no longer. Keeping her head low, she scrambled on all fours to the window.

"Emma, stay down," Katie's father said as she raised her head slowly and peered out the window.

"I believe we're safe now," she said, staring at a bullet-riddled body lying on the front lawn. Rosemary Shaw was standing over the man, gun smoking, apparently having fired the last shot. Emma's father and his new deputy were walking toward her, guns still drawn.

When they rolled his body over and seemed satisfied that he was dead, the sheriff ordered, "Drag him out of sight of the family, Wesley, and then go for the coffin wagon."

"Yes, sir," Wesley said. He looked up and saw Emma at the window, and their eyes met. Wesley was tall with blue eyes that twinkled, and he had a chiseled chin. *He looks very heroic*, Emma thought. He tipped his hat at her, and Emma moved from the window, embarrassed.

The sheriff walked back inside. "It was Grimes, John," he said, "and it's over. He'll never harm another."

"A fitting end to the life of an evil man," Mr. Leavitt said.

"I wish you weren't a prosecuting attorney," Joseph said.

"Today has been excessively frightening, my son, but the good Lord was watching over us."

Mr. Leavitt shook the sheriff's hand and thanked him for protecting the family. Curious once again, the boys jumped up and ran to the window. By now there was nothing to see, save a trail of red blood against the white snow.

Katie looked at Emma and mouthed the words, "My thanks to you as well."

"You're welcome," Emma whispered squeezing her hand.

When they arrived home, Emma's stepmother was back with a million questions about the blood on her husband's pants, so Emma went to her room and took the book she'd been reading along. As she finished *Moonstone*, she realized that reading about a crime was a far cry from being caught in the center of one. She'd been frightened out of her wits when the shots rang out, fearing that perhaps her father had been hit—even wondering if she might be next.

Being a female detective is a dangerous game to play—though an exciting one, to be sure. Emma was curious to know more about this brave Wesley Hatch fellow who bore no wedding ring on his finger. *I'm just shy of seventeen, and if the look we exchanged is any indication, he may wish to court me. Perhaps Father will provide us with an introduction.*

Two

Katie

It was a cold day in February as I sat at the small wooden desk in my room, making entries in my diary. Mother had given me one of the new fountain pens with its self-contained ink, and I still marveled that an inkwell was no longer needed. The cast iron fireplace was not keeping me warm, so I rose from my desk and added several pieces of coal to the glowing embers.

Attempting to again concentrate on my writing, I heard my brothers, Andrew and Jacob, in the room next to mine, horsing around as usual. Andrew is eight-years old, bright, with a forgiving heart. Five-year old Jacob is creative, impish, and delights in playing tricks. I adore them both, but they're a handful. Rapping on the common wall we share and raising my voice, I said, "Can I get some peace and quiet around here? I don't want to hear another peep out of either of you."

I heard Jacob call out, "Peep."

That does it. I stormed from my room into theirs and found them collapsed on the floor, laughing. I wanted to be angry with them, but I couldn't. "That's enough, boys," I said, attempting to look stern. Andrew rose from the floor and hugged me around the waist, then Jacob joined us.

"Sorry, Katie," Andrew said, eyes filled with contrition.

"Me too—but not really," Jacob responded with a twinkle in his eye.

"What's that you say?" I tickled them until they couldn't catch their breaths. We heard Father clomping up the stairs. "Quick, let's hide," I said, and we jumped into the wardrobe and shut the door.

Father walked in and began looking for us, knowing full well where we were. "Hmm," he said. "What's become of my boys? Are they under the bed? No, where could they be?"

"We're here, Father!" Jacob said, swinging wide the door.

"Well, I declare, I never would have thought to look for you in the wardrobe," he said, smiling. "Boys, Aunt Ada is preparing breakfast, and your mother is waiting for you downstairs. So, off you go." He turned to me. "I'd like to speak with you."

"In my room, please, Father, it's warmer there."

We sat at my desk chairs, and Father said, "I have a proposal that you may find intriguing."

"What is it?"

"Let me preface it by asking if you read the papers of January 12 alerting us that the Utah Central railway tracks from Farmington to Ogden are now complete."

"I did read that, Father."

"I'm inviting you to accompany me to Salt Lake City via train through Ogden."

I leaped from my chair, tipping it over. "I've never ridden a train before. What an adventure that would be! When do we go?" I asked, the words spilling from my mouth.

"Early morning on the tenth of this month. Let me inform you why I selected that particular day."

"You have my full attention, Father, though I should be pleased to go anytime you specify."

"The day I've chosen promises to be unlike any other. I spent last evening discussing matters of business with my friend, Hector C. Haight."

"I'm friends with his granddaughter, Julia."

"I hadn't forgotten that. You may remember that Hector is our Council Member from Davis and Morgan Counties in the Utah Territorial Legislature, and he tells me that a vote is scheduled February 10th on a bill that proposes to grant women the right of suffrage. He's invited the two of us to attend the meeting."

I could scarce catch my breath. "You've rendered me speechless."

Father smiled. "That's very unusual for you, Katie. Hector says the bill has overwhelming support and will pass handily through the legislature, though acting Governor Stephen Mann has not been in support. Hector confided that it has taken several days of arm twisting to get him to sign the amendment."

"We'll be present? In the very room when the vote is called?"

"You and I will meet Hector in the Rose room on the second floor of the Salt Lake City Hall where the legislature meets. Julia will accompany him, and the four of us will sit in back and observe the proceedings."

I was so happy that I twirled about the room.

Father laughed. "I'm pleased I've engendered such joy."

I smiled and asked, "Is that a copy of the *New York Herald* under your arm?"

"It's the January 23rd issue, and I've marked an article for you titled 'Women in Council.'"

He handed me the paper, and I read aloud, 'In logic and in rhetoric, the so-called degraded ladies of Mormondom are quite equal to the women's rights women of the East.'

"What do you think?" Father asked.

"I wondered when the men of the East would reach that conclusion."

Father laughed. "Let's get breakfast."

****

I could hardly sleep the night of February 9th, thinking about the day ahead. The next morning, I poured water into the wash basin and splashed my face. I shook with cold, wiping my face with a

29

cloth. I went again to my wardrobe to select what I hoped would be just the right apparel to attend a legislative session. Since it was a more formal occasion, a black skirt seemed the appropriate choice. I weaved my hair atop my head, ringlets dropping down the sides of my face.

Father was waiting downstairs, and Aunt Ada had prepared a light breakfast to take with us on the train. She didn't look happy that I was going but said nothing. We would travel from Farmington north to Ogden and backtrack south to Salt Lake City. A round-about way to be certain, but there were no rails running south from Farmington.

Father helped me into my heavy coat, and I added gloves and a bonnet. Joseph would take us by carriage to the 'whistle-stop' station where we would board the train. "You look quite dapper in your top hat, Father," I remarked. "I don't believe I've seen those gray pants with the black stitching down the sides. Are they newly purchased?"

"You are quite observant, and yes, they are."

"They pair well with your black coat and gold vest," I said as we boarded the carriage.

"I wish I were riding the train with you and Katie today," Joseph muttered.

"You'll have your chance, I promise," Father said as we rode. "Today we honor our sister suffragists."

"Can't we men be suffragists as well?"

"A point well taken, my boy, and yes, many males in the Utah Territory might well be considered suffragists, including me."

"I hadn't thought of it that way," I said.

When we reached the tracks, a sign read 'Board here.' We got out of the carriage, thanked Joseph, and saw the black smoke of the train coming 'round the bend. As it approached, I could see a large metal device on the front of the locomotive. "What's the purpose of that?" I asked, pointing.

"It's used to deflect obstacles on the track that might otherwise derail the train and is referred to as a cowcatcher."

I saw a man in blue overalls and a scruffy shirt leaning out the window where the engineer sat, thinking that he must be the one to stoke the coal. The train stopped, and the conductor laid out steps to the rust-colored passenger car. The sign on the door read 'Utah Central Railway.' We climbed on board and were hardly in our seats when the train lurched forward.

The train gradually picked up speed, and we flashed through miles of Douglas fir and aspen, a light snow on the tree branches. When we reached Ogden, Father suggested we sit in the observation car for the journey to Salt Lake. I was only too happy to oblige, climbing the small stairs, and feeling a sense of awe at my first train trip.

"Father," I asked as we settled in and gazed out the large windows, "it seems to me but a short space between when Bathsheba Smith demanded the right of franchise in last month's meeting and today when the legislature will take a vote."

"There were many meetings, events, and protests that led to today's vote, but you are correct that it's easier than what the women in the East are experiencing in their bid for suffrage."

"Why is that?"

"Two reasons, I believe. First, the men of the West trekked across the plains with women who pulled their own handcarts and drove wagons with teams of horses. They suffered hunger, death, and privations along the way with the men. It's impossible to view Frontier women as delicate, fragile, or lacking judgment, because that simply hasn't been our experience."

That makes sense to me, I thought, hearing the train whistle as we approached a crossing. "And the other reason?"

"The other has to do with the reorganization of the Relief Societies that expanded women's influence in every ward congregation in our church and granted them a voice. There are now 100 such societies across the Utah Territory."

"I had no idea there were so many," I said, the changing landscape outside capturing my attention. "See, Father, we're approaching the Salt Lake station."

"We'd best make our way downstairs," he said as the train slowed. "Be careful, my girl."

When we reached City Hall, I saw several women and men standing outside with signs protesting today's vote. They shouted at us and passed out pamphlets as we walked through the crowd. One of the women was particularly vocal in her opposition and seemed to lead the others. "Do you know who that woman is, Father?" I asked.

"Her name is Jennie Froiseth."

"Is she an anti-suffragist?"

"No, she is a passionate suffragist who believes there should be no votes for Mormon women until the practice of polygamy is eradicated."

"Why punish the women? I don't think I follow that logic, Father."

"Nor do I, but we must hurry along."

I quickened my pace. My parents didn't engage in plural marriage; neither did Julia's nor Emma's, but others of our faith did. Polygamy had become a practice of the Mormon Church in 1842, though not required. Less than twenty-five percent of us engaged in polygamy, and I found my mind confused over the issue.

We walked inside and moved to the back of Representative Hall, waiting for the session to begin. Mr. Haight introduced us to Abram Hatch, the representative who proposed the Women Suffrage Act. "It's an honor to meet you, Mr. Hatch," I said, as he shook hands with me and Father. I sat down next to Julia and gave her a hug. "Can you believe this is happening?"

"An historic event," she said. "I'm so pleased we're here together to watch it."

A few moments later, roll was called, and after it was determined that a quorum was present, the chaplain offered a prayer. A message from the Legislative Council, of which Mr. Haight was a member, was read on the proposed amendment. On motion of a Mr. Reese, the House concurred with the Council amendment. I was a witness to history being made.

A message from the acting governor that was addressed to the house in care of Orson Pratt was read into the record. The letter declared that on this day, Mr. Mann had approved and would sign the act 'conferring upon women the elective franchise.' I wanted to cheer at those words, but I dared not. *The women of Utah were at last being taken seriously.*

As the reading of the letter continued, Mr. Mann expressed his doubts over the advisability of the passage of the amendment, but then said in view of the 'unanimous passage of the act in both the House and Council,' he had approved the bill. I looked over at Father who smiled and put his arm around my shoulders. When the house took a brief recess, we left the room.

Father shook hands with Mr. Haight and said, "Thanks to you and others who made this vote possible."

Hector smiled, clapped him on the back, and bid us goodbye. "I'm pleased you and Katie could attend, John."

I hugged Julia, and Father and I left for the station.

On the train ride home, my mind revisited both the public and private hurdles that had been overcome to make it possible for the women of the Utah Territory to secure the vote. I knew that while the Suffrage Act enfranchised women, it didn't allow them to hold office. It was a hopeful beginning.

****

The following afternoon, I found myself alone in the house with Mother who was sitting in the parlor, reading. There is no one quite as articulate or intelligent as she when not suffering from the exhaustion her pain inflicts. I lingered a moment and then walked over and sat in a chair facing her. Even from there, I could smell her perfume, a light floral scent that I loved. She looked up at me, smiled, and returned to her book.

I sat for a moment and feigned boredom until she put her book down and asked, "Do you wish to engage in conversation, Katie?"

"Yes, Mother. I have a question for you."

"Please continue. You may ask me anything; you know that."

"I don't understand the practice of polygamy in our religion."

"Please come sit next to me on the sofa and let's talk," she said, putting her arm around me. "Some in the East have proclaimed Mormon women who live in plural marriages to be degraded. Nothing could be further from the truth. Eliza Snow, for example, is one of the most vocal and articulate women among us."

"I observed that when I attended last month's meeting. She was inspiring."

"I'm going to tell you something that may help, but you must promise not to share it with anyone else, even Emma, because it's a private matter and I cannot verify its certainty."

I leaned in, listening, and couldn't imagine what was coming next. "I promise, Mother."

"There are some who know Sister Snow who whisper that the reason she can't bear children is because she, like other women who live among us, was ravaged by the Missouri mobs after Governor Boggs issued his Mormon extermination order in 1838."

I stared straight ahead, lowering my voice to a whisper. "Who would do something like that?"

"Men who are evil and wicked," my mother said, her voice breaking. "In Sister Snow's situation, the practice of polygamy has been a blessing and allowed her the opportunity to marry, have a home, and receive financial support."

I furrowed my brow, attempting to process what I had heard.

"It is a complex question with no simple answers. But according to the Book of Mormon, the standard doctrine of our Church is monogamy, and I believe you'll see the practice of plural marriage end in your lifetime. For some women, polygamy may not be a blessing, which is also true of monogamy. In society at large, women live with the pernicious evils of prostitution and abandoned children."

I cuddled up under her arm, and we sat, saying nothing. I rubbed my forehead and closed my eyes, a tightness in my chest. I loved Aunt Eliza and couldn't begin to comprehend her resilience and courage.

Emma

The streets of Farmington were quiet, and a light snow had begun to fall as Emma drove her surrey through town on her way to the Archer Ranch. Emma wanted to tell her cousin Anne what Katie had shared with her about the meeting at the legislature. A short ride later, she reached the large stone farmhouse, pulling her horse to a stop in front. Emma's step was light and her spirit buoyant as she walked up the short set of steps. She raised the heavy metal knocker and let it fall against the wooden door. Emma waited, stamping her feet to keep them warm, but there was no answer. *That's odd.* She saw Anne peeking through the white lace curtain covering the door. "Anne," she said. "May I come in?"

When Anne cracked opened the door, Emma was greeted by a tear-stained face. "Whatever is the matter?" She paused. "Is Charles about?"

Anne shook her head no.

Emma gently took her arm, and they walked to the sofa. Anne turned her face away as Emma waited for her to speak and couldn't imagine what had transpired.

When Anne had regained her composure, she declared, "You must tell no one what I am about to tell you."

"You may trust me."

"Give me your pledge, Emma."

"I do."

"Charles approached me this morning and said he had something important to discuss with me. As we sat together, he removed a telegram from his pocket he'd received from a friend in Salt Lake advising that Governor Mann signed the suffrage bill into law February 12."

"That's what I came to talk with you about. Katie and her father were present in the meeting, and I thought you'd be as jubilant as I was to hear the details."

"I would have been if I'd heard it from you first. Charles, on the other hand, found the news distressing. He advised me that suffrage was unwholesome and unnecessary and that women were already represented by their fathers and husbands."

"Katie's aunt Ada believes much the same, Anne. Such unenlightened positions."

"Charles didn't stop there. He said that women were not meant to speak from the pulpit or lecturer's platform."

"Susan B. Anthony lectures around the country, and I'm certain Eliza Snow will one day speak from the general pulpit," Emma said. "He's mistaken."

"I assured him that my only desire was to be a good wife, and soon the mother of his child," Anne said, patting her growing stomach, "but told him I didn't agree that women should refrain from casting ballots."

"How did he respond?"

"He flew into a rage and shouted that what I thought was of little consequence. He reminded me that he was my husband and head of our household. He said when we married, I had agreed to obey him." Anne stood and began pacing the floor.

"Each person, male or female, is entitled to an opinion."

"When I said something similar, he told me I was nothing more than a ridiculous woman. He grabbed me and began shaking me."

"He has no right to do that," Emma said, shocked and outraged.

"But he did it nonetheless." Anne cried again and said, "That's when he struck me across the face, leaving this bruise on my cheekbone."

Emma had noticed the bruise when she came in but assumed Anne had fallen against something. "Charles gave you the bruise?" she asked angrily.

"Yes," Anne said, her cheeks burning red, eyes wet.

"He has no call to hit you under any circumstance, but especially when you're pregnant. You must not put up with this."

She hung her head.

"Anne," Emma asked quietly. "Is this the first time he's struck you?"

In a hushed voice devoid of emotion, she whispered, "No."

"We must put a stop to it," Emma said, rising.

"I forbid you to say anything of this matter to anyone, Emma, especially your father. To do so would only increase my husband's anger and add to my shame."

"What about speaking with Uncle Peter?"

"No, not my father either. He will remind me that he advised against marrying Charles. The two of them don't get along with each other."

"I know they've had words."

"Father and Charles got into a terrible argument over an investment Charles made, and things have been even worse between them since."

"But you must speak with someone about the way Charles treats you. He may hurt you again."

"No, he won't because I'll be more judicious with my words, I assure you," she said not looking Emma in the eye.

If Anne believes she can control a man like Charles with the use of words, she's mistaken, Emma thought.

"Let's speak no more of this, Emma. I will soon have the baby to consider."

Am I to do nothing about what Anne has confided in me?

"Come into the kitchen," she said, "and we'll enjoy cornbread and a bit of my father's sarsaparilla," she said. "It's quite good."

Emma couldn't believe Anne had switched gears from abused wife to hostess so easily. *It's shame that motivates her.* Emma sat at the table and began biting the inside of her cheek, obviously distressed.

"All will be well, Cousin," Anne said. "Please don't trouble yourself."

Too late for that, Emma thought as they ate, chatting about nothing of consequence from that moment forward.

After they finished, Emma made her exit as soon as it was polite to do so, assuring Anne she would see her again soon. On her way out, she spied a half empty bottle of whiskey tucked away into the sideboard. She knew Anne didn't imbibe, and while Charles maintained that he never touched the drink, Emma surmised that was but another of his charades, along with the obvious pretense of being a model husband.

When Emma reached home, her mood was dark, and she felt lightheaded. While she had agreed to tell no person what Anne had revealed, that didn't include Palumbo. She went directly to the barn where she kept a pair of riding trousers at the ready. Pulling them on under her skirts, she walked over to her Palomino's stall, slipped the bridle over his ears, cinched the saddle around his belly, and led him from the barn.

The two of them rode for miles, the late afternoon sky burning a bright orange. Emma closed her eyes and took a deep breath. *There's nothing more comforting than walking and talking with Palumbo.*

Emma spoke aloud the sordid details of what she'd learned about Charles's treatment of Anne. Palumbo listened and whinnied, shaking his head from side to side as if he didn't understand it either. Emma couldn't abide hypocrites nor those who mistreated others, and it seemed that Charles was both. Her nostrils flared and there was a tightness in her eyes. She kneed Palumbo in the sides and off they raced, going as fast as she dared.

A few hours later she was back in the barn, wiping the sweat from her horse's flanks. She threw a blanket over him and sat on a bale of hay and cried quiet tears for her dear cousin, Anne. Palumbo gently nuzzled her back, and Emma stood, kissing the white star on his forehead.

Walking back to the house, the evening air was cold on her skin, and a full moon was making its rise in a now star-studded sky. When she reached the house, her stepmother was sewing. "Oh, my dear," she said, as Emma came through the door. "We were worried about you."

"I'm not feeling well and will retire early," Emma said, climbing the stairs to her room, removing her clothing, wrapping a heavy blanket around her. She slept fitfully that night.

It was after eight the next morning when Emma's sister, Christina, woke her with a hot cup of cocoa and a warm muffin.

She's a beautiful woman, Emma thought, *blonde hair, cobalt blue eyes, the very picture of self-assurance and kind as well.* Emma bit into the muffin. "It's delicious. Thank you, Christina."

"You're most welcome," she said respecting Emma's privacy by not asking questions she would be unable to answer. Christina closed the door and said, "Please let me know if there's anything else I may do for you."

"Thank you," Emma said, draining her cup and recalling the lines she and Katie had memorized from the first woman's rights convention held in 1848 in Seneca Falls, New York. The convention had adopted the Declaration of Sentiments which paraphrased the Declaration of Independence, stating, "We hold these truths to be self-evident: that all men and women are created equal."

There's much more to equality for women than the vote. There's the right to be treated with respect. She vowed then and there that she would keep a watchful eye on Charles Archer and his shenanigans. He had no idea who he was up against.

Three

Katie

I was applying the finishing touches to a Valentine's card that I'd embellished with small bits of white lace, penning the words across the bottom, 'With love and devotion to my mother.'

Father sat in the room with me reading the newspaper. "Valentine's Day is becoming quite the business in the East," he said. "According to this article in the *Times*, New Yorkers are paying exorbitant prices for Valentines, some of them costing up to $500 each."

"I can't imagine a card elaborate enough to command such a sum," I said.

"Nor can I, but always remember that heartfelt is best. Your mother will appreciate your lovely creation."

Gazing at my simple card, I dreamed that one day I might receive an elaborate Valentine from a handsome and dashing gentleman. Would he be tall with curly black hair that fell across his face? I could almost picture such a man. I sighed, knowing I wasn't allowed to be out with boys until I reached the age of sixteen in October.

Father reminded me that we'd be departing for dinner within the hour. "I'll go see to your mother and make certain Ada has the custard ready," he said, leaving the room.

Hector Haight had invited us to dine with him, along with his son Horton David, and Horton's wife Louisa, a dear friend of my mother's. Hector had recently completed the addition of a two-story rear wing onto his home with a two-story porch that faced south which he planned to operate as the Haight Union hotel. Mother told me the addition came replete with a formal dining room where we would dine this evening.

I went to my wardrobe and selected attire suitable for the evening. I chose a red silk dress with a full skirt and white lace stitched along the lower length of the sleeve. Concerned that the dress may not go well with my red hair, I pinned it under a full white lace bonnet.

When I descended the stairs, Mother was waiting. "You look splendid, Katie," she said.

"Thank you. I have something for you," I said, handing her my card.

"It's lovely, and I can't tell you how much your sentiment means." We embraced just as Father walked into the room with flowers for both of us, two for me and a bouquet for my mother. "Oh, my Dear," Mother said. "Thank you." She kissed him on the cheek.

"We'd best be off," he said, tucking the dish of custard under one arm and my mother under the other.

It was frosty outside, but not snowing, as we made our way to the white top carriage and sat inside. "How are you feeling this evening, Mother?" I asked.

She sat a little straighter and put a hand on one knee. "I'm looking forward to the festivities and determined to enjoy myself," she said.

While she exuded calm, I knew she was practicing a skill she'd learned to help manage her pain. As she closed her eyes, I was grateful Louisa would be with us this evening. The two of them were close, and I knew Louisa would be appropriately attentive without making my mother feel helpless.

I admired Louisa's strength and sense of self-reliance. Her husband was often called away on church business of one sort or another, and she was left to manage all household matters as well as their growing family. They had borne seven children, counting my friend Julia and a daughter, Matilda, who died before reaching her first birthday.

41

As we rode past the granary, Mother commented that the Relief Society had gleaned and stored, at last count, 149 bushels of wheat. The women had also gathered wool caught on wire fences carding it into hats and making quilts for the poor among us. "It's quite the operation," she said, "and President Sarah Harvey Holmes is in charge."

I marveled at the growing sphere of women's influence in our small town alone.

When we arrived at our destination, we got out of the carriage and walked inside the newly completed structure. I couldn't believe the transformation since my last visit some months ago. The dining room was stunning with its mauve wallpaper and floor to ceiling buffet that Father told me had been built out of pine and feather painted to give the wood the appearance of brown oak. The top half of the cupboard was glass and held beautiful china cups with matching plates stored below.

We took our seats at the dining table and I saw a silver-grey metal chandelier hanging from the ceiling with seven candles ensconced in holders. "Observe closely," Horton said, lowering the chandelier, lighting each candle and raising the chandelier again, using some type of pulley. I watched in amazement.

We were beginning our dinner of roasted mutton, potatoes, and vegetables when a telegram arrived for Hector. "What could this be?" he asked, opening the envelope the delivery boy handed him. As Hector read the words on the page, a smile broke across his face. "I have news! Utah no longer comes second to the territory of Wyoming."

We looked at him, puzzled.

He waved the page in the air, and said, "Utah is now the first place in the nation where a woman has cast a ballot. Seraph Young was the first to vote today in a municipal election on her way to work as a schoolteacher."

We joined him in a round of applause and a hearty hurrah.

He raised a glass of apple cider and asked us to join him in a toast. "To the women of Utah," he said.

"Hear, hear," we agreed, clinking glasses.

Hector said, "We must be careful not to take our political good fortune for granted. The territory of Utah is under the control of the Federal government, and there are those who wish to suppress the Mormon vote. If they prove to be successful, women may lose the right to vote in Utah."

I was surprised at his words and realized my naivete when it came to the world of politics. Before I became a voter, I was determined to increase my civil education.

"But tonight," Hector continued, "we celebrate the women's victory."

The mutton was cooked to perfection and seemed to melt in my mouth. The roasted potatoes had the right consistency, crisp on the outside and soft on the inside. All in all, it was one of the best meals I'd eaten.

We polished off the main course and were enjoying the custard when I noticed Mother's energy was flagging, and she appeared to be slumping. Louisa looked at her, and then at me. She could see it too. Father was deep in conversation with the two Haight men as I stood and approached his chair.

I whispered, "I believe the time has come to take Mother home."

He took one look at her and agreed.

Louisa stood. "Thank you to our dear friends for joining us in the evening's festivities," she said. "A very Happy Valentine's Day to you all."

"It's been our pleasure to be with you on this auspicious occasion," Father said, standing. "An unforgettable evening for which we express our most sincere gratitude." Turning to my mother, "Elizabeth, my darling," he said, offering his hand, "it's time to take our leave."

She almost collapsed in his arms as she stood. Louisa retrieved Mother's cloak and bonnet, and all three men helped her out to the carriage, where she attempted to stand on her own before entering. But her knees hitched under her small frame.

"Are you well, Mother?" I asked.

"My head feels as if it is spinning," she said. "I'll be fine when we arrive home. My thanks to all of you," she said waving a handkerchief and saying goodbye.

As we rode home, the cold night air did Mother some good and she was a little better when we arrived, though still wobbly on her feet. Father and Ada helped her to bed. *Why can't I do anything for her? There must be something.*

I went to my room and returned to my stack of medical books, searching again for answers to the cause of my mother's chronic illness. After a few hours of discouraging research, I found nothing that explained her symptoms.

Desiring to record the evening's events, I picked up my diary and began writing. I put pen to paper and realized that as glorious as it was that the women of Utah had won the right to suffrage, and several had actually cast a ballot today, there was still much to be done for our sister suffragists in other parts of the nation. It was incumbent on the women of Utah to get involved in the struggle. I'd written down something Elizabeth Cady Stanton, National Woman's suffrage leader, had said: "Every truth we see is ours to give the world, not to keep for ourselves alone."

Emma

Spring had come to the foothills of Farmington, and the purple and yellow wildflowers were in bloom against the green backdrop of the mountains. White, wispy clouds punctuated the blue sky, and the City of Roses was at its finest.

Emma stood alone at the front of the Rock Chapel, peering out the window at the radiant sunshine and waiting for Sunday services to begin. She had arrived early, allowing her a moment for quiet reflection.

Turning away from the window, Emma gazed down the long, rather narrow room and recalled the day church members united their voices in prayer seeking the Lord's assistance to build this fine edifice...

The entire ward, including the children, had donated all monies they could spare for months to a building fund. Coming up woefully short, they sought God's divine guidance.

A few days after their fervent prayers, a huge storm violently struck the town. It rained for days on end, and a heavy wind toppled trees. Emma was only eleven at the time and remained indoors all day, fearing to go outside.

The next morning, the storm abated. The townspeople ventured out to assess the damage and found a large rockslide a few blocks from the location designated for the new church in a street also filled with sand and gravel. What a mess.

But they soon saw the miracle for what it was. Enough rock had tumbled down the mountain to build a new chapel, and the extant sand and gravel could serve as mortar.

When the construction commenced, the men used ox teams to haul rocks that were then laid to build the walls. Emma remembered serving men food and water that the Relief Society supplied. Members of the ward congregation toiled two long years to complete the chapel.

On January 9, 1864, Brigham Young had traveled to Farmington to dedicate the building. What a day of jubilee and rejoicing it had been. Emma especially loved the Farmington brass band. No one involved in the creation of this chapel would ever take its construction for granted...

Anne tapped Emma on the shoulder. The chapel was filling with people.

"Do you mind if I join your family nearer the front today? I've been asked to sing a hymn prior to the bishop delivering his sermon. Charles will remain on our usual bench."

"Of course, you may. Please come sit by me. I love hearing you sing."

Following an opening hymn and prayer, a quiet spirit of reverence filled the room during the administration of the sacrament, our sacred ordinance for partaking of bread and water in remembrance of Christ. It was Anne's turn to sing.

She walked up a few steps to the white podium on the left, and took her place at the rostrum, nodding at her accompanist to begin. Her voice rose in song, and Emma's breath caught in her throat as she listened to the hymn 'God is Love.' No one moved as Anne intoned the familiar words, 'Earth with her ten thousand flowers.' Not even the babies stirred as she sang with the voice of an angel.

Emma turned discreetly in her seat to look at Charles, who seemed oblivious to his wife's melody, scribbling something on paper. *What's he doing that's so all-fired important?*

Anne finished her song and sat next to Emma.

The bishop spoke next, taking his text from the Bible, I Corinthians chapter 13. "Charity," he said, "meaning love, is gentle. Love is kind, is not puffed up, and is not easily provoked. That's what we strive for daily in our families."

The love spoken of did not describe the way Charles treated Anne; sometimes he was kind, and other times mean. *Was he listening to this?* Emma couldn't resist glancing again in his direction. Still scribbling, paying no attention to what was being declared over the pulpit.

When the bishop concluded his talk, and the closing prayer was offered, Anne rose to join Charles.

Emma said to Anne, "Your song was divine. Thank you." Then she paused, not wishing to sound critical. "Charles seemed to be quite busy making notes about something or other as the bishop spoke."

"Charles desires to expand his influence by encouraging legislation that will reinforce and support our cattle business—and that of others, of course," she added.

Emma attempted to understand his priorities, or lack thereof, in her estimation.

"I'm proud of his ambition," Anne said, raising her chin. "And you must pay no mind to what we discussed the other day, Emma. I spoke out of turn about what was anomalous behavior for Charles."

Emma very much doubted that. Anne walked away, and it seemed to Emma that perhaps it was Charles's ambition that had drawn Anne to him. Emma recalled the words of Shakespeare's Lady Macbeth from the play she and her schoolmates had been recently reading. 'Vaulting ambition, which o'er leaps itself, and falls on the other side.' She wondered if that might describe Charles. *What did the future hold for Anne?*

"Emma," her father spoke.

"Yes, Father?"

"I see Wesley Hatch approaching. He was the deputy posted outside Katie's house when Fred Grimes was killed."

As if I need reminding. Emma smiled to herself.

"Would you care to meet him?"

"I would, please," she said.

When Wesley reached their bench, Emma's father said, "Emma, may I present my deputy, Wesley Hatch. Wesley, my daughter Emma."

Emma stretched out her hand, and Wesley took it in his and bowed slightly. "Miss Gregory," he said. "It's a pleasure."

"Mr. Hatch," she replied and curtsied. "The pleasure's all mine." Their hands touched, and Emma felt something shoot straight through her. Wesley's eyes told her he experienced something similar. It wasn't until her father cleared his throat that they let go of each other's hands. "I'll leave you two a moment to get acquainted," he said.

Emma began the conversation. "I was impressed with the professional way you comported yourself at the death of Fred Grimes." *What a silly thing to say*, she chided herself. *He must think me a fool. Why are you so tongue-tied?* Her throat grew thick.

Wesley returned a cordial smile and said, "Thank you, Miss Gregory. The true professional that day was Mrs. Rosemary Shaw."

"I'd have to agree with you there, Mr. Hatch. Do you find it odd that the Pinkertons hire female detectives?"

"I believe women are quite capable in whatever they choose to undertake. My grandmother pulled a handcart with six children across the plains with no one to assist her."

A wonderful answer, Emma thought. *I'll try another question and gauge his response.* "I'm sure I would admire your grandmother, and I'm delighted that women have recently received the right to suffrage."

"I'm also pleased with the new law. As you know, in our faith women have always had the right to vote 'yay or nay' along with the men when someone is called to a position. It seems to me a natural extension of that existing religious right to extend women the ballot."

Emma hadn't thought of it that way, and she appreciated his words. He was no Charles Archer; of that she was certain.

"I wonder if I may call on you sometime."

"I'd like that very much."

"I'll speak with your father about when I may come see you," he said, tipping his hat and walking away.

Emma closed her eyes, standing stock still, unaware of anything or anyone around her.

"Emma," Katie interrupted, "Are you quite well?"

Emma turned. "Fine, fine, yes."

"You're positively glowing, my dear. Does this have anything to do with your conversation with Mr. Hatch? I observed the two of you from across the chapel." Katie grinned.

"Is it that obvious?"

"Perhaps only to someone who knows you as well as I do. Did he ask to see you?"

"He did," Emma said, reaching out and holding Katie's hand.

"A gentlemen caller, how wonderful. You must tell me all about it when he courts you."

Her father came to take Emma home and she told Katie good-bye.

The walk home was several blocks long, and Emma enjoyed each step she took alone in the warm sunshine, leaving her family to walk ahead of her. *What a glorious day*, she thought, skin tingling. *And are those birds singing?* "Yes," she said aloud, heart beating rhythmically to their sweet notes.

Wesley is handsome, brave, spiritual, and supports the expanding sphere of women. What more could I ask for? Emma's heart was light as she skipped ahead, catching up with her family, trusting Wesley would come by soon.

Four

Katie

I was finishing a bit of mending when I heard a blood-curdling scream come from the yard. I tossed my sewing aside and ran outside to find Joseph lying on the ground, desperately crawling away from Yancy, our new black quarter horse. Father had hold of the reins and was calming the rearing horse as I raced to Joseph's side.

"Katie!" he screamed. "It's my knee. Yancy kicked me with his hind leg!"

I dropped to the grass beside him to have a look. His pants were torn, and his knee was bleeding and already beginning to swell. "Don't move," I said. "I'll go fetch the doctor." I hoisted my skirts and ran several blocks to the small office that bore the name 'Dr. Axel Persson,' hoping to find him in.

When I arrived, he was on his way out, medical bag in hand. The two of us near collided at the door.

"What is it, Katie?" he asked, taking me by the shoulders and setting me right on my feet again.

"It's Joseph. A horse kicked him, and his knee looks awful."

"Let's take my buggy and go to him. Climb aboard."

I wedged in beside him and he snapped a whip lightly over the large bay horses.

Minutes later, we rode into the yard. Father was at Joseph's side comforting him, and Yancy was chuffing against the fence, head down.

Dr. Axel walked across the dirt and sat next to Joseph. "Let me see that knee," he said, using scissors to cut away the overalls around the wound. Joseph moaned in pain at the doctor's touch. "It doesn't appear to be broken, but it's likely fractured. Our first concern is to do what we can to prevent infection."

He took a bottle of distilled camphor from his bag, preparing to pour it over the wound. As he opened the vial, the aroma was clear and piercing.

"Will it sting?" Joseph asked.

"No, it will cool your wound and begin to reduce the growing inflammation, my boy."

I held Joseph's hand as the doctor poured the oil. Doctor Axel turned to Father and said, "I'll administer a bit of morphine to assist in controlling the pain while I suture the wound."

Despite the morphine Joseph grimaced in pain as Doctor Axel closed the skin with his needle.

The stitching completed, Father and Dr. Axel carried Joseph inside, easing him up the stairs and into his room. I followed along, making certain Joseph was comfortably settled in bed. "Will you have to bleed him?" I asked, worried. "I've read about that procedure in some of my medical books."

"The once orthodox treatment of using leeches and fomentations has fallen into disfavor and has no value compared to circular compression and perfect immobilization of the limb," Dr. Axel stated, removing some sort of cotton from his bag. Noting my curiosity, he said, "This is surgical gauze treated with carbolic acid which seems to drop the mortality rate of patients."

I watched as he placed the gauze on the wound, then wound the end of a large bandage under the knee, carried it round the limb, bringing it over the same part two of three times, finishing it off with a turn or two. "Now, Joseph," he said, "you must lie still and stay off your leg as much as possible for two weeks, giving it time to heal. I leave it to you, Katie, to remove the bandage daily, apply this fresh gauze and restore his bandage, wrapping the knee as I did."

"I will do just as you ask."

"Two weeks?" Joseph asked weakly.

"Yes, my boy, and following those two weeks, you must use a walking stick or cane for two more."

"Such a long time," Joseph said. "The July 24th celebration is coming in under four weeks." He sounded sleepy, turning his head to the wall.

"Let us kneel and pray for him," the good doctor said.

I knew he was a firm believer in prayer and often knelt at the bedside of a patient in supplication for help from a power greater than his own.

He concluded the prayer, we rose, and he said, "Let's leave him to sleep now." The three of us crept from the room.

"Thank you," Father said shaking his hand when we arrived at the front door. "I will come by your office and settle up in a few days."

"Thank you, John. There's no rush; I know you're good for the payment."

"May I walk you out to your carriage, Dr. Axel?" I asked.

"Of course, you may, Katie."

I loved Dr. Axel Persson. As the town doctor, he was a familiar sight, riding through Farmington in his horse and buggy. Some of the children thought he looked a bit like Santa Claus, with his white hair and rosy red cheeks. His tummy was so round that he sometimes used it as a writing desk, and he loved to pass around a bag of peppermint candy and tell stories. He was known for his compassion, sitting at the bedside of the sick all night using old home remedies paired with words of encouragement to help his patient recover.

"One of the best things you can do for your brother is to cheer him while he lays healing," he said to me. "He has had quite a shock to his system, and it is common for those in his circumstance to become discouraged."

I hadn't thought about the way a patient's mind and heart are connected in the healing process.

"Sit by his bedside, play games with him, invite his friends over. And feed him lots of johnny cake." He winked.

I laughed. "I want to be a doctor just like you."

Without skipping a beat, he said, "Studying to be a doctor is a wonderful aspiration, my dear. Come by my office anytime, should you wish to discuss the practice of medicine further."

"Thank you, Doctor Axel. I look forward to it."

****

Within three weeks, Joseph was up and about, walking without a cane. Though he still favored his uninjured leg, he had healed sufficiently to participate in his favorite holiday. Our family boarded the train for Salt Lake City the evening of July twenty-third to stay with Cousin Sophia.

As the morning of July 24th broke, we heard a cannon firing and a large bell ringing. Those were our signals to begin our annual celebration of the day commemorating the pioneers' arrival into the Salt Lake valley in 1847. I had been asked to ride on the City of Farmington float along with other girls my age, including Emma. Her father would pull the decorated wagon using a team of horses.

After performing my morning washings, I donned a long white parade dress with green trim, pulling my hair back in a bun. Since I was the tallest among us, I would stand and hold the large green parasol over my head, shading my friends who would sit on the top tier of the float. I fussed with my clothing and checked and rechecked my hair in the mirror, a fluttery feeling inside.

I walked downstairs and Joseph let out a low whistle. "You look beautiful, my sister."

"Thank you." I curtsied and smiled. "When do we leave?"

"As soon as we finish breakfast," Mother said.

"Would you care for something to eat?" Sophia asked.

"No, thank you. Is your speech ready for later, Father?"

He smiled. "Yes, it is, and don't worry, I will make you proud."

"You always make me proud."

I walked into the parlor and stood in front of the window, waiting for the others. When everyone was ready to go, we made our way to Main Street where the parade would begin. Emma was already there.

"The float looks lovely," I said, noting the bunches of flowers draped along the sides of the white cloth. Wesley Hatch rode up on his horse, paper roses serving as a blanket for his saddle. He was wearing a bolo hat, suit, and cravat, and looked quite handsome. He would accompany us, riding behind our float. He tipped his hat, and Emma smiled, all her attention focused on him.

He climbed down from his horse and lifted each of us onto the deck of the float. When we were settled and my parasol was raised, Sheriff Gregory tugged on the reins of the team and we began our slow walk to get in the parade line.

An open carriage carrying the town's dignitaries led the procession, our float coming after several of the others, all followed by a brass band. Young men pulling handcarts came behind the band. Joseph watched from the sidelines, his knee almost healed, as his friends dragged the handcart my father had used when he crossed the plains at the age of twelve.

Father often told stories of Mormon families being driven from their homes in Nauvoo, Illinois, many of the men whipped, or killed, and their homes burned. In the peaceful setting where we now lived, it was difficult to imagine the horrors and trials our parents and grandparents had endured. *These are the people we remember every July 24: Our blessed, honored pioneers.*

As the procession went down Main Street, residents lined the streets and cheered, the children waving as we passed. The brass band struck up a favorite song and all of us in the parade and on the sidelines began singing aloud the familiar words: "Put your shoulder to the wheel push along, do your duty with a heart full of song."

When the parade returned to its origin, I could see Father sitting at the podium, reviewing his notes. With Wesley's help, we got down from the float and stood amongst the rest of the town, waiting for the orations to begin.

"July 24th is the best holiday ever and never disappoints," Emma whispered to me.

We listened to several speakers, Father being the last. He began by reminding us that it was the mercy of God that had made our desert home "blossom as the rose." He concluded a few minutes later with something W.W. Phelps, early leader and writer, had said in 1851: "The 24th of July, the Mormon Thanksgiving; for more land, more light, more learning. Honored and blessed be the ever-great day." Father paused and said, "Let's go to the supper."

We all cheered at that. It was time to eat, and I found myself ravenous. I was looking forward to a large, outdoor supper, followed by dancing in the bowery. Our dances added to the religious significance of the day, as we merry Mormons danced in gratitude for the opportunity to reside in these lovely vales and practice our religion in peace.

I turned to speak with Emma and found that she had wandered over to where her father and Wesley stood. They seemed to be in love, and I was happy for my friend.

Emma

Emma's family continued the July celebration, gathering at long tables and benches for a supper of chicken, mutton, beans, pies, and puddings. Emma's grandmother joined them, and her father had invited Wesley as well. After Emma's mother died giving birth to her, Grandmother Phoebe had been her support.

"Grandmother," Emma said, "I believe you've met my friend and Father's deputy, Mr. Wesley Hatch."

"Ma'am." Wesley rose from the bench and said, "It's an honor to see you again."

"Thank you, Mr. Hatch. I know you've been courting my granddaughter." Emma's grandmother never minced words when it came to Emma.

"Yes, Ma'am. It's been my honor to do so these past five months."

"Your intentions are honorable, then?"

Wesley declared in a firm voice, "They are indeed."

"How old are you, if I may be so bold?" Grandmother asked, jaw set, brow furrowed.

"Twenty-two."

"Emma is not yet eighteen, and she can't marry until she reaches eighteen."

"Yes, Ma'am. She told me that."

"I understand you work for my son-in-law as a deputy and that you came from Salt Lake. Why leave Salt Lake for Farmington?" Emma's grandmother seemed poised to continue the relentless barrage of questions.

"Sheriff Gregory offered a promotion and pay raise, and I prefer a small town to a larger city."

"Would you care for beans and corn on the cob, Grandmother?" Emma asked, hoping to deflect the conversation.

"Yes, thank you, my dear."

"I'd be pleased to answer any other questions you have of me," Wesley said.

"That will do for now. But should marriage be in your future, the two of you must remember that a lasting marriage takes more than love. It requires time, effort, and patience."

"Yes, Grandmother," Emma said.

After supper, Wesley and Emma lingered a moment alone, and the rest of the family proceeded to the bowery for the evening's dancing. The juvenile dance would come first, and the stated purpose was to 'socialize the children and teach them steps they would use later in life on similar occasions.' It also helped them feel they were an important part of the celebration.

When Wesley and Emma reached the hall, the children were singing 'All Things Bright and Beautiful,' which concluded the juvenile dancing. As the younger ones walked away, the brass band struck up a tune. Wesley escorted Emma to the floor where they danced, performing rills and quadrilles. Between dance numbers, the crowd sang and some offered humorous toasts, lifting glasses of apple cider amid the laughter. It was a lively evening.

At last came a waltz. Wesley took Emma in his arms, and they glided across the floor to the sounds of 'The Blue Danube.' As Wesley held her, Emma found herself lost in the music and his gentle touch.

Emma's father interrupted their reverie with a tap on Wesley's shoulder. "I'd like the next dance with my daughter."

"Of course, sir." Wesley said, stepping back. But the music stopped, and the band took a short break.

"I'm feeling quite flushed and could use some night air," Emma said to Wesley. "Do you mind, Father?"

"Go ahead, but don't be long. And see if you can find your brother, David, while you're out. He's somewhere in the yard with his friend, Jack."

"Yes, Father."

When Wesley and Emma walked outside, the night was lit with stars and the moon was beaming overhead. He put his arm around her shoulders, and she leaned into him as they walked.

"I see David and Jack there, and they appear to be striking matches," Emma said.

"I suspect they have firecrackers, which could prove dangerous."

David blew the match out when he saw Emma and Wesley.

"What's that you have there, boys?" Wesley asked.

"Just a couple of firecrackers," David said.

"Do you know how to use them?" Wesley asked.

"Sure, what's to know?" Jack retorted. "You light the fuse and they go pop."

"See this long, white scar on my hand?" Wesley asked.

"Yeah, I see it."

"Burn I got from a firecracker when I was about your age. Hurt like the dickens."

David and Jack looked at each other and back at Wesley.

"Permit me to share some pointers about firecracker safety," Wesley advised, stepping between them. "First, make certain you stand clear of any of those trees. When you put the match to the fuse, toss the firecracker in the dirt. After it's cooled off, soak what's left in this bucket of water. Do either of you have gloves?"

"No, sir," David said.

"Here, you may use mine," Wesley said. "Let's light these crackers together."

David and Jack had two firecrackers each. After they finished setting them off, David turned to Wesley and said, "Thank you, Mr. Hatch. I like you."

"Thank you, David," Wesley said, tousling the boy's hair. "I like you, too."

Emma stood back and watched, noting that Wesley was good with the boys, and they respected him. *He'll make a fine father.* "Off you go, David and Jack," she said. "Back to the bowery with you."

"Beat you there," Jack said and took off.

"No, you won't," David countered, running after him.

Wesley and Emma stayed behind and gazed up at millions of stars. "Look, there's the big dipper," Wesley said.

"And there's Orion. Such a wonderous night." All her senses were heightened.

"Emma, when I'm in your presence, I feel something I don't understand."

She turned and looked at him. "I feel it too, Wesley. You seem to have, I don't know, a familiar spirit."

He smiled. "Perhaps we knew each before."

She moistened her lips and said, "I don't know if that's why I feel a connection to you, but I do."

He drew her in for a kiss, and sparks flew between them.

Emma took a step back and ran a finger across his lips. "We'd best go back inside."

"Wait one moment, please," he said, turning to face her. "Did I mention that I spoke to your father about us last week?"

"No, you didn't."

"I asked for your hand in marriage, my darling, after you reach the age of eighteen."

Emma was breathless. "What did Father say?"

"He sat me down and proceeded to interrogate me. Said he loved you and that he wanted only the best for his daughter. Then, he leaned across his desk, looked straight at me, and said I'd better be an honorable husband to you and a solid father to our children or I'd have him to answer to. He removed the gun from his holster and laid it on the desk between us. I got the message."

"After all that, I'm surprised you're still here."

"Wild horses couldn't keep me away. All my life, I've waited for someone like you, Emma. Thanks be to God, I found you."

Emma kissed him gently on the lips again.

He got down on one knee and took her hand in his. "Will you marry me?"

"Oh, yes," she said.

Wesley stood, took a box from his pocket, and removed a gold ring. He placed the ring on her finger and said, "It was my grandmother's."

"It's exquisite," Emma said, turning it to catch the light. "You were quite certain I'd say yes, weren't you?" She grinned.

"I was, perhaps, optimistic."

Emma laughed. "One of the things I like best about you. Let's go share our good fortune with the others."

When they reached the bowery, Wesley strode up to the band leader and asked for a moment after the song finished. The music stopped and all eyes were on Wesley, except Katie's. She was looking directly at Emma's finger.

"May I have your attention, please," Wesley began. "Emma will you come up here with me, please?"

Her mouth was dry, and her pulse quickened as she approached.

"After receiving her father's blessing, I have asked Emma Gregory to marry me. She has consented to become my wife for time and for all eternity."

The crowd drummed their feet against the floor, shot their hands into the air, and cheered. Wesley lifted Emma from the floor and swung her around to the delight of those looking on.

Katie, Julia, and a gaggle of Emma's friends rushed to her side, squealing and hugging her. Emma pretended to faint, and they all laughed.

"Show us the ring," Katie said.

Emma beamed, held out her hand, and some good-natured jostling followed as the girls tried to get a closer look at her ring finger.

"It's lovely," Katie said. "My heartiest congratulations to you both."

The band's drummer rapped his sticks against the cymbals and called, "Everyone take the floor for an engagement dance."

Adult dancers and children filled the floor and the band struck up a polka.

Emma and Wesley danced one number, left the floor, and sat next to Grandmother Phoebe. "Do we have your blessing, too?" Wesley asked.

"Yes, my children, you do. You're a lucky man, Wesley Hatch, and I trust you know that my Emma is a gem without price."

"Yes, Ma'am, she is," he said looking into Emma's eyes. "I'll take good care of her and love her with my dying breath and beyond."

The two of them wrapped Grandmother Phoebe in their arms and hugged her close to their hearts.

Five

Katie

At the conclusion of our July celebration, Sophia and I watched from her front porch as my family climbed into a carriage bound for the train station. Father's smile was hesitant as he waved good-bye, and I knew he didn't like departing without me. Sophia had invited me to remain so I could accompany her to the August county elections. It would be the first time she voted, and I couldn't wait to observe the procedure.

When Father questioned the advisability of my staying behind, I smiled and reminded him that he had only himself to blame for my interest in politics. No argument there.

"Katie will be fine with Sophia," Mother said, and so they left Salt Lake for Farmington without me.

As an attorney, Father had been trained to see both sides of every question, and he delighted in taking a position that he guessed would be in opposition to mine, merely for the sport of engaging me in debate. Neither my mother nor my brothers enjoyed these heated discussions, so they left the room whenever we were at variance with one another.

Looking back, I suppose our political discourses began when I was thirteen, and the country was preparing for the 1868 presidential elections. Father followed the news closely and regularly discussed it with me. He advised that if he were to choose a party, it would be Republican.

After reading over the positions of both parties, I asked him what sense it made that the Republican party supported suffrage only in the south, agreeing to let northern states decide whether to franchise negro males.

"While I agree with you in principle," he declared, "the democratic Presidential candidate, Horatio Seymour, wants to overthrow reconstruction altogether, since he says it was the radical Republicans that forced it on the South."

"Then," I stated, "I don't believe I could support the position of either party."

"This is the democratic process and our two-party structure," he said, "where sometimes we choose the lesser of two evils. It's an imperfect system, and change takes time."

Though soon-to-be-President Ulysses Grant had taken no part in the campaign that year, and made no promises, the Republican campaign theme had been, 'Let us have peace.' And in the end, the election had been won with that mantra.

"You appear lost in thought," Sophia said, bringing in a silver tray with hot blueberry muffins.

"They look so tasty," I said, grateful to be the only one spending time with Sophia. Today, we would be permitted breakfast in peace.

With my mind still consumed with politics, I said, "I was delighted earlier this year when Congress passed the fifteenth amendment granting Negro men the right to vote, and President Grant signed it into law. But why didn't the nation's women get the right to vote at the same time?"

"That's an excellent question," Sophia said between bites. "It wasn't for lack of trying. Leaders of the national movement, Susan B. Anthony, Elizabeth Cady Stanton, and many others, worked tirelessly to include woman's suffrage in the amendment with no success."

"Imagine what good we might do if all the women in the country could vote," I said, fanning myself against the heat of the day.

"Female suffrage is under legislative consideration in most states outside the South, but no state legislature is yet convinced it's the right thing to do. It's not just the men, Katie; there are many women who don't wish to vote."

"I confess I don't understand that."

"Even in my Fifteenth Ward Relief Society, views on women voting run the gamut. While some of our sisters declare themselves fully in favor of women's rights, others agree that they will vote for good men, though they have no interest in politics. Still others assert that they refuse to vote because they find politics beneath them."

"It seems to me that refusing to participate in civic matters precludes meaningful change."

Sophia reached over and patted my hand. "You are a Leavitt through and through," she said, "and I'm delighted, but we must try and understand the positions of others."

I nodded. "You're right, of course."

"Speaking of the positions of others, are you aware that Utah has initiated a two-party system?"

"I thought voters supported the candidate they favored, who ran with no political affiliation."

"All that changed when William Godbe established what he calls the 'Liberal party' earlier this year."

"Isn't Mr. Godbe a former member of our religion?"

"Yes. He started his own church last year. The Godbeite Church is also known as the Church of Zion, and earlier this year, Godbe decided to form a new political party with the stated goal of selecting what he called 'independent candidates' for the Salt Lake City municipal election. His organizers claimed the occasion was a meeting of the 'people.' My neighbor, Maxwell, attended, along with a crowd of others, and nearly hijacked the meeting."

"The kind of thing, I suspect, that prompts some women to find politics beneath them." I was enjoying our conversation immensely.

"A very frustrated Godbeite named Kelsey asked them to leave, which they did. Those who remained designated what they deemed an independent municipal ticket, thus forming the Liberal Party."

"What's the name of the other party?"

"It's called the People's party, and it was the People's party that championed woman's suffrage and secured the right to the ballot. Following the passage of the legislation, Sarah Kimball declared in a Relief Society meeting that she had waited patiently a long time, and now that we were granted the right of suffrage, she would openly declare herself a woman's right's woman."

"I like that."

"She called on us to back her up, and many of us did, including me."

"I'm honored to call you Cousin."

"Thank you, my dear," Sophia said. "I'm pleased you remained to accompany me as I cast my first ballot."

"You have no idea how much it means to me."

Sophia smiled and looked startled. "See the time," she said looking at the clock. "We've spent hours discussing politics. May I offer you a change of pace? Would you enjoy doing some shopping downtown?"

"I'd like that," I said, collecting my bonnet.

When we reached downtown, we found large crowds of men and women holding mass political rallies. On one corner, signs declared that the people were gathered in support of the Liberal party. On the other corner, members of the People's party were holding signs and calling out their preferences for candidates. A great deal of tension existed between the two groups.

Having had enough of politics for one day, Sophia and I slipped into the Zion's Cooperative Mercantile Institute store looking for shoes from 'The Big Boot' shoe factory that had opened earlier this year. I was astounded at the large selection we found. One of the clerks told us the factory had manufactured 83,000 shoes since ZCMI opened. I had no trouble finding myself a fashionable new pair of black boots and a blue pair for Mother. We made our way home for supper and retired early for the night.

The next day dawned clear and warm, and it was the August first election. Today's election would be memorable, because it was the first time the women of Utah would vote in a territorial election. Sophia had told me that it would also mark the first time in the nation women voted with unrestricted suffrage rights. It was anticipated that thousands of women would turn out to vote today.

I donned a green dress with ruffles down the skirt and white lace at the bodice, adding a white hat, my hair pulled back neatly behind my ears. Sophia had dressed in a light blue skirt, accompanied by a matching blue top with large lapels and white cuffs. As we prepared to leave the house, Sophia gave me a sunflower, pinning it to my dress. "It's lovely," I said. "Thank you."

"This flower has special meaning today, Katie."

"How so?"

"In 1867, Kansas suffragists used the sunflower, their state symbol, in a suffrage campaign. Since that time, yellow has become the symbolic color of the national woman's suffrage movement."

"I'm pleased to be wearing a sunflower, Sophia."

"I thought you might be. Today, we show our colors."

While the *Salt Lake Herald* had suggested in yesterday's paper that quietness be the order of the day today, as Sophia and I walked to the Council Hall we found the streets crowded and the mood festive. Several bands, including the 10th ward brass band and Olsen's string band were outside dispensing first-rate music. People seemed good natured, and a few of them jostled about, telling jokes. I noticed that the men were generally showing the utmost respect to the women.

A separate entrance to the hall had been opened and many ladies were lined up, their heads close together, chatting. There was a sense of camaraderie that pervaded the group.

Sophia and I got in line with the others and saw a sign that read, 'Voters proceed.' As we waited, raising our parasols for shade against the hot sun, she turned to me and whispered, "Several of my friends intend to vote for women for public office."

"But women can't yet run for office," I said, puzzled.

"That's true, but their goal is to make a statement that they should be allowed to do so. While I agree, I didn't want to throw away my first vote."

Once we made our way inside, we saw lines of women winding down several flights of stairs. On the landing below sat a metal ballot box with glass on either side that had been placed on a small round table, an American flag upright at the side. A dapper looking gentleman sporting a black moustache and wearing a black hat stood at the side of the table, book in hand, recording the names of those who voted. He raised his eyebrows when he saw me, so I moved to the side when it was Sophia's turn to mark her ballot. She looked in my direction as she dropped it inside the box, eyes filled with confidence.

Today I participated in the new order of things.

The two of us left the hall jubilant, walking through the streets arm in arm, as we called out together, "Hurrah for the women of Utah." We received answering hurrahs from all around us.

Sophia said, "Mark my words, Katie, suffrage will be an important topic in Relief Society meetings across the territory. I've heard that Sarah Kimball is preparing a course on civic education, and we will be encouraged to study the workings of government and participate in civic affairs."

"Will women attend political conventions as well?" I asked.

"I expect we'll be represented at all local and county conventions. I know I'll be present," she said, "and you should join me."

Emma

Katie had told Emma about the August election, and she looked forward to casting a ballot when she reached the age of twenty-one. Today she was more interested in finalizing her wedding plans. Emma wore a simple dress, the kind she often wore around the house, a print fabric with a high neckline and long sleeves. She also wore a shawl against the November cold. Emma tapped her foot, smoothed the cream-colored apron that lay over her dress and looked at the clock on the wall. Wesley wasn't late—at least not yet.

Her father had let them use his office, away from the hubbub of the family's comings and goings. Emma appreciated this room, with its black leather chairs studded with silver nails, ornately carved wooden desk, and an American flag standing in the corner. On the wall hung a picture of a smiling young Emma with her first dog, Ruby.

The new bell her father had installed at the front door jangled. *That must be Wesley*, she thought, a wide grin covering her face. Wesley and her father strode across the parlor, conversing in serious tones.

Her father came into the room and took a seat in the gray chair behind the desk, indicating that Emma and Wesley should sit in the leather chairs facing him "Pardon the interruption, Emma. I need to speak with Wesley, but you may find our discussion of interest."

"Tell me more, Sheriff," Wesley said.

"There was a train robbery on the evening of November fourth in Nevada about five miles west of Reno. It was Nevada's first robbery and too close to Utah in my book."

Wesley let out a low whistle. "Which line, and where was the train coming from?"

"Central Pacific from San Francisco. The express car held a load of Wells Fargo sacks filled with twenty-dollar gold pieces, value about $41,000. The shipment was on its way to Virginia City to make payroll for the Yellow Jacket Mine."

"Piles of money," Wesley said.

"Yes, although they left several silver bars behind, probably because they were too heavy for the sacks."

"How did the robbers pull it off?" Emma asked, curious.

"As the train was leaving the station, three masked men climbed on board and unhitched the engine and express car from the remainder of the train. There were five robbers already on the train who then joined the others, whereupon the varmints locked the brakemen and the guards in the mail room, using a double-barreled shotgun."

"Must have been some pretty bad hombres," Wesley said.

"As it turned out, the leader of the band was a Christian Sunday school superintendent by the name of John Chapman."

"A Sunday school superintendent?" Emma asked. "I never would have figured someone like that for a robber."

"There's no explaining some folks' actions, Emma. There's those who look good to the outside world who are shady characters in their hearts. You never know what those types might be capable of doing."

Emma's mind went to Charles Archer, another scallywag. She wanted to tell her father her concerns about Charles, but she had promised Anne and so she remained silent.

"How did they get the train to stop?" Wesley asked.

"'Bout five miles west of Reno, near a location called Hunter's Station. Other members of the gang had put rocks and logs on the tracks so the engine and express car would have to stop there."

"Had it all planned out," Wesley said.

"Did the train ever reach Reno?" Emma asked.

"Yes, thanks to the quick thinking on the part of the train conductor who let the rear half of the train coast downhill. The robbers had already made their getaway by that time, and the engineer and fireman reconnected the rear and front of the train, then lit out for Reno, reaching the station only thirty minutes late.

"When the train reached Reno, law enforcement officials were immediately on the case, and several days later, they apprehended the gang and most of the gold. Turned out two of the men were stage robbers, who applied their experience in robbing stages to robbing trains."

"We live in a new world with the advent of the railway," Emma said.

"Truer words were never spoken, my girl."

"But surely an event such as a train robbery is rare, Father."

"In my estimation, we're at the beginning of an increase in railway crimes, Sheriff," Wesley said.

"Case in point, twenty hours later and a couple hundred miles further down the track, another train robbery happened on the same train on the same day."

Emma leaned forward, curious. "Are we in danger here, too, Father?"

"The state of Nevada is near enough that it was once part of the Utah Territory, so we should be prepared," he replied. "The driving of the Golden Spike last year marked the end of an era. The output of our mines has increased sevenfold since the railroad's completion. According to one estimation, more than a million dollars in gold, silver, copper, lead, and zinc has been taken out of the Utah mines this year."

"I'd say that makes us an eventual target for robbers," Wesley said.

"The immigration of new settlers is increasing too," Emma said. "It used to take three months to come to Utah by wagon from the East, and now it takes less than a week by train.

"With rapid change comes both the good and the bad," her father said. "It behooves us as officers of the law to be vigilant, Wesley."

"Yes, sir."

"I'd be happy to help in any way I can, Father," Emma said.

"What did you have in mind?" he asked.

"I could work undercover like Mrs. Shaw did. Perhaps ride the rails and keep an eye out."

"That may be a bridge too far for the time being, Emma," her father said. "But let's keep it in mind. Now, I'll go so the two of you can talk." He stood. "Have you set a date for the blessed event?"

"Next June, the first of the month," Emma said.

He looked at his daughter, a wistful expression on his face. "I leave you to your conversation."

"Discussing our wedding seems anticlimactic after the revelation of train robberies in Nevada," she said to Wesley.

He took her hand in his. "There is nothing more important to me than you in all the world. What would you think about getting married at the Haight hotel, followed by dinner and a reception on the lawn? We could travel to Salt Lake the following day and have our union sealed for eternity in the Endowment House. That would allow some of my family members, who are not of our faith, to attend our wedding."

"It's a wonderful idea," Emma said, placing her hand absently on his knee. "I'd like to have the wedding party arrive in separate carriages the day of the party to heighten the fun."

"I leave all those details to you," he said, leaning over and kissing her on the cheek. "I can't wait for us to be husband and wife. I have something I'd like to show you. Let's get your cloak and bonnet."

They left the house and walked several blocks north and then east to find the foundation and outer walls of a building. "What will this be when it's finished?" Emma asked.

"Our new home," he said, turning and touching her face, smiling. "Your father and I have been working on it since July when you agreed to marry me. The men from our ward helped us haul quartz and granite rocks from the canyon that we used to construct it."

As they walked across the dirt, he said, "When it's finished, the walls will be more than thirty inches deep, lined with adobe bricks that we'll plaster over and whitewash."

"It's more than I expected," she said, noting the spool turned pillars waiting to be put up on the porch.

Wesley took her hand in his. "It will be complete by the end of April, and we'll have May to furnish it."

"It's lovely, and a delightful surprise."

Six

Katie

I watched the sun rise in a sky painted orange and pink, thinking it looked a bit chilly outside for late May. *Emma's wedding is next month, and it should be warmer by then.* The rest of my family remained in bed as I dressed, donning a simple linsey-woolsey dress with denims underneath. I moved quietly down the stairs and out to the porch where I put on boots fit for hiking in the foothills.

When I reached the canyon, I walked uphill, making my way through the dirt and brush until I'd gone far enough to see the waters of the Great Salt Lake shining in the distance. I took a cleansing breath and sat on my favorite rock, treasuring the peace and quiet.

I love the meadows and canyon springs of Farmington, and I adore my family, but I want to live in the city with Sophia. There, I've said it aloud, and clouds didn't gather, and lightning didn't strike. I smiled.

I worried about Mother's health although I knew she was in capable hands with Ada. My parents had already agreed that when I turned eighteen, I could move to Salt Lake and attend the University of Deseret. I wanted to leave a year early following my seventeenth birthday instead, which would be an unanticipated expense for my parents—unless I could live with Sophia.

I broached the idea with her, and she was supportive, suggesting that I wait until after my birthday in October and the holidays were over. I hadn't yet discussed this with my parents.

In my pocket I carried a letter from Sophia I'd collected at the post office on my way to the canyon. When I opened the envelope, two articles fell out, along with her letter. I read her letter first.

> *Dearest Katie,*
>
> *I hope this letter finds you well. I have heard some wonderful news that I could not wait to share with you. In late June of this year, Mrs. Elizabeth Cady Stanton and Miss Susan B. Anthony, who are, as you know, the president and vice-president-at large of the National Woman Suffrage Association, will stop in Salt Lake City for a visit on their way to the Pacific Coast. I understand they wish to help us celebrate the passage of our recent legislation conferring the franchise upon Utah women.*
>
> *Isn't it grand? A meeting is to be organized in the old tabernacle, and I, of course, plan to attend. I'm inviting you to join me, and I will pay for your train ticket. Would you like to come? I do hope so.*

I stopped reading and put Sophia's letter aside, trying to take in what I'd just read. *Susan B. Anthony and Elizabeth Cady Stanton coming here? To Salt Lake City?* I shook my head and couldn't believe it. *Would I like to come to the meeting? I would like nothing more, thank you, thank you!* I picked up the letter and finished reading.

> *I've also enclosed two articles I believe you'll want to read. The first is an open letter I read in the New York Times, written by Almira Lincoln Phelps, an avowed anti-suffragist. Her words are disturbing. The second is a petition I found in the editorial section of this month's Godey's Lady's Book and Magazine, and it's addressed to the U.S. Congress. The anti-suffragists have become more vocal since the Wyoming*

and Utah Territories have granted women the vote. We have our work cut out for us supporting our sister suffragists in the East.

I look forward to hearing from you about the upcoming June meeting.

With love,

Your cousin Sophia

I read the petition addressed to Congress first. It remonstrated against votes for women and was signed by nineteen women who oppose the vote. These women were using their rights of petition and remonstrance to influence legislators against legislation granting women the franchise.

I'd heard there were women who claimed the suffragists' new doctrine of individual rights violated the fundamental principle that 'the family is the basic unit of republican government.' I was especially puzzled by that one. *How does giving the women the vote hurt the family? I would think it enhances the overall education of its members in civic matters.*

I read the open letter from the Times next. Mrs. Phelps stated that, "the feminine silent masses oppose woman suffrage, a measure agitated in the regrettably revolutionary tradition of female Thomas Paines."

Why shouldn't women speak up as Paine did? I wished we had only men to contend with in winning the right to suffrage, but there were women as well.

The day was growing warmer, and when I looked at the position of the sun, I suspected it was well past eight o'clock. My stomach was grumbling and wanted to go home for breakfast. I folded the contents of Sophia's letter and articles, put them back inside the envelope, and made my way down the hill.

When I reached home, the others had finished breakfast, and my brothers were on their way out to do chores. "Is there anything left for me?" I asked.

Mother smiled. "Of course, my dear. Sit down and I'll get you something."

"Thank you, Mother. Just eggs and an apple, please. I have the most wonderful news I received in a letter from Sophia," I said.

"What does she say?" Father asked.

"She's invited me to come to Salt Lake at the end of June and attend a meeting in the old tabernacle and offered to pay my train ticket."

"It sounds like a matter of some importance," Father said.

"Susan B. Anthony and Elizabeth Cady Stanton will be speaking."

Ada frowned and left the room. "Revolutionaries," I heard her mutter under her breath.

Mother took my hand. "What a wonderful opportunity."

"Sophia also sent me anti-suffrage literature, so I'd be better informed on the opposition. Did you read Mrs. Phelps's open letter in the *Times*, Mother?"

"An insult to women everywhere, including the women of Utah," she said, disgusted.

"Without doubt," Father agreed.

"May I go to Salt Lake for the meeting? Perhaps I'll even meet Miss Anthony and Mrs. Stanton."

"I hope you do, and you may go." Mother smiled.

"I agree," Father said.

Now might be a good time to ask about moving to the City. "Father, Mother, I'd like to propose something else for your consideration."

They looked at me quizzically.

"You've offered to pay for me to attend the University of Deseret when I reach eighteen."

"We have," Father said.

"I'd like to leave one year earlier when I turn seventeen in October. I'll wait until the holidays are over."

Father crossed his arms over his chest and leaned back in his chair. Not a good sign. Before either one of them had a chance to respond, I continued, "It wouldn't require additional expense, because Sophia would allow me to live with her."

"You'll be leaving us soon enough," my father said.

"I'll only be a few hours away by train, and I'd come home often. Please, before you answer, would you take time to discuss my request?" I asked, appealing to my parent's sense of logic and fairness.

After a long moment of silence, they consented.

"Would you care for more honey on your cornbread?" Mother asked, rising and placing her hand on my shoulder.

"Yes, please," I said.

I finished eating and went to my room, my thoughts turning to Emma. I wouldn't see her as often either after I moved to Salt Lake, but Emma and I were as sisters, and we'd remain close no matter where we lived. We'd be spending a great deal of time together over the next few months since I was the Maid of Honor at her upcoming wedding.

Emma

Emma walked onto the upstairs porch of the Haight Union hotel where she could see for miles and miles. The hills were littered with trees still bearing late spring flowers, and a gentle breeze was blowing – a picture-perfect day for a June wedding. Emma was grateful for Wesley, who was considerate and didn't take matters into his own hands. When she wanted to talk, he listened. Emma smiled at her good fortune.

They would spend their first night in this room as husband and wife. Emma sat on the bed and patted it, finding it comfortable enough, but she was nervous and wondered what being together would be like. Neither of them had experience in this area. She'd discussed her fears with Wesley on several occasions, and he'd said, "I promise to be gentle and loving."

Emma thought about his blue eyes, kind face, and strong arms. She wanted him to hold her in the worst way. But that would have to wait. It was time to get dressed for the wedding.

She pulled her hair back in a chignon, revealing her mother's white pearl earrings. She put on full length white gloves and slipped into the wedding dress, with its lace-layered high neck and three-quarter length sleeves. The dress flounced to the floor, sweeping the tops of her white shoes. She placed a matching cap in the shape of a small flat crown on the top of her head. Katie had helped her select the dress and, just for today, Emma didn't mind looking like a princess.

She walked downstairs to make certain everything was ready. Grandmother Phoebe had created a three-tiered chandelier cake covered with white and blue frosting and a small spray of yellow flowers on top. Emma was sorely tempted to run her finger across the bottom of the cake and taste the frosting, but she resisted. White paper chains and flowers decorated the tables.

Emma looked outside and saw the first guests coming up the street. She hurried back upstairs so as not to be seen before it was time to make her entrance. She smiled out the window when she spied the entourage of carriages approaching with members of her wedding party. Wesley and Katie were in the front one, and Katie held a large spray of pink yarrow flowers in her hand for Emma. Wesley was dapper in his black suit and boutonniere. The remaining bridesmaids and groomsmen followed in three carriages. The guests assembled on the lawn were surprised and pleased at the sight of the carriages, clapping their appreciation.

After getting out of the carriages, the wedding party stood with the guests, waiting for the processional and the bride's entrance. Emma watched Katie primp her hair and smooth down the sky-blue dress Grandmother Phoebe had made. Grandmother had also created the white and blue floral-patterned dresses for the other bridesmaids. To top off their gowns, Emma had presented all four bridesmaids with cream-colored fans to hold in their hands.

The bishop, who would marry them in the civil ceremony, stood at the head of the group.

When everyone was in place, Emma came downstairs and walked in on her father's arm, stepping along an elongated, white piece of home-spun silk. One of the local fiddlers played the wedding march, and Emma glowed, acknowledging her guests with a smile.

Emma and her father stepped aside for a moment and lighted a candle that was sitting on a small table in memory of her mother, Joyce. Tears of sadness and joy glistened in Emma's eyes as the flame sparked. Emma's father sat down, she took her place next to Wesley, and the bishop thanked everyone for coming to share in the celebration.

He began by reading Emma's mother's favorite poem, 'How do I Love Thee,' by Elizabeth Barrett Browning, concluding with the words, 'I love thee with the breath, smiles, tears, of all my life; and, if God choose, I shall but love thee better after death.'

Wesley read vows he'd written for Emma. "You are my heaven on earth, Emma, and I will be your true friend forever, keeping you close to my heart."

It was her turn. "I'm certain you're the right man for me, Wesley, because I'm my best self when I'm with you."

The couple joined hands as the bishop read the traditional vows, pronouncing them man and wife. Wesley placed another gold ring on Emma's finger, and they kissed each other on the lips. The small crowd sent up a hurrah.

The party moved inside for dinner, the scent of tantalizing chicken with roasted potatoes and vegetables piercing the air. After they filled their plates and took their seats, the bishop offered an apple cider toast. "To the happy couple," he said. "We love you, and God loves you. May your future be bright."

Emma's father gave the next toast declaring, "This wedding ceremony is only the beginning of your nuptials, for tomorrow you will be sealed for eternity in the endowment house. Listen closely to the words you hear and the promises you make. Your happiness depends on those to whom you are united."

When everyone had eaten their fill, Wesley and Emma cut the cake, placing a piece into the other's mouth, leaving bits of blue frosting smeared on each other's faces. The guests laughed as Emma wiped frosting from Wesley's face, and he returned the favor. Christina and Cousin Anne cut the rest of the cake and handed it out to the guests. Anne had left her baby at the Whitman Ranch with their long-time housekeeper, Alice, so she could help Emma with the wedding.

After dessert, the tables were cleared away and the dancing began. The bride and groom led off with a few country dances and ended with a minuet. The celebration continued until about ten in the evening, then Emma's father stood and said, "Please come and wish the happy couple well on your way out, and thank you for coming."

Charles and Anne were the last to offer their congratulations. As they approached, Emma heard Charles speak harshly to Anne under his breath, chiding her for one thing or another.

"Charles, I'd appreciate a word with you," Emma said taking his arm and stepping out of ear shot. Looking him right in the eyes, she said, "I've overheard more than once the things you say to Anne. If you talked to me that way, I'd knock you into tomorrow, and don't think I couldn't do it."

Charles took a step back and seemed shocked at her words. His face turned an angry red. "How very ladylike of you," he said, sarcasm dripping in his voice. "This is what comes of giving women the vote."

Emma laughed. "You've known me for years, Charles, and as such you are aware that I usually speak what's on my mind. I didn't begin doing that a year ago February." Emma walked away without giving Charles another opportunity to respond.

He went to Anne, grabbed her arm, and steered her toward the door.

"What was that all about?" Wesley asked.

"I'll tell you another time."

Wesley took her in his arms. "Are you ready to go upstairs?"

Emma blushed. "As ready as I'll ever be."

Wesley insisted on carrying her up the stairs—although running would be a more accurate description, which made her laugh.

Their first night together was wonderful. She loved being in his arms, her head close to his heart, and they slept later than usual the next morning. Then they dressed and packed, checked out, and went to their new home. When Emma walked in the door, she still couldn't believe the house was theirs.

"I have a surprise for you," Wesley said.

"What is it?"

"A new resort has opened southwest of Kaysville. It's called Lake Side, and it's supposed to be quite the place. I hear tell that for 25 cents each, we can ride the City of Corrine, a steamboat going to Lake Point on the south shore. What do you think?"

"It sounds like an adventure. Let's go."

"Bring some bathing clothes and towels for sitting in the sand and sunning. This will be our honeymoon, Emma." Then he looked at his feet. "I regret that I could only afford two days away from work."

Emma kissed him on the cheek. "We have the rest of our lives to be together, and I'll enjoy spending time with you on the beach."

They left that morning. The remainder of the day was spent pushing their toes in the sand and sitting under a large umbrella, watching the waves lap against the shore. *This is the best honeymoon ever*, Emma thought.

Seven

Katie

It was nearing the end of June, and I was sitting in the Ogden train station waiting for my connecting train from Farmington to Salt Lake City, thinking about what a glorious event Emma's wedding had been. After the train chuffed into the station I boarded and took my seat. Looking around the interior of the car, I noticed two women sitting together a few rows ahead of me who looked to be somewhere in their fifties. Was it possible?

The older of the pair had a motherly look about her, round face, and a bit overweight. Her hair was wispy white, curled in neat rows across her head and was cut short above the ears. Her eyes were bright, and she wore a shawl about her shoulders, with a small Christian-cross hanging down her neck. It had to be Mrs. Stanton.

Next to her sat Miss Anthony who had a rather stern look, straight brownish hair parted down the middle and pulled back behind her ears, a simple shawl covering her shoulders. She glanced my way and I found her eyes piercing and determined. The two heads of the NWSA were on the train with me?

I wasn't crass enough to interrupt their conversation, but before we reached the City, I saw them leave their seats and move to the back platform of the train. I stepped outside as well, making myself as unobtrusive as possible. Emma wasn't the only one who was audacious enough to listen in on the conversations of others.

The two suffragists spoke of their Western lecture tour which had been initiated to take their cause to the Pacific Coast. They expressed pleasure in shaking hands with women in the Wyoming Territory who had won the right to vote first. And while the two of them had obviously traveled the country a great deal, they spoke with wonder and awe about their first journey to the West and the 'far-famed' Great Salt Lake.

They raised the topic of plural marriage, proclaiming that while it was their desire to support suffrage, they didn't want to appear to condone the practice of polygamy. Mrs. Stanton said, "I'm pleased we reached out to the New Movement, the Godbeites, first; it shows where we stand on the matter."

"I was astonished when Brigham Young invited us to speak tomorrow at the old tabernacle," Miss Anthony said.

I could see parallels between our two separate groups in Utah and a deeply divided national woman suffrage movement. I knew Lucy Stone was the person who headed the competing group, the American Woman Suffrage Association, and she objected to what she viewed as the confrontational tactics of the National Woman's Suffrage Association.

When we pulled into the station and prepared to disembark, Anthony said, "We will soon meet the second group of women in the United States who won their battle for the ballot, the women of Utah."

As we reached the steps of the train, I offered to lift their bags down the stairs and they graciously accepted.

After we reached the station's platform, Anthony asked, "What is your name?"

"Kathryn Leavitt," I said, shaking her outstretched hand.

"May I ask if you are aligned with the suffragists?"

"Whole-heartedly, though I'm still too young to vote."

Stanton asked, "What aspirations do you have for yourself, my girl?"

"One day I will become a doctor."

Stanton smiled, pleased, her white hair waving in the soft breeze.

Anthony said, "Thank you for your help; it's good to meet a sister suffragist."

"It's my pleasure," I said, feeling part of them. I watched the two of them walk away, arm in arm, thinking how strong, determined, and outspoken they were. I so admired them.

The next evening, I sat next to Sophia in the old tabernacle, waiting for the leadership of the NWSA to address our gathering, making the following note in my journal: *June 29, 1871, Thursday evening. Susan B Anthony and Elizabeth Cady Stanton visit Salt Lake City to address a gathering of what looks to be almost 300 women, which includes several of our Mormon women leaders.*

Following a few introductory comments, Stanton launched into a discussion of political equality for women, asserting that she would rather be a woman among the Mormons "with the ballot in my hands than among Gentiles [non-Mormons] without the ballot." In Utah and Wyoming, she argued, for the first time in the "history of the world" there was "true Republicanism": men and women "enjoying equal political rights."

Stanton's praise seemed to come as a surprise to many who had expected attacks on polygamy. Stanton was against any form of marriage that was bound up in oppressive male domination, whether it be monogamy or polygamy.

Anthony seemed more distant and reserved and didn't commit herself to seeing positives in the practice of polygamy, even for those women who were widowed or divorced and lacked visible means of support. She'd also been reluctant to include Utah suffragists in the NWSA which I hoped would change over time. It seemed to me that Miss Anthony was a practical woman and was first and foremost motivated by achieving national suffrage.

After the five-hour meeting ended, Sophia and I went back to her home in the Avenues. As we sat with our shoes off, rubbing sore feet, and drinking lavender tea, she asked, "Do I detect an air of disappointment about you? Or are you merely tired?"

"It may be disappointment."

"What's on your mind?"

"This may sound strange, but yesterday morning when I met Mrs. Stanton and Miss Anthony, I was elated, having heard so much about them. They were larger than life in my eyes, I suppose. After hearing them speak, they became human, knowable, and I felt let down somehow."

Sophia smiled. "A lesson well learned, Katie, if a little painful. It's easy to admire those in positions of prominence, who invariably have their faults and foibles just as the rest of us. Never put someone on a pedestal, because when they fall off, it will hurt you more than it does them."

"What do you mean?"

"There have been those who left our faith when they found our leaders were fallible. Take Brigham Young, for example. A visionary man, who founded Salt Lake City, the second president of our church, and the first governor of the territory. And, I believe, the first one to tell you, he makes mistakes along with the rest of us."

"What kinds of mistakes?"

"Let me give you an example. At one point, he told farmers in the valley to grow sugar beets instead of grain, and he even built a sugar house south of Salt Lake City. Some people invested heavily in beets and ended up losing money. A few of them may have lost their faith, because Brother Brigham was wrong."

I paused. "I guess I don't think he should be wrong if God is guiding him."

"Sometimes God encourages us to try something new and leaves us to work the details out for ourselves. It's how we grow. President Young tried something new, and it failed, so he learned something."

"Dr. Axel told me when he used a compression bandage on Joseph that doctors don't bleed patients anymore. I suppose that even in the practice of medicine we do the best we can until something better comes along."

"That's an appropriate parallel, Katie. Feeling any better?"

"Much," I yawned, covering my mouth. "Pardon me."

"Take yourself to bed, and I'll clean up here."

"Thank you, Sophia," I said, giving her a hug.

"Good night, my angel. Sleep well. We have an enjoyable week ahead of us."

Later that week, Stanton's and Anthony's criticisms went too far in my opinion. Stanton wrote a letter from Salt Lake City criticizing religious leaders from Moses to Brigham Young and advocated that women establish "their own constitutions, creeds, codes, and customs."

"What a ridiculous notion," I said to Sophia.

"While we want women to expand their sphere of influence, there is no need for separate constitutions and creeds," she added. "Better to work together than be pulled apart."

In a speech delivered later that same week, Anthony commented that "she had as good a right to receive revelations, direct from God" and that "revelations which came exclusively to men would never satisfy her."

Sophia said, "In our faith, each person, man or woman, has the right to receive revelation and is encouraged to obtain his or her own witness about revelation from any source."

"I wonder what Eliza Snow thinks about all this?"

"I've heard her say that the interests of men and women are the same; that man has no interests separate from that of women, and however it may be in the outside world, our interests are all united."

"I'm in accord with Aunt Eliza, and her words remind me of the old Liberty Song: By uniting we stand, by dividing we fall."

"Precisely."

My head was spinning. "Sophia, may I sit at the piano and play?"

"Of course, you may. You have no need to ask."

"I find that music has the power to calm my mind, which I could use about now."

"Do you know the old hymn, 'Be Still My Soul'?"

I nodded and took my seat at the piano, taking a cleansing breath. "Your voice has such a rich timbre. Would you mind singing along?"

We played and sang together, "Be still my soul, the song of praise on Earth." The sun spilled through the window, brightening the room.

Later that week, on July 6, Anthony and Stanton boarded the Southern Pacific railroad for San Francisco, having met with women of all faiths. Katie heard they had acknowledged to women of the Relief Society that they had been received very kindly by the women who filled their meeting halls. They had also visited several Mormon homes, where they later said, they met refined, lovely women.

Emma

Katie sent a letter to Emma telling her all about Miss Anthony's and Mrs. Stanton's visit. Emma had found Katie's account fascinating, particularly after she heard Eliza Snow's words read aloud.

Today Emma was on the back porch, churning butter with one hand and holding a book with the other, sitting as close as possible to the thick adobe walls of her home to keep cool. It was still early, and the day was already warm and promised to be a scorcher. Wesley stood a few paces away in the yard pumping water into two large buckets for the horses.

When he finished, he hauled the buckets over to the porch and sat next to Emma. "What's that you're reading?" he asked.

"Re-reading," she said. "Poe's *Murders in the Rue Morgue*."

"One of my favorites. Can we talk?"

"Of course," she said, putting her book down.

"My duties as a deputy have consumed me these past days, and I haven't inquired about this year's July 24th celebration in Ogden. It was quite the event, I understand."

"If I had but two words to describe the day they would be 'hot and crowded.' Throngs and throngs of people filled the streets."

"How did the festivities compare to last year's celebration in Salt Lake?"

"No comparison at all, because last year we got engaged."

Wesley reached over and held her hand. "It's been the best year of my life."

"Mine too." Emma smiled. "The day's grand procession was moving, especially the pioneers and the Relief Society sisters. My favorite was the special program that followed at the bowery in Union Square."

"Was it the brass bands and choirs that stirred you the most?" he teased.

Emma socked him in the arm and laughed. "You know very well it would have been listening to David McKenzie read the address Eliza Snow prepared for the occasion."

"What did she say?"

"The *Deseret News* printed a copy of her address yesterday, and Father presented me with a copy. Stay right there and I'll retrieve it. I'd like to read you a few bits. Some of what she said was in reaction to comments Mrs. Stanton and Miss Anthony made last month when they visited Utah."

"While you fetch it, I'll water the horses and be right back, so don't go away," he said touching her face, smiling. "Let's meet up inside where it's cooler."

A few minutes later, the two of them snuggled together on the sofa, and Wesley said, "I'm all ears. Go ahead."

Emma unfolded the paper and began reading Eliza Snow's words:

> *"The day we celebrate is a very important one. The arrival of the Pioneers in these valleys is an event which history will repeat with emphasis to all succeeding generations. It formed the starting point—the commencement of a delightful oasis in the desert wilds of North America—of establishing a midway settlement between Eastern and Western civilization, a connecting overland link between the rich agricultural products of the Atlantic and the undeveloped mineral treasures of the Pacific."*

"She has a way with words," Wesley said.

"One of our best writers, and I can attest that both men and women applauded loudly and often, especially when she said that Utah was not only a home for exiles of our faith, but for the oppressed of all nations. Reading on:

"*[we are] a reservoir of freedom and religious toleration, where the glorious flag of liberty now waves triumphantly, and where the sacred Constitution which our noble forefathers were instrumental in forming under the inspiration of the Almighty, shall be cleansed from every stain.*"

"Patriotic," Wesley commented.

"I'm pleased to have a copy of her remarks that I'll keep for our daughters to read one day."

"And sons too. I hope we are blessed with many daughters and sons."

"You know I want a large family. Moving down the page to where she begins addressing the women.

"*Ladies, please allow me to address you by the more endearing appellation of sisters. We have the privilege of uniting with our brethren in twining a garland with which to decorate the stately brow of this auspicious day. Why should we not? What interests have we that are not in common with theirs, and what have they that are disconnected with ours? We know of none, and we feel assured that they have no more interests involved in the settlement of these valleys than ourselves. Who is better qualified to appreciate the blessings of peace than woman? ... And where else, on earth, is female virtue held so sacred, and where so bravely defended? Facts answer, nowhere!*'

"Like that last part about female virtue being bravely defended," Wesley said.

"I thought you might," Emma answered, "for you are one of its noblest defenders. And listen to this section:

86

"Who can doubt that Mormon women are equal to any and all emergencies? The great questions relative to woman's sphere, which are making some stir in the world abroad, have no influence with us. We realize that we are called to be co-workers with our brethren in the great work of the last days. Although we are not at present living up to all our privileges, and fulfilling all the duties that belong to our sex, the field is open before us, and we are urged to move forward as fast as we can develop and apply our own capabilities.

"I embrace the idea of developing my capabilities along with being a wife and mother," Emma said.

"I support you in both spheres."

"I'm fortunate you turned out to be the man I believed you were when I married you. Not all women are so lucky."

Someone began pounding on the door, shouting, "Wesley, Emma, are you in there? Open up!"

"Sounds like my father," Emma said, putting the paper down.

"So it does." Wesley crossed the floor to the door. "Must be urgent." He opened the door.

"I have troubling news."

Emma stood. "Whatever is it, Father?"

He walked over and put his arms about her shoulders. "Your Uncle Peter is dead."

"D…dead." She shuddered, the image of her uncle and Anne's father fresh in her mind. "But how? Why?"

"We're not certain yet, although on the face of it, it looks as if his heart gave out."

"He's always been so healthy."

"Never been sick a day in his life," her father said.

"How is Cousin Anne holding up?"

"Not well, as you might imagine."

"Are you certain it was his heart?"

"Dr. Axel has yet to examine him post-mortem, so I'm withholding judgment."

"What else do you think it might be?" Wesley asked.

"Peter's chest pains and palpitations, as Anne described, fit a heart attack. But there are additional symptoms which is why we need Dr. Axel."

"I must go to Anne and comfort her," Emma said. "Is she still out at the Whitman ranch?"

"The coffin wagon is on its way, and she's there waiting with her father's body."

"I'll accompany you," Wesley said, reaching for his hat.

"Not yet. I must speak with Anne woman to woman. Give me two hours alone with her."

Emma ran to the yard and hitched a horse to the surrey. As she was preparing to climb inside, she heard Katie's voice behind her. When she turned and saw her friend, Emma began to sob.

Katie took her hand and asked, "What is it, dear friend?"

"It's Uncle Peter. He's dead."

"I am so sorry! Whatever happened?" Katie asked, reaching in her bag for a lace handkerchief, offering it to Emma.

Emma wiped her eyes. "It appears to be a heart attack, but we don't know for certain. I'm on my way to the Whitman ranch to see what I can do for Anne."

"Is there anything I may do for you?"

"I haven't even inquired why you came to see me?"

"I'm not certain myself, but I had a feeling I should drop by."

"A tender mercy. Thank you for coming, and I'm sorry I broke down."

"Nonsense. It was just what you needed to do."

Emma wiped her eyes. "Thank you."

"You said no one knew for certain regarding the cause of your uncle's death?"

"While it appears to be a heart attack, there are symptoms my father wants Dr. Axel to investigate." Emma paused. "Katie, there is something you can do for me."

"Anything."

Emma couldn't imagine her healthy uncle dead for no reason. "Would you stop by Dr. Axel's office and get his impressions on the post-mortem, letting him know that your presence is at my family's request?"

"I'll go there now and see what I can find out. He allows me to come observe his work on occasion."

Emma thanked Katie, climbed into the carriage, and laid her whip over the horse's head, riding off in a cloud of dust.

Eight

Katie

I arrived at Dr. Axel's office as the coffin wagon pulled up outside. It was covered in black curtains with a large matching drape that cascaded down both sides, and the top was constructed of wood that was painted black. The cushioned seat in front for the drivers had a curved metal footrest and the horses were also black in color. It was the dreariest thing I'd ever seen. I walked into the office while the men unloaded the box with Peter Whitman's body inside.

"Katie, hello," Dr. Axel said. "I wasn't expecting you today."

"The Gregory family asked that I come by while you perform an examination on Peter Whitman's body."

"Very well. Come inside, and I'll share my conclusions after I take a look at him."

I sat waiting as Dr. Axel completed his examination. He finally poked his head out of the curtained door in the next room, and invited me in. As I entered, I was relieved to see that the deceased eyes had already been closed. I don't like looking into the eyes of dead people. "Do you know how he perished?"

"Perhaps. Come here and have a look at his face. See the dried drool?"

"Yes," I said taking a closer look.

"Drooling is not a typical symptom of a heart attack."

I nodded as if I knew that. "What's this dry brown material on his chin? Is it mud?"

"You make a good observation. I thought it might be at first, but it appears to be an herb of some sort. Come view the brown residue through my microscope."

I peered through the large gold-colored microscope with the small lighted candle shining on the lens. "What type of herb to you suspect it is?"

"I'm not certain yet, but it may be poisonous."

"Do you think Peter Whitman accidentally ingested it?"

"It's more likely that someone gave it to him without his knowledge. No one eats foxglove on purpose."

I paused, recoiling from the doctor's words. "So, he may have been murdered?"

"It will be up to Sheriff Gregory to investigate from here, but yes, it's possible. Is the family gathered at the Whitman ranch now?"

"Yes."

"Let's ride there in my buggy and provide them with the results of my examination."

"Thank you, Dr. Axel. I appreciate going along with you." We climbed into his buggy and several miles later reached the entrance to the ranch where I spotted a few deer grazing in the field off the road. When we reached the gate, a ranch hand opened it and waved us through.

As we rode, I spotted a few wild turkeys, hundreds of cattle, and dozens of horses. Peter Whitman had claimed approximately 150 acres when he established the Long View Ranch twenty years ago, and it had since become quite the operation. It required several ranch hands to run the place and was much larger than the Archer ranch.

We soon arrived at the main house where a tan fence surrounded the yellow brick and stone farmhouse, and green curtains framed the window. Doctor Axel pulled the horses to a stop. We climbed out of the carriage and walked up to the door, knocking loudly.

A tear-stained Anne opened the door. "Come in, please," she said, leading us into the parlor where Emma, Wesley, Sheriff Gregory, Charles Archer, and Anne's brother, Daniel, greeted us.

"Thank you for coming Dr. Axel," Daniel said, rising and shaking his hand.

"I'm deeply sorry for the loss of your father," the doctor said.

"Thank you. It came as quite a shock this morning when I went into his room to rouse him and discovered him unresponsive."

Anne reached up and took her brother's hand. "Do you believe our father perished as the result of a heart attack?" she asked Dr. Axel.

"While that's a possibility, I've discovered other signs that indicate he may have been poisoned."

"What kinds of signs?" Charles asked, joining the conversation.

"I saw what appeared to be dried dirt on his face that turned out instead to be some type of herb."

"There are several poisonous plants indigenous to our area," Emma said.

"Indigenous. You're pretty smart, Emma...for a woman." Charles smirked.

Wesley walked over and slammed him against the wall. "Don't insult my wife," he said, eyes flashing. "I'll wager she's a lot smarter than you are, Archer."

Charles flushed red, balled his fists, and lunged at Wesley.

Sheriff Gregory stepped in between them. "Both of you, take it easy. We don't need fisticuffs erupting today." The two men moved to opposite corners of the room and stood, glowering at each other. "If Dr. Axel's assumption has merit, Peter's bedroom is a crime scene, and no one is allowed in that room until I return tomorrow."

Alice, the family housekeeper, said, "I'll see to it, Sheriff."

Emma motioned for me to join her in the kitchen, leaving the men and Anne to talk amongst themselves. "Let's go outside, Katie," she whispered.

As we stepped off the porch, I turned to Emma, eyes flashing, and said, "I was incensed when Charles insulted you."

Emma stopped walking and said. "He says and does far worse to Anne."

"What do you mean?"

"Anne made me pledge to tell no one, but I won't keep her secret any longer. Charles strikes her, speaks cruelly, and abuses the drink—which she told me not long ago."

I was at a loss for words momentarily. "He's a deceptive miscreant who must be stopped at all costs."

"I agree, and perhaps this is our opportunity."

"What do you mean?"

"If Uncle Peter was poisoned, Charles is not above suspicion."

My face turned pallid. "Then he's a dangerous man."

"If Charles is the culprit, the remnants of poisonous flowers may be in his shed. We need to search the Archer ranch, and this may be the perfect opportunity while he and Anne are here. Will you come with me?"

I didn't hesitate. "Of course. Do you have a gun with you?"

Emma hiked her skirt to confirm that she carried it strapped to her leg. "My surrey is in the side yard, and I believe we may depart now without being missed."

We rode Emma's surrey to her home as fast as the horse could carry us, left it in her yard, and walked briskly to the Archer ranch. Emma wanted to leave no trace of our presence outside the Archer ranch, should Charles and Anne return unexpectedly.

When we reached the house, we made our way around back, searching for the shed. We found it, tried the door, and it was locked. "We may be out of luck," I said.

"Don't despair," Emma said, reaching into her pocket and removing a lock pick. She turned the lock, and we went inside.

"Clever and very resourceful," I said, noticing that the shed was large and replete with tools.

Emma spotted something and called, "Over here, Katie."

"What is it?"

"See these dried purple flowers?"

"Foxglove. Leaves are extremely poisonous if ingested."

"Is there any way to determine whether this is the herb used to kill Uncle Peter?"

"I slipped a small sample in my bag of the herb Dr. Axel was examining under the microscope, so let's see."

Emma crushed a small sample of the Foxglove on the workbench and I placed mine alongside. It seemed to be a match. "What now?"

"We report our findings to Father and Wesley," she said, selecting one of the dried plants, cutting off a small branch, placing the plant behind a large shovel.

We heard a noise from inside the house. "They're home," I whispered.

"Come with me and don't make a sound. We'll make our way through the trees in the side yard and escape undetected."

We crouched down and crept along the side of the house and could hear Charles and Anne conversing in the kitchen, their words unintelligible. Then we made a break for the woods. While Emma didn't seem bothered by our current circumstance, my fear was considerable.

When we at last reached Emma's home we were out of breath. Sheriff Gregory and Wesley came outside to meet us.

"Where have you two been?" Sheriff Gregory asked, worried.

"We've been doing some sleuthing," Emma answered, "and I believe you'll want to see what we've uncovered."

Wesley's concern was palpable, and I knew the three of them had much to discuss. Time for me to take my leave. "My family is expecting me home."

Emma hugged me, "I appreciate your assistance today."

"It was a pleasure watching you work," I said, bidding them all farewell.

94

Emma

After Katie went home, Emma, her father, and Wesley ate a light supper of bread, cheese, and fruit while Emma told them about her visit to the Archer ranch and the foxglove she found.

"Why would Charles want Peter dead?" Wesley asked.

"My hypothesis," Emma said, "is that with Uncle Peter gone, and Anne one of his only two heirs, Charles will have access to the revenue the ranch generates."

"Utah doesn't have a law allowing married women to own property, but it's been the practice for the past several years," Wesley said, "so, the control of Anne's share of the ranch's revenue belongs to her, right Sheriff?"

"Yes, and the legislature is discussing a married person's property act, which will formally give married women property rights."

Emma buttered a slice of bread. "While it may be that Anne owns the revenues, it will be Charles who runs the show. He insists that all decisions are left to him and he may have money problems. Anne confided that she'd come across a paper on Charles's desk when she was cleaning his office. Seems he put a heavy mortgage on the ranch to invest in a diamond mine."

"Heard about that diamond mine," her father said. "It's since gone belly up."

Wesley let out a low whistle. "We may have ourselves a desperate man."

"Let's assume for a moment that Charles wanted Peter dead." Her father leaned forward in his chair and steepled his fingers. "And perhaps used foxglove to do it. We need to determine how he got Peter to ingest it." He stood and stretched. "Let's give it some thought overnight. Both of you meet at the ranch at eight in the morning. Emma, I've underestimated your powers of deduction. Well done."

"Thank you," she said, shoulders back, a high color in her face.

"Oh, and one more thing. Charles approached me earlier today after you left, whispering that if anyone had a motive to poison

Peter, it was Hank Thompson, the ranch foreman. He's getting on in years, and I guess Peter wanted to replace him, so we'll need to speak with him. Emma, you interview Alice while I search Peter's room, and Wesley, you'll talk to Hank. See you in the morning," he said, taking an apple with him and walking out the door.

The next morning, after the three of them met at the ranch, Wesley made his way down the winding road to the show barn to find Thompson. When Wesley walked inside, he was surprised at the size of the place. It was huge, dirt floors, wooden rafters and dozens of metal pens filled with cows. He'd never seen the insides of a working ranch this large before. Impressive, he thought, as he wound his way past the horse stalls in search of Hank Thompson.

"You Hatch?" a man asked without turning around.

"That's me."

"They told me you was coming." The man turned and shook hands with Wesley. "Hank Thompson, Long View Ranch foreman. Don't believe we've met."

Wesley took his hand, noting the killer grip. "Good to meet you. I'm the deputy sheriff investigating Peter Whitman's murder. Can we sit?"

"Sure. You okay sittin' on a bale of hay?"

"Sure."

Thompson's back popped when he threw down two bales. Then, they sat down facing each other.

Thompson glared at him. "What's that there notebook for?"

"Helps me remember conversations."

He grunted. "Go ahead, ask your questions."

"All right. What'd you do before you came to the ranch?"

"Farm hand for a hay and cattle business out in Texas."

"What brought you here?"

"Heard they was looking for a Ranch Hand Manager. Top notch place to work with good pay. After talkin' with Mister Whitman a time or two, he determined I'd make a fine supervisor. Helps that I know most all there is to know 'bout horses and cattle."

"Sounds like he was lucky to get you."

"Reckon he was."

"I understand you've become more like family than a ranch hand."

"Miss Anne tell you that?"

"Yes."

"I've gotten close with both her and Mr. Daniel. Nothing I wouldn't do for the both of 'em." He leaned forward with one hand on his knee and looked hard at Wesley. "Neither one of 'em would hurt a flea."

"You friends with Archer too?"

He snorted. "Don't care for him, dodgy fella. You can call a horse a duck, and it don't change anything."

"Mind if I ask how old you are?"

"My age ain't no secret. I'm 71."

"Ranch work is tough; you ever think about hanging up your spurs?"

"Nope."

"Did Mr. Whitman ever speak with you about retiring?"

"He might could have a time or two, but I ask you, what would I do instead? Can't dance, never could sing, and it's too wet to plow." His deep laugh was filled with sarcasm.

Wesley made a note. 'Whitman talked with Thompson about retiring, and he declined.' "Tell me more about the night your boss died."

"It was rainin' hard outside. I come in the house for dinner and stayed the night in the house."

"Was that unusual?'

"Yep, but it was comin' down in sheets outside. We all turned in early, 'cept Mr. Whitman. I didn't know anythin' more until mornin,' when I heard Mr. Daniel shout, and I run upstairs." Thompson rubbed the back of his neck. "When I knew for sure Mr. Whitman was dead, I rounded up the boys to carry his body out." His muscles quivered, and his voice shook.

Wesley stopped and gave him a moment to collect himself.

He cleared his throat. "Let's keep movin'."

"Anything look odd or out of place in Mr. Whitman's room?"

97

"Not that I could see. Newly opened bottle of sarsaparilla on the table and one drained glass. He kept a stockpile of the stuff in the cellar, bottles numbered. Pretty particular about it."

"Anything else you remember about that night?"

"Nope. That's about it in a nutshell."

"Will you be staying on at the ranch with Mr. Whitman gone?"

"Course. Now, if there's nothin' else, I got work to do."

"That's all for now." Wesley stood and they shook hands again.

Meanwhile, Emma went looking for Alice. When Emma walked into the kitchen, she could smell banana muffins, her favorite.

"Please sit, and I'll get you some muffins," Alice said.

"They look delicious. Thank you." Emma smiled, hoping to put her at ease.

"Would you care for something to drink?"

"Milk, please."

Alice placed a large, cold glass in front of Emma and sat down across from her.

Emma took a large bite of muffin that melted in her mouth. "These are delicious."

"It's an old family recipe that come from Northern England."

"They're lovely. Thank you. My Uncle Peter's death must have been terrible for you too, Alice."

She nodded, looking down at her hands.

"You and Mrs. Anne are close too, I believe."

"She's very kind."

"And Mr. Daniel?"

"A good man and a fair boss."

"What about Mr. Charles?"

Alice scowled. "I don't like speaking ill of no one, but he doesn't treat Mrs. Anne with respect."

Emma wasn't the only one who'd observed that behavior.

Did Mr. Whitman have anything to eat or drink before retiring for the evening?"

"When I closed the door to his room yesterday, I saw a bottle of sarsaparilla on the nightstand. Mr. Whitman loves his sarsaparilla and keeps a labeled stock in the cellar."

"I've enjoyed drinking it at Anne's before. Can you take me down to the cellar?"

She looked puzzled but agreed. "I'll get the key from the pantry."

Emma ate the last of the muffin and finished her glass of milk.

"This way," Alice said, leading her down the steps, candle in hand.

When they reached the bottom, she opened the door and lit the candles on the wall. Emma walked into the now well-lit room and saw a rounded stone roof and a dark brown pine floor with two large shelves filled with bottles of sarsaparilla.

Emma noticed a detailed inventory of the bottles posted on the wall. It seemed that when a bottle was pulled from the shelves, the date was noted. She looked for yesterday's date. No bottle had been crossed off the list that day.

"I'm finished here," Emma said. "Thank you." They walked back upstairs and met her father coming into the parlor with Daniel. Emma sat down, and Alice went into the kitchen, as the sheriff began questioning Daniel.

"What happened on the night in question?" he asked.

"Father went upstairs to the balcony off his bedroom. Said he wanted to keep watch over the ranch, what with the rain pouring down hard. I went to bed, as did Alice, and Hank slept on the couch. Father didn't want him going back out in the rain, which was growing worse by the minute."

"Was Hank up when you went to bed?"

"Yes, as I remember it, he was. Anne and Charles were here too. Came out for the day and spent the night in the spare room. Brought the baby with them. Anne fried up some of her chicken for dinner and Charles brought sarsaparilla from the general store."

"Did you hear anyone go up the stairs that night?"

"I'm a sound sleeper, always have been, so I can only speak for myself. I didn't leave my room until early the next morning."

"You're the one who found your father."

"He was still sitting outside, head resting on his chest. Thought maybe he'd fallen asleep, but he was already dead. Wish I'd looked in on him earlier. Maybe I could have done something."

"What did you do when you realized he was deceased?"

"Went to the stairs, called for Anne and Charles, and they came running. When I informed Hank, he got some of the boys to carry Father's body down the stairs for the coffin wagon."

"That's all, Daniel. Thank you."

He rose, shook the sheriff's hand, and left the room. By that time, Wesley had joined them, so the three sat and compared notes, the sheriff beginning with his search of Whitman's room.

"Nothing unusual in the bedroom," her father said. "Peter liked to keep his things neat and tidy. Always a stickler for detail, that one. What about Thompson? Get anything useful out of him?"

"Not much. Doesn't care for Archer, though," Wesley said. "I don't think Thompson's our man."

"Alice despises Charles," Emma said. "She's heard him mistreat Anne, as have I."

"Daniel told me the Archers were in the house that night," the sheriff said, "giving Charles opportunity."

"There's something else," Emma said. "The sarsaparilla Uncle Peter drank the night he died didn't come from his personal stock. Charles must have brought it in, taking it upstairs after the others went to bed."

"Saw that half-empty bottle on Peter's nightstand," the sheriff said.

"That, paired with the foxglove found in the shed points in his direction," Emma said.

"I'll go upstairs and bring the bottle down, and the two of you take it to Dr. Axel and see if he can find traces of foxglove. If he does, we've got our man."

An hour later, Dr. Axel confirmed the presence of foxglove in the sarsaparilla. Wesley and Emma informed the Sheriff who went to the Archer ranch, cuffed Charles, and led him away.

As they watched him go, Emma held a crying Anne, who had collapsed in her arms.

Later that evening, Emma, Wesley, and her father discussed all that had transpired in a single day.

"This case wrapped up fast," Wesley said.

"It's unusual to resolve a murder this quickly," the sheriff agreed. "It's a sad situation. Peter's dead and Archer's in jail."

Emma said, "I'm concerned about Anne and her baby who's only four months old. Her life's in shambles; she's depressed and requires support. I insisted the two of them come and stay with us, at least through the holidays."

"I hope she agreed," Wesley said.

"She did."

Nine

Katie

I'd made pumpkin bread with bits of chocolate for my family and decided to take Emma a loaf. When I arrived, she opened the door, stepped out onto the porch, and thanked me. "Smells so good. You know how much I love your pumpkin bread, and it's still warm. I'd invite you in, but Anne doesn't want anyone to see her right now."

"I understand," I said. "Merry Christmas, dear friend."

"And to you as well," Emma said, giving me a warm hug that lasted longer than usual.

"How are you doing?" I asked.

"Things are difficult here."

"Why don't we have a walk and talk after Christmas?"

"I'd like that."

"See you soon," I said, waving and walking home through the snow.

It was Christmas Eve. Ada had knitted seven new Christmas stockings that were red with white lace at the top and arranged them neatly along the mantle. A tall green pine, glowing with candles, stood in the corner of the room, and underneath lay one small present for each of us to open this evening.

After enjoying a hearty meal of ham and trimmings, we moved into the parlor, taking our places at Father's feet to listen to him read Charles Dicken's *A Christmas Carol*.

By reading selected passages, he had managed, over the past few years, to time his oration to just over an hour. As Father began with the words, "Marley was dead," Jacob curled up next to my mother, his eyes round, and we all listened to the tale with rapt attention as if we'd never heard it before.

After reading both the beginning and thick middle of the story, with the appropriate level of drama and wild hand gestures, Father reached the ending:

"Scrooge was better than his word. He did it all, and infinitely more; and to Tiny Tim, who did not die, he was a second father. He became as good a friend, as good a master, and as good a man, as the good old city knew, or any other good old city, town, or borough, in the good old world. Some people laughed to see the alteration in him, but he let them laugh, and little heeded them; for he was wise enough to know that nothing ever happened on this globe, for good, at which some people did not have their fill of laughter in the outset; and knowing that such as these would be blind anyway, he thought it quite as well that they should wrinkle up their eyes in grins, as have the malady in less attractive forms. His own heart laughed: and that was quite enough for him.

"And it was always said of him, that he knew how to keep Christmas well, if any man alive possessed the knowledge. May that be truly said of us, and all of us! And so, as Tiny Tim observed..."

Father paused so Andrew and Jacob could repeat in unison, "God bless us, every one!" We all clapped.

"Your rendition of the timeless tale grows better each year," Mother said to Father, clasping his hand in hers. Turning to me, she said, "Please go to the piano, Katie, and let's sing our most beloved carol of the season."

I sat down and the family gathered around, holding hands as they sang, 'Joy to the World.' Then Father read to us from the Book of Luke.

When he finished, Jacob asked, "Is it time for presents now?"

Mother laughed. "Right after the Christmas pudding."

"Yum," he said, gobbling his down as quickly as possible. "Hooray," he said, "Now we open the presents."

I laughed, took his hand, and we sat next to the tree. The others soon joined us.

Our gift opening tradition began with the youngest and proceeded up the line to me. Jacob's eyes sparkled when he found a tin soldier inside his gaily wrapped package. Andrew opened a clockwork toy, and Joseph, who is blessed with an analytical mind, received a jigsaw puzzle.

When my turn came, Mother said, "After you open your present, Katie, we'll provide an explanation for our choice."

My curiosity was aroused as I opened the flat package wrapped in gold-colored paper. Inside, I found a train ticket to Salt Lake City with no date attached. I paused and looked at my parents. "Is this what I think it is?" I asked, astonished.

"What's Katie talking about?" Joseph asked.

"We'll discuss it later, Son," Father said. "We need to speak with Katie first."

My brothers bid us a sleepy goodnight, and Ada said, "I shall retire now as well."

"A very merry Christmas to you, Aunt," I said, walking across the room, giving her a hug. "Thank you for the lovely Christmas stockings. They are a treasure."

"You're welcome, and a Merry Christmas to you."

After she left, I turned to Father and Mother, looking at them expectantly.

"Let's begin with my friend Edward Sloan," Father intoned.

"Sloan? The editor of the *Daily Herald*?" I said. *Where were they going with this? Why him?* My eyes narrowed.

"The very one," Father said. "You may not know that he has conceived the idea of a women's paper."

"Such as the ones they have in the East?" I asked, moving my chair closer to theirs.

"Precisely. The paper is to be published semi-monthly and will be titled the *Woman's Exponent*."

"What kind of content will be printed in the new publication?"

"Edward tells me the paper will contain summaries of current news, articles on topics of interest—such as woman suffrage —" he smiled — "educational matters, household hints, poetry, and reports of the Relief Societies of Utah."

"It sounds as if Mr. Sloan is anticipating a broad readership of women."

"He's preparing a prospectus outlining the goals of the publication that he'll send to every Relief Society, seeking subscriptions. He'll also place a piece in the *Herald*, I believe in April."

Mother asked, "Katie, do you recall reading a poem published recently in the *Herald* titled, 'Tired Out'? It was a rather melancholy piece that found its way to the front page."

I thought for a moment. "I do remember reading it—quite impressive."

"The composer of the poem, Lula Greene, has had experience editing a gazette in Smithfield, Utah, and Mr. Sloan has asked her to be the editor of the new paper."

"How would you like to meet Lula Greene?" Father asked.

"Why would she want to meet me?" I asked, surprised.

"Over the next several months Miss Greene and her committee, which includes Eliza Snow, will be looking for typesetters, and Mother and I thought, given your desire to move to Salt Lake and live with Sophia for a time, this might be work that would capture your interest."

A light-hearted feeling floated around my head. *Was it possible that I would not only realize my wish to move to Salt Lake, but work on the first woman's paper ever published in Utah? Such an opportunity! Will Miss Greene find me worthy to join her staff? Can I succeed in this endeavor?* I attempted to maintain a sense of calm while my stomach churned.

"Is this proposal of interest, Katie?" Father asked.

"It exceeds my wildest dreams."

Father and Mother looked at each other and smiled. "We will expect you home once a month for two or three days at a time," she said.

I went and sat next to her, putting my arms around her. "I'll come home as often as you like. I love you, Mother, and you too, Father, and I'll miss you and the boys. I count myself fortunate to have been blessed with parents such as you and saying the words 'thank you' seems inadequate to express how appreciative I am."

Father cleared his throat before saying. "We've been in correspondence with Sophia about your move to live with her and have settled on March, less than three months hence."

I detected no small degree of stress in his voice. How difficult this must be for the two of them. They were putting my happiness ahead of theirs. "March sounds ideal, Father. Would it be acceptable for me to correspond with Lula Greene in advance of the move?"

"Capital idea. I'll speak with Edward about it day after tomorrow."

"Thank you, Father." I could see exhaustion filling my mother's eyes.

"May I help you up the stairs, Mother?" I asked. "It's growing late, and tomorrow is Christmas Day, a busy one."

"I'll escort your mother upstairs," Father said, extinguishing all the candles on the tree. "Please put out the last two candles on the table before retiring."

"I will, Father. Good night to both of you."

"Good night, Katie," he said. "Sleep well… and may God bless us, everyone."

Emma

After the holidays ended, Anne left Emma's house and made the Longview Ranch her permanent residence. The bank had foreclosed on the Archer ranch to pay the debts, and she'd been forced out. In late January, Charles pleaded guilty to killing Peter Whitman in exchange for life in prison with no possibility of parole. He'd acted on the advice of his attorney in order to avoid the death penalty and was now rotting in the Utah Territorial Penitentiary.

Emma knew Anne would never visit the man who'd murdered her father, none of his former friends wished to see him, and he'd shamed his family. *His must be a tortured existence*, she thought. *Charles could live like this for another fifty years.*

Emma was finding it difficult to believe that money was all that motivated Charles to kill Uncle Peter. There had to be more to the story and Emma wanted to know what it was.

She began by looking into the investment Charles made that had gone sour, traveling to the office of the *Salt Lake Herald* to research newspaper clippings. Turned out Charles was part of what they were now calling 'The Great Diamond Hoax.' Emma read that a Kentucky grifter and his partner pulled off a scam and announced in 1870, "We have found it! The greatest treasures ever discovered on the continent, and doubtless the greatest treasures ever witnessed by the eyes of man."

I remember reading about that now, Emma thought. The mine was called 'The Mountain of Silver,' and bankers, miners, and investors, like Charles, 'flocked to get a piece of the action.' Last year, the *San Francisco Chronicle* had reported that it was 'the most gigantic and barefaced swindle of the age.'

Many people were duped and lost money—it wasn't only Charles. Emma doubted that few, if any, had turned to murder to recoup their losses. Charles could have come clean and admitted he'd invested in a scam, but it seemed he hadn't. The only way to find out what Charles was thinking was to go to the source. Emma decided to pay him a 'family' visit while she was in Salt Lake, taking a streetcar to the Sugar House neighborhood where the Penitentiary stood.

Upon arriving, she asked to speak with the warden, and after a lot of fast talking and a little arm twisting convinced him to let her meet with Charles. A jailer escorted her to his cell, opened the door, and stood guard outside. Charles was alone.

"What in blazes are you doing here, Emma?" he asked.

"Thought maybe you could use a little company."

He looked down at his hands. "No one else wants to see me. Why do you?"

"Because I don't understand, Charles, and I want to. We've had our differences and I despised the way you treated Anne, but I never figured you for a murderer."

"Neither did I. Guess the devil got hold of my heart."

"What happened?"

"After we lost everything, I went to Peter and asked for help until I could get back on my feet. He called me a 'no account,' reminding me that he'd warned me against making the investment. Claimed he wanted to make sure a scallywag like me never influenced his grandchild, saying he'd make certain Anne divorced me."

It wasn't only about the money. Charles believed he would lose his family as well.

"I begged Peter for more time, and he said he'd give me a month. I tried but came up empty handed. I figured my next best recourse was to get rid of him and take the ranch, so I poisoned him and tried to make it look like a heart attack. You know the rest of the story."

"Any remorse?' Emma asked.

"Killing Peter was evil, and I wish I'd never done it. Too late for that now, though. Talked with the prison chaplain and said I wanted to repent of what I'd done."

"What did he say?"

"Told me there was no repentance for taking another man's life, so I guess I'm stuck. Ashes to ashes and dust to dust, the good Lord won't take me, so the devil must," he said. "I only have this life to live for, not the next, Emma. When my child gets older, I want to see him, tell him how sorry his daddy is, and what a horrible mistake he made. Please help me persuade Anne to let our child pay me a visit after he's old enough."

"I'll give it some thought."

"That's all I ask."

Emma went outside to find a streetcar. On the train back to Farmington, Emma felt more conflicted than she'd expected to about Charles. She believed in redemption, and there seemed to be none for Charles.

Several days later, she took her surrey to the Longview Ranch to see Anne, leaving one evening after dinner with plans to stay the night. She had no intention of telling Anne about her visit with Charles. Maybe someday.

By the time she reached the ranch, it was dark outside, and Anne was standing on the back porch, watching a full moon cast its eerie shadows across open fields.

Emma walked over and stood next to her. Neither one said much for a time.

Anne spoke first, "I can feel my nerves prickling up and down my skin."

Emma held her hand. "Do you wish to talk?"

"Not now, and perhaps not ever."

"Why don't we sit on the porch swing," Emma suggested.

They sat down and Anne said, "My husband's in jail, and I'm on my own with my child. Could things get any worse?"

Emma placed her arm around Anne's shoulder. "You're a capable woman, Anne, with no shortage of skills. You have a home here with your brother, own half the Longview, and you have a precious child. Most importantly, you're no longer living with abuse. These are things to be thankful for."

"My child and I will endure the pitying tongues, wagging about Charles killing my father and me being left alone. People will say whatever they want, and I can't stop that. But Charles wasn't a Whitman, and my child, Peter Whitman II, is."

"That's what matters most."

"I'm glad you're my cousin, Emma." A deep breath shuddered through Anne's body. "For the moment, all I want to do is to curl up in my childhood bed and sleep for days." Alice came out to the porch and invited them in, offering lemon tea and hot scones before bed.

On the way to the kitchen, Emma and Anne walked by the family portraits hanging in the hall. Anne stopped in front of the one of her Grandmother Whitman who stood straight and proud. She said, "My grandmother was a strong woman whose husband died when she was in her early fifties." Anne began talking aloud to the picture. "I wish I'd known you, Grandmother. Father told me you sang, just as I do. I want to be as resilient as you were."

The next morning, Emma told Anne good-bye, grateful Anne would be cared for by her loving family. When she climbed into the carriage, she spotted Hank Thompson watering the horses. "How are you, Hank?" she asked.

"Gettin' old, Mrs. Emma. But don't you worry none – I'll take good care of the place for Mr. Daniel and Mrs. Anne until I can find 'em a new Ranch Manager."

"What will you do then?"

"Still got family in Texas. Want to spend what time I got left with 'em."

"I wish you God speed," Emma said.

He tipped his hat. Emma climbed into her surrey and left for home.

Ten

Katie

I was waiting to board a train, two valises in hand, enjoying the March sunshine. I'd told my family good-bye at home, asking Emma to take me to the station where she'd let me off moments ago. We promised to write each other often.

I stood alone next to the track, recalling my first train trip two years earlier in 1870, the day the suffrage act passed. *The world continues to change rapidly, and I along with it,* I thought. *Not only will I be a working woman tomorrow, I begin my study of chemistry at the University of Deseret in May.* I paused for a moment, contemplating the radical change ahead.

"You're up to the task," I said aloud, listening as the word 'task' echoed off the hills. *Sometimes I wish I were less self-reflective.*

After Father spoke with Edward Sloan in December, I posted a letter to Lula Greene introducing myself, offering congratulations on her new position as editor and making application for a position as a typesetter. I checked the post office daily looking for a letter from Lula. In mid-January, that letter arrived.

While I awaited my delayed train, I removed Lula's letter from the new beaded handbag Mother had embroidered for me, unfolded it and, reread it again.

Dear Katie,

Thank you for your recent correspondence. Over the next few months, Eliza Snow and I will be planning for the new paper. When I informed her of your interest, she recommended we hire you as a typesetter. We also hired Martha Hughes who is now a typesetter for the Desert News. She comes to our publication with experience and will help you learn the skill.

You indicated that you will be moving to Salt Lake in March and living with your cousin. I will be moving there shortly myself, staying with my Uncle Lorenzo. He has offered to let me use his parlor as an office until Mr. Sloan constructs a small office for the Exponent near the Herald. I look forward to meeting with you in Salt Lake in March.

My regards,

Lula

I folded the letter and placed it back in my handbag, looking forward to our meeting tomorrow.

The train came rolling into the small station and braked to a stop. I strode over to the passenger car where a kind porter helped me load my bags on board. After finding a seat, I looked out the window and waved farewell to Farmington. I'd be back of course, but home would never be the same again.

Sophia was waiting for me at the Salt Lake station and I was pleased to see her. She hugged me and loaded my valises into a carriage. As we bumped along, I saw a streetcar on the dusty street being pulled by a team of mules.

"Does Salt Lake have streetcar service?" I asked.

"I'm not certain why this one is out today; the first cars won't be available for transport until June."

"How exciting," I said. "In less than three months I'll have access to a streetcar which will give my budget a boost."

"So you shall," she said, smiling.

We soon reached her home in the Avenues. *I love this part of town that is my home too—at least for the next two years.*

Sophia showed me to my room. I looked around, happy with my surroundings, especially the cream-colored bedspread with yellow daisies.

"You have access to the whole house except the shed out back, which is where I paint. That's by invitation only." Sophia laughed.

I hugged her. "I'm grateful to be living with you."

I slept fitfully that night, anticipating my first day on the job. After a light breakfast, I made my way to Lorenzo Young's residence for my prearranged appointment with Lula Greene. He escorted me into her temporary Exponent office and invited me to have a seat. The room had a table and some writing materials, several books, a few magazines, and three chairs. There was a bed in the corner.

Moments later, two women walked in.

"You must be Katie," one of them said, reaching for my hand. "I'm Lula Greene. Please call me Lula."

"Thank you. It's a pleasure to meet you."

"Katie, meet Martha Hughes, the typesetter I told you about."

"Call me Mattie," she said shaking my hand. "All my friends do." She looked about my age, or perhaps a few years younger. She had curly hair that was cut short above the ears. Her face had a pleasant shape to it, and the hint of a smile was permanently displayed across her lips. Mattie's eyes had an inquisitive look about them, as if she were ready for anything.

"Lula told me you were an experienced typesetter," I said, shaking her hand. "As I novice, I'm grateful to learn the skill from you."

"You'll pick it up quickly, and it will be fun working side by side. I was just on my way out, but I'll see you soon."

Lula began our discussion by handing me a sheet of paper, saying, "I've composed this introductory editorial for the first edition of the paper, and I'd appreciate it if you'd read it aloud. It helps me to hear my words spoken."

Lula leaned back and closed her eyes, listening as I read aloud.

"The women of Utah today occupy a position which attracts the attention of intelligent thinking men and women everywhere. They are engaged in the practical solution of some of the greatest social and moral problems of the age but have been grossly misrepresented through the press, by active enemies who permit no opportunity to pass of maligning and slandering them; and with but limited opportunity of appealing to the intelligence and candor of their fellow countrymen and country women in reply."

Lula interrupted. "I may decide to make an addition to that part, but I'll consider it later, so please continue."

I nodded and read on, "Who are so well able to speak for the women of Utah as women of Utah themselves? It is better to represent ourselves than to be misrepresented by others! For these reasons, the publication of the *Woman's Exponent*, a journal owned by, controlled by, and edited by Utah ladies, has been commenced.

"This will be the first paper of its kind in the intermountain west!" I said, excited.

"It's an important moment in our history," Lula said. "Please continue."

"The aim of this journal will be to discuss every subject interesting and valuable to women. It will contain a brief and graphic summary of current news, local and general, household hints, educational matters, articles on health and dress, correspondence, editorials on leading topics of interest and will aim to defend the right, inculcate sound principles, and disseminate useful knowledge. Utah, in its Female Relief Societies, has the best organized benevolent institution of the age; yet, but little is known of the self-sacrificing labors of these Societies. In *Woman's Exponent*, a department will be devoted to reports of their meetings and other matters of interest connected with their workings; and to this end the Presidents and Secretaries of the various Societies throughout the territory are requested to furnish communications which will receive due attention."

I interrupted again with a comment. "I like the idea of including reports of meetings in the paper. It will make the more far-flung areas of the territory aware of what local Relief Societies here are doing."

"Exactly, and Eliza Snow, who, as you know, is in charge of all our Relief Societies, will be a contributor to our paper—when she has leisure from her numerous duties."

"That will be a gift to us all," I said. "Reading on…

"*Woman's Exponent* will be published semi-monthly, each number containing eight pages, quarto. The following low rates will place it within the reach of all, and the hope is that it may be made so valuable that it will be found in every family in Utah."

"What do you think of the aims of our new publication?" Lula asked, her eyes bright.

"Wonderfully broad purposes, and you've expressed them so well. What will the paper cost to purchase?"

"The terms, strictly in advance, are $2 per copy, while ten copies per year may be bought at the reduced rate of $18.00."

"It sounds reasonable, and I hope we sell many papers."

"While we may not make a great deal of money, we do need to break even." Lula stood and said, "I'm pleased you'll be working with us, Katie. I can tell you and I will get on famously."

That was my cue to leave. I thanked her for her time and interest, left the house, and made my way home, anxious to tell Sophia about all that had happened. *My first job!* I didn't skip through the streets, but I wanted to.

While all of us worked hard to have the first issue of the paper published in April, various delays in our receipt of type and paper prevented its issuance until June 1, 1872.

The first words on the page proclaimed that women were now admitted to fifty American colleges. *I am proud to be one of those women.*

Our publication also disputed the 'news' that Susan B. Anthony had declared before the Cincinnati Convention met, that if it gave her the cold shoulder, she would go on to Philadelphia and pledge the ballots of the women of America to U.S. Grant.

Ridiculous, I thought. The *Exponent* countered by saying that "the supposition is fair that Miss Anthony possesses too much good sense to have made any such declaration." Ours was a newsworthy paper, and I appreciated our support of Miss Anthony.

Even the *Salt Lake Tribune*, which had initially scoffed at the Exponent's prospects, admitted that the publication was "the greatest stride the Mormons have yet made in literature, being well edited, and quite newsy." Other newspapers responded favorably to the first issue as well and were generally encouraging. *Not bad for our first effort.*

A few weeks later, when I went to bed one night, instead of dreaming about deadlines, I dreamed about Emma. I awoke toward morning thinking about the letter she'd sent last month telling me she was pregnant. "I've never been so happy,'" she'd written.

I'd been happy too, and I was to be the baby's auntie. I sat up in bed with the distinct impression I needed to go to Emma. I tried to dismiss the feeling, but it wouldn't go away. I got up, dressed, and took a streetcar to the train station.

Emma

Emma could already feel her body changing, even though her baby wasn't due for another five months. She'd done her best to hide her condition, as her stepmother had counseled, although Emma considered that an outdated convention. The women in her ward congregation noticed anyway, smiling and nodding as they passed by in the hall. Emma felt as though she were part of some special sisterhood, and she loved it.

Sarah, a neighbor who lived down the street, was also with child and was coming over this morning to compare notes. Emma was looking forward to her visit. Wesley was in Ogden and wouldn't be home for hours.

As Emma finished dressing, something inside didn't feel quite right. It wasn't the same as the morning sickness she'd experienced. Her body felt weak all over, and her head ached. A searing pain punched through her stomach, and Emma gasped.

She moved to the bed, easing her body onto the cover, clutching her stomach. She slowly laid down, willing the pain to go away. The pain subsided, and she was relieved, taking a deep breath. It's fine, she said aloud. But moments later, it returned with a vengeance.

Emma knew she needed to go for help. She rolled over to her side and rose slowly. As she stood, Emma felt weak and faint, lying down again. *This will never do.* The room started spinning, and everything went dark.

When she awoke, Sarah and Christina were with her and so was Doctor Axel. The pain was still there. He was calling her name. "Emma? Emma, do hear me?"

"Yes," Emma said, trying to raise her head, noticing that she was back in bed and most of her clothes had been removed.

"Just lie still," Sarah cautioned, applying a wet cloth to her head.

Dr. Axel took Emma by the hand and said softly, "You're going to lose this baby, and there's nothing I can do to change that. I must deliver it."

Emma was devastated at his words. "No, no," she said aloud, and Christina took her by the hand.

"I know how much you want it, but too much damage has been done, and you're bleeding. It's your life we need to save now," he said, gently lifting Emma's legs and placing a large sheet underneath her body.

Emma turned away and wept, stomach cramping.

Christina gripped her hand, "I love you, Emma," she said.

"Emma," the doctor said, "I need you to bear down and push it out for me."

She did as she was told and felt a huge gush. It was over; her baby was dead. Emma lay shaking on a blood-soaked sheet. Christina and Sarah carefully removed the sheet and took it outside to burn. Emma felt numb all over. She didn't even know if it was a boy or a girl. Doctor Axel said the baby had been born too early to tell. But her baby was gone, and part of her had died with it.

An hour later, she heard Wesley's voice in the front room. The doctor was telling him she'd lost the baby. Oh, how Emma hated the word 'lost.' It sounded as if she were somehow to blame, and she should have done something more.

She heard the doctor say, "Emma has hemorrhaged, and it will take several days for her to regain her strength. We're fortunate she's still with us."

Wesley dashed into the bedroom.

When Emma heard him coming down the hall, she closed her eyes, and turned her face to the wall.

He came in, sat gingerly on the bed, and said, "Please look at me, Emma. I love you."

She turned toward him, cheeks burning, and like a dam bursting, tears rushed down her face.

He took her in his arms and held her close.

"I'm glad you're here."

"I'm sorry I wasn't with you," he said, eyes filled with regret.

"Losing the baby was the worst thing I could ever imagine," she sobbed.

"The worst thing would have been losing you," he said. "We'll try again."

But Emma feared she might never have another. She knew of women like that.

A short time later, Emma heard a knock at the front door. *Who could that be?* Whoever it was, she wanted to see no one—until she heard Katie's voice. *What was she doing here?*

"Oh, Emma," Katie said, coming into the room and throwing her arms around Emma. The two of them cried until they could cry no more.

Emma sat up, wiped her face. "I'm so relieved you've come, but what brought you here?"

"The Spirit did, Emma," Katie said. "I had the distinct impression I should come to you, so I caught the first train out."

"Heavenly Father knew," she whispered, eyes wide.

"He did."

"That makes me feel like it's not my fault," she wept.

"Oh, dear friend, it's not," Katie said, holding her again. "I'm so sorry about the baby."

Emma held Katie's hand and confided that her greatest fear was she would never bear another child.

"Losing one baby doesn't mean you won't have more," Katie said. "Sadly, miscarriages are all too common though rarely discussed. Please take heart."

Emma's body relaxed a little, and she took a deep breath. "You've given me hope."

Katie stayed overnight at her home and returned the next morning.

"You've brought the sunshine with you," Emma said as Katie handed her a bouquet of roses.

"May I offer you peppermint tea? I've brought some of Mother's cornbread to go with it. Did you eat at all yesterday?"

"No, and that looks good."

"I've brought honey as well. Let me prepare your plate."

The two friends sat, saying nothing, drinking tea, and eating warm cornbread with honey; together again. Emma heard a robin sing outside the window, and she drifted off to sleep.

The next few days passed slowly for Emma. Katie returned to her job in Salt Lake, and Emma lay in bed, working to regain her strength. She was rarely sick, but this was something else again. Even after Dr. Axel examined her and declared her able to return to her duties, Emma remained in bed, telling herself every day to get up and get on with it, but she simply wasn't up to the task. She was still grieving the loss of her child.

Eleven

Katie

It was a warm day in September and not a cloud in the sky. Having finished my chemistry classes for the morning, I made my way to the offices of the *Exponent* where one of the ladies handed me a short statement Eliza Snow had recently written. "You may find this of interest," she said, walking away.

Wondering what she meant, I took the page and read Sister Snow's report that Brigham Young wanted "a good many [sisters] to get a classical education and get a degree for Medicine."

Reading over the brief statement, I was elated. In a little more than two years I'd complete my studies at the University of Deseret, then it was off to medical school. I thought about Sister Snow's comments and wondered if Brigham Young might address the topic during next month's General Conference.

Since I'd moved to Salt Lake, Sophia and I hadn't missed a session of our faith's semi-annual General Conferences. It was always a happy time for me, an uplifting reunion, as well as a time of spiritual growth. In my world, science and religion co-existed harmoniously with each other, and I embraced both aspects of my life.

When I arrived home that evening, I wrote a letter to my parents asking them to join us for conference in October, which they happily agreed to do and said they would bring my brother Joseph along as well.

A few weeks later, I was with four of my favorite people, walking to the conference. The trees in the Wasatch Mountains to the East were replete with fall colors, red and yellow leaves interwoven with various shades of green. There was a fall nip in the air, and the mood on the street was cheerful.

We soon spotted the slate, turtle-backed dome of the tabernacle and walked through one of the ten entrances to the building, looking for seating on the main floor. It didn't matter where we sat, because even in the gallery, the acoustic qualities of the hall were remarkable.

We found seats downstairs in the middle of the room, the golden colored pipes of the tabernacle organ in full view. At 700 pipes, it was one of the largest organs in the world and one of the most resonant. The choir had already assembled in their chairs below the organ, and I could see George Carless, the choir's director, waiting in the stand.

The program began with the choir singing. I closed my eyes and listened to their divine voices fill the hall. It was a stirring experience and one I never tired of.

Following the open prayer, we listened for mission calls that might come from the pulpit today. They often came without warning and were a surprise even to those called to the work, as the voice of Brigham Young or Heber C. Kimball said: "Hosea Stout, called to open the Chinese mission," or "Orson Pratt to England." Others were asked to settle in more than 350 places outside Utah.

When Brigham Young stood to deliver his address, I held my breath. We all listened as he declared:

"If some women had the privilege of studying, they would make as good mathematicians as any man. We believe that women are useful not only to sweep houses, wash dishes, and raise babies, but that they should study law...or physic...The time has come for women to come forth as doctors in these valleys of the mountains."

121

It was a remarkable moment, and the right place at the right time for me. Utah women had seen too many mothers and children die in childbirth, and having female doctors in the church might improve their chances, since male doctors didn't usually treat women.

A few weeks, later I returned to Farmington to celebrate my eighteenth birthday. My friends were coming this afternoon and I was looking forward to seeing them again.

I walked into the house and my brothers sang out in unison, "Happy Birthday, Katie!" Each of them had made a card that they presented to me in turn.

"Read our cards aloud," Jacob squealed. "Mine first."

"I'd be honored. From my brother Jacob: "Roses are read, violets are blue, you are kind, and I love you.

"Thank you, my little one. I appreciate your gentle sentiment," I said, squeezing his hand.

"Now mine, Katie," Andrew said.

"Roses are red violets are blue, God made you beautiful, and I love you."

"I adore it. Thank you, Andrew."

He grinned from ear to ear, pleased with his verse.

"Now yours, Joseph," I said, opening the card and reading. "Roses are red, violets are blue, what to say next, I cannot construe."

We all laughed. "Very clever," I said.

"Happy birthday," he said, smiling, "to my favorite sister."

Father offered a blessing on the food and we ate eggs sprinkled with cheese, cornbread, sliced oranges, and hot cocoa.

"I have a card for you too," Ada said, placing it beside my plate. "Please read it later."

"Thank you, Aunt. I will."

"Your father and I have two gifts for you, Katie," Mother said.

"The first is this small blank book in honor of your eighteenth birthday," Father said, "It has your name and the date imprinted in gold lettering on the cover. We'll ask your friends to write their birthday wishes inside, and Mother and I will add a note as well."

"What a lovely memento," I said, turning the mauve book over in my hand.

"We also secured a copy of *Lorna Doone: A Romance of Exmooren*, by the English author Richard Doddridge," Mother said, handing me the book.

"Thank you, Mother," I said, face beaming. "I've wanted to read this novel since its publication."

"I'll be curious to know whether you like the story. While Joseph and Andrew clear away brunch, please go upstairs and read for a few hours while we decorate the dining room. I want you to be surprised at what we've planned."

"What a special day you've arranged," I said. "Thank you."

I picked up my new novel and walked up to my old room, anxious to begin reading. But as I placed the memory book on my desk, I wanted to write a poem instead. I wrote and then scratched out words, writing and rewriting my thoughts, finally penning this on the last page of my new book.

> The leaves of Autumn shine with orange glory,
> And faces beam with joy this radiant morn.
> In my fancy, I sketch the shape of my life's story,
> Gazing at a dream I know not of.
> My visions come in colors both dim and bright,
> The beauty of the day, the darkness of the night.

I read my words aloud, the last two lines reminding me that life wouldn't be a sketch under my control. *While it will be far from ideal, it will be a wondrous journey.*

Joseph knocked at the door. "We're ready for you, Katie."

When I saw the dining room, I was stunned. Ribbons of blue and white had been strung from the corners of the table up to the chandelier overhead, forming an arch. Blue ribbons draped down the table, dividing it into thirds, and four tapered candles were spaced along the top of Mother's best white lace cloth.

"I don't know what to say. It's beyond description."

"Come look at your cake," Mother said. "It is three-layers filled with raspberry and chocolate, covered with a white icing."

"My favorite." White china plates for the guests were stacked next to the cake along with silver forks.

"You've planned everything down to the last detail, Mother," I said, smiling. "It's lovely."

"I'm glad you're pleased," she said, clinging to the edge of a chair.

"You require a rest, dear sister," Ada said, taking Mother's arm and leading her away.

"Enjoy the festivities, Katie," Mother said. "I'll be down later."

"I love you, Mother," I called after her. Several knocks came at the door.

Emma, Julia, and Sarah were the first to arrive, and they oo-hed and aahed at the lovely decor. Wesley and another man I didn't know stood behind Emma. "Katie," Wesley said, "This is my friend Thomas Forrest. He lives in Salt Lake and came to visit for a few days."

"Welcome, Mr. Forrest," I said, extending my hand.

"Miss Leavitt," he said, taking mine. "It's a pleasure to meet you."

I looked into his warm face with its large round eyes and saw kindness. His hair was black and curly and wisped under a gray top hat. I admired his smooth face that had no whiskers or sideburns. He dressed smartly in a dark gray suit with a black crisscross pattern and a navy-blue cravat standing out on his white shirt. I found him quite handsome.

Thomas offered his arm, and we went outside. It was a little chilly, but still warm enough to play croquet. My friends giggled at the two of us, causing me to blush to the roots of my hair.

After nine wickets and two stakes were embedded in the grass, Emma, Wesley, Thomas and I took up our mallets to begin the game while the others sat at a small table waiting their turn. We began knocking our wooden balls through the small hoops, keeping score. I often played this game with my brothers and prided myself on the ease with which my balls passed through the wickets. Thomas and I were soon evenly matched, winning one game each.

"I congratulate you, Miss Leavitt," he said, "on your skill at the game."

"Thank you." I smiled.

Rather than playing a third game to determine the winner, we stepped aside so the others might play. Thomas and I talked, and he told me a bit about his family, saying he was taking pre-law classes at the University of Deseret. I told him I was studying chemistry at the same institution.

"Perhaps we'll see each other there," he said.

"Perhaps we shall."

Before retiring, I read the contents of Ada's card, in which she wrote, "While you and I do not see eye to eye about women's suffrage, and never shall, you are my treasured niece, and I cherish our relationship."

"I love you, Ada," I said aloud, smiled, and blew out the candle. I hoped to speak with Emma soon to see what more I could find out about Thomas Forrest.

Emma

Emma had told Katie all she knew about Thomas before Katie returned to Salt Lake. "I wonder if they might be right for each other," Emma said aloud as she rode her horse into Grandmother Phoebe's yard. When she reached the porch, she ran her hand along the stones her grandfather had used to build this home, hand cutting the timbers that supported the structure. He'd died four years ago from the ague fever, and Emma missed him.

Grandmother had invited Emma to dine for the noonday meal, and she was glad of the opportunity. As she walked inside, she saw steam rising from hot, buttery scones topped with strawberry preserves. Just right for a chilly November day.

"Please sit down, and I'll bring you some stew," her grandmother said, standing at the cook stove.

Emma's mouth watered as she waited for the savory stew with its generous portions of mutton, potatoes, onions, parsley, and carrots. "It smells delicious," she said.

Grandmother Phoebe said, "Have I ever told you about Betsy? We were childhood friends in the small town of Greene, New York, where I was born."

"I don't believe so," Emma said, mouth full of scone.

"The two of us have corresponded since my family joined the church and came West, and her family moved to Boston. I recently received a letter from her with an invitation. In her letter she said that neither of us was getting any younger, and she wanted to see me again. I'd like to see her as well; we enjoy a rare, life-long friendship."

"Is she coming to Salt Lake?"

"No, she's invited me to go to Boston next month."

"What a wonderful opportunity, Grandmother," Emma said, eyes bright. "You must go."

"You're right. At 63 years of age, I'm not getting any younger, and I'd like to travel while I still can. I've told Betsy all about you for years, and she's invited you to come along, offering to pay for our trip."

Emma laid her spoon down and stared at her grandmother. "You're inviting me to accompany you to Boston?" she asked in a loud voice.

Phoebe laughed. "You're my only granddaughter, and I want us to do something memorable together."

"I've never been further than Salt Lake, and a trip East would be glorious." Emma's eyes danced.

"How do you think Wesley will respond to the idea?"

"Wesley is very busy with his deputy duties, and I'm certain he wouldn't mind."

"December is a particularly cold time of year in Massachusetts, but Betsy would like us to attend a special event with her at Faneuil Hall on the 15th of the month."

"What is it?"

"Lucy Stone has organized a centennial observance of the Boston Tea Party with the aim of promoting woman's voting rights. Betsy is a member of the American Woman's Suffrage Association, and Lucy is its president."

"We could support our sister suffragists in the East."

A smile spread across Phoebe's wrinkled face. "I hoped you might feel that way. Fair warning, though, it will take us almost a week to make the train trip. It's going to be a long journey there and back, and we'll spend two weeks in Boston. Altogether, we'll be gone over a month."

"Will you find the trip tiring, Grandmother?" Emma asked, concerned.

"I was thirty when I rode for months in a dusty wagon from Nauvoo to Salt Lake, and thirty-four years later, now I can make the trip by train in a week. I may be old, but I'm still blessed with enough stamina to ride the rails," she said, determined.

"Of course, Grandmother, and if you need assistance, I'll be there."

"Then, it's settled. We leave December fifth. Betsy has checked and seats on the train are still available."

"My valise will be packed and waiting," Emma said, breathless. Not only will we visit Boston, but we'll see the countryside of our nation as we travel."

"That we will, my girl, and I'll be pleased to view it this time from the window of a train."

Emma rose from the chair and put her arms around her grandmother. "Thank you for the opportunity. I'll be a steadfast traveling companion."

"I have no doubt of that, Emma. I have no doubt."

When Emma and Phoebe boarded the train in Ogden a few weeks later, neither realized that Betsy had booked premium tickets until the porter showed them to their compartment with its plush red seats. He demonstrated how the seats converted into snug sleeping berths and said, "I'll be back this evening to make up your beds and will see to it that you have fresh linens daily. You'll also have access to our dining car."

Emma took a step back, shaking her head. "I can't believe our good fortune."

"I am as amazed as you are." Phoebe smiled, fanning herself. "I'll find our trip relaxing, not tiring."

A week later Betsy picked them up in her coach. As they climbed inside, she held Phoebe in her arms as if she might never let go. "It's so good to see again you at last," she said.

"I'm surprised you recognize me; I've changed so much."

"You still have a lilt in your step and those same blue eyes filled with determination. I'd know you anywhere. This must be Emma."

"Grandmother told me so much about you on our trip. It's good to meet you."

"You look just like your grandmother did at your age."

"You are little changed from the girl you were then, Betsy," Phoebe said.

"Life has been kind to me. I hope you enjoy your time here in the Boston area."

"The ride here was so much more than I expected. Perhaps for the first time in my life, I felt pampered," Phoebe said.

Betsy smiled, "You deserve it, my friend. On our way home, we'll stop by Boston Commons, the oldest city park in our country which boasts about 50 acres. The trees will be bare of leaves at this time of year, but I believe you'll still find it an impressive place to take a short stroll. After that, I thought perhaps Emma might enjoy stopping by the Old Corner Bookstore on Tremont street."

Emma enjoyed visiting the Commons, and she could hardly wait to see the bookstore. When they walked inside, she had never seen so many books in one place in her life.

"The store is not only home to several booksellers, but a few publishing houses also have their business here," Betsy said. "Several authors have used the store as a meeting place, including Charles Dickens, Nathaniel Hawthorne, and Longfellow."

Emma felt like she'd died and gone to heaven as she walked among the stacks, looking for a book she wished to purchase. She found a copy of *The Revelations of a Lady Detective*, published in 1864. The book marked the first appearance of a woman detective in literature. Emma stood breathless as Betsy purchased a copy for her.

After a few more days spent exploring the city, December fifteenth dawned cold in the city of Boston, the day of the Women's

Tea Party. As they dressed, Phoebe asked Emma, "Did you know that Lucy Stone was the first Massachusetts woman to earn her bachelor's degree?"

"I didn't know that. What a wonderful accomplishment."

When they reached the streets downtown, Phoebe, Betsy, and Emma walked arm in arm until they reached Faneuil Hall, a favorite meeting place of America's revolutionary leaders.

"Samuel Adams delivered one of his orations here," Betsy said, "and others who encouraged our independence from Great Britain. This building has been a marketplace and meeting hall since 1743. Just imagine, if you will, the cradle of liberty."

Emma stood on the sidewalk and craned her neck at the historic old building with its red brick walls, bank of rounded windows on each floor, and at its crown, a white cupola. "We're part of history today, Grandmother."

"So we are, my girl," she replied.

The three ladies made their way inside and found seats in the gallery, taking care not to sit behind one of the white supporting posts. A man by the name of Thomas Wentworth Higginson, who Betsy whispered was a well-known historian, essayist, and Unitarian Minister, presided at the event.

When it was Lucy Stone's turn to speak, she strode smartly up to the podium and discussed taxes, associating them with the right to vote. Last night Betsy had told them that several years prior, Stone refused to pay her city taxes because she didn't have the right to vote. The town constable auctioned off her household items to pay the tax.

She proclaimed, "Great Britain never dared to do to the colonies what Massachusetts does to the women of this state today," creating a parallel of the predicament of the Thirteen Colonies with the disenfranchisement of women."

Phoebe whispered, "Here in the state of Massachusetts, and in all other areas of the country save Wyoming and Utah, women are taxed without representation."

It was a stirring meeting, and the room was filled with like-minded women.

But a few weeks later, Betsy stormed into her house with a copy of the January 3, 1874 issue of Harper's Weekly. "See here," she said. "Nast has drawn a cartoon satirizing the suffrage movement and the Woman's Tea Party."

Emma looked at the drawing and saw that he'd sketched two people pouring tea into the Boston Harbor, standing aboard a small rowboat named The Mayflower. The figure on the right was obviously meant to resemble a stern Susan B. Anthony, pouring tea into the Boston Harbor, looking as if she were hosting a tea party at home.

On the left of the drawing, stood a man dressed as a woman. "How disparaging," Emma said. "The man has a moustache and sideburns paired with a hair net and bonnet."

"Indeed," Phoebe said, snorting in disgust. "With all else that's offensive about the cartoon, he promotes the ridiculous notion that suffragists are not feminine."

The caption under the drawing read, "The New England Woman's Tea Party, believing that 'Taxation without Representation is Tyranny,' and that our Forefathers were justified in resisting Despotic Power by throwing the Tea into Boston Harbor, hereby do the same."

"A demeaning caricature," Betsy said. "I should like to give him a piece of my mind. What a disappointing conclusion to an awe-inspiring meeting."

The next day, it was time for Emma and Phoebe to return home. "Thank you for your hospitality," Emma said to Betsy. "It was a lovely Christmas."

"You've been a joy to be with," she replied. "I hope one day you'll realize your dreams of becoming a female detective."

"I'll remember our trip to Boston as long as I live," Phoebe said. "It was so good to see you again," she added, hugging Betsy goodbye.

Betsy's carriage took them to the train station, and after they boarded the train, Phoebe turned to Emma and said, "A memory made and shared lasts a lifetime."

Twelve

Katie

Following a harsh winter, spring arrived in Salt Lake City. An assortment of yellow, purple, and pink flowers blanketed the entrance to Sophia's home. Several of her best spring landscapes were displayed on easels set about the house and we were expecting a crowd. Sophia had placed a small advertisement in the *Herald* last week, hoping to attract customers beyond those who were already familiar with her work.

I was the one assigned to collect the money. As her assistant, I'd dressed simply and was sitting at a small, round table in the parlor waiting for potential customers. Gazing around the room, I found myself worried. *Is Sophia selling her art because she lacks money? Should I be paying something for my stay?* After mulling over my concerns, I decided to put the question to her directly. "Sophia," I asked, "Do you want me to pay room and board?"

"Of course not," she said, looking surprised. "The pleasure of your company is payment enough. Why do you ask?"

"I wondered if perhaps you were selling paintings to raise money."

"No, my angel, I part with my art because I want to send it into the world where it may bring joy to others."

"I was afraid you'd been adversely affected by the financial panic that began last September."

"I sold my railroad stock two months prior to the collapse, concerned that the shares may be overvalued. Their price had risen so much in the past five years that I did very well, but I was one of the lucky ones."

I was relieved her financial circumstances were solid.

"Several people are coming up the walk, our first customers. Katie, I neglected to place the cake knife by the trifle. Would you get it, please?"

Sophia and I had made the dish together, beginning with dry sponge cake, layering it with custard and berries, and adding whipping cream on top. Our cakes looked and smelled delicious.

A man came through the door wearing a white shirt with crimson, white, and green striped trousers. He looked quite stylish. *Could that be Thomas Forrest?* I stood, walked over, and touched his arm. "Hello," I said.

He turned around, surprised. "Hello yourself." He beamed. "How are you, Katie?"

"Doing well, thank you. I didn't expect to see you here."

"I saw the ad in the *Herald* and thought I'd have a look."

"You've come to the right place; Sophia is a talented artist."

"How do you know her?"

"She's my father's cousin."

"A very nice residence," he said, glancing around.

"I live here with her now. How are your pre-law classes?"

"Coming along. You're studying chemistry, I believe?"

"Yes, and I'm a typesetter for the *Woman's Exponent*."

"My mother reads that paper, and it's well-written."

"Would you like me to show you Sophia's art?"

"I'd like that," he said, offering his arm. "Thank you for being my guide."

I took his arm, smiled, and could feel my pulse pounding in my throat. "Let's begin with this mural. While it's not for sale, it is, in my opinion, Sophia's masterpiece."

"It's large and so colorful," Thomas said as we reached the mural, admiration in his voice.

"Sophia began painting it about five years ago, wanting to depict immigrants who came to the Valley to make it their new home."

Thomas examined the painting more closely. "Seems to be appropriately titled, 'An American Dream,' but there are more people shown here than pioneers, farmers, laborers, and railroad workers. Who are they?"

"The painting includes two generations of Sophia's family who emigrated from Wales."

"Impressive," Thomas said.

"Look—Sophia is taking out her brushes preparing to paint something new."

"Why does she paint while she has customers?" Thomas asked.

"She's found that people love watching her create from whole cloth."

"I don't think I've ever observed an artist at work."

"Let's stand over there where we can get a better view," I said.

As we watched, Thomas said, "She is skilled indeed."

"I think so too." His hand touched mine, and I blushed up at him and smiled.

"I believe I'd like to purchase this small landscape," he said a little later, selecting a picture of the Wasatch foothills in the fall with snow-capped mountains in the distance. In the forefront, stood a small brown home set among fields of golden hay scattered about in bales.

"Of course," I said, setting it aside. "Before you leave would you care for some trifle?"

"I would, yes, if you'll join me."

"I'd be delighted," I said, walking to the dining room table and cutting a piece for each of us. "Let's take ours and sit in the kitchen away from those mingling about the house."

After we sat down, he cut into his trifle and said, "This is excellent." He took another large bite. "One of the best trifles I've tasted."

"Thank you. Sophia and I made it together." I reached up and brushed a few crumbs from his chin. "You don't want to walk about the city with cake on your face."

He laughed. "No, I don't. Thank you."

"Would you care for apple cider?"

"Yes, please." As I poured, he said, "Tell me about you."

"What would you like to know?"

"Everything," he said, reaching over and putting his hand over mine, "beginning with, were you born in Farmington?"

"Yes, my grandfather was one of the early settlers. What about you?"

"Salt Lake born and bred, and my family lives not far from here. I have two older brothers." He smiled. "We're a noisy bunch, but a deeply religious family. My father served a mission for our church in Canada."

"How does your father make his living?"

"He's an attorney, along with two of my uncles. Seems to run in the family. If memory serves, your father is a prosecutor."

"For Davis County."

"And yet you want to be a doctor."

"I'm called to the work," I said, wondering how he'd respond to my assertion.

"Forgive me for being forward, but are you interested in marriage and children as well?"

"Oh, yes, very much," I said, skin tingling.

After we finished eating, Thomas took my hand in his and kissed it.

Sophia came into the kitchen. "Hello," she said to Thomas. "I don't believe we've met."

"This is my friend Thomas," I said. "Wesley and Emma introduced us."

He stood, and with a slight bow, said, "Ma'am."

"Please, call me Sophia."

"I admire your art, and Katie has set aside a piece for me to purchase."

"Thank you. I'd be happy to ring it up while she collects her bag."

I looked at the clock. "Where has the time gone? I need to get to the train station."

"Where are you going?" Thomas asked.

"Farmington."

"I'd be happy to take you to the station in my carriage, if you'll allow me the privilege."

"I'd like that very much," I said in a soft voice. I dashed up the stairs to collect my bag, and moments later, Thomas and I were on our way.

"I've enjoyed getting to know you better," he said as we rode.

"I'm pleased and surprised that we ran into each other today."

When we reached our destination, he helped me out of the carriage and lingered a moment, gazing into my eyes. My heart melted in my chest. Then the rain started.

"Do you have an umbrella?" he asked, putting his up over my head. By now, the rain was coming down in sheets.

"At Sophia's, and a lot of good it will do me there." I laughed.

"Here, take mine."

"You'll get soaked."

"Then allow me to walk you to the platform."

"That would be nice. Thank you."

"Ready? We go on three: One, two, go," he said, taking me under his arm.

We ran through the rain, dodging puddles and laughing.

When we reached the train, Thomas helped me up the steps with my bag and came inside to make certain I was comfortably settled. "You're such a gentleman," I said, eyes shining.

"I'll see you soon."

The conductor called, "All Aboard!"

"I'd best be off," Thomas said, hurrying down the steps.

As the train pulled away, he waved and smiled a manly grin, standing underneath his umbrella in the rain.

He's so handsome, I thought. He was on my mind all the way to Farmington.

Emma

It was Sunday morning, and Emma was sitting in the Rock Chapel with the rest of the congregation preparing to sing the closing song. She could see Katie sitting with her family in the back of the room talking with the Haight family. At the choir director's signal, the organist began playing, 'Did You Think to Pray?' For Emma it was merely another hymn, until they sang the words, "When sore trials came upon you, did you think to pray?" Eyes wet, she looked around the room and saw so many mothers with babies. Emma had been praying fervently to conceive again after her miscarriage. *Still nothing.*

When the meeting ended, Emma waited while Wesley and the others filed out of the chapel. She wasn't in the mood to speak with anyone, not even Katie.

While Emma sat alone, Aurelia Rogers approached the pew she occupied. Sister Rogers had recently reached the age of 39, and Emma knew her as a firm supporter of women's suffrage and a woman of great faith.

"Do you mind if I join you?" she asked.

Emma moved over. "Please do," she said, trying to force a smile.

Even as a child, Emma had known the Rogers family, who'd lived in Farmington since the early days. Emma's father told her that young Aurelia Spencer had learned to be a mother at twelve after her mother died, and she and her older sister took care of four younger siblings. Their father had been called by the Church to take charge of missionary work in Great Britain.

Sister Rogers turned to Emma and said, "As we sang the closing hymn, I felt prompted to share something with you."

Emma turned to her, curious.

"You may know that after marrying at the age of seventeen, I gave birth to twelve children. Only seven survived infancy. When three of my precious little ones died, one following the other, I fell into a deep despair and nearly lost my belief in God."

Emma was surprised. *I imagined her faith to be unwavering no matter the circumstances.*

"I'm aware, Emma, that you lost a baby and have been struggling to conceive," she said. "Please don't despair." Sister Rogers held Emma's hand. "Life can be very trying, and we often don't know what the Good Lord has in mind for us until later. But this I'm sent to tell you: His eyes are upon you, and He hasn't forgotten you."

Tears rolled down Emma's cheeks.

Sister Rogers folded Emma into her arms and held her close. "It took time for me to overcome my malaise and believe again after the death of my children, but I've come to appreciate how precious life is, and I know we must nurture the young among us no matter who they are."

Emma paused, enjoying the comfort of Sister Rogers's kind arms before sitting up and saying, "There are mothers in our congregation who struggle every week to manage their young ones. I could help."

"I believe they'd appreciate your kind assistance. We're all mothers in Zion, Emma. Eliza Snow has impacted the lives of many children throughout the territory."

Emma remembered the day she'd met Eliza Snow when she was with Katie in the Salt Lake suffrage meeting. For the first time, Emma understood why Aunt Eliza wished to be addressed as Aunt.

"The Lord loves you, Emma," Sister Rogers said with firm conviction. Then, she rose and walked out of the chapel.

Emma didn't yet know what it all meant, but she felt comforted.

Early the next morning, Katie came to Emma's house. Wesley was out riding with their neighbor Hezekiah, as was their habit each day. Emma made muffins, and the two women talked and laughed, enjoying themselves immensely.

Emma's neighbor Hezekiah burst through the door without knocking. "Come quick, Emma," he shouted. "It's Wesley. I'll take you to him."

Emma ran outside, leaving Katie behind.

When they reached the pasture, she found Wesley lying prostrate, moaning in the dirt. Dr. Axel was tending to him. Wesley's right leg was in shreds, and there was blood everywhere.

"What happened?" Emma asked, falling to her knees, holding Wesley's head in her hands.

Hezekiah said, "We were riding at a gallop when a large coyote jumped in our path, spooking the horse. He reared, stumbled and went down rolling on Wesley, crushing his leg. I went for Dr. Axel and came for you."

"I'm going to have to take his leg off," the doctor said. He opened his long amputation box that held a variety of knives, an amputation saw, bond nippers, a tourniquet, tweezers, scissors, and a hey saw.

Wesley moaned and seemed unaware of what was taking place.

"Are you certain?" Emma asked.

"I'm afraid there is no saving that leg. It's beyond repair."

Emma grimaced. Wesley was a strong, active man, and losing his leg would devastate him. As the doctor readied to perform the surgery, Hezekiah sat next to her.

"The morphine has taken hold," the doctor said. "You may wish to turn your head while I do my work."

Emma looked away, and while she couldn't see what Dr. Axel was doing, she could hear flesh and bone being cut away.

In a circular-cut sawing motion—to keep Wesley from dying of shock and pain—the doctor quickly cut off his leg, and Wesley awoke, screaming.

Emma sat in a state of shock, still holding Wesley's head in her hands, looking down at the stump where his leg used to be. Thankfully, he'd passed out.

"I'll wrap the wound in gauze laced with carbolic acid," the doctor said. "That will help him heal." When he finished applying the gauze, he placed a stocking over the stump.

Hezekiah carefully picked Wesley up in his large arms and carried him to the buckboard, placing him on a blanket in the back.

"Emma," the doctor said, turning to her, "Wesley's recovery will take time, and you must know that he'll retain sensation for a time in a limb that's no longer there."

What a miserable experience that will be, to experience an itch he wants to scratch in a leg that no longer exists.

"It will be several months before he's sufficiently healed, and he'll experience grief over the loss of his limb. When he's ready, I'll fit him with a prosthetic, but for now, he needs as much rest as possible. He should sleep until morning."

Emma sat dazed. It had all happened so quickly.

Dr. Axel took her hand. "There's one more thing, Emma, and I'm sorry to have to tell you this," he said. "One of his testicles was trampled, and he may never father children."

Emma nodded as if she understood, a queasy feeling in her stomach. Time to get Wesley home. Emma thanked the doctor, hoisted her skirts, and climbed into the buckboard with Hezekiah.

Neither one of them spoke on the ride home.

When they arrived, Katie walked outside and came over to the wagon. A look of horror crossed her face when she saw Wesley lying immobile, his leg gone.

Hezekiah took Wesley from the wagon, carried him into the house, and lifted him into bed. "I'll be back to check on you both in the morning," he said. He tipped his hat and left.

Emma collapsed in a chair while Katie brewed peach tea and Wesley slept. As they sipped their tea, Emma said, "Dr. Axel told me that Wesley may never father children." Though still in shock, Emma had a remarkable calmness about her. "I don't need to tell you how devastated I am and will remain so for quite some time. But I'm grateful for my conversation with Sister Rogers yesterday morning."

"I saw the two of you speaking. Aurelia Rogers is a woman I much admire."

"I do as well, and she never misses an opportunity to help the young ones."

"What did she tell you?"

139

"She said she'd lost several children, had fallen into despair, and almost abandoned her faith. She counseled me to hold on to mine. If she hadn't spoken with me when she did," Emma said, looking off in the distance, "Dr. Axel's news might have extinguished my faith. Instead I feel some sense of peace knowing that the Lord is there to comfort me when faint or discouraged."

"She was inspired," Katie whispered, squeezing Emma's hand.

The two of them held each other, as words to a beloved Mormon hymn filled Emma's mind. 'Gird up your loins, fresh courage take, our God will never us forsake. And soon we'll have this tale to tell, all is well, all is well.'

The next morning Emma woke to the sounds of Wesley writhing in agony. "Emma, Emma," he called. "The muscles in my leg are throbbing." He reached down to clutch his leg and found nothing there. "What happened? What happened?" he shouted.

Emma sat up, held his hand, and in a soft voice asked, "What do you remember of yesterday?"

"I remember the horse falling on top of me and a crushing pain in my leg. Dr. Axel administered something for my pain." Wesley paused, a horrified look on his face as the truth of the matter sank in. "He took my leg."

"Yes, my love," she said, kissing him on the forehead. "I can't imagine how devastating the loss of a limb must be. But if he hadn't removed your leg, you would have died, and I simply couldn't have borne that," she said.

Wesley rolled into her lap and sobbed like a baby while Emma held him and stroked his hair, telling him over and over that she loved him.

A few hours later he took a deep breath and said, "I'm hungry. Would you get me something to eat?"

"Anything you like," she said kissing him. Emma decided not to tell him about the problem with fathering children yet. He had enough loss to manage.

"What would you like to eat?"

"Johnny cake, eggs, and cocoa," he said, grimacing in pain.

"I'll cook that and add pear slices."

"My favorite fruit," he said, looking again at the stump. "You no longer have a whole man," he said in a whisper.

"Wesley Hatch without one leg is better than any other man with two. We'll weather this storm together," she said, a confidence in her voice she did not yet feel.

Part Two

"I believe in women, especially thinking women."

Emmeline B. Wells

Thirteen

Katie

Thomas and I had spent as much time together as convention allowed over the past ten months, and the days had flown by. We studied together or discussed the latest civic events over dinner. We enjoyed simple things the most, such as lying in the lush grasses in the park, laughing and pointing at swollen white clouds set against the brilliant blue of a Utah sky. I'd laugh and say, "This cloud looks like a bear, and that one's a dragon." He'd smile and hold me close.

When we were together, no one else mattered. This evening he'd invited me to dinner at his boarding house, asking that I dress for a night on the town. With a twinkle in his eye, he said he had a surprise that I would enjoy following dinner. I chose a dress with a light green bodice, yellow ruffles at the neck, and peach colored flounces adorning the skirt.

When I heard the bell ring, I came down the stairs and found him standing at the door. He looked dashing in his black suit and top hat, mauve vest, and white ruffled shirt. "Madam," he said, removing his hat, "you look lovely."

"Why thank you, sir," I replied, smiling.

"Enjoy your evening," Sophia said.

We walked outside and climbed into his carriage. I asked, "Will you reveal the surprise now?"

"No." He laughed. "After dinner, but I promise it will be well worth the wait."

The evening was surprisingly cool for the middle of June as we rode to Fanny Brook's boarding house. I'd never been there, but I knew of it, as did most people in Salt Lake City.

"Allow me to tell you a bit about the Brooks family," Thomas said as we rode. "They were the first Jewish family to settle in Utah. I suspect it may not have been a simple matter to feel included when they first arrived in 1864, but they have since become respected and valued members of the community. Fanny is largely responsible for their growing businesses."

"She sounds like a person I want to know."

"She's outspoken, filled with energy, and yet she's diplomatic. Fanny speaks her native German, as well as French and English. Her first baby died along the plains after she and her husband left Nebraska and joined a wagon train West. Life hasn't been easy here either, and she's experienced her share of hardships and tragedy."

"She's thrived despite difficult circumstances. I admire that and suspect she favors women expanding their spheres of influence as she has."

"She certainly does. Permit me to tell you a story about the unstoppable Fanny Brooks and Brigham Young that occurred in 1868, when he asked church followers to give preference to Mormon businesses. Fanny demanded a personal meeting with him, with the outcome being that he encouraged members to continue to patronize her businesses and even donated land for a Jewish Cemetery in Salt Lake. That's the kind of woman Fanny is."

When we arrived at the boarding house, Fanny herself met us at the door. She looked about forty, her brown hair worn about chin length and tucked behind her ears. She wore long pearl earrings and presented herself as the professional she was.

After Thomas introduced us, she showed us to the dining room where a small table for two was set with white linens, silverware, and china. The fluted glasses were filled with apple cider.

"Since this is a special occasion, I'll serve your meal," she said, placing a plate of trout almandine topped with parsley and lemons in front of each of us.

"This is delicious," I said after taking my first bite.

"I prepared it myself."

"Fanny is known for the personal touches she provides her customers," Thomas said.

She nodded and walked away. "Enjoy your meal."

As we ate custard for dessert, Thomas said, "Please catch me up on Wesley. How's he doing?"

"He walks with a prosthetic and his limp is marginal. Sheriff Gregory has given him a desk job, but it's been a trying time for both Wesley and Emma."

Fanny approached with more cider. "Pardon the intrusion. I couldn't help overhear your conversation. Has your friend fallen on difficult times?"

"My friend's husband was thrown from a horse. His leg had to be amputated, and the doctor believes he may never father children."

"Remember Hannah in the Bible?" Fanny asked. "She was in despair because she couldn't conceive. Sarah, Rebecca, and Rachael who came before her suffered the same affliction, but Hannah was the one of the three who accepted God's promise with faith." Fanny raised both arms, looked up and said, "God will provide." She placed her arm on Katie's shoulder and left the room.

I loved her words, 'God will provide,' and thought of my friends who had adopted children. *Sometimes God provides in one way and sometimes in another.*

We finished our meal and went to the carriage. "Now are you going to tell me where we're going?" I asked

He smiled, pleased with himself. "To the theatre."

"You know how much I enjoy the theatre. What's playing?"

"*Around the World in Eighty Days.*"

"I've heard so much about it. I'm pleased that many of the great actors of our time are beginning to come to the Salt Lake Theatre."

"That's due to the quality of the theatre itself and the education and sophistication of our audiences. Back East, they refer to the building as the Cathedral in the Desert."

"It's a fine structure, and I love the gas lamps. I wonder if tonight's production includes a live elephant. That would be wondrous."

"Perhaps," he said, placing his hand over mine. "We shall see."

We arrived at the Doric style theatre and assumed our seats along with almost 1,500 other people. I read Thomas the brief synopsis of the play printed in the program:

> *"Stampeding elephants! Raging typhoons! Runaway trains! Unabashedly slapstick! Hold onto your seats for the original amazing race! Join fearless adventurer Phileas Fogg and his faithful manservant as they race to beat the clock! Phileas Fogg has agreed to an outrageous wager that puts his fortune and his life at risk. With his resourceful servant Passepartout, Fogg sets out to circle the globe in an unheard-of 80 days. But his every step is dogged by a detective who thinks he's a robber on the run. Danger, romance, and comic surprises abound in this whirlwind of a show as five actors portraying 39 characters traverse seven continents in an adaptation of Jules Verne's story, published in 1873."*

"It promises to be an entertaining evening," Thomas said.

Indeed, it was. We reveled in Phileas Fogg's adventures in London, Paris, Bombay, Hong Kong, and a trip to San Francisco by steamer. I laughed so hard I could barely catch my breath through the dancing, singing, and romance.

"I marvel at the idea of flying machines," I whispered to Thomas. "Do you think it's possible?"

"Who can tell?"

After the play concluded, we all rose to our feet and offered the performers a standing ovation. *I love the community feel of the theatre, for here there are no divisions among us. What an evening it has been.*

"We have one more stop on the way to Sophia's," Thomas said, checking his pocket watch.

"I can't imagine what it might be; it's already been a perfect evening."

Thomas pulled the horse to a stop near one of our favorite parks in the Avenues. "Look at those stars," he said stepping out of the carriage and offering me his hand. "Let's walk to that bench on the far side of the park."

It was a lovely night as we strolled hand in hand.

After we sat down, Thomas kissed me and said, "I've found my world in you, Katie, and I need search no further." He got down on one knee and opened a box, a ring gleaming inside. "Will you do me the honor?" he asked. "I've already spoken with your father, and he approves."

I leaned down, kissed him, and tugged him up next to me, "Yes," I said, my heart pounding. "I love you."

He kissed me and said he loved me too.

"When?" I asked breathless.

"Let's be practical for a moment now," he said taking both my hands in his. "In less than a year, we will have both completed our studies at the University of Deseret, and we could marry then. I plan to apply to the Georgetown Law school in Washington D. C., and you've mentioned your desire to attend the Women's Medical College in Philadelphia."

"I have, yes. Romania Pratt attends there, and I'd know someone."

"I'm not certain I know who she is."

"She's married to Parley P. Pratt, Junior."

"Him, I know. Why does she wish to become a doctor?"

"After bearing seven children, one of her sons lived just a few days, and her only daughter died before reaching the age of two. Sophia told me that after one of Romania's close friends also passed, Romania was determined to educate herself in medical school. Following Brigham Young's conference talk, urging women to become doctors, she asked him for a blessing and left last year for Philadelphia."

"Who's caring for her children?"

"Her mother. She journeys home periodically to see them. Speaking of travel, how would we manage a long-distance marriage with you in Georgetown and me in Philadelphia?"

"The trip takes less than two hours by train, and we could spend every weekend together."

"Are you certain you'd be satisfied with that?" I had my doubts and wondered if being married and living long distance might be difficult. It didn't seem practical.

"I don't see why not."

"I wouldn't want to be with child until after I received my degree."

"There are ways around that."

"It sounds like you've thought of everything."

"You know me," he smiled. "I create plans, and I make alternate plans to cover every eventuality."

"One of the things I love about you." I smiled.

"Then it's settled. Let's plan on next spring."

Emma

Emma had received a letter from Katie telling her that she and Thomas were engaged. Emma believed the two of them would be a good match. Thomas was supportive and didn't seem threatened by Katie's independence. Emma set Katie's letter aside and resumed sorting through a stack of Wesley's medical bills. With doctor bills and prosthetics costs mounting, Emma needed to find a way to supplement Wesley's income.

Emma had wanted to be a detective for as long as she could remember, reveling in the surprise of collecting and discarding puzzle pieces until a crime was unveiled and a criminal brought to justice. Her ears never failed to ferret out a secret. Without discussing it with anyone, she corresponded with Rosemary Shaw at the Pinkerton Detective Agency in Chicago, hoping she would remember their brief encounter in the case of Fred Grimes five years ago. *Five years,* she thought. *Has it really been that long ago?*

Emma wrote to Mrs. Shaw and presented a plan for employment. Mrs. Shaw had reached back with a train ticket to Chicago and the promise of an interview.

Emma later found herself fidgety on the more than twenty-hour train ride from Ogden to Chicago. On this trip, she'd sleep sitting up with strangers instead of traveling in a compartment with service as she had with Grandmother Phoebe. *Doesn't matter one bit*, she thought, a smile splashing across her face.

She'd discussed her plans with Wesley before packing her valise, and he had barraged her with questions. But at the end of it, he had to admit they needed more money.

Tomorrow, Emma would meet Alan Pinkerton and the Lady Pinkertons, or 'Pinks.' She had compiled a few newspaper clippings about Mr. Pinkerton, wanting to be prepared in advance for the meeting. This is what she knew about him:

Alan Pinkerton had founded the detective agency that bore his name in 1850 after emigrating from Scotland. He had begun his career working for the Chicago abolitionists, his home serving as a stop on the Underground Railroad. Later, after coming across a band of counterfeiters and spying on their movements, he turned them over to the local sheriff and soon became the first police detective in Chicago. Later he founded his own agency.

What an interesting journey he took to arrive where he is today, Emma observed, *but then everyone must begin somewhere, even me.*

In her correspondence with Rosemary Shaw, Emma learned how Pinkerton had come to hire females. Rosemary had written:

Six years after the agency was established, Kate Warne, a widow, walked into Alan's office and asked him for a job. She was very persuasive, and he'd always been interested in defying convention. It took him less than twenty-four hours to hire Kate, who became our nation's first female detective.

At that time, very few females held jobs outside the house, and still don't. Being a detective is certainly still not considered woman's work. Kate died in 1868, and I knew her only a few years. While she appeared demure, she was a master of disguise who could change her accent whenever she wished, infiltrate social gatherings, and cry on cue. Kate even foiled an early plot on Abraham Lincoln's life, refusing to rest until he was out of danger. She was the beginning of the Lady Pinkertons.

Emma regretted that she'd never known Kate Warne. What a woman she must have been, a true pioneer. Emma read on in the letter:

You should be aware that rumor has it some of our top male agents are hoping to persuade Alan to reconsider hiring women since many of their wives do not like their husbands working alongside women. But while Alan Pinkerton is alive, I can assure you that action will never take place. If you hire on with us, your position is secure while he lives.

I have arranged for you to stay overnight at my boarding house at no expense. I look forward to seeing you again soon. And please, refer to me as Rosemary.

Emma thought. *I knew I liked her when I met her. It is so kind of her to offer me a place to stay for the night, and since I've packed my own food for a few days, this trip should prove to be relatively inexpensive.* Emma gazed out the window at the plains of Wyoming, thinking she had yet a long way to travel. She put her things away and closed her eyes, though sleep eluded her for several more hours.

The next day, a very tired Emma arrived at the Chicago station, the undisputed railroad center of the country, and it was massive. Rosemary met Emma outside and welcomed her. They boarded a streetcar pulled by horses, passing through a district darkened with soot, the result of the huge fire that had struck the city two years ago in 1873. The destruction was widespread.

When they arrived at headquarters, Rosemary escorted Emma to Alan Pinkerton's area. The office furniture consisted of a large brown wooden desk and chair, and across the room a small leather divan and chair. Emma noted that the desk had several compartments filled with papers of one sort or another.

Mr. Alan Pinkerton came in moments later, and Rosemary introduced Emma. He had a full beard, rather large ears, and eyes that brooked no nonsense. Emma sat up straighter as he took a seat on the chair opposite and got right to the point. He stressed the need for "well-directed and untiring energy and a determination not to yield until success is assured." He asked Emma if she had those qualities.

"I can assure you, Mr. Pinkerton that I do," she said raising her chin. "My father is a sheriff, and he raised me with the determination not to yield. I also have excellent deductive skills and can size people up in a hurry. I helped my father apprehend a killer and put him behind bars."

"That's impressive. Any other reasons you need a job?"

"My husband is a deputy sheriff who was injured, and his leg had to be amputated. To be blunt, our medical bills are mounting, and we need money. You will find me intelligent, quick-witted, with an ear for discerning secrets. I will be an asset to your firm."

"I'm sorry to hear about your husband. Rosemary tells me you live in Utah. Are you moving to Chicago?"

"I'm of the firm opinion that you need a permanent agent in the Utah Territory where crimes are increasing, especially in Salt Lake City. I'm also a short train ride from Wyoming, Nevada, and Colorado should you need someone there in a hurry."

"I'm intrigued," he said. "Are you Mormon?"

"Yes, I am. Does that present difficulties?"

"Do you mind going into bars?"

"While I don't imbibe, if I need to go into a bar to question a suspect, I will do that."

"I'm an avowed atheist. Is that a problem for you?"

"My faith in God runs deep and sees me through difficult times, but what others believe is their own affair."

"We understand each other." He leaned back in his chair, steepled his fingers, and said, "Let's see how well you keep up with innovations as they relate to the commission of crimes. A bank robbery occurred two days ago in a small-town in Vermont. Shortly after 10 pm, the cashier of the bank and his wife were awakened by men in masks. The leader of the gang reportedly said to the cashier, 'You can probably guess our business. We want you to go to the bank with us and let us in. Keep quiet, and you should not be hurt.' All four men carried weapons, and the cashier's wife was very frightened." He paused and looked at Emma. He seemed to be waiting for a reaction.

"Interesting," Emma said, appearing unphased. "I'm listening. Do go on, please."

"The thieves found the keys to the bank in the cashier's pocket and, leaving one of the gang members to keep watch over the cashier's wife and child, the others took him to the bank that he had locked about twelve hours earlier after the bank closed for the day.

"When they reached the vault, the cashier opened it but told the thieves he couldn't open the safe inside. Was he bluffing?"

Emma thought for a moment, and said, "No, I don't think so. I suspect the bank had installed one of the new clock locks."

He smiled. "You are correct. I find you knowledgeable and determined. I will hire you because you can get a job done," he said, standing.

Emma stood as well. "Thank you, Mr. Pinkerton," she said. "I will not disappoint you."

"I'm quite certain you won't," he said. "Rosemary will take care of the necessary paperwork." He left the room.

Emma turned to her and whispered in a low voice, "I'm in! I can't believe it."

Rosemary laughed a gleam in her eyes. "Welcome aboard. Let's go collect your badge."

Emma embraced her. "If you hadn't put in a good word with Mr. Pinkerton, this wouldn't have been possible. I'm grateful."

"It's important that we ladies stick together, Emma. When first we met, I was impressed with your enthusiasm for detective work." She smiled.

They walked down a short hall, and Rosemary removed a tin badge from a cabinet. As Rosemary pinned the badge to Emma's dress, she repeated, "I'm a Pink, I'm a Pink," unable to believe her good fortune.

"This is to be worn only in matters of official business," Rosemary warned, "for you will be undercover most of the time. Outside the circle of those closet to you, take care not to let others know you're an agent, and swear those you know to secrecy. Your life may depend on it."

Emma agreed, letting the seriousness of her new situation sink in.

After spending the night at Rosemary's, Emma boarded a train for home, a shiny new badge tucked inside her handbag. She was almost too excited to think as the train passed out of the city.

As the train clicked back and forth down the long track, Emma closed her eyes, reviewing the hurdles she'd overcome to make her new employment possible. She'd taken a chance reaching out to Rosemary, traveled across the county on her own, and presented an employment plan that Mr. Pinkerton had found palatable. She gave herself a hug. "Well done," she said under her breath.

Fourteen

Katie

Mattie Hughes and I sat next to each other in the *Exponent* office, waiting for a staff meeting to begin that Lula had called. Mattie and I were discussing a Supreme Court decision made in March, Minor v. Happersett, 1875. We knew that our friends in the East must be sorely disappointed. "I hoped our sister suffragists might triumph with this case," I said.

"Sadly not," Mattie replied. "The court has ruled that the United States Constitution doesn't grant women the right to vote, and in this instance, a female citizen of the state of Missouri, even though Missouri law granted rights to vote to a certain class of citizens. The NWSA has been forced to revise their strategy."

"They'll be compelled to pursue a constitutional amendment to achieve voting rights for women."

"A far more difficult path."

"It appears as though Lula is ready to begin the meeting." I glanced around the room, noting we had several visitors today. Our paid staff on the paper was small and consisted primarily of the editor, business manager, and typesetters. The women who wrote articles, fiction, or other newsworthy items were generally volunteers. *Even though our paper is an essential voice for the women in our territory, it doesn't generate much income*, I thought. We were blessed with many fine female writers who graciously donated their time.

Lula had moved to the front of the room and stood alongside a woman I hadn't met. She was small in stature, no taller than five feet I supposed, and weighing less than 100 pounds. Her hair was black, earrings amethyst, and she wore a blue tulle scarf that matched her eyes. As I looked at her hands, I noticed several rings on her fingers. I guessed her age to be mid to late forties. *Who is she, and why is she here?*

Lula began speaking, "Allow me to present Emmeline B. Wells, an accomplished and talented contributor to our paper."

I'd seen her name on general notices about the Relief Society or grain storage, but that was about the extent of it.

Lula continued, "Emmeline has written several excellent articles for our paper under the 'nom de plume,' Blanche Beechwood."

This small-framed woman is Blanche Beechwood? I'd read several of her articles without realizing there was someone else behind the name. While I understood it wasn't unusual to write under a pen name, especially for women, I had never met a writer who'd done it. I was impressed.

The Beechwood article I most admired had appeared in one of last year's issues and was titled 'Real Women.' I still remembered her urging women to seek the qualities of "real" womanhood which she had described as having five components: an active mind, common sense, knowledge for themselves, respect for individuality, and a desire to enlarge their experience.

I hoped then, as I do now, that I possess each of those qualities.

Lula said, "My favorite Blanche Beechwood quotation is this: 'I believe in women, especially thinking women.'"

We all clapped in agreement, including Lula, who went on to say, "It may surprise you to learn that Emmeline has another literary persona she uses to write her fiction and poetry. Ladies, meet Aunt Em."

This woman is Aunt Em too? I adore her reveries and soliloquies. What a range of writing abilities she enjoys.

"You will soon become better acquainted with Emmeline Wells," Lula announced. "As of the November issue, Cornelia Horne's name will be removed as business manager from our masthead, and the name Emmeline B. Wells will appear in its place as associate editor."

The noise of surprised voices circled the room.

"I can assure you that Emmeline has a cosmopolitan outlook on life and champions woman's suffrage," Lula said. "Emmeline, will you please introduce yourself?"

Emmeline began by saying, "For those of you who may not know me, please allow me to tell you a bit about myself. I'm a former schoolteacher, my family is largely grown now, and I've been married three times. My first husband abandoned me and the second one died, so I asked Daniel H. Wells to marry me and became his seventh wife. I wanted more children and a place to call home," she said.

"The written word is in my blood. When my daughter, Emmie, was younger, we organized the Wasatch Literary Association and often held those meetings in my home. The girls enjoyed excursions to Brighton Canyon, Saltair, and theatre parties at the Salt Lake Theatre, and I loved to entertain friends. Those were the good years before my husband's business faltered, and we lost everything."

Emmeline Wells is no stranger to hardship.

"Since that time," she said, "I've learned to depend on my own resources and become self-reliant. Now I'm a working woman, just as you are, and proud of it. I must warn you, though, I'm told I can be somewhat caustic at times, but I'm fully repentant afterward," she said, a twinkle in her eye.

We all laughed at her self-deprecating humor.

"I'm dedicated to continuing to make the *Woman's Exponent* a credible paper," Emmeline said, "and I look forward to getting better acquainted with each of you."

An auspicious beginning.

Mattie Hughes and I looked at each other, and I whispered, "this is a woman to be reckoned with."

"I know her, and you are correct," she said. "Emmeline Wells will be a wonderful mentor for both of us. You should go introduce yourself."

"I'll speak with you later."

It was Lula who introduced me. "Emmeline," she said, "may I present one of our typesetters, Katie Leavitt."

"How do you do," I said. "It's an honor to meet you."

"Why don't we sit for a minute and you may tell me something about yourself," Emmeline offered.

I told her where I'd grown up, who my family was, and that I planned to attend medical school next spring. I also told her I was engaged.

"Does your soon-to-be husband support your decision to attend medical school?" she asked.

"He does. After we marry, he'll attend law school in Georgetown while I earn my degree in Philadelphia."

"So, you'll live apart?"

"Yes, for two years."

She looked at me and said, "I'm a firm believer in the efficacy of prayer. May I be so bold as to ask if you have prayed about the decision to marry then live apart?"

Her question took me back, and I said, "I pray over almost everything, but I confess I haven't prayed over the timing of our marriage. I was concerned when he first suggested it."

She held my hand gently in hers, looking at me with piercing blue eyes. "Do you recall a song whose lyrics were published in last November's issue of the *Exponent* titled, 'As Sisters in Zion,' by Emily H. Woodmansee?"

"It's one of my favorites."

"I refer you to the ninth stanza: 'Oh! Naught but the Spirit's divinest tuition—Can give us the wisdom to truly succeed.' My advice to you, Katie, is to seek confirmation from the Spirit about the timing of your marriage."

I paused. "I'll do that. Thank you."

"Come speak with me anytime," Emmeline said, standing, "You'll find in me a friend." She walked away to meet the others.

Lula approached saying, "I should like to know your impressions of Emmeline, Katie."

159

"She's wonderful. I find her smart, resilient, and yet nurturing."

"An apt description, and she has other talents as well."

"What do you mean?"

"Eliza Snows tells me that Brigham Young is considering placing Emmeline in charge of the grain-saving program for the Church, which would be a huge undertaking."

Is there anything this woman can't do? "But she just started as your associate editor. When do you think he might do that?"

"I suspect next year, but please keep this information to yourself for now. Something else might be coming up for one of our other Relief Society leaders. You've met M. Isabella Horne, I presume?"

"Just once. Sophia introduced us."

"She plans to throw her hat in the ring for Vice-President of the Utah Silk Association, and I should be surprised if she did not succeed."

Placing women in these types of positions was almost unheard of in the East, and I was proud of our Western sisterhood.

Over the next few weeks, I observed women from all over the city crowding into Emmeline's office, sometimes daily. As they came to discuss their concerns and problems, she proved to be a good listener and wise counselor when they asked her advice.

I spent weeks fretting over the timing of my marriage to Thomas. When I sought guidance from the Spirit, something didn't feel quite right. Thomas was the man I was to marry, but the timing was wrong. I needed to complete medical school first.

But how would he respond to that? *He may not be in support, and I couldn't blame him for that. And in that event, I may risk losing him altogether which would break my heart and his as well.* One night as I lay awake again, unable to sleep, my mother's favorite scripture in the book of Proverbs came to mind, and I repeated it aloud in the quiet of my room. "Trust in the Lord with all thine heart; and lean not unto thine own understanding. In all thy ways acknowledge him, and he shall direct thy path." I had my answer, and I needed to trust it would work out. My mind and body relaxed, and I fell asleep.

The next morning, I thought about how best to speak with Thomas. Christmas was fast approaching, and I was leaving for Farmington for the Christmas holidays. *I don't want to have this conversation at what's supposed to be the most joyous time of year.* It would have to wait until after the first of the year. I rehearsed what I might say, and what his response could be in return.

I left Salt Lake City early the morning of December twenty-second, and after arriving home, enjoyed lunch with my family. I missed them all, but most especially my mother. She's the one I seek with imponderable questions, and she somehow finds a way to guide me in the right direction. Mother seemed better today and was looking forward to Christmas.

After lunch I walked through the snow to Emma's, hoping to find her at home, but she wasn't there. Wesley told me she'd been sent out on a job, and he didn't expect her back before nightfall. This was her first assignment as a Pink and I could hardly wait to hear all about it.

Emma

Emma had ridden to a small town adjacent to Farmington after the local sheriff sent a telegram to the Pinkerton office requesting an agent. It was chilly when she dismounted, hands cold despite the fur gloves she wore. Emma led Palumbo to a watering trough near the Sheriff's office, and after breaking the ice, permitted the horse to drink his fill. "There you go, boy," she said, patting his nose and tying him to the hitching post.

When she walked inside, a man with a badge asked, "What can I do fer ya, little lady?"

"Are you the one who sent a telegram asking for a Pinkerton agent?"

"Might be. And just how would you know about that?" he asked, looking puzzled.

"I'm the agent," she said showing him her badge.

161

"They sent me a woman?" His face registered shock. "Didn't even know Pinkertons hired females," he snorted.

Emma clenched her hands, bemoaning the fact that she got this attitude from males far too often in her line of work. "Lady Pinkertons have been employed since the Civil War," she said. "Are you Sheriff Thompson?"

"That's me."

Emma opened a small pad, removed a pen from her handbag, and sat down. "Let's get started, shall we?"

He sat next to her and asked, "Are you a widow?"

"No, and my private life is none of your affair. I'm here in a professional capacity."

"Hope you know what you're doin'," he said, shaking his head and looking doubtful.

Ignoring his comment, she said, "Let's began with the night in question."

He began filling in the details. "Happened two nights ago," he said. "One of the female residents of our hotel found blood in the washbasin that three of the rooms share in common. She was scared clean out of her wits, and she alerted Mrs. Mabel Timms, owner of the place, who come runnin' to my house right around dinner time and banged on the door." He leaned forward in his chair.

"After I arrived, I searched the rooms and found one of 'em locked. I pounded on the door, but no answer, so Mabel unlocked it, and we went inside. A woman was lying face down on the floor, name of Daisy Miller. She worked in the tavern below the boarding house. When I touched her body, it was cold," he said. "Seemed she'd been dead for quite some time."

"Did you notice anything unusual in the room?"

"There were rumpled linens on the bed. Looked like Daisy had been changing 'em."

"Perhaps her killer surprised her," Emma said.

"We turned the body over and counted five stab wounds to her face and chest."

"Based on the number of stab wounds, I'd say the person who attacked her did so in a rage. He was after something."

162

"I was thinkin' the same thing," he said.

"I'll go to the tavern and see what I can find out," she said, closing her notebook, "and be back with a report."

Emma went to the local hotel that had been constructed over the tavern. Before entering its doors, she touched the six-shooter wrapped about her waist. Once inside, she found an attractive woman standing behind a feather painted brown bar, wearing a plain dress and apron. "What can I get you?" she asked, wiping the counter.

"Information, if you please," Emma said, removing the badge from her handbag. "I'm here investigating the death of Daisy Miller."

"My name's Kitty," she said, "and Daisy was my friend. I'll help you any way I can."

"Thank you," Emma said. "Were you the one tending bar that night?"

"No, that would be Jack."

"Is he here?"

"In the back. I'll get him."

A few minutes later, Kitty returned with Jack. "You want a drink?" he asked Emma.

"Do you have any sarsaparilla?"

"One of them teetotalers, eh? Might be bottle or two around," he said, reaching behind the bar.

As he poured the sarsaparilla, Emma asked, "Did you hear anything down here the night Daisy Miller died?"

"I was pourin' drinks for some of the boys when we heard what sounded like a muffled scream comin' from upstairs. It was a woman's voice, and she seemed to be crying for help. Then we heard a loud thud and another scream that turned into a whimper," he said, hocking chewing tobacco into the spittoon.

"One of the men said, 'What's goin' on up there?'

"'That's the hotel upstairs,'" I said. 'Sounds like a family fight to me.' So, we all went back to drinking."

Emma struggled to keep her face impassive as she said, "Let me understand this. Several of you men heard a woman scream for help, followed by a thud, and you did nothing?"

"If it were a family fight, it weren't none of our business," he said, winking.

Kitty looked at Emma and said, "Daisy was one of our 'ladies of the tavern,' if you know what I mean."

Emma knew just what she meant, and it made her angry that women were forced to support themselves in that manner.

Jack said, "It wasn't until the next morning when they found the blood that we got to wonderin' if somethin' could have happened that night."

Emma turned to Kitty. "Would you take me up to Daisy's room, please?"

"Sure," she said, looking at Jack.

"You go on ahead, sweetheart. I'll mind the store for ya."

When Kitty and Emma reached Daisy's room, they saw a braided rug covered with blood stains and a small brown bureau behind the iron headboard. "Do you know if Daisy kept anything of value in the bureau?"

"Just her clothes. She kept the important stuff under her mattress."

"Has anyone taken a look?"

"Not that I know of—just thought of it myself."

"Let's turn it over." Underneath the mattress, they found an empty money pouch.

"Daisy had money she'd been saving, wanted to go back where she come from. Someone must have stole it."

"The suspect likely entered while she was changing the linens and adjusting the mattress. When she tried to ward him off, he stabbed her."

"Such an awful way to die," Kitty said, shuddering.

"Yes, it was. Any idea who might have done it?"

"She had one male friend, not a customer, who'd been boarding with us for a time. He worked hauling hay at one of the farms. Every week, he sent what he earned home to his father who lives down south in St. George. Johnson is a right fine man who wouldn't hurt a flea. Miss Mabel will vouch for him."

164

Emma made a note.

"Come to think of it," Kitty said, "I haven't seen him around the past few days."

"I'll ask the sheriff to send someone out looking for him. I'd like to speak with some of the other lodgers now."

"You might try Mrs. Morton down the hall. She doesn't miss much that goes on around here."

"Which room is hers?"

"That one down there, number 10."

"Thanks for your help."

"Go easy on her. She's been in a state of shock the past few days, what with Daisy getting murdered right down the hall and all."

When Emma knocked, an elderly woman opened the door a crack. "What do you want?" she asked.

"I'm a Pinkerton detective assisting the sheriff in the matter of Daisy Miller's death."

"Already told him everything I know."

"Do you mind if I come in for a moment and ask you a few questions? I won't stay long."

"Suit yourself," she said opening the door wider. "Got a small table and two chairs over there in the corner, so have yourself a sit," she said turning up the lamps.

After a bit of prodding from Emma, Mrs. Morton recollected that she had seen Daisy alive and well just before three o'clock that afternoon. "She came upstairs with that young southern kid, bout twenty-one I'd guess. Daisy had her coat on, so she must have been out. I told her I was going to the general store, and I locked up my room and left. She must have been stabbed soon after that," Mrs. Morton said, shaking.

Emma placed her hand over Mrs. Morton's.

"That's all I know," she said. You might want to talk to the hotel manager. He likely knows more about the kid. He hadn't been here long."

Emma thanked her, went to the front desk and asked, "Are you the manger?"

"Yes, Bill Simmons. Are you a Pinkerton?" he asked, looking at her badge.

"Investigating Daisy Miller's murder. Just spoke with Mrs. Morton, and she told me about some boy from the South who's been around lately. Said you might know more about him."

"He come from Alabama, I think, with money and no prospects. He drifted into the hotel about a week back after he saw the cardboard sign on the downstairs door. His name was Bob Burton, and he asked if I could spot him fifty cents a night for a room which he thought he could pay at the end of the week. He told me that if he couldn't raise the money, he'd give me his pocket watch.

"I agreed to let him stay and told Daisy he was down on his luck, so she found him, took him into the kitchen, fried up some ham and beans. She even pressed his clothes, saying it might make it easier for him to find a job."

"Very generous of her," Emma said.

"She always did have a heart of gold," he said, wiping his nose on his sleeve.

"Do you know where he is now?" Emma asked.

"No, I don't."

"Could you show me his room, please?"

"Yes, ma'am, I can."

When they reached the door, it was locked, but Bill had a key. "Go ahead on in," he said, motioning for her to enter first.

Emma looked around the small room, got on her knees and peered under the bed. She saw blood-stained clothes rolled up in a ball and pulled them out. "Take a look at these. Must have changed before he left," she said opening the closet. Sure enough, it was empty.

Bill looked shocked.

"I think we've got our killer. Now we need to locate his whereabouts."

"Well, I'll be," he said. "You're good."

"Just doing my job. I'll go to the sheriff's office and submit my report."

"Hope they catch the guy," he said, rubbing his temples.

"That man took advantage of Daisy's kindness and killed her when he had the opportunity. A despicable act of murder if ever there was one."

Bill nodded, a sad look in his eyes.

Emma left the hotel and walked to the sheriff's office to let him know what she'd found, knowing she'd be glad to leave this town.

When she arrived home, Wesley had supper waiting. "Just leftovers," he said.

"I'm happy to have food of any kind. It's been a long day," she said, removing her hat, gloves, gun, and holster.

"Got some of that chicken vegetable soup you made yesterday for Sunday dinner with cold bread and stewed fruit."

"Just right," Emma said, washing her hands and sitting next to him at the table in the kitchen. *Wesley seems a bit despondent today,* she thought, *as he sometimes is over the loss of his leg.* As they ate, she asked, "Did you have time to get to your carving?"

Since Wesley had taken a desk job, his day typically ended at sundown. He had begun carving birds, finding it therapeutic, and he'd become skilled at it. On occasion, it took him as many as two hours to complete one toe. When he was satisfied with the carving, he painted it.

"I completed a new one today," he said rising from the table, pride in his voice. "Let me show you." When he came back, hobbling with his cane, he held a Merlin bird in flight.

"Oh, Wesley," she said, taking it gently in her hands. "It's exquisite and your best work yet. Look at those colors," she remarked, "brilliant blue wings, light brown and white body, and those beady black eyes. The Merlin is my favorite bird."

"Which is why I created it or you," he said, leaning over and kissing her. "Turn the stand over that the bird rests on and read the inscription."

Emma read aloud, "Carved by Wesley Hatch to Emma, Xmas, 1875."

167

"I had to abbreviate the word Christmas due the size of the stand."

She smiled and kissed him long and deeply. They very much enjoyed the remainder of their evening together. Wesley's accident had not impaired their love making.

Fifteen

Katie

I sat alone in the parlor at Sophia's, making an entry in my diary. *Saturday, January 1, 1876, the new year, begins. I've lately been accepted at the Women's Medical College in Pennsylvania and will begin my studies in June.*

The words looked a little overwhelming in print, and I'd need time to digest the upcoming changes in my life. *I'll be leaving Sophia's, my job at the* Exponent, *friends in the City, my family in Farmington, and… perhaps… Thomas as well.*

I put my pen down. He was coming to have a conversation for which he was wholly unprepared. The truth of the matter is that I was unprepared as well.

His knock soon came at the door, and I knew Sophia would answer, as we had agreed. "Come in, please," Sophia said.

When I saw him, my hand went to my heart, and I greeted him with a hug, almost melting in his arms. I wanted him to hold me and never let go.

"I'm off to the studio to paint," Sophia said. "I'll leave the two of you alone."

Thomas and I were so caught up in each other we barely noticed her exit.

"I've missed you," he said, breathing into my hair.

"Please come in."

"Whatever is the matter?"

We went hand in hand to the parlor and sat next to each other. I touched him lightly on the arm and he gave me a long and satisfying kiss. "We're good together, Katie," he said. "This year promises to be life-changing for us."

"Please hear me out and keep an open mind." I drew my finger across his lips. "You're a wonderful man, Thomas Forrest, and you've shown me what love can be."

He appeared confused, which I understood. I took a deep breath and said, "Would you consider postponing our marriage for two years until I complete medical school?"

He released my hand and said, "Why wait?"

"I've given the matter much prayer, Thomas, and I believe it's important I finish medical school before we marry."

His face went blank. "You've taken me by surprise, and I need time to think about what you're proposing. Perhaps we should take a few months apart and speak again in the spring."

I knew what this might mean for the two of us. "If that's what you want, I understand, but know that I love you and that will never change. Remember the day we splashed through puddles in the rain? Oh, how I loved that moment, and when I close my eyes, I feel the same way about you now as I did that day."

He looked sad. "I know we both wanted our engagement to work, Katie, but sometimes wanting something isn't enough to make it happen."

"You're right," I said, tears running down my face. "It's not, and if you must go, know that I will forever be your friend." Thomas wiped away my tears with the palm of his hand and neither of us spoke for several minutes. Then, the strangest thing happened as his face changed from a mixture of anger and sadness to one of contemplation. I moved a little closer and laid my hand over his.

He turned to me with the softest eyes. "I love you, Katie, and the judge," he said, pointing to the heavens, smiling, "finds on behalf of the plaintiff."

"You're willing to postpone our nuptials?"

"We'll stay engaged and won't marry until we finish our advanced degrees in July of 1878, with the following stipulation: Whenever we're together, we'll require a chaperone. I have difficulty not making you mine even now." He smiled.

"One day, I will be yours forever." I kissed him again, eyes wet with joy.

"This conversation has left me famished. Have we anything to eat?"

I grinned. "Right this way," I said, leading him to the kitchen. "Sophia prepared cold bread with ham and cheese and a pudding to top it off." As we ate, I said, "I have an idea for one of our meetings in the East after we depart for our respective schools."

"I'm all ears," he said, wolfing down another slice of bread.

"As you know, the city of Philadelphia is hosting an 1876 Centennial Exposition that begins May tenth. Why not leave Salt Lake and travel to Philadelphia for the opening ceremonies? You could leave for Georgetown from there?"

"I support your timing. Sounds fun."

"I understand there will be a Woman's Pavilion, despite last year's disappointment when the women who helped raised funds for the Exposition were informed there would be no room in the main hall for their contributions."

"Surely, you jest," he said, looking at me between bites of pudding.

"I do not. The women decided to construct their own pavilion to showcase women's contribution to the arts, education, industry, and domestic life."

Sophia came in from her studio and asked, "Did I overhear the words 'Woman's Pavilion'?"

"Yes, you did," Thomas laughed. "I'm clearly outnumbered in this household. Please come join us."

"Thank you, just pudding for me. Katie, did you know that the women of Utah will have an exhibit in the Pavilion?"

"I didn't. What a wonderful opportunity."

"November last, Eliza Snow was notified of an appointment to participate in the Woman's Pavilion and invited to take charge of gathering items from the women of Utah for exhibition at the fair. She assembled a committee made up of both members of our faith and representatives from other established faiths and sent out a Circular. I believe I have a copy here in the drawer. Yes, here it is. Listen to this: 'We are generally requesting all creditable specimens of women's work, both useful and ornamental, from a necklace to a carpet, and natural curiosities of our own collecting.'"

"That circular must have generated a sizeable response," Thomas said.

"It has," Sophia said, "but due to limited funding, only a small sample of what's being collected will reach the Exposition."

"That's unfortunate," I said.

Sophia's eyes twinkled. "It may not surprise you to learn that Eliza and her committee are planning Utah's own centennial celebration by way of a territorial fair to be held this summer, so she can display all the goods collected."

"That sounds like Aunt Eliza," I said, "and I regret that I won't be able to attend the territorial fair."

"Ah," Sophia said, "but you'll be present at the celebration in Philadelphia, so be certain you don't miss our exhibit."

When we finished eating, Thomas said, "I must be going; I have studying to do." He turned to me and said, "You've certainly started the New Year off with a bang."

"I love you, Thomas, and I'm pleased with our conversation today."

"As Shakespeare said, all's well that ends well." He kissed me on the cheek. "I'll see you at the University Monday."

I stood on the porch and watched him go, knowing my heart would always be his.

In March, tragedy befell our family when Mother died. I was holding her hand as she took her last gasp of rattled air, and I felt my world shatter with her passing. Dr. Axel told our family that her weakened body could no longer coexist with her mysterious illness, saying "I know none of you were ready to let her go, but she was ready to leave. She's gone to a better place, and you will see her again."

That evening I wrote in my diary, distraught that I had once again failed to save a family member's life. I sensed my mother's presence in the room. I could see her clearly in my mind's eye, and she was happy, her body no longer a burden. She smiled, blew me a kiss, and disappeared. I wept.

Emma

Emma was anxious to catch up with Katie, who'd been devastated at the loss of her mother. *I know how hard she tries to keep a stiff upper lip when horrible things happen. She pushes her feelings aside so she can cope from day to day. If, and when, she's ready to talk, I'll listen.*

Emma looked out the window of the train, happy to be nearing the end of the long trip from Ogden to Chicago. The Pinkerton Detective Agency, pleased with Emma's handling of the Daisy Miller case, wanted to give her instruction on the investigation of bank robberies, so they'd paid her ticket to Chicago. It hadn't been cost prohibitive to add on travel to Philadelphia where she'd join Katie for the Centennial International Exposition, the first World's Fair to be held in the United States.

Emma thought about how Katie had persuaded Thomas to postpone their nuptials for two years while she attended medical school. *It's so like Katie to want to have the best of both worlds whenever possible, and I don't believe she could have borne the loss of both Thomas and her mother at the same time.*

An hour later the whistle blew, and the train began pulling into the Chicago station. Emma stood to collect her things, grateful that Rosemary Shaw would be waiting on the platform to transport her to the Pinkerton offices. As she left the train, the June sun shone hot with nary a cloud in the sky.

When they reached the office, Emma learned that she was to meet with Robert Pinkerton, not Alan, so they went to his office and Rosemary introduced them. He was a bit taller than his father, hair slicked back with light sideburns. His moustache was thick and a bit droopy, his nose prominent.

He dismissed Rosemary and told Emma to sit down, saying, "I'll get straight to the matter at hand, Mrs. Hatch. We're here to educate you on the investigation of bank robberies, so I'll begin with a recent one to illustrate a point."

Emma found him curt and did not care for his tone of voice as he addressed her. She took a deep breath and took out her note pad.

"You may have read about the Northampton National Bank heist that occurred this past January. It was the largest bank robbery ever, the thieves making off with more than $1.5 million in cash, bonds, and other securities. Our company was hired four days after the heist to find the thieves, and this is what we learned," he said.

"In the middle of the night, prior to the early morning robbery, men, carrying dark lanterns, broke into the home of a man named Whittelsey, a cashier at the bank. They bound and gagged the other members of the household and beat Whittelsey until he gave them the combination to the vault. The thieves apparently knew that the night watchman left his post at 4 a.m., leaving the bank unguarded until it opened for business."

Robert paused and looked at Emma. She caught a look of disdain in his eyes. *If he's concerned that I'm not getting the appropriate level of details, he needn't be*, she thought, wishing Alan were conducting the training instead.

"Sometime after 4 a.m.," Robert continued, "the robbers took Whittelsey to the bank, opened the vault, took everything inside, and made their getaway. A few of the men left by carriage, and others took the train to New York. While I'm confident we'll find the perpetrators eventually, my gut tells me there's a mastermind behind it all. The detailed plan was well executed. As if it had been rehearsed beforehand."

"A mastermind, you say," Emma observed, interested.

"Yes. In other words, the intelligence directing the scheme behind the scenes, the one responsible for organizing and planning."

Emma understood the definition of mastermind but said nothing.

"Robbers in general, while threatening and violent, are often not all that bright, so always be aware that in addition to the gang of thieves, there may be a mastermind behind it all. He might be someone you'd least expect to be involved in the commission of a crime, say a well-mannered gentleman who may visit the bank beforehand to observe its layout."

Someone whose social standing is deceiving, Emma thought.

"I don't believe you've yet had a major bank robbery out West, but that day will come soon, and when it does, if you're the first on the scene, remember that no one is above suspicion."

"Thank you, Mr. Pinkerton, I shall."

"There are a few other things of note to ask potential witnesses to the crime. Try and get them to recall the approximate height, weight, build, and any distinguishing characteristics of the bandits. Make certain a witness is telling you what he personally observed and not what someone else in the bank remembered. Witnesses can be unreliable."

Emma's eyebrows raised at his last statement, and she admitted to herself that she hadn't fully appreciated the potential unreliability of eyewitnesses whose memories might be affected by the trauma of the crime they'd experienced. She'd be more cautious in the future.

Robert stood, thanked her for coming, and dismissed her.

Does he treat me this way because I'm a woman? She recalled Rosemary's observation that Robert did not favor hiring women agents. *One day his father will pass,* Emma thought, *and he'll take charge of the agency, and I suspect the Pinkerton policy of hiring women and male minorities will cease.*

Rosemary was waiting outside the door when Emma walked out. "Let's go somewhere for lunch," she said. "You may not know that Chicago is a city known for its food. As far back as 1860, we had 27 restaurants, though the great fire of 1871 left only five in the city directory. We recovered quickly, however," she said with pride, "and as of last year, we had 176. Do you care for Italian food?"

Emma hadn't spent much time dining out, and she didn't want to appear provincial. "Italian sounds delicious," she said, smiling.

"Good. Let's dine at Bona Caesar on Madison Street, my treat, then I'll take you to the train for your journey to Philadelphia."

When they arrived at the restaurant, Emma looked over an unfamiliar menu and selected the mushroom Florentine pasta, which turned out to be delicious. Rosemary gave her a taste of the garlic parmesan pasta she'd ordered. "So good," Emma said, her mouth full.

"Let's top off our meals with cannoli covered in chocolate."

Emma enjoyed the cannoli most of all.

The two ladies went back to the office for a few hours before Rosemary dropped Emma at the station. She boarded an evening train to Philadelphia, another twenty-hour ride stretching ahead of her, and slept much of the way.

Somewhere around three pm the next day, Emma reached the train station at Prime Street in South Philadelphia that Katie told her had been reconstructed to manage the increased traffic of the Centennial Exhibition. When she got off the train and went inside, she found a large and intricate station that offered services such as restaurants. *Amazing*, she thought, looking around, and she heard a familiar voice.

"Emma, over here." Katie waved, a huge grin on her face.

The two of them hugged, happy to see each other.

"Isn't it strange," Katie said, taking Emma's valise, "that we two are together in Philadelphia? Could you have imagined such a thing when we were young?"

"Never." Emma smiled.

"How did your meeting go in Chicago?"

"It was fascinating, and I'll tell you more about it later."

"Let's go catch a streetcar to the boarding house where I live and get you settled. You must be tired from your long journey."

When they arrived, Emma saw an old mansion that had been turned into a small boarding house. In the sitting room, two armchairs rested on either side of the fireplace, and a blue-grey rug covered a brown oak floor. She liked the small ceramic clock on the mantle and the two green vases filled with fresh flowers placed on either side of the clock. In the center of the room was a large round table on which an afternoon tea service sat, and Emma could smell scones cooking in the kitchen.

"Let's take your things upstairs, then come back down for lavender tea and scones. They will be smothered in jam," Katie said.

"No need to ask twice," Emma laughed as they ascended a narrow set of backstairs. The room was large enough to hold two small beds, a chest of drawers, an old wardrobe, and a washstand with a mirror. It was a bit sparse, but comfortable. "Do you have a roommate?" Emma asked.

"No, I'll live alone for the next two years. You're welcome to take the bed on the left," Katie said, placing Emma's valise on the floor. "It will take at least two days to see the fair, and I'm excited to show you around."

"You and Thomas attended the opening ceremonies last month, I believe."

"We were two of the ten thousand people who participated on the terraces of the Art Gallery where speaker stands were erected. It was incredible, Emma. President Ulysses S. Grant spoke, and an orchestra played national anthems from at least a dozen countries. A huge choir sang several songs, ending with the 'Hallelujah Chorus,' and the ceremony ended with a 100-gun salute. I was speechless at the end."

"That's remarkable."

"Wait until you see the Exposition. The landscape at Fairmont Park is huge, covering more than 200 acres. There are five main buildings and 250 additional structures, including the Woman's Pavilion."

"How will we cover such a distance?"

"There are rolling chairs and an elevated railway to help us maneuver the grounds. It's quite fun."

"Should we pack a lunch?"

"No need. There's a lunch counter on the grounds and a variety of restaurants that include the American Restaurant, a German restaurant, and two French restaurants. We must try the food at the

Restaurant Lafayette. I'm anxious for you to sample two new treats: sugar popcorn and soda water."

"I don't even know what those items are," Emma laughed.

"You will soon enough, and you'll find them delicious."

"As tired as I am, I don't know if I can sleep, just thinking about it all." But sleep she did.

The following morning, Emma and Katie boarded a trolley to the fair. Katie had purchased tickets for each of them in advance at a reasonable cost of 50 cents each. "Let's begin at the Main Exhibition Building," Katie said when they arrived. "It's the largest building at the Exposition and you'll be amazed to know that it covers more than 20 acres."

When they reached the main pavilion, Emma was taken aback. The iron-trussed building was mammoth and included four high towers at each corner. She guessed each tower was at least 70 feet high. The interior walls were whitewashed, and the woodwork was painted in blues, greens, crimsons, and gold.

"Let's move to the center stage first and see the American exhibit," Katie said. "The foreign exhibits are arranged from the center out and have been set up in order of their geographic proximity to our country, with China and Japan at the outer ends."

At the American exhibit, Emma saw textiles, historical relics, cutlery, china, and furniture. Great Britain had jewelry, silver, and pottery from Doulton and Company, while Switzerland had lines and lines of clocks, watches, and music boxes. They made their way to the Western entrance to the building and found new inventions: the electric light, a typewriter, and a telephone. Visitors stood in awe, mouths literally hanging open as they learned how the inventions operated.

"The typewriter reminds me a bit of a treadle sewing machine," Katie said, "with its foot being used as a carriage return."

"You're right," Emma said, "and look how it sits on a table and is painted black with floral decorations, also similar to a sewing machine."

"See here," Katie said, "for 50 cents, you may have a letter typed on the machine that you can mail to Wesley. Wouldn't he be surprised?"

"He'd love that. Let's come back tomorrow after I have more to tell him. I'm caught up in the moment and feel as if I've stepped into the future," Emma said.

"I know," Katie said. "It's simply beyond description."

"Let's go see what China has to offer," Emma said. When the two women walked to the outer edges of the building, they found a Chinese court with an entrance that took them into what looked like a pagoda, decorated with carved and painted dragons. The showcases held porcelain, vases, and silk screens. On the outside, there was a large exhibit of intricately carved furniture, including two elaborate bedsteads.

"I've always wanted to visit China, and now I feel as though I've had a taste of it."

"It's like taking a trip around the world."

Emma was fanning herself against the heat.

"It looks as if you're getting warm," Katie said. "I have just the thing. Let's go next to the Cataract exhibit."

"What's that?"

"It's a hydraulic exhibit that features a system of pumps that creates a simply breathtaking water fountain which not only supplies energy to the exhibits nearby, but it will also give us an opportunity to sit for a while and cool off."

After visiting the hydraulic exhibit, Emma and Katie walked to the lunch counter and ate a late lunch of bread, cheese, and a new type of root beer, labeled 'Hires.' It was delicious. When they finished, Emma asked, "Where do you suggest we go next?"

"Let's go to the Memorial Hall and Art Annex. It's a permanent building made of granite, brick, glass, and iron, and I'm told it cost the state of Pennsylvania $1.5 million to construct. I haven't seen it yet because I wanted to wait and see it with you. That will consume the remainder of our day. Tomorrow, we'll come back and begin with the Woman's Pavilion so we can see the exhibits from the ladies of Utah. Are you in agreement?"

"Yes, of course. You're the guide and doing a splendid job of it."

Upon reaching Memorial Hall, they entered through a rotunda filled with statues. There were two large galleries and several smaller ones on either side. Emma and Katie enjoyed paintings, lithography, architectural design, and mosaics. Photographic displays filled an entire building with landscapes of the Arctic, Yellowstone Park, and the Holy Land.

"Wesley would adore this," Emma said. "This is what I want to write to him about tonight when we return home."

"How are his carvings coming? Katie asked as they walked. "He's very talented."

"He has some beautiful specimens of birds, and he's taken up oil painting as well."

"Sophia told me she believes the creative process is the same, regardless of the kind of art being produced, whether it be painting, poetry, or music."

"That makes sense to me. I can't wait to write to him about the art we've seen."

That evening Emma penned a letter that she intended to have put on the new typewriter tomorrow and mail.

> *My Dear Wesley,*
>
> *I wish you could be here with me in Philadelphia at the Exposition! It's like nothing I've ever experienced. I'll write first about what I think may interest you most, the Art Annex. There I saw works of some of the most famous sculptors of Italy, including two called, 'Children Blowing Bubbles' and 'Girl at the Bath.' My favorite was 'A Child's Grief,' which made me cry, as I wished we had one of our own little ones to comfort.*

Emma dabbed at her eyes and continued.

> *I'm sure you've noticed that this missive is not in my hand; rather it was typewritten by a new machine! One of several new inventions here, including an electric light.*

Tomorrow, we shall see the Woman's Pavilion. I understand that more than 75 women have obtained patents for their inventions that are on exhibit, one of them being a six-horsepower steam engine which powers six looms and a printing press! I'm so pleased the women of Utah are also represented here, and I look forward to seeing their creations.

I leave here the day after tomorrow and expect to be home by the end of the week. I miss you.

With love, Emma

Sixteen

Katie

This morning over breakfast, my friend Romania Pratt shared a well-known story about the Women's Medical College that occurred seven years ago. It was referred to as 'the jeering episode.'

"One day in November of 1869," Romania said, "a group of students from the Women's College attended a lecture at Pennsylvania Hospital. During the address, the male medical students proceeded to throw spitballs at the women, make cat calls, jeer, and refer to them as She Doctors."

"What a disgusting experience," I said, surprised.

"At first blush, yes," Romania said, handing me a copy of a diary page a woman named Sarah Hibbard had written the year after the incident. "I'd be interested in your opinion."

I read:

> "...the conduct of the male students...needs no comments further than to say that their loss was our gain, for certainly they did lose and certainly we did gain...if these poor fellows had sought to do us a favor, they could not have done it more effectively than they did in their conduct towards us during those sessions.

"The incident united the women rather than intimidating them," I interjected.

"Not only those women, but the rest of us who've attended the college since that day. It's become a memory we share. You may not know that one of last year's graduates, Clara Marshall, became the first woman on the staff of our hospital."

"I can only imagine what she must have gone through to get there," I said, shaking my head.

"Clara also has a broad knowledge of drugs and medical remedies. She arranged the pharmaceutical display at the Centennial Exposition."

"I saw the exhibit, and it was fascinating. It makes me proud that it was one of our own who assembled it."

"You see," Romania said with a smile, "you're becoming one with the women already."

I laughed, grateful for Romania. *She's a year ahead of me in school, and it's a blessing to have someone here from home who also knows the ropes in Philadelphia.* We had one other woman from Utah with us, Ellis Ship, who'd begun her studies at the Women's College last November.

Ellis is eight years my senior and left three small children behind in Salt Lake City to attend medical school. She told me that after passing her first-year examinations, she would go to Utah to see her children before returning to complete her degree. I knew Ellis didn't have much money, but she told me she was going to take in sewing and guard the hall of cadavers at night to pay her tuition and board. I admired her courage and determination and believed I'd found a life-long associate.

Tomorrow, my June medical studies commenced, and I wanted to have a closer look at the interior of the Women's Medical College. I took a streetcar to North College Avenue where I found the new building that had been constructed last year in 1875. It sat next to the Woman's Hospital of Philadelphia.

When I arrived, I went first to the library which I knew would be my new home for the next two years. After wandering through the stacks, I went out to the hall and soon arrived at the chemistry laboratory, passing a space dedicated to microscopy.

As I continued to make my way around the building, I saw the dissection rooms, where I paused and took a deep breath. While I'd observed Dr. Axel dissecting a cadaver a time or two, I'd never done such a thing myself. *I hope I'll be up to the task,* I thought.

Romania was very skilled in the art of dissection, and the manner and style with which she worked was often used as a model for others, which I found impressive. Another medical student said that "the sight of eight stark, staring bodies, of every age and color, stretched upon as many tables, was not reassuring to say the least." I shuddered and moved on.

I went next to one of the lecture halls and sat in the center of the empty seats, thinking about what the next two years might bring. *You're at the beginning of your journey to fulfill your calling as a doctor.* I thanked God for guiding me here.

The next day I returned to the lecture hall that was now filled with women also seeking medical degrees. Our first class was obstetrics, and I'd been told the professor was a master teacher. She started her lecture by saying, "Today you begin your studies at the first school in the world established specifically for the purpose of training women for the degree of doctor of medicine, so congratulations. Philadelphia is also home to our nation's first hospital and is world renowned as the City of Medicine."

We all nodded and smiled at our good fortune.

"But make no mistake," she said. "Your acceptance into the medical world will be fraught with peril. Our own county medical society denies admission to our graduates."

Her words surprised me, and I wondered if I'd face the same lack of acceptance when I returned to Utah. I hoped not, given the proliferation of the Relief Societies, and the men's support for suffrage.

The professor continued, "It's still assumed in some circles that women are unfit to practice medicine, because they claim we lack sense and mental perception and are contemptuous of logic," she snorted.

184

How insulting and purely primitive, I thought, and we were all aghast.

"On that grim note," she said, "welcome to my class on obstetrics, where we will generally use demonstration clinics in our studies. One day, I hope we'll attend to women who are prenatal and be present at live births."

My next class was physiology taught by Frances Emily White, a 'shockingly modern thinker,' or so we'd been told. We have several men on our faculty, including the notable surgeons W. W. Keen and John B. Roberts. The Dean of the college, Rachel Bodley, is a woman.

I wrapped up the day with discussions of germ theory and epidemiology, and my head was buzzing by the time I left. I was in a state of sheer exhaustion when I returned to the boarding house and collapsed into bed.

Each day was endless, and so like the ones that followed, that the weeks passed in a blur. I often worked late into the nights, holding a human skull in hand, marking its lines or memorizing lengthy Latin names associated with every bone in the body. I reviewed my notes on the most recent laboratory experiment, getting precious little sleep. It seemed the only rest I had from my labors was the one day every month I spent with Thomas.

****

I had finished my first year of medical school the day I traveled to Washington D.C. in April of 1877 and learned of a new woman's rights' champion. Thomas and I searched for a restaurant in the Georgetown historic district, not far from where he attended law school. It was a lovely spring day as we strolled arm in arm along the Potomac River.

"I've missed you," he said, taking my hand in his and looking at me with those gentle brown eyes that never failed to warm my heart.

"I've missed you," I said, flushed.

Before long, we reached the heart of Georgetown. I love this gentrified neighborhood.

Thomas said, "We'll enjoy lunch today at the historic City Tavern. Many of our country's founding fathers, including George Washington, Thomas Jefferson, and John Adams were known to frequent this establishment. The food is quite good, and I used some connections to secure a private table for lunch."

As we dined on a delicious meal of striped bass and cooked vegetables, Thomas told me he had recently participated in a Moot Court at the University that involved arguing imaginary cases for practice. "I found," he said, "that I revel in oral arguments made inside a courtroom."

"Do you suppose one day you might want to be a prosecuting attorney?" I asked between bites.

"No, I believe I'd be more interested in being an attorney for the defense."

"That's because you champion the underdog," I said, pride in my voice.

"Sometimes I believe you know me better than I know myself," he said, leaning over and kissing my cheek. He took another mouthful of fish and said, "By the way, one of our moot court judges was Mrs. Belva Lockwood who graduated from here four years ago, class of 1873. She attempted to gain admittance to the bar of the Supreme Court last year, but the justices refused to admit her, stating that none but men were permitted to practice before them as attorneys and counselors."

My back stiffened, and I shook my head. "The prejudice that proliferates against women."

"An example of backward thinking," Thomas said. "Mrs. Lockwood is now single handedly lobbying Congress for the right to argue before the court, and I suspect she'll win."

"A pioneer to be sure, what do you know of her background?"

"When she introduced herself to my class, she said she'd been left a widow at the age of twenty-two with a three-year old daughter. She earned a degree and taught school in New York State before moving here and marrying an elderly civil war veteran by the name of Ezekiel Lockwood. When his health failed, she came to

186

law school. But listen to this. On the day she graduated, the men in her class declared they wouldn't graduate with a woman, and they took her law school degree from the hands of President Ulysses S. Grant, the institution's ex officio head at the time."

"Ruffians." I frowned. "Makes my blood boil."

"Make no mistake, Mrs. Lockwood has only grown stronger through her struggles since that day. She's quite fearless."

"I'd like to meet this courageous woman one day."

"I hope you do. She is, of course, an ardent supporter of female suffrage."

After we finished lunch, Thomas took me to the train station, and we said our goodbyes. Only one more year of studies left, and we'd earn our advanced degrees.

At the end of August, I received a telegram from Utah. *That's unusual*, I thought, turning it over in my hands. *I hope all is well at home.* The message was from Sophia advising me that Brigham Young had died August 29, 1877, at the age of 76. The news of his passing saddened me as I remembered the day that he'd called Utah women to go to medical school, a life-changing experience for me. He was a visionary leader in many ways and a master organizer.

Emma

Two weeks after Brigham Young's death, Emma attended an afternoon Relief Society meeting in the Rock Chapel. President Sarah Holmes reported to the women that 25,000 people had taken their last farewell of Brigham Young in the Tabernacle. She dabbed tears from her cheeks and said, "I know you were acquainted with President Young, who visited Farmington often. He loved having his own room here at the Haight Union Hotel."

Sister Holmes paused for a moment and said, "It seemed appropriate at such a time as this to ask Louisa Haight to share a special blessing she received at the hands of Brother Brigham. This is a sacred event for her, and she rarely speaks of it, but on his passing, she has agreed to do so. Louisa, please come forward."

Louisa stood and looked around the room, her dark hair parted down the middle and pulled back from her face. She walked to the front and cleared her throat, hands clasped in front of her. "Permit me to begin by saying that Horton worked at the behest of Brigham Young for many years, making fifteen trips back and forth across the plains in search of both needed goods and freight, as well as assisting emigrants seeking passage to the Valley. He and Brother Brigham were fast friends, and we shall miss him."

The ladies were appreciative of the many sacrifices her husband had made for the Church.

"What most of you don't know," Louisa said, "is that after our first baby boy was born dead, a doctor traveled to Farmington from Salt Lake and, after thoroughly examining me, told us that I would never bear a live child." Tears stood out in her eyes as she recalled the memory.

Emma stared at Louisa, surprised, aware that she had successfully delivered ten children. Emma placed her hand over her heart, waiting for the rest of the story.

Louisa continued, "President Young, upon hearing what the doctor said, came to our home, laid his hands on my head, and blessed me that I would become the mother of a large family. So, at a time when I was distraught and had almost lost hope, Brigham Young came to our aid with a blessing from God. My husband and I will be forever grateful for his prophetic words."

When Louisa sat down, there wasn't a dry eye in the room. *Perhaps there's hope for Wesley and me as well?* Emma wondered, recalling the scripture about faith preceding the miracle. She determined to speak with Sister Haight after the meeting ended.

After thanking Louisa, Holmes read from an article Emmeline Wells had written in last February's issue of the *Exponent* titled 'Courage Under Difficulties.' "Sister Wells wrote this," she said, "and I quote:

"There is an old proverb that in war, you should keep your powder dry and trust in Providence... keep your courage up, never let your spirits shrink... and face the music with indomitable resolution, asking for wisdom and guidance from our Father in Heaven, in the name of the one who passed through the most fiery ordeal and came off conqueror over death and the grave."

Emma listened closely to the words about trusting in Providence and knew she and Wesley needed a blessing. *We must seek the mind and will of the Lord on our behalf,* Emma thought, *and we haven't done so.*

"Sisters," Holmes continued, "Emmeline concludes her article with an admonition to those of us who are the mothers of daughters, so please heed her words.

"Mothers, you are doing your daughters the greatest injustice when you allow them to come to years of maturity without placing in their hands a power of some sort by which they could, if necessary, be self-supporting. They are not fit for wives or mothers, and if they remain single, they will lack that solidity of character which will help them maintain any position of responsibility or trust."

A hush fell over the room, and Emma suspected that while some women agreed with Emmeline's admonition, others may not, believing that they and their daughters could always depend on their husbands for support. Emma was relieved she possessed the means to pay off medical bills, and she loved her chosen profession as a Pinkerton agent. *You never know when the unexpected might occur.*

Another sister stood and offered a new recipe for marble cake, and Emma made notes. She and Wesley loved a good cake.

The last speaker delivered a report from the Silk Society and asked for volunteers willing to wind the silk from the cocoons, using their spinning wheels to make dresses, scarves, ties, and shirts. That task is far better than raising the worms, Emma thought, making a face and recalling the day she'd placed tree limbs all over a shelf so the worms, who were then four to five inches long and as thick as two fingers put together, could go into their cocoons.

After the meeting ended with prayer, she waited for those who wished to speak with Louisa, and as she was leaving, Emma approached her. "Do you have a moment, Sister Haight?" she asked.

"Certainly. Would you care to step over here where we will have more privacy?"

When they were out of earshot, Emma asked, "Do you think your husband would be willing to give Wesley and me a blessing? My father could assist him."

"He'd be honored. Horton has given blessings to many. May I ask, is this about bearing children?"

"It is. You may have heard that I miscarried once, and after Wesley lost his leg, the doctor told us he may never father children."

"You've received a medical opinion; now let's see what the Lord has in mind for you. Would next Sunday be convenient?" she asked, placing her arm about my shoulder as we walked outside.

"Next Sunday would be just right, thank you."

"Do you mind if I accompany my husband?"

"That would be wonderful, and I'll invite Grandmother Phoebe as well."

"I love your grandmother, and I think she'd very much want to be present for the blessings. Horton will prepare himself in advance, and we'll both come fasting. May I suggest you all do the same."

"Yes," Emma said, her voice quivering with emotion, "and thank you for sharing your inspiring story today."

"The only purpose in sharing our stories is to help others." She gave Emma a hug, who shamelessly cried in her arms.

The following Sunday, Horton and Louisa came by Emma and Wesley's home. Emma liked his white, handlebar mustache and generous eyes. "Shall we use this chair?" he asked.

"Yes," Wesley said, carrying it into the parlor.

"I'd like to offer you a blessing first," Horton said to Wesley. "Brother Gregory, do you have the consecrated oil?"

"Right here," Emma's father said, removing it from his pocket and pouring a little on Wesley's head, declaring that the oil had been consecrated for the healing of the sick. Then laying hands on Wesley's head, Brother Haight offered a blessing, telling him that the Lord loved him and was pleased with his steadfast dedication to the gospel. He said, "I bless you that your wounds may be healed, and you will father children."

When it was her turn to receive a blessing, Wesley moved to the sofa and Emma took her place on the chair. Brother Haight told Emma that she'd been blessed with the courage of her grandmother, the resilience of her father, and the curiosity of her mother. The part about her mother filled Emma with joy. He declared that her faith was a gift from ages past, and it would never leave her. He ended the blessing by saying, "I promise you, Sister Hatch, that you will yet be a Mother in Israel and bear children."

The spirit that burned in Emma's heart was strong. When Brother Haight concluded, they all sat for a moment in an air of quiet contemplation and reverence.

Grandmother broke the silence saying, "I know you've all been twenty-four hours without food, so if you'll permit me, I've prepared a light meal." She went into the kitchen, returning with her delicious cold bread, cheese, strawberries, and cake. *Food has never tasted so good*, Emma thought, and wondered aloud how long it might be before she would be with child. Brother Haight counseled patience.

Seventeen

Katie

I was in my room reading about the ongoing efforts in Washington to introduce legislation that had been designed to take away the right to vote from the women of Utah. We were grateful for the support of papers in the East such as the influential *Woman's Journal* and the Philadelphia paper *Woman's Words*. The editors of these papers condemned the proposed legislation as being both discriminatory and illegal, and I agreed. The National Woman's Suffrage Association was concerned enough about the women of Utah that they'd appointed three of their members to watch over our rights, and one of them was Belva Lockwood. *We can't do better than she*, I thought, pleased to have a lawyer of such stature as one of our champions.

It had become crystal clear to the NWSA that an amendment to the Constitution granting women the franchise was necessary.

Onward and upward we go, I thought, picking up a *Deseret News* article that had been published two months ago, titled 'Woman Suffrage in Utah,' December 19, 1877. Emma had sent me a letter and included a copy of the article.

It stated that our paper in Philadelphia, *Woman's Words*, had sent Emmeline Wells information she'd requested in order to mount a petition drive in Utah. *I'm proud of my former associate and mentor at the Exponent, who last year took over the paper as chief editor.*

Miss Anthony appreciated the value of the *Woman's Exponent* as well and had declared: "It is impossible to estimate the advantage this little paper gives to the women of this far western territory. From its first issue it was the champion of the suffrage cause, and by exchanging with women's papers of the United States and England it brought news of women in all parts of the world to those of Utah."

I adore Miss Anthony. She's a selfless champion for women here and overseas.

The *Deseret News* article went on to state that Emmeline Wells had organized a meeting at her office at the Exponent with "some of the most prominent female leaders of the City" to organize a campaign."

Emmeline had been elected chair, and the group had made plans to first canvass Salt Lake City and then the entire territory of Utah.

Emmeline is becoming well known and well thought of in our nation's circle of intellectual women journalists. It was even rumored that one of them, Sarah Andrews Spencer, Washington correspondent and Secretary of the NWSA, wanted to invite Emmeline to the next Washington Convention. *She'll be the right one to represent Utah.* I smiled. *There's so much going on at home that I want to be part of.*

But first I was looking forward to attending the thirty-year anniversary of the Seneca Falls Convention in Rochester, New York, July 19. Lucretia Mott would be the featured speaker, and she was the reason I wanted to attend. She was growing frail, and this would almost certainly be my last opportunity to listen to this pioneer woman's rights leader and abolitionist.

I took a deep breath and laid my reading aside. Next month, Ellis Ship and I would graduate with our Doctor of Medicine Degrees. I was looking forward to completing my education, and I could hardly wait for March to arrive. Thomas wouldn't finish his Master of Law Degree until early July, and I wanted to remain in the East to attend the Seneca Falls Convention. Then we'd go home to Utah.

Ellis told me she'd written Eliza Snow about the possibility of setting up a School of Nursing and Obstetrics next year in Salt Lake

City after Ellis completed another year of training at the University of Michigan. The purpose of the school would be to train licensed midwives, and Ellis had invited me to join her. Certain that Aunt Eliza would help make this worthy dream a reality, I agreed. Ellis believed it was the crowning joy of a woman's life to be a mother, and this school would be an ideal way for her to combine both her love of medicine and children.

Our friend Romania Pratt had graduated the year prior, and she was the first Mormon woman to earn a medical degree. Instead of returning home, she'd spent this year in Boston, focusing her studies on the eye, ear, nose, and throat. I missed Romania and had been to Boston once to see her. She told me my friend from the *Exponent*, Martha Hughes, would soon begin studying medicine at the University of Michigan. *Mattie will make an excellent doctor.*

A few months later, my valise with my degree tucked inside was stored securely at the Grand Central Depot in New York as I sat inside the Rochester Unitarian Church, waiting for the July Seneca Falls Convention to begin. I was on pins and needles anticipating Lucretia Mott's address. I looked at the podium, and I could see a gleam still in her eyes, despite the burden of her 85 years.

When she began her reminiscences, the audience listened with delight as she recounted an illustrious journey with the woman's movement. She pled for woman's equal, civil, religious, educational, and industrial rights, as well as an equality of political exertion, and a right to use all the sources of this power equal with man.

She declared, "Place woman in equal power, and you will find her capable of not abusing it! Give her the elective franchise, and there will be an unseen, yet a deep and universal movement of the people to elect into office only those who are pure in intention and honest in sentiment! Give her the privilege to cooperate in making the laws she submits to, and there will be harmony without severity, and justice without oppression."

I held my breath as I listened for more.

"Make her, if married, a living being in the eye of the law—she will not assume beyond duty; give her the right of property, and you may justly tax her patrimony as the result of her wages. Open to her your colleges—your legislative, your municipal, your domestic laws will be purified and ennobled. Forbid her not and she will use moderation."

Her words were powerful. She said, "I believe in the scripture: Behold, a new heaven and a new earth, for old things have passed away." She was a woman of both faith and feminism, which is precisely how I saw myself.

In her closing remarks, Lucretia Mott said she wished to "add her expression of gratitude to the Unitarian society who had so kindly given us the use of their edifice." The convention arose in her honor and on behalf of us all, Frederick Douglass, the well-known social reformer and abolitionist, bid her 'good-bye.' My heart filled with emotion as I watched her leave.

I'd listened to the woman I'd come to hear and was deeply impressed. Thomas was waiting for me outside the church and we had a few stops to make before leaving for Utah the following day. Our first would be Coney Island, the seaside resort that was the Eastern counterpart to our own Saltair, and since this was our last day in the East, we wished to take advantage of every moment we had left.

We hopped a steam railway to West Brighton, where for 35 cents, we rode the Prospect Park & Coney Island Railroad to the Culver Depot terminal at Surf Avenue. Across the street from the terminal stood the 300-foot Iron Tower, which had been bought from the 1876 Philadelphia Exposition. From the top, we were treated to a stunning birds-eye view of the coast.

Our second stop was Manhattan Beach where we wandered around its grand new hotel that was filled with restaurants, ballrooms, and shops. I selected a few gifts to take home to my brothers, and we dined on a delicious meal of prime rib and potatoes. When it was time to retire, we enjoyed a luxurious stay overnight at the hotel, sleeping in separate rooms, of course. Thomas's generous mother had paid for our lodging.

The next morning, we rose early and made our way to Grand Central Depot, whose name never disappoints with its three towers that represent the three participating railroads. The interior was grandly designed and meant to look like a palace, a fitting gateway to this exuberant city.

We boarded our train, and I found myself filled with mixed emotions about leaving the East, which shouldn't have surprised me, but it did. Once inside, I sat next to Thomas, holding his hand, reflecting on the past two years.

"You're very quiet this morning," he said, brushing my arm with his fingers which always made me tingle. "What are you thinking about?"

"I've spent the past year focused on earning a degree, looking forward to graduation and the day we'd return to Utah. Now the day has arrived, and all I can think about is how much I'm going to miss the City of Brotherly Love, with its Liberty Bell, Declaration of Independence, and fascinating culture. It's been a grand experience living in Philadelphia, and I don't believe I've relished each day as I ought to have."

Thomas took my hand in his. "It's easy to get so caught up in the future that we fail to appreciate the present."

"I fear that's what I've done," I said, "but no more. Today is the beginning of our lives together, and I don't want to waste another day living in either the future or the past. I'm determined to be present in my own life each day, come what may."

Emma

Emma looked at the calendar in the kitchen and noted the date. According to Katie's last letter, she and Thomas had left New York for Utah yesterday, and Emma couldn't wait to have Katie closer to home. She was tapping her fingers on the table when Wesley came into the room. *He's getting around so well on his new leg,* Emma thought. *His limp is barely noticeable.*

"Good morning," he said, kissing the top of her head. "How are you this morning?" Without waiting for a response he said, "I know

196

you don't have a case right now—how about taking a much-deserved break?"

Emma looked at him and smiled ruefully.

"Perhaps you might like to read a novel?" he suggested. "But not about detectives, please."

Emma laughed. "I fear the art of deduction is in my blood."

Wesley smiled. "Fortunately for us and our finances, it is. I'm going to boil eggs; would you care for some?"

"Yes, please," Emma said, slitting open a letter she'd received the last evening from Chicago. After reading it through, her brow furrowed and she muttered, "What on earth is going on?"

"What is it?" Wesley asked, turning from the ice box.

"A Pinkerton manager is coming through Utah on his way to Wyoming, and he wants to meet with me in Ogden to conduct what he's calling 'a field office review.'"

"That's a bit unusual, isn't it?"

"Yes, it is. I send copies of my case files to the Chicago office, so they're aware of my activities on their behalf. Makes me wonder," she said.

Wesley placed a plate of eggs, cheese, and cold bread in front of her. "Do you think there's a problem?" he asked, slicing a peach in her bowl and adding a dash of milk.

"It may be nothing," she said. "I don't want to get ahead of myself, so I'll wait and see what comes of the review."

"When is it?" he asked as they ate.

"Two days from now."

"What's the guy's name?"

"John Peterson, and he's one of Robert's right hand men. I met him once, and there's something I don't trust about him," Emma said, eyes flashing.

"Your instincts are usually accurate. Where's the meeting?"

"He wants me to meet him in a bar by the train station."

"I despise it when you have to go into bars for meetings."

"I will come prepared, never fear," Emma said.

"Guess I'd better get to work. See you this evening," he said, wolfing down one last piece of bread.

"Give Father my best, but don't tell him about the review just yet."

"Will do." Wesley placed his Stetson atop his head, kissed her on the cheek, and walked out the door.

Emma was concerned about the ongoing rumors that Robert wished to do away with the female detectives. He didn't possess his father's open mind, of that she was certain. Emma had heard that Robert's brother, Will, had worked with the first female Pinkerton detective, Kate Warne, in Kansas City. Emma understood they'd been a good team, but she sensed that if it came to a matchup between Robert and Will over retaining females, Robert would emerge victorious.

A few days later, Emma sat in a small bar in Ogden, waiting for Peterson. She was dressed in a long tan skirt and cream-colored shirt, badge pinned to her chest. Her gun was strapped to her side, resting in its holster, and she intended to convey the impression that she was not someone to be trifled with. Emma had arrived early so she could case the place and size Peterson up when he came through the door. She had selected a table away from several rowdy and drunk ruffians, who eyed her suspiciously.

"What can I get you?" a woman bartender asked, coming to Emma's table and wiping it off.

"Water, please."

"That's it?" she asked, looking surprised.

"That's it, thanks," Emma said, taking out paper and pen and making notes on her latest case, a copy of which she hadn't yet sent to Chicago, waiting for resolution that had come only yesterday.

A few weeks ago, Emma had found a barn full of stolen goods in a neighboring town that she traced to a local peddler. Suspecting he had accomplices, and that the trail didn't end with him, she put a few of the local businessmen under surveillance. Sure enough, two of them were helping the peddler fence the merchandise. Emma turned her findings over to the town's sheriff, and he later arrested all three. They were now sitting in jail awaiting trial.

She looked up from her notes as the bar doors swung open, and a man of medium height with black hair, a pot belly, and beady eyes walked in. He was dressed in a black and gray suit. Emma believed it was Peterson.

When he looked at her and saw her badge he walked up to the table. "Mrs. Emma Hatch, I presume?"

Emma rose and shook his hand. "Yes. Mr. John Peterson?"

"Indeed," he said, taking a seat, as the barmaid walked over again. "What'll you have?"

"Beer," he said, looking at Emma's glass of water. "Want something else?" he asked.

"No, this will do it for me. How was your train trip?"

"Uneventful, which is just the way I like them." He took a large drink of beer. "Let's get to it, shall we?"

"Let's do."

"I spoke with Rosemary Shaw about you before I left," he said, leaning forward.

"And?"

"She tells me you're a solid agent and that your investigative skills are second to none."

"Thank you. I'd like to think so," Emma said.

"Mrs. Shaw also reported that you once jumped off a horse, tackled a man, and wrested his gun from him."

"I did," Emma said, wondering if his compliments were sincere or designed to catch her off guard.

"You're quite brave. For a female of course," he added.

There it is. Saw that one coming. "All in a day's work," she replied, leaning back in her chair, not rising to the bait. "I often work undercover as well, when the situation calls for it, and I have a case filled with disguises."

"I would expect nothing less from our women employees."

One of the desperados wandered past their table on his way to the bar for a refill and asked, "Heard you two a talkin'. So you let a woman do your work for you?" He looked disgusted.

"She doesn't do my work for me," Peterson said. "She works for my company"

"Is that a badge I see pinned on her chest?" he asked

"It is," Emma answered for herself. "I'm a Pinkerton agent."

The guy sneered. "I heard them Pinkertons hired negros and females, but I never met one afore."

"Well, now you have," Emma said. "Lucky you." She laid her gun on the table.

He clenched his fists, snorted, and went to the bar.

"Comport yourself carefully around men such as these," Peterson said under his breath.

"I can take care of myself."

"That may be, but you will do as I say. Remember that you represent the Pinkerton agency—at least for now."

"What are you implying?"

"I'm implying nothing," Peterson growled. "I'm stating clearly that I agree with Robert that our agency is no place for women."

"Does this mean you've come to fire me?"

"No," Peterson said, backing down from his position. "But one day, I hope to be part of removing all you Pinks from the agency. I tire of listening to the complaints from the wives of our men who must work with female agents."

"What is it that disturbs them?" Emma asked, curious.

"Oh, I think you can guess, Mrs. Hatch. They don't want their husbands cavorting with other women."

"Cavorting, you say?" Emma asked, surprised.

"Things have been known to happen, believe me."

"And it's the female agent's fault, then."

"Of course. They're a distraction, Mrs. Hatch, and I believe one day Robert will get rid of all of you."

"Not as long as Alan Pinkerton is in charge," Emma said. "Are we finished here?" She stood.

"Not yet. I've brought copies of a few rap sheets from our Rogue's gallery, and I want you to have a look at them."

Emma resumed her seat, and he handed her the material. The Pinkertons were well known for their Rogue's gallery which consisted of a collection of mug shots and case histories used to keep track of wanted men. Emma checked the photos for distinguishing marks and scars and went through the newspaper clippings. She soon found information that matched the profile of the peddler she'd reported to the sheriff.

"This one," Emma said, handing Peterson both his picture and her paperwork on the case she'd completed. "He's behind bars at the moment, awaiting trial."

Peterson read through the case file she'd handed him and begrudgingly grunted the words, "Well done, and now we're finished. You may go."

"Good-bye, Mr. Peterson," Emma said. She stood, walked out of the saloon, and without another word, made her way to the Ogden train station. She couldn't wait to get home and send a missive off to Rosemary.

Eighteen

Katie

Thomas and I had spent the past few weeks preparing for our upcoming wedding. There was still so much to be done, and I was feeling overwhelmed. We'd been trying to find a place to live somewhere not too far from his widowed mother, Rebecca, who lived north of downtown Salt Lake. I'd been in her company several times, but we'd never been alone together.

I admitted, but only to myself, that I sometimes found my future mother-in-law a little intimidating. Rebecca was a tall woman with strong posture, who made her presence known whenever she entered a room. She was intelligent, loved to read and discuss everything, sometimes to the point of exhaustion. Rebecca had three sons, Thomas being her youngest.

When I went to her home, she was awaiting my arrival. "Come in, please, Katie," she said, opening the door before I'd knocked. Her white-blonde hair was parted down the middle and pulled back behind her ears, and she wore the pair of earrings her husband had given her the day they married.

"Thank you, Mrs. Forrest," I said, entering her lovely home.

"Please, call me Rebecca. We'll be family soon, you know."

I smiled.

"I already think of you as the daughter of my heart, Katie," she said, holding my hands in hers, "and I want to offer you love and support."

I sensed she would become an important part of my new life here, and meeting alone with her made me realize how warm she could be. *Thomas tells me she loves listening to the minds of young children*, I thought, looking into her eyes, *and I'm guessing she'll be a caring and engaging grandmother*. When I entered the parlor, she offered me lemon tea and cakes, and we began our conversation about the wedding.

"Where would you like to hold your wedding dinner following the temple ceremony in the Endowment House?"

"We're considering dinner on the second floor of the Walker House, in one of the public parlors. Their kitchen is so large they can easily accommodate both their guests and our wedding party."

"An excellent choice, my dear. Their bakery is divine, and I'm told the carving room contains a steam table with covers for keeping the meats and vegetables hot. Will your family spend the night there in the hotel before we travel to Farmington the next day for your reception?"

"No, they'll stay with my father's cousin, Sophia."

"Thomas tells me the two of you are close."

"I'm living with her again until the wedding." My mind wandered for a moment, and I thought about how different my marriage would be if Mother were still alive. *Oh, how I miss her every day.*

Father had remarried the year after she died, and his new wife, Marilyn, was nice enough, I supposed. She'd agreed to let Ada remain in the house, which was generous, even though the two of them don't get on well. Father told me Ada pretty much keeps to herself these days which made me sad. Even though Ada and I rarely saw eye-to-eye, I appreciated all the help she'd given Mother.

Marilyn had redecorated the house, which was her prerogative, but it didn't feel like the home where I grew up. Andrew and Jacob were fond of her, though, and that was the most important thing. Joseph had married a few months ago and left Farmington for Southern Utah. My nuclear family seemed to have splintered, and I felt as if I were on the outside looking in.

Rebecca took another bite of cake, telling me about a home on her street that had been put up for sale. "You and Thomas might be interested in having a look," she said. "It's rather nice."

"Thank you, but Thomas and I have decided to live in the Avenues."

"I see," she said, unable to conceal her disappointment.

I wanted to live near her but not on the same street. It was important that Thomas and I create our own lives together, and I hoped Rebecca would come to understand that because I wanted us to be fast friends.

"Thank you for the delicious tea and cake, and I regret rushing off," I said, rising, "but I must be on a train to Farmington this afternoon."

"You're welcome anytime, my dear," Rebecca said, hugging me good-bye. "I look forward to the two of us coming to know one another better."

A few hours later, Thomas dropped me at the train station. I'd promised Father I'd stay overnight this time, and I was determined to make the best of my visit. When I reached the Farmington station, it was my brother Andrew who awaited my arrival. He gave me a big hug when I stepped inside the carriage. At sixteen years old, he'd become a handsome young man. "It's so good to see you, Katie." He grinned.

"I've missed you," I said. "How you've grown."

"Did Father tell you I've decided to go to law school in two years?" he asked.

"No, he didn't. After Thomas and I marry and get settled, you must come and let him share his experiences at Georgetown with you."

"I'd like that, Katie. Next spring, I begin my pre-law classes at the University of Deseret."

"We'll have the opportunity to see you much more frequently, which gladdens my heart." Horse and carriage carried us over streets strewn with gold and orange leaves. *Fall is my favorite season of the year in Farmington, and I've always seen it as a time for new beginnings.* I looked around and took a deep breath of clear air.

"When do you begin your practice of medicine?" Andrew asked.

"Next spring as well. I want time to set up house and be with Thomas first."

As we approached Julia Haight's house, she was standing in the yard, dousing potted flowers with a watering can. When she saw us coming, she waved and walked to the street. Andrew pulled the horse to a halt, and I stepped out of the carriage. It was good to see my old friend.

Julia hugged me and said, "You must come inside and say hello to Mother. She's lately received wonderful news, and I'm certain you'll want to hear the details."

"I'll take your things to the house," Andrew offered, "and you can walk home when you're ready."

"That would be lovely," I said. "Thank you." When I went inside the Haight home, I saw Louisa standing at the stove, stirring a pot of soup.

"Katie," she said, putting the large spoon down and wrapping me in her arms. "It's wonderful to see you again."

Being in Louisa's presence reminded me of my mother. Louisa seemed to sense my thoughts when she touched my cheek and said, "I know. I miss her, too, love."

Tears ran down my face, and Julia offered a handkerchief.

Louisa said, "I understand you and Thomas will marry next month. What a joyous occasion it will be and thank you for the invitation to your reception."

"It wouldn't be the same without you. And speaking of happy events," I said, "Julia told me you have news to share."

Louisa's eyes brightened. "On August 11, Sunday last, the local Farmington Ward Primary Association was formally organized. Sister Aurelia Rogers was sustained as president, and Helen M. Miller and I were sustained as her counselors. We are the very first primary in the Church at large, Katie. It's high time we had an organization dedicated to teaching the children."

This was wondrous news indeed. "How did this come to pass?" I asked.

"Aurelia Rogers has been thinking about this for a while, concerned that our younger children in the community have too much unsupervised time, particularly the younger boys who are often mischievous and unruly. One night, while praying for guidance, a voice reminded her there was an auxiliary organization in the church for all ages, except the children."

"She's always been a woman of faith," I said.

"She puts it into action," Louisa said. "Aurelia met with President John Taylor soon after and received permission to operate a church organization for children. With the assistance of Eliza Snow, the first primary was officially organized last Sunday in the Rock Chapel. Eliza will assist us in spreading the Primary to other church congregations."

"What a marvelous beginning," I said, "and right here in Farmington. But you must be even busier than ever."

"The three of us have been visiting every home in the ward, and we're inviting all 224 children between the ages of six and fourteen to come to the first meeting to be held Sunday, August 25. After that, we'll meet weekly on Saturday afternoons with the children. We've asked other sisters to assist us."

"What lessons will you teach?" I asked, curious.

"The children will be taught lessons on faith, obedience, prayer, punctuality, and manners. Specifically, the boys will be encouraged not to take fruit from orchards and melon patches, and the girls will be exhorted not to hang on wagons."

I smiled and said, "Those are much needed messages to be sure."

"Music will also become an integral part of our program, as will recitations, gardening projects, and lessons on home arts. We also plan to hold an annual fair."

"What a promising beginning for the youngest among us, and you'll do a wonderful job."

"Thank you." Louisa looked at the clock. "I must go," she said. "I still have several homes to visit before the day is out. Julia, will you please finish the soup? Katie, it's been such a treat to see you." She tied a bonnet under her chin. "Now that you've finished medical school, you must come to Farmington more often." Louisa slipped a shawl around her shoulders and left.

I turned to Julia. "My family is awaiting me at home."

"I'll walk along with you," Julia said. "The soup can wait. We haven't yet had an opportunity to speak with each other." As we walked, she took my arm in hers. "You and Thomas have a wedding coming up." She smiled. "Thank you for asking me to be one of your bridesmaids at the reception in Farmington."

"I'm honored you accepted. We'll be married in just about two more months, after postponing our marriage for more than two years. Thomas has been so patient."

"I'm happy for you, Katie."

On October 27, 1878, Thomas and I were married for time and sealed for eternity in the Endowment House, and it was Emma who accompanied me through the sacred temple ceremony. I was grateful to have her by my side along with my family. Even Joseph made the trip from southern Utah.

That evening, family and friends gathered at Delmonico's for a delicious steak dinner. Several of my former colleagues from the Exponent came, and I was delighted to see them, especially Emmeline Wells. I invited her to sit at our table next to me and Thomas, Emma and Wesley.

After offering her heartiest congratulations, she put her fork down and said, "Something has just occurred to me."

I gazed at her, curious.

"Zina and I will be traveling to Washington D.C. in January, and we're looking for a copyist to accompany us and keep notes. You'd be the ideal candidate, Katie, but fair warning, we'll be gone almost a month. Are you available?"

"Let me give it some thought and discuss it with Thomas."

Emmeline nodded and said, "We'll be staying at the Riggs house, which serves as headquarters for the National Woman's Suffrage Association. We'll hold a planning meeting at the home of Belva Lockwood before meeting with President Rutherford B. Hayes and his wife."

"I'd hoped to meet Mrs. Lockwood one day," I said.

"Here's your opportunity," Thomas interjected, "and I predict the two of you will get on famously."

"You must go, Katie," Emma said.

"You're both right," I said. "So yes, I'd love to go, Emmeline. Thank you." *And I'm to meet the president and his wife as well*, I thought, trembling. I reached over and held my new husband's hand, grateful for his encouragement.

Emma

It had been snowing for days, and frozen drifts covered the roads as Emma and Wesley prepared to enjoy a quiet Christmas Eve at home. They'd finished the chores early and were toasting their feet in front of a warm fire, waiting for the apple pies to finish cooking. Holly berries sat amid green branches dressing the mantle, and the red and white Christmas stockings Emma had knitted were hung with care. In the corner of the room glowed a tree with all the trimmings.

Emma was pregnant, but she hadn't told Wesley. She hadn't told anyone, because she feared it might not last. *What if I miscarry and lose another child? That would break his heart and mine as well.* But if she waited much longer, the size of her growing belly would give her away. She delayed, reaching into a dish on the table, offering Wesley a piece of peppermint chocolate.

"This is delicious," he said. "Merry Christmas, my angel."

"Merry Christmas," she said, plucking up her courage. She turned to Wesley and said, "I have something to tell you."

"What is it?" he asked, accepting another piece of chocolate.

Emma took a deep breath. "I'm with child."

Wesley jumped from the couch and almost fell, steadying himself on his good leg. He raised his fist into the air and shouted, "Yes! We did it." He tugged Emma up after him and began twirling her around the room.

She laughed at his enthusiasm.

"How far along are you?

"Three months."

He stopped and looked at her. "Why didn't you tell me before?"

"I wanted to make certain it was real, Wesley," Emma said. "What if I can't carry a baby to term?" Her face turned ashen.

Wesley gathered her in his arms. "This time you will. I can feel it," he assured her.

"I hope you're right. I guess I've let my fear overrun my faith."

"It's because we've been through such trials. But this is what God promised us, Emma. It's what He promised. It's time to read our Christmas Eve scripture from the Book of Luke," he said, picking up his Bible. He opened to Luke chapter 2 and read,

"And there were in the same country shepherds abiding in the field, keeping watch over their flocks by night.

"And, lo, the angel of the Lord came upon them, and the glory of the Lord shone round about them; and they were sore afraid.

"And the angel said unto them, Fear not; for behold I bring you tidings of great joy."

Wesley paused and said, "Similar to that sacred Christmas Eve so long ago, when Christ our Lord was born, this is another remarkable Christmas Eve, Emma. God is telling us to put away our fears and accept His tidings of great joy."

Emma broke down and sobbed, first with a sense of relief, then joy. *He's right*, she thought, grateful that she could be vulnerable with the person she loved most in this world. "What would you like to name our baby, if it's a boy?"

"Twins run in my family, Emma. What if we have a boy and a girl? It could happen, you know."

Emma hadn't considered that possibility and she glowed at the idea. "Twins," she said. "If we have a girl, I'd like to name her Joyce, after my mother."

"Of course," he said. "And what about our little boy?"

"We'll call him Wesley Hatch II after his father, and he'll be a man of great faith, just as you are."

Wesley kissed her. "Such a gift that would be." They sat still, savoring the moment, listening to the fire pop and crackle. A bit later, he yawned and inquired, "Are you ready for bed?"

"I am," she said. "I'll remove the pies from the cook stove, let them cool, and be right behind you."

"What time are we eating with your family tomorrow?"

"Just after noon."

"Time for us to enjoy our own Christmas morning together. I have a special gift for you, though nothing can compare to the gift you've just given me."

"Must I wait until morning?" she asked, eyes twinkling. Emma suggested each year that they open their gifts on Christmas Eve.

"Yes, you must, my darling."

Wesley

The following morning, Wesley awoke first and rolled from the bed, leaving Emma fast asleep. He edged down the stairs on his prosthetic leg, closed the door to the house behind him, and moved to the small shed he'd built on the back of their property. Wesley removed the padlock, went inside, and looked around. Being in his tiny workshop gave him a sense of fulfillment and peace; it was here where he created his art.

Collecting the small bird from the table he'd carved for Emma, he wrapped it in bits of paper, hoping she'd be pleased with his offering. He went back inside and gently woke her with a kiss on the cheek.

"Good morning." Emma stretched. "You're up already?"

"I couldn't wait. How are you feeling?" he said, concerned, touching her belly gently.

"A bit nauseous, but it'll pass. What's that gaily wrapped package you have there? Is it for me?" she asked, sitting up in bed.

"It is."

When Emma opened the package, she found an elegant carving of a black and white baby eagle with a yellow beak, wooden wings raised, as if preparing to take flight.

Emma turned the eagle over, viewing it from all angles. "It looks so real," she said with admiration.

"The thing I like about birds is they represent the freedom of flight, and in their wings live a sense of new possibilities."

"You're very poetic this morning," Emma said.

"There's method in my madness," Wesley said, grinning.

"Whatever do you mean?"

"This bird represents something, namely, your freedom."

"I confess that I still don't understand." She looked at him quizzically.

Wesley swallowed hard and prepared to share his proposal. What will Emma think? He determined to begin with a question. "What is it that you like least about your job as a Pinkerton agent?"

"Well, I love almost everything about it. I like looking for puzzle pieces, solving problems, and bringing villains to justice. I'm also fond of the thrill of the chase."

"And the Pinkertons are your source for the cases."

"Yes, of course they are," she said, looking puzzled.

"Stay with me for a moment. What's the one thing that concerns you about your employer?"

"That they'll close down the female detective branch of the agency after Alan dies."

"I've listened to that worry more than once. What the Pinkertons have that you need most are connections with law enforcement. True?"

"Yes, that's true."

"Here's what I'm proposing, and I'm going to ask that you don't give me a response until after we return from Christmas lunch with your family. Will you do that?"

"If it's important to you, yes I will."

Good, he thought. *She's agreed to consider it, which is a happy circumstance, because what I'm about to say will no doubt come as a surprise. Although my argument has been bolstered by the news that she's pregnant. Here goes.* "Permit me to suggest that you resign from your position with the Pinkertons and open your own detective agency with me. As a deputy sheriff of several years, I have the connections you need with law enforcement. The remainder of the necessary skills, you already possess."

Emma had a blank look on her face. "While I won't give you an answer just yet, I do have several questions."

"I'd expect nothing less." He smiled.

"What about your job with my father in the sheriff's office?"

"I'd keep my desk job, which is not all that demanding, and use my time after work to search for cases across the whole of the territory that I'd assign to you. You've worked as a Pinkerton for several years, providing a stellar resume."

Emma said nothing and still appeared surprised at the idea.

"There's something else I believe you'll find appealing about opening our own agency. When you deliver our babies, you'll have the time to care for them as you've always wanted to do."

Emma looked at him with gratitude.

"We'll find and hire a male agent to work under your direction. He can come here to you for training and assignments when I'm at home to assist."

"It might not be easy to find a man who's willing to report to a woman."

"There are many good men looking for jobs right now, and if he needs the work, he'll agree to our criteria for the position. I can assure you that there will be none of this 'looking to me when he should be addressing you.' I think we can make a go of it, Emma, and all my medical bills are paid now."

"You've thought everything through, Wesley," she said, pride in her voice.

"I learned everything I know from you." He smiled.

Emma laughed heartily. "What do you think my father will have to say about this?"

"I've taken the liberty of discussing it with him already."

"Of course, you have." She smiled. "And…"

"He supports the idea, if you're in favor of it. The decision rests with you, Emma."

"There's much I like about the proposition but resigning from my job is a big step."

"Which is why I don't want you to give me your answer until we return from Christmas lunch, so let's get dressed. See," he said, walking to the window and raising the curtains, "the sun is shining outside, and the ice is melting."

Emma walked over and stood beside him, "What a beautiful Christmas morning."

The two of them donned their winter coats, and Wesley hitched the horse to the buggy, giving her a hand inside. He kept gazing at her out of the corner of his eye, wondering what she might be thinking. But, like the good detective she was, her face remained impassive, and she gave nothing away.

When they pulled up outside Emma's family home, he said, "I'll give the horse water while you carry the pies inside. Don't fret about the gifts; I'll bring them in too."

"Wesley," Emma said.

"Yes?" He turned to her and waited.

"Your idea is brilliant, and my answer is yes."

Wesley could hardly believe his ears. "So, we're to open our own agency?"

"We are, and together we'll make it a grand success. It'll take time, and much effort, but we'll get there." She hugged him and said, "I love you. I knew when I met you that you were the man for me."

He kissed her.

"Let's go inside," Emma said. "We have good news to share with my family, and my brother, David, will be thrilled to learn he's to become be an uncle."

Nineteen

Katie

Thomas was keeping me company while I loaded my trunk with several warm woolen dresses, checking them off my packing list as I went. It was a chilly January day and promised to be cold in the East as well. The clothing colors I selected were in the dark blue, brown, and gray categories, in keeping with the season and the formality of upcoming events in Washington D.C. at the National Woman's Suffrage Association of 1879.

"Katie," Thomas said.

"Hmm," I said over my shoulder, distracted.

"What's on your mind this morning?"

"Why do you ask?"

"You don't seem yourself. Are you troubled about something?"

I put my things down and sat next to him. "I'm not certain what kind of reception we'll receive in Washington."

"Go on," he said.

"I'm looking forward to the women's convention, and both Emmeline and Zina Williams will be speaking, so it's not that."

"Emmeline's on the NWSA's advisory board, correct?" he asked.

"She is."

214

"I suspect the invitation to speak at the national convention is due in large part to the women of Utah being progressive on the suffrage question," he said with a sense of satisfaction that I appreciated.

"That, and the fact that Emmeline generated large petitions asking for the passage of a Sixteenth Amendment to the Federal Constitution, in the hopes of enfranchising all women."

"A true advocate."

"She is, but I can't shake the feeling that we're walking into a political lion's den."

"You may be right. Apart from the NWSA leadership, you three may be viewed as provincial Mormon women from the West."

"I don't think I'm prepared for that," I said, folding my arms across my chest, thinking of the wonderful days I'd spent with Thomas in our nation's capital where we were treated just as everyone else.

"Given that Emmeline Wells and Zina Williams are both plural wives, they may be viewed as curiosities."

"Curiosities," I said, incensed. "They're intelligent, articulate, and independent women, not curiosities."

"I know that, and you know that, but others cling to a religious bias regarding all members of our faith, polygamist or not, so be ready." He put his arm around my shoulder and said, "I stand behind you, remember that."

"I'll miss you," I said.

"I'll miss you, and what an adventure this will be for you, Emmeline, and Zina."

"You're right," I said, rising and returning to my packing, trusting that three pairs of boots would be enough. I locked my trunk.

"Let me take that for you and put it in the carriage. I'll meet you outside."

I gazed around the room to make certain I hadn't forgotten anything. Guess not. Then I went to the wardrobe, removed a long, gray woolen cloak, and hurried downstairs. I paused at the front door, feeling pleased with our new home. It was spacious, comfortable, well-decorated, and had room for little ones. I opened the door and strode through the wet snow to our carriage.

It was cold outside, and I could see Thomas's breath take shape in the air as he laid reins on the horse. When we arrived, he loaded my trunk into the train and kissed me good-bye.

Emmeline and Zina soon came aboard, and we traveled first to Ogden, then made our way East. Emmeline was fascinated by the journey; she looked out the window and declared, "When I crossed these plains in 1848, could I ever have imagined that my return east would take me to the highest levels of government, where we'll be pleading for religious tolerance?"

"It's a huge responsibility we bear," Zina said.

I said nothing and hoped that Thomas was wrong about us being viewed as curiosities. *We need to be known for who we are, and not as flat characters in someone else's hypothetical story,* I thought as we made the long journey.

When we reached Washington, we went to the Riggs House, where we'd be living for the next month. This small, but elegant hotel had been built in 1856 and managed by Jane Spofford and her husband since 1876. I knew Jane was an active suffragist, and Susan B. Anthony usually lodged at the Riggs House whenever she was in Washington. *What a pleasure it is to stay here.*

"Such impressive and luxurious accommodations," Emmeline said as we made our way to our rooms and settled in for the night.

The next evening, we met at Belva Lockwood's home for a planning meeting that had been called in order review the agenda for tomorrow's opening session of the woman's conference. I was thrilled to meet Belva, letting her know that she and my husband shared an alma mater. She shook my hand and generously recalled meeting Thomas, speaking highly of him. She introduced us to Sara Spencer, another one of the NWSA members whom Anthony had appointed to help support the Utah women.

The meeting lasted several hours, and Emmeline was appointed to the committee on resolutions and Zina to the committee on finance. We were treated very graciously. "We have much to learn from you great leaders who have been laboring in the cause of woman's enfranchisement for more than thirty years," Emmeline said.

216

The next day, we went to the convention at Lincoln Hall, which sits on the corner of 9th and D Streets. It was constructed of bricks that had been scored with stucco to look like stones. I knew the Hall featured one of the finest auditoriums in our Capitol, and when we reached the auditorium, we were invited to sit on the platform.

As we sat down, it became obvious that we were indeed a curiosity to many of the women delegates who packed the hall. Zina said, "Dear me, what an awful thing to be an elephant. The ladies all look at me so queer."

I agreed with her and whispered, "I find their stares unnerving." The crowds seemed to assume that all women from Utah practiced polygamy, which was odd.

Emmeline turned to us and said, "I suffered far worse than this when we were driven from our homes in Nauvoo, and we'll get through this small inconvenience as well. Chin up; you young ladies are pioneers of another sort today."

Over the next few days, large crowds gathered wherever we went, having read much about the Mormons. While I wasn't used to receiving this kind of treatment, and didn't care for it one bit, I had a small inkling of the discrimination my parents and grandparents had endured. *If they can do it, so can I.*

The day came when Emmeline and Zina spoke to the convention and I made a note of the date, January 10, 1879, and wrote, "the hall is filled to capacity."

When Emmeline rose to speak, she took the opportunity to chastise Congress for seeking to remove the ballot from Utah women. "Congress had better heed what wrong is contemplated to be done by taking away the only safety we enjoy," she warned. "The women of Utah have never broken any law of that Territory, and it would be unjust as well as impolitic to deprive us of this right."

Zina followed, reinforcing what Emmeline had said and asking the women of the convention to aid us in our fight to retain the ballot.

Sara Spencer spoke in support and reminded the delegates that even though the NWSA didn't support polygamy, it was "preferable to the licensed social evil, which is being advocated by many of our bloated public men."

I paused to think about the 'licensed social evil' Sara was referring to, knowing it was prostitution, which was not illegal, and there was no interest in Congress changing that. The hypocrisy of it came rushing to my mind. Members of Congress often referred to the practice of polygamy as barbaric and had passed laws making it illegal, while turning a blind eye to the evils of prostitution and women being sold as sex slaves. *There's something wrong with this picture.*

Emmeline's remarks prompted the convention to draft a resolution for President Hayes, in which the women reproved the government for refusing "to exercise federal power to protect women in their citizen's right to vote in the various States and Territories," and chastised them for permitting the "exercise of federal power to disenfranchise the women of Utah."

A bold declaration, I thought, thankful for the support of our sister suffragists in the East. Emmeline and Zina were appointed to join Sara Spencer, along with Matilda Gage, to present this and other NWSA resolutions to President Hayes.

Perhaps not surprisingly, the American Women's Suffrage Association (AWSA), that Lucy Stone headed, used their publication *Woman's Journal* to ridicule the National organization for admitting Mormon women.

Matilda Gage, who was also editor of the *National Citizen* and *Ballot Box*, defended our attendance at the convention and said, "It ill becomes the *Woman's Journal* to cast a slur upon those women whose married life is not in accord with its ideas of right, for Lucy Stone's own married life... is a protest against the laws of marriage as recognized by the Christian Church and the Commonwealth of Massachusetts."

Before meeting with President Hayes, Emmeline and Zina worked on the declaration they planned to make on behalf of the Church of Jesus Christ of Latter-day Saints. This memorial was to be read in both houses of Congress, and they chose their words carefully. "The best outcome," Emmeline said as the two women worked on the resolution, "would be the full repeal of the Morrill Act, but given the recent Supreme Court ruling, the hope that Congress will overturn it seems fruitless."

So, short of that, Emmeline penned the memorial to state that she was asking Congress to "enact such legislation as will securely legitimize our children and protect our names from dishonor by preserving unbroken the existing relationship of families." That seemed an essential protection for the families in our church who still practiced polygamy in the Utah Territory. Without such legislation, existing families might be ripped apart, the women left without support, and the men jailed. That would serve no one.

I didn't accompany Emmeline and Zina over the next three weeks as they visited members of Congress, but I recorded their observations when they shared them with me at the end of each day. Emmeline complained that Senator Allen G. Thurman refused to even put the petition before the senate which I found appalling.

Zina said that when they met with Attorney General Charles Devens, his response was much the same, and she called him "a crusty old bad man." That made me laugh.

"But," Zina continued, "he got some wholesome truths from us."

I was proud of their resilience and courage as they endured rejection.

The next step was to present our memorial to the President, and this time, I was invited to go along. Emmeline began the conversation by charging him with neglecting the women of the country in his annual messages. Then she presented the petition on polygamy.

He appeared sympathetic, and said, "These words have proven to me the misery that would follow if the Morrill Act is not repealed." He asked his wife Lucy to come meet us and invited Emmeline and Zina to present their important matters to the Lady of the White House. She listened and spoke to us in a sisterly manner.

"Lucy Hayes was very polite," Emmeline said that evening, "and she is a lovely woman. The kindness which we received from her, and other noted women, always will remain a pleasant memory of my first visit to the national capitol."

I sensed a sub-rosa aversion on the part of President Hayes and suspected he would oppose even our modest appeal. But we had done what we had come to do, and Emmeline had proven herself an expert in winning friends and building bridges for our Latter-day Saint sisters.

On the train ride home, Emmeline said, "I thank God I was the first to represent our women in the Halls of Congress. This has been a pivotal life experience for me."

Zina said, "I hope I have said nothing wrong."

"You did very well, my dear," Emmeline reassured her. "Upon our return home, we will take up the subject of the ballot more energetically in its general sense than ever before through our continued public speaking and writing."

I knew she'd be true to her word.

Emma

Emma was reading a recent article that had been reprinted in the *Deseret News* titled, 'The Mormon Question in Congress.' She was intrigued by the position of the *New York Graphic* newspaper, which declared that they'd been moved by the "plea of the lady delegates from Utah."

"Listen to this," she said to Wesley.

"Now we see the question of putting down polygamy is not a simple question of putting down a crime. A whole society is based upon this custom, which has existed for more than a generation. Endeavor to root it out with fire and sword and you break the bonds of society, you make paupers of the industrious, wealthy, and self-supporting persons; you declare thousands of women who are innocent of any intentional wrong to be common harlots, and you condemn innocent children to bear the infamous brand of illegitimacy. Granting that polygamy is

now and has been a crime, is this not too great a price to pay
for its suppression?

"It's well put, and I believe their assessment is correct," Emma said.

"I ran into Thomas in downtown Salt Lake yesterday, and he told me that following the ladies' visit, the Judiciary Committee drafted a bill to legitimize the offspring of plural marriage up to a certain date, which also authorized the president to grant amnesty for past polygamy offenses that are now against the law."

"That's welcome news."

"Our legislative representative George Q. Cannon didn't urge passage of the bill."

"Do you know why not?"

"He and others who influenced him were apparently not ready to concede that polygamy had been declared an illegal practice despite the Supreme Court Ruling."

"I hope they don't come to regret that decision."

A knock came at the door. "That must be our man," Emma said. They were waiting for their latest job applicant to arrive, having already interviewed five candidates interested in working in their newly formed detective agency, 'The Defenders.' Emma loved the name they'd chosen.

"What's this one's name?" Wesley asked.

"Burt Savage."

When he came in, Emma noted that Mr. Savage was a man of about thirty with neatly trimmed brown hair, an attractive aquiline nose, and a deep white scar that ran down the side of his forehead. What impressed her about him was his genuine smile. *But would this man make a good detective?* "Tell us something about yourself," Emma said.

He looked directly at her when he spoke. "Might as well start with how I got this here scar on my face, since I seen the both of you lookin' directly at it. One day I was ridin' my horse along a dirt path next to a dry ditch when I spotted this n'er do well fella comin' toward me on foot. When he got up next to me, he pulled a gun, cocked it in my direction, and ordered me to climb down and empty my wallet. Weren't no way I was givin' my hard-earned cash to that varmint, so I pulled the reins back hard on my horse, makin' him rear up so high on his hind legs that the both of us almost went down. That's when I leaped off my horse backward, landing butt first right on top of the rascal and knocking him out."

"That was daring," Wesley said. "So how'd you get the scar?"

"When I got up, I stumbled on the root of a tree and hit my head on a rock. I survived, and the lowlife didn't."

"That's an incredible story and shows your bravery. What else qualifies you for a job as a detective?" Emma asked.

"I'm a hard worker, a quick thinker, and honest as the day is long. I served a Mormon mission in the Eastern states, so I know how to talk with all kinds of people, and I'm as loyal as they come."

"Say," Wesley asked, "aren't you the guy who got a commendation for a rescue you made up Logan canyon in the winter of '75? Your name sounds familiar."

"One and the same."

"What happened?" Emma asked.

"It was pouring rain and the lightning was flashing that day," Savage said.

The man loves telling a good story, and he remembers details, Emma thought.

"I watched this guy get throwed from his wagon when his mare stumbled in the mud. I could see his head was bleeding, and he looked badly injured. Just as I climbed down from my horse, a lightning bolt struck one of the wagon wheels, and it caught fire. I run over, pulled the man from the mud, and dashed away with him lickety split, just as the wagon burnt to a crisp. Never met a man as unlucky as that one."

"You risked your life to save his," Emma said.

"Anyone would a done the same thing," he said, coloring.

And he's modest, too. "No, actually there aren't many people who would risk their personal safety to rescue another," Emma said. "An unselfish act, in my book. Do you mind if I call you Burt?"

"Course not, ma'am."

"Are you working right now?" Wesley asked.

"I've been farmin' with my dad, but our crops failed this year, and I have a wife and two little ones to support. That's why I'm here, and I'm a quick learner."

"To be clear, you'd be reporting to my wife and not me. She's the Pinkerton Detective."

Burt let out a low whistle. "That's impressive," he said.

"How do you feel about reporting to a woman, Burt?" Emma asked him directly.

"Don't make no never mind to me, ma'am. I was raised with an older sister, and I spent my whole life listenin' to her tell me what to do."

Emma laughed. *He has a sense of humor as well. Him, I can work with.* "Would you mind stepping outside on our covered porch while my husband and I consult?"

"I'll just take a seat on one of them brown rockers."

When Emma and Wesley discussed their new applicant, they found they were of one mind about hiring him. "He'll require training," Emma said, "but I trust him, and integrity is the most important quality in my book."

Wesley agreed.

"Would you mind letting Burt know he's been hired, and I'll begin composing my resignation letter for the Pinkertons."

"Not at all," Wesley said, walking outside.

A minute later, Emma heard a whoop and a holler come from the porch. *Sounds like Burt is pleased with the offer of his new position.* She smiled.

Twenty

Katie

Ellis Shipp had established her medical practice in a room of the Old Constitution Building, a five-story, low rise structure that sat in the heart of downtown Salt Lake City. I was coming to meet with her to discuss joining her office. She had recently run an ad for her practice in the *Exponent* that read, 'Special attention given to obstetrics and diseases of women.' Ellis was devoting her efforts to the women and children of the city, and I wished to do the same.

She often said, "Society, through ignorance and sins of omission, is responsible for half of the infant mortality rate as well as for the many deaths and disabilities of mothers." It was a travesty that required correction.

When I reached her office, she welcomed me warmly. "Katie." She smiled. "It's such a pleasure to greet you again."

I hugged her and took a seat across the desk.

She asked first about Thomas. "Has he commenced his legal work?"

"He decided to join the VanCott practice after they made him a lucrative offer. It surprised me, because I've always thought of him as a defense attorney, but he assures me he'll have many wrongs to right working with businesses and litigation resolution."

"I'm certain he's right," Ellis said, handing me a paper. "Let's begin with a discussion of rates. Understand that some of my patients have little to no money to offer, so I charge $25, 'when convenient' for my services. That service includes prenatal care, delivery of the child, as well as ten follow-up home visits, and I sometimes cook and clean for the new mothers."

"It's a wonderful standard of care, Ellis."

"Thank you, Katie. I make it a rule to give every woman who comes under my care the same treatment that I would give my own daughter. I give the same care to the poor that I do to the rich, where I know I will get something for it. Do those conditions sound as though they will suit you?"

"They do."

"Then welcome to my practice," she said, taking my hand in hers.

"I'm delighted, thank you. Have you opened your School of Obstetrics and Nursing?"

"I've been teaching the first classes in my home and promoting the more progressive techniques of midwifery. As you know, in our faith, perhaps even more than in some others, our women wish to be attended by a woman when they give birth. There are three female doctors in town, and you and I are the only two delivering babies, so there still exists a great need for midwives."

"I understand the women's preference is shared by their husbands who consider it offensive for a male to attend a woman in childbirth."

"Precisely, and for thousands of pioneer babies, midwives such as Mother Sessions was the first voice they heard." She smiled. "Did you know that Patty Sessions continues to serve as a mid-wife in Bountiful? She's almost 84 years old."

"I didn't know she was still delivering babies. What a blessing she's been to many."

"If you're ready to get started, I have a patient for you to attend to. Her name is Esther Brown, and she has five children, the last of whom did not survive birth. I've been providing prenatal care, but

225

my time is limited with the new school and the care of my own children. I'm concerned about Esther's age and condition," Ellis said, "and I want to provide her with a doctor of your caliber. We experience success or failure with our patients in a matter of seconds."

"I'll stop by and see Esther on my way home."

"Thank you, Katie. Please tell her I sent you."

Twenty minutes later, I pulled my carriage in front of Esther's bungalow. When I knocked at the door, a man who I assumed to be her husband answered. He had a panic-stricken look on his face.

"Are you with the Relief Society?" he asked.

"No, I'm Doctor Katie. Ellis Shipp sent me."

"Thank the Good Lord," he said, opening the door. "Esther's gone into labor early."

"Please get me some soap and a pan of warm water," I said removing a bichloride solution from my medical bag.

"I'm Ben. Follow me."

When we reached her room, Esther's pupils were dilated, and she was clearly frightened out of her wits. "Who are you?" she asked.

Ben said, "This is Doctor Katie, and you'll be in good hands with her. She's a real doctor. I'll go fetch that warm water."

I took hold of her clammy hands and said, "I'm here to attend you."

"I'm so frightened, Dr. Katie. I lost my last one."

"Let's get you into this short undershirt and petticoat," I said, rifling through her closet. I found a pair of warm stockings and bedroom slippers and placed them on her feet. By that time, her husband had returned with soap and warm water.

We removed her dress, and she put on the undershirt and petticoat. I washed my hands with a chlorinated lime solution and cleaned the skin of her abdomen, thighs and external female parts, using the warm water. Then I applied the bio-chloride solution to prevent infection. I looked for a clean sheet that I tied to the bed post, so she could pull on it with each pain, knowing it would provide her with support. By now, night was coming on, so I lit a candle and offered a prayer in my heart.

Esther sat up in bed, screamed, and grabbed the sheet. "Push, Esther," I said.

She pushed several times, then the heavy bleeding started. No, no, no, I said to myself, reaching for a clean compress, noting that some of her membranes had ruptured. I staunched the bleeding, took out my stethoscope, and listened for the baby's heartbeat, noting fluctuations.

"I'm going to need forceps," I said, removing them from my bag.

Esther began to tremble through her pain. "That's how my baby died last time," she moaned.

"We're not going to lose him," I promised, noting that her cervix was fully dilated, and the baby had dropped into the birth canal. I reached gently in with the forceps and carefully maneuvered the baby out.

When I had him in my arms, I spanked his bottom lightly, started the all over cleaning, and he began to cry. I exhaled, not realizing I was holding my own breath. "You have a strong baby boy," I said, clipping the umbilical cord and handing him to his mother.

"He's fine," she exclaimed holding him close, "just fine. There's not even a bruise on his face. You're a miracle worker, Dr. Katie."

"Your new baby's the miracle." I smiled. "Let's remove that undershirt and petticoat and get you into a clean nightgown." When she looked comfortable, I asked, "Would you and Ben please join me in a prayer of gratitude?" They nodded and bowed their heads, as I offered a heartfelt prayer, knowing it's what Dr. Axel would have done. I rose from my knees, went into the kitchen, and made a pot of soup for the family.

An hour later, I bid them good-bye, letting them know I'd return for several post-natal visits. I wandered wearily from the house and sat in my carriage not moving a muscle. I knew more than anyone that mother and son had almost died. In the end, I'd been able to save both lives, and it was in that moment I knew in the very depths of my soul that being a doctor was my life's calling.

Emma

Dr. Axel had confirmed that Emma was carrying twins and determined one baby was a boy and the other a girl. As a physician well-skilled in the use of a stethoscope, he had the keenness of ear to detect a difference in faint sounds. He told Emma, "If the pulsations are in excess of 130, the child will most certainly be a girl; if less than that number, it will be a boy." After listening intently for a time, he smiled and said, "You have one of each." Emma and Wesley had been ecstatic.

Emma heaved her pregnant body onto a kitchen chair and took several deep breaths, exhausted. Next month, she was due to deliver. After discussing the impending birth of their babies at length, she and Wesley had decided to employ a midwife for the delivery, with Dr. Axel standing by in case of complications. He recommended Patty Sessions, telling them "Sister Sessions in not only an experienced and highly acclaimed midwife, but she's deeply spiritual as well. You can't go wrong with her."

Patty had agreed to travel the six miles to Farmington from Bountiful, where she'd lived for several years, having left Salt Lake to be nearer to family. Emma was alone in the house when she heard a carriage pull to a halt outside. Soon a knock came at the door. "Come in," Emma called from the couch. Must be Sister Sessions.

When she came through the door, Emma beheld a woman who had to be eighty years old, if she was a day. Her face was wrinkled and weathered, and she wore a dark bonnet that completely covered her hair with a navy bow tied under her chin. Her face had the gritty and determined look of someone who'd lived a long and trying life, but her eyes were alive and gentle.

"Please sit down, Sister Sessions," Emma said.

"Call me Aunt Patty; all my women do. If you don't mind me saying, you could pop any day, my girl."

Emma laughed and said, "I hope you're right because I can

228

barely maneuver around my own home. There's apple juice and cake on the counter that my husband Wesley prepared before he left for work, so please help yourself."

"Thank you, I will." Patty sat down and offered to tell Emma about her life as a midwife. "I've been doing midwifery since I was seventeen, and this year I'm 84. I still deliver three babies a week most weeks, and I earn about $2 a delivery. The year after I came to the Salt Lake Valley, I delivered 248 babies. I've kept track of every birth I've attended, and I've delivered over 3,000 babies with only two difficult cases."

"That's an impressive record, and you're a celebrated midwife. Would you mind disclosing the nature of one of those difficult cases?"

"You're a curious one, aren't you?"

"I'm afraid so." Emma smiled.

"It may be hard to hear in your condition."

"Nonetheless, I'd like you to tell me."

Patty reluctantly agreed. "Once back in 1853, I attended a woman by the name of Sister Roads. She was dangerously sick, and I soon found that I could do nothing for her. The child's arm was born before I was sent for. I then proposed to have a doctor. She said she'd been butchered once by a doctor, and she would not have a doctor. Neither would she have any lobelia to soothe her muscles.

"I remained with her all night, but the next day, things were no better and we became alarmed. We sent for the doctor, even though Sister Roads had refused, but he wasn't home. By the time he came, she was dead."

Emma looked stunned.

"Sister Roads's story will not be your story, my dear girl."

"I believe you're acquainted with Dr. Axel?"

"I am, and I have a great respect for him."

"He's agreed to be on hand in case I experience any difficulties."

"A wise contingency against the unexpected. Tell me a bit about yourself, Emma. Have you other children?"

"No, these two are my first, though I lost a baby to a miscar-

229

riage. My husband lost his leg in an accident, and Dr. Axel despaired that Wesley would never father children," Emma hurried on. "But then Horton Haight promised him in a blessing he would father children and that I would be a mother in Israel." Emma cried. *My emotions are so close to the surface, and I'm blathering.* She pulled herself together and said, "I'm looking forward to becoming the mother of little offspring, lavishing upon them my tenderness and affection."

"That you shall do, dear one, for you are under the protection of God's angels. I myself have had angelic visitations that are too sacred to discuss," she said, looking right through me. "Now, you must take yourself to bed. Let me assist you upstairs."

When they reached the bedroom, Emma's water broke, spilling onto the floor. She turned to Patty, a look of panic in her eyes. Her babies were coming almost a month early. It was only May 15.

"Never fear," Patty said. "You'll do fine, and while birthing your babies will be painful, it is well known that we women endure pain and sickness with more fortitude than men."

Several excruciating hours later, Patty held baby Wesley in one arm and Joyce in another, telling Emma she needed perfect quiet for the next several hours. When Wesley got home, Patty granted him a five-minute interview with Emma, then shooed him away downstairs.

"But she seems to be doing so well," he protested.

"However well she feels, she needs quiet. Excitement is dangerous, and no other visitors are permitted for the next several hours," Patty proclaimed firmly.

Under protest, Wesley did as he was told.

For the next two hours, Emma lay on her back with her lower limbs extended and her head low. Patty told her, "You may change to a side position as you desire, but for the first four days, you ought to lie upon your back as often as possible."

"How long must I wait before sitting up?"

"After the fifth day, you may sit propped up in bed with pillows behind you for an hour at a time. You should not sit up in a chair until the top of the womb has descended into the pelvic cavity which will occur sometime between the tenth and the fourteenth day. Even during the third and fourth weeks, you should lie down or recline upon a sofa much of the time."

Emma hoped she had the patience to do as she was told, and after nursing her little ones, dozed in and out. Patty cleaned the room, removed Emma's soiled clothes, and closed the door quietly behind her.

When Emma awoke several hours later, it was Grandmother Phoebe who brought Baby Joyce and Baby Wesley to her to nurse. "They're just beautiful, Emma," she said proudly, "and how precious. Which one was born first?"

Emma smiled. "Joyce came into the world fifteen minutes ahead of her brother," she said, pleased to see her beloved grandmother who had come to stay for a month to look after her and the babies. *We're a real family now.* For the first time since giving birth, Emma heaved a deep sigh of relief. *Thanks be to God.*

Twenty-One

Katie

I was riding the train to Ogden to listen to my friend, Romania Pratt, speak in the Ogden City Hall. She'd recently written an article for the *Exponent* stating that it was a 'woman's duty and privilege to do whatever she can that will promote the advancement and elevation of her sex.'

Along with Ellis and myself, Romania had become a busy practitioner of medicine, her specialty being eye and ear infirmities. A committee headed by Relief Society leader Zina D.H. Young, who was a midwife, had asked Romania to offer education in obstetrical science. She provided instruction at an office at the *Exponent* and had also begun advocating for the establishment of a local hospital.

Advertisements for Romania's classes had begun regularly appearing in the pages of the woman's paper, declaring,

> '*Mrs. Romania B. Pratt, M.D., continues her interesting and instructive free lectures to the Ladies' Medical Class every Friday afternoon, as usual, at this office. All ladies desirous of obtaining knowledge of the laws of life and how to preserve their health and rear children, how to determine the cases of illness, should improve these opportunities and not fail in punctuality.*'

I'd listened in on more than one class and found her a master teacher. Her articles on hygiene had become a regular feature in the paper that had grown in scope and influence under Emmeline Wells's editorship.

As the train chuffed along, I sat back my seat, closed my eyes, and was reminded of my new friend, Belva Lockwood, and her recent victory in Washington DC. On the motion of Washington Attorney Albert G. Riddle, who had long been her champion, Belva Lockwood had become the first woman admitted to the Supreme Court Bar in March of this year. It's about time! An article I read indicated she had recently been sworn in amidst 'a bating of breath and craning of necks.' Picturing the response of others to her bold move made me smile. *I miss my sister suffragists in the East.*

When I reached the train station, I disembarked and threaded my way carefully downtown. Though I passed several upscale restaurants, I was aware of Ogden's current rough and tumble character, and I determined to keep my wits about me. It was a city where one might witness gambling, robbery, and even the evils of prostitution on the streets. Ogden was a railroad town, and Emma told me it reminded her a good deal of Chicago.

By the time I reached City Hall, the auditorium had almost reached capacity, so I took a seat on the back benches. There was a large audience of women in attendance today.

When Romania stood to speak, she offered a commanding presence, and a hush fell over the auditorium. Her brown hair was pulled back from her face and dropped in ringlets to her shoulders. Her dress was yellow, and several of the rest of us wore yellow hats, ribbons, or banners.

I knew Romania to be an intelligent and determined woman as well as a caring mother. She'd told me once when we were in medical school that on one of her infrequent trips home that her two younger sons hadn't recognized her, which broke her heart. It took time for them to become reacquainted.

Romania began her address by speaking to the women about the importance of being self-sufficient, telling them, "Knowledge feeds and fattens on itself, and it is good to become self-sustaining and have a complete knowledge of some branch of work."

I looked about the room and noted her audience was listening in rapt attention, and many were nodding their heads.

Romania continued, "A woman must work her way up to the position she desires to fill in life, while keeping in mind that her mission as a mother is a sacred one."

That's one calling I have yet to fulfill, I thought, hoping it wouldn't be long before I had a child.

Romania turned her attention to suffrage. "Why not let capacity and ability be the test of eligibility to vote and not sex? Our duties as suffragists are to inform ourselves and instruct each other in the science of government, to interest all our friends in the movement, and convert our fathers, brothers, and husbands to the fact that we can understand and wield an intelligent power in politics, and still preside wisely and gracefully at home."

Romania was also an ardent suffragist and was concerned, as was I, about the political noise regarding taking away the woman's right to vote. I had learned lately that the liberal party in Utah was making plans to disenfranchise our women next year, asking that their names be removed from the voter rolls. One of those names was Emmeline B. Wells, who I knew would not take that assault on her rights sitting down.

I wanted to stand and cheer for Romania, but I contented myself with enthusiastic clapping along with the others. She finished her address, and I made my way through the crowd to the front of the room to say hello and congratulate her on a rousing speech.

She came forward and gave me a hug. "Katie," she said with enthusiasm, "I didn't see you in the auditorium, and I'm so pleased you came."

"I arrived just as the meeting began so I sat in the back. I had a post-natal visit this morning, and I reached here later than expected."

"It was good of you to come at all."

"I wouldn't have missed it. I was particularly gratified by your remarks on suffrage."

"I fear that over the course of the next few years that the federal government will succeed in taking away our right to vote."

"Having spent time in Washington earlier this year and observing the process, I'm quite certain you're right. We've been voting for several years now, and I'll be incensed if that vote is taken from us."

"And well you should be. I heard you went with Emmeline and Zina Williams to Washington, and I read some of the subsequent articles about the trip. I hope one day to attend an NWSA convention."

"You'd be an asset, and I believe you'd enjoy Susan B. Anthony in particular."

"I'd like to meet her. By the way, how's Ellis doing?"

"Extremely busy, just as you are. There's such a high demand for female doctors and midwives that we can't keep up with it all."

Out of the corner of my eye, I could see several women waiting to speak with Romania, and so I said, "I'll leave you to converse with the others and see you again at the *Exponent* offices for one of your classes. I've enjoyed reading your articles."

"Thank you, Katie."

Emma

Emma, Wesley and the twins were on their way to Salt Lake City to attend the General Conference Jubilee, celebrating the passage of fifty years since the Mormon Church had been organized in 1830. As they traveled the muddy roads in Grandmother Phoebe's large carriage, Emma held tightly to her precious now-ten-month-old little ones.

Wesley is a wonderful father, she thought looking at him. *He's very involved, and he adores the twins, which is a good thing, since it takes both of us to manage the babies.* Even changing diapers and washing them out was not beneath Wesley, and Emma and Katie had discussed how unusual that was for a male.

He had fashioned two highchairs for the twins that had turned legs, rails, stretchers, and a shaped seat. Each chair had a little footrest, and Wesley had bolted straps to the chairs to prevent Joyce and little Wesley from pitching out of the chairs headfirst. He even carved tiny birds into the arms which delighted the children, 'bird' being among their first words.

The little family planned to stay with Wesley's brother, Byron, and his wife, Virginia, in Salt Lake City during conference and were grateful when they at last reached the City and were able to get the children down for a nap.

The next day, the twins remained at home with Auntie Virginia and her three children while Emma and Wesley attended a preliminary meeting in the newly completed Assembly Hall downtown on Temple Square.

Emma looked about the room, impressed with the magnificent ceiling and its frescoes. It was a chilly day, and she was glad the building had been designed with steam heat. The hall was brilliantly lit, despite an overcast day, thanks to many gas lamps and a huge central gas chandelier. It was incredible. She spotted Thomas and Katie across the hall and waved.

They listened as Mormon Church President John Taylor announced the theme of the jubilee celebration. He reminded the 3,000 crowding the hall that in ancient Israel, the year of jubilee was celebrated by a time of general rejoicing and forgiveness in which debtors were released from their obligations and prisoners were set free. "In a like manner shall this modern-day jubilee find its celebration," he said.

Wesley and Emma looked at each other, not understanding what that really meant but knew there would be more to come tomorrow.

The following day, they sat in the drafty Tabernacle with no heat, along with at least 7,000 others. Emma was moved when President John Taylor stated, "In this year of jubilee we ought to do like the ancients and take off the yoke from those who are in debt to the Perpetual Emigration Fund, and unable to pay, and release them from their bondage."

236

Emma's eyes grew large when the actual sum was announced. It was proposed that the church remit half of the indebtedness to the fund which helped poor emigrants from all over the world come to the Salt Lake Valley. That indebtedness stood at $1,604,000. It was further explained that this action was to be taken for the benefit of the poor, and not for those who were able to pay. When the proposal was brought to a sustaining vote, the full congregation voted unanimously in favor of the motion. Emma knew what a blessing this would be for the poor among them.

After they left the Tabernacle, Emma and Wesley wandered down Main Street, avoiding the many grog shops that served beer and whiskey. The wide, tree-lined streets were dusty, rather than muddy, and Wesley commented that some of the downtown merchants were adding asphalteum in front of their stores, which was of particular benefit to the ladies. They stopped at the ZCMI store to purchase bows, ties, and new straw hats. Summer was fast approaching, and everything was at bedrock prices to suit the city and conference visitors.

"Let's stop at the Eagle Emporium," Emma said. "I need some new braid pins."

"Salt Lake is becoming a metropolis," Wesley commented as they walked. "At least in the downtown area, though I see a few cows on the loose over there." He laughed.

"Salt Lake City certainly has its fair share of bicyclists," Emma said, dogging a rider who had come onto the sidewalk with no regard for those on foot. "Bicycling has become a craze; perhaps I should get one myself."

"Emma, watch out," Wesley said as they began to cross the street, and the coach from Sandy went barreling by.

"I wish the stage drivers would be more careful," she said, dusting off her dress. "It's quite dangerous on these City streets. While I love visiting here, I prefer living in Farmington."

Wesley put his arm about her waist. "Emma, see this circular on the pole. A circus is coming to town this summer. There are to be bareback riders, a traeial cyclist, two giants, and a lion tamer who actually puts his head in a lion's mouth."

237

"That's either brave or foolhardy, and I can't decide which." She laughed. "Do you want to come back in July? We could attend both the circus and the July 24th parade."

"We should give that some thought," he said. "For now, let's get back to the twins."

Joyce and little Wesley would celebrate their first birthday in May, and Auntie Virginia and Uncle Byron wanted to begin the celebration today, so she had baked two cakes for the occasion. *How the time has flown*, Emma thought.

When they came inside, their precious little ones were crawling all over the house and up to no end of mischief, pulling pots and pans from the cupboards and pounding on them with spoons. Emma hugged them both and helped Auntie Virginia add a healthy layer of frosting to each cake, wondering what new toys she might buy for the twins.

She was grateful that their detective agency continued to thrive. Emma often said to Wesley, "Thank goodness for Burt Savage." She liked having Burt do the leg work and report his findings to her, leaving Emma to do the investigative research while the twins napped. She found that she enjoyed delegating to another some of the more unpleasant aspects of detective work.

Wesley came into the kitchen. "Today's party promises to be fun for young and old alike," he said, placing the children into chairs, scooting them up to the table, and tying safety dish towels around their waists. "Byron has agreed to play his fiddle, which will delight their three children as well as our twins." There promised to be plenty of singing and dancing today.

Emma's family was in town for conference as well, and Father—or Papa as the twins called him now—and Patricia would be coming to the party. Emma paused and wondered why she'd never referred to her stepmother as 'Mother,' but she'd always been Patricia. Now she was 'Gammy' to everyone, which she adored. David, who'd grown into a fine young man, was Uncle David. The twins loved it when he dropped to the floor on all fours and played 'horsey' with them, bucking and neighing to their small hands clapping. Grandmother Phoebe was coming, too.

After the party was over, and while the twins slept, the adults spoke of April Conference and the Jubilee celebration. "I understand," Emma's father said, "that following conference, thousands of head of sheep and cattle will be distributed to the worthy poor."

"It's a season of love and brotherhood," Wesley said.

"It's a time of love and sisterhood as well." Emma smiled. "The General Relief Society now numbers 300 local branches, and they go about doing charitable work for others."

"That's impressive," Wesley said.

"I've heard," Virginia said, "that Eliza Snow may be officially appointed General President of the Relief Society as early as June."

"I saw her shopping downtown at ZCMI this afternoon," Emma said, "her signature large pocket watch on a gold chain draping down her dress."

"Eliza is not only accomplished and meticulous, she's feminine and loves elegant, high-fashion clothes," Grandmother said.

"I didn't know that about her," Emma said.

"Sister Snow is an intellectual who leads by the force of her intelligence, and every word she uses is well articulated, even at the age of 76," Grandmother said, smiling.

"So true," Virginia said, eating another bite of cake.

Two months later, Emma read in a *Deseret News* article that Eliza Snow had been named as the new General President of the Relief Society, with Zina D. H. Young as her first counselor. She told Wesley, "Katie knows Zina Young as a midwife and has heard it said that Sister Zina is all love and sympathy, drawing people after her by reason of her tenderness."

"It sounds like the two women will be a good complement to each other."

"I appreciate these bold, outspoken, and spiritual women. No one can doubt that our women are intelligent, informed, and articulate. We deserve to retain the right to the ballot."

Emma and Katie were outraged as the managers of the Liberal Party in Utah actively engaged in a campaign to disenfranchise the women. The matter had been brought before the Supreme Court of the Territory on a 'writ of mandamus' to compel the Registrar of Salt Lake City to 'strike from the list of voters the names of the following persons: viz, Emmeline B. Wells, Martha M. Blythe, Mrs. A.G. Paddock, and others.'

Katie told Emma that Emmeline Wells was incensed, and Belva Lockwood had sent her a dispatch under the date of September 28, 1880, stating, "Stand by your guns. Allow no encroachment upon your liberties. No mandamus here."

Emma later read a communication in the *Woman's Exponent* from M. Isabella Horne, a woman of considerable character and force. Her communication on the mandamus:

> "*I wish to express my indignation at the movement now being made to disenfranchise the women of Utah, basing their argument on the very weak plea that women do not pay taxes. Now, I claim that women do pay taxes with their husbands, as they are partners in the property which they hold; for if the man dies, the woman is called on to pay taxes on that property, the same as before. It is not the individual that is taxed, but the property, whether owned by the man or the woman.*"
>
> "*Another plea is that women are not citizens. If not citizens, what in the name of common sense are they? Will some wise man, who knows more about women than women know about themselves, explain? Have not women labored hard and endured hardships to build up this Territory and make homes for their families? Their labors as citizens have been acknowledged by our legislators, and they gave them the right of franchise, which privilege they have enjoyed and honored for ten years. Now an opposition is made by one whose title should imply manhood—but witness the cowardice of the act to attack women whom men profess to defend.*"
>
> "*This affidavit asserts that women are not legal voters, demanding that the names of all women be struck off the registration list of voters. I cannot tell you with what contempt*"

I look upon men who seek to oppress the weak because they have the might. Shame on such an American citizen!'

Emma agreed with her compelling arguments, and when the matter was brought before the court, the court refused to mandamus the registrar to remove the names of women from the registration lists, and the women voted.

We've won this round, but there are more battles to be waged.

Twenty-Two

Katie

With cupped hands around my eyes, I peered out the window of our warm home at a daunting January blizzard. The snow was blowing across the roads, and I could hear the wind howling through the streets of the Avenues. I shivered and wrapped up in a blanket on the sofa, wondering if Romania Pratt, Zina Young, and Ellen Ferguson were faring any better in the New York weather.

The three ladies were attending the Woman's Suffrage Convention and I was disappointed I'd been unable to accompany them. I had several patients who were due to deliver babies, and they were my priority.

Thomas came into the room and placed a steaming cup of chamomile tea with honey in front of me. "Thought you could use this."

I smiled at his generosity and thanked him. "Do you have a moment?" I asked.

"Of course." He sat next to me on the sofa.

"I can offer better assistance to more women if I join the staff at the soon to be completed Deseret Hospital," I said putting the cup down. "What do you think?"

"I read where the Catholic sisters had decided to vacate St. Mary's Hospital, and I believe the Relief Society took over the building?"

"Under the direction of Eliza Snow, the women have been accumulating operating funds and purchasing the necessary supplies to open a new hospital."

"A sizeable undertaking. Where did they acquire the financing?"

"From a variety of sources, including subscriptions, donations from primary children, and even benefit concerts. In-kind contributions have produced blankets, pillows, quilts, and towels."

"I imagine fundraising will need to be an ongoing effort. Do you know when the hospital is scheduled to open?"

"July of this year, and Martha Hughes will be joining the staff as a physician."

"Your friend from the *Exponent*?"

"Yes." I smiled, remembering our collaboration with fondness. "After graduating from medical school, Mattie came home and opened a private practice in a new wing of her old house that her stepfather built. She'll be moving to the new hospital, and I'd like to join her. Romania and Ellis will serve there as well."

"An outstanding assembly of female doctors," Thomas smiled. "You're a credit to your profession, Katie," he said, placing his arm about my shoulder.

"Thank you," I said, anxious to add 'mother' to the top of my medical resume. I had been trying to get pregnant since we married with no success. A few false starts, no results, though we hadn't lost hope. My mother had been slow to conceive and still bore four children.

"It seems to me," Thomas continued, "that joining the staff of the hospital will also provide you with more flexibility, allowing you time to help with the suffrage movement. I know you regret not being in New York with the others this month."

"I do," I said wistfully.

I later read a letter Romania wrote to the *Exponent* about her time at the Woman's Suffrage convention and especially loved her description of Susan B. Anthony that fit her to a tee.

Romania wrote: *Everybody who is not as mean and green with prejudice and jealousy, as a tomato worm, cannot help admiring and liking Miss Anthony. If she is terse and decided and hits the nail a peeling clip square on the top of the head, is not that the way to do, when we are in dead earnest to accomplish anything?*

Miss Anthony would be pleased that women were being elected to assist in preparing a new constitution, once again urging Congress to admit Utah as a State. Participation in the convention will be a new departure for women, and I have no doubt it will be good political discipline, especially in parliamentary law and usage.

Thomas said, "I hope we have more success in achieving statehood than we did ten years ago in 1872. The effort to be admitted as a state is even more urgent with the impending passage of the Edmunds Act. Congress is expected to approve it in March. I've heard from my friends in Washington that President Arthur doesn't want to sign the bill, but he won't veto it either, so it will pass into law. The bill will place Utah's electoral process in the hands of the President."

"It goes without saying that many men and women in Salt Lake City are supporting the Edmunds Act in order to take away the vote from polygamous men and women."

"These are divisive times."

"Wouldn't it be wonderful if Congress passed a bill outlawing prostitution, forbidding anyone who practiced it to vote? There's a cause worth fighting for."

Thomas laughed. "If that happened, I imagine the nation would lose several congressmen."

"I believe you're right."

"I knew you were an activist when I married you, and I proudly back your efforts. Keep up the good work."

I kissed him, grateful for the way he supported me.

A few months later, Thomas and I went to the Salt Lake City Hall and sat in the back of the room at a legislative assembly meeting where a joint resolution was passed authorizing a constitutional convention to begin April 8, 1882. For the first time, among the seventy-two delegates, there would be three women who would take part in framing the new constitution: Mrs. Emmeline Wells, Mrs. Sarah M. Kimball, and Mrs. Elizabeth Howard. "We will be well represented," I whispered to Thomas.

The delegates to the convention met for seventeen days before the convention adopted the constitution. Emmeline assured me that the women's work was every bit as satisfactory as that of the male members, and there was no friction between the groups whatsoever, which I found gratifying.

I had the opportunity to vote on the proposed constitution in May, and it was ratified by the people of Utah on the 22nd of the same month. A memorial was submitted to Congress asking for admission to statehood, and we held our collective breaths waiting for a response. But Congress offered no response, so statehood was denied.

I was sorely disappointed, but not surprised. Setting my suffrage concerns aside the moment, I began preparing to move my practice to the hospital.

Franklin D. Richards dedicated the Deseret Hospital in July of 1882 with Eliza Snow, President; Zina D.H Young, Vice-President; and Emmeline Wells, secretary. Romania Pratt was a member of the Executive board, being a visiting surgeon for the eye, ear, nose, and throat. Dr. Ellen B. Ferguson was the resident physician and surgeon. *A hospital funded, opened, and run by women is unheard of—and yet here we are.*

Martha Hughes helped set up training classes for nurses and lectures on obstetrics and a few months later replaced Ellen as the resident physician. During our first months of operation, the hospital served, on average, between 12 and 20 patients a month. We treated illnesses such as typhoid fever, rheumatism, diphtheritic tonsillitis, and other maladies.

I lost my first patient to typhoid. Mary was a young mother with a husband and three children. He brought her to the hospital with a fever that worsened in the evening, a general malaise with headache, a furred tongue with red edges and tip, and a relatively slow pulse. Her symptoms fit the words Eberth used to describe the typhoid bacillus two years ago. Since we had no vaccine for typhoid, I isolated her from others and watched her closely keeping her as comfortable as possible.

A few weeks later Mary became agitated and delirious. Her husband Jim and I were in the room, each of us holding one of her hands when she passed. He sobbed, laid his head on her chest, and I stood helplessly by, watching his anguish. That night as I grieved over her untimely death, my brother Adam's passing returned to my mind, and the nightmares of his death began again.

A week later Romania asked to speak with me. "You seem distressed, Katie," she said. "Does this have anything to do with the recent death of your patient?"

"I trained to be a doctor so I could spare lives, not lose them, Romania. I tried everything I knew to do," I said, looking down at my hands.

"We do whatever is humanly possible, Katie. When I lost a patient, I was forced to realize that my patients have a Savior—and it's not me."

I looked at Romania. For the first time I realized that I'd held myself accountable for the life and death of others ever since we'd lost Adam.

"My dear Katie," she said, taking me in her arms. "It's not your fault that Mary died. You did everything any of us would have done. The patients are in our Lord's hands, and while we do our best to assist Him, sometimes all we can do is hold fast to our faith in a life beyond this one."

I stood and hugged Romania. That was the last dream I had about Adam.

Emma

Emma received Katie's letter about her patient's death from typhoid. *Katie has always been hard on herself when it comes to caring for others. May this new perspective relieve her pain.*

246

The following morning, Emma was in her office waiting for Burt Savage. She'd sent him to investigate a rancher by the name of Jim Marshall who lived a few hundred miles south of Salt Lake City around Panguitch. Emma and Wesley had received reports from some of the local ranchers that Marshall may be up to no good, and they were paying the agency to investigate. Burt had hired on at the Marshall ranch to see what he could find out.

When Burt arrived, he was tired from the long and dusty trip to Farmington. Emma offered him biscuits, cheese, and water. "Thank you, Mrs. Emma," he said. "I'm hungry and a mite parched, but boy howdy did I learn some good stuff." He took another swig of water.

Emma filled his cup again. "Do tell."

"The local ranchers sure as shootin' don't trust him, that's fer sure. One of 'em told me, 'I wouldn't trust him out of my sight, or in my sight, if his back was towards me. Sin and debauchery are plainly written all over him.' And I have to say as how I agree with him."

"Sounds like a sinister character," Emma said, making notes. "What does he look like?"

"Has a hatchet shaped face, tall, with beady eyes that are set close together. And he abuses the drink."

"What do you think he's up to?"

"If I had to guess, I'd say cattle rustling."

"How did you reach that conclusion?"

"A small-time outlaw by the name of Mike Cassidy who steals cattle is also workin' on the Marshall ranch. Looks like he's got his-self a young apprentice, name of Robert Leroy Parker."

"I've heard of Mike Cassidy, but not Parker. What do you know of him?"

"His mother, Annie, oversees the Marshall dairy ranch, and af-ter I gained her trust, she flat out told me it was Cassidy that give Robert a pistol and taught him how to use it. Annie also said as how she feared Cassidy had taught her son some of the finer points of cattle rustling."

"Such as?"

"Usin' a creative branding iron."

"What's Annie like?"

"God-fearin' woman. She's devout in her Mormon religion and loves her family. Robert is the oldest of her thirteen young uns."

"Sadly, it sounds as if he's headed down the wrong path."

"Yep, but it may not be the first time."

"What else do you know of his exploits?"

"Three years ago, at the raw age of thirteen, Robert Parker had his first run-in with the law. Word is he let hisself into a closed shop, stole a pair of jeans, and left a note sayin' as how he'd come back later to pay for 'em. The clothier pressed charges anyhow, and Parker was arrested, though he was later acquitted by a jury. Accordin' to his mama, that run in with the law left him angry with the legal system and any people in authority over him."

"I'd say he has the beginnings of a desperado."

"His mama agrees with you. After she told me she was sure somethin' shady was goin' on at the Marshall Ranch, she said she planned to take Robert, and move the two of em' back to the Parker Ranch in Circle Valley."

"I fear the die has been cast for young Robert Leroy Parker," Emma said taking notes, "and we may eventually learn he's turned to a life of crime."

"Might take him a few years, but he'll get there."

"Are you at the point where we should send the local sheriff out to the Marshall Ranch and check on Mike Cassidy?"

"I reckon we should give it another month or so, while I work on diggin' up more dirt."

"No one suspects you're working undercover?"

"No, ma'am. You know me; I'm sly as a fox."

Emma smiled. "Yes you are, Burt. Keep a close watch on all of them and tell the local sheriff when you're ready."

"I will. Think we got ourselves a bad combination here." Burt tipped his hat and walked out the door.

Emma looked at the grandfather clock. It was almost time to pick up Joyce and little Wesley, but she had one more stop to make on her way to Christina's. It was with a heavy heart that she walked several blocks to the Horton Haight home to tell Louisa and her family good-bye. Louisa had acted as both an aunt and mentor to Emma, and she would miss her.

Emma's father told her that President John Taylor had called Horton at the age of fifty to move to Idaho and preside over a ward congregation in the Goose Creek Settlement area near Oakley. Of course he'd agreed to go, and Louisa had as well, reportedly quoting from the Book of Ruth proclaiming, "Whither thou goest, I will go," even though she was well aware that she was leaving behind a beautiful home, farmlands, friends, and a comfortable life.

This move will be not be easy, Emma thought, admiring Louisa's faith and that of her family. They were all going to Idaho, even the married children. It was back to the dust and the sagebrush for them, and they faced a long and tedious journey to the place where Horton and his sons had already built log cabins. Emma imagined that in addition to her community and friends in Farmington, Louisa might miss serving in the primary most of all.

When Emma reached the Haight home, Aurelia Rogers was already there. She held in her hands a touching document for Louisa that she said had been designed and executed with pen and India ink by Professor A. J. Phelps of Bountiful.

Across the top of the framed document, printed on what looked like a flowing ribbon, were the words 'Con Amore,' which Emma knew meant 'with love.' On the top left, a small ribbon with the word 'Farmington,' and on the top right, 'July 8, 1882.'

The bottom middle of the document held another beautifully designed ribbon with the word 'friendship,' and to the left and right of the ribbon the poem:

True friendship is a gordian knot.
Which angel hands have tied.
By heavenly skill its texture wrought.
Who shall its folds divide.

249

Aurelia read the rest of the document aloud to all who had come to bid Louisa a fond farewell:

> '*A Testimonial presented to Mrs. Louisa Haight by the Farmington Primary Association of Davis County. In consideration of the great Care, Love and Kindness she has manifested while serving as the first counselor to Aurelia S. Rogers, which she did since its organization August 11, 1878. As duty requires you to labor in another part of the vineyard, you will please accept this as a token of the love and esteem in which you are held by us. And we assure you that you will always live in our hearts as a noble, kind, and dear friend.*'

Sister Rogers presented the testimonial to Louisa.

Louisa's tears ran freely as did Emma's and most of the women present.

"Do you recall that first eventful day our primary was formed?" Aurelia asked Louisa.

"The local citizens who passed the meetinghouse reported hearing the children singing the songs of angels."

"Oh, how I shall miss you, dear friend," Aurelia said, and the two embraced one more time.

As Emma looked at Louisa, she thought of the blessing she and Wesley had received at Horton's hands. Such a miracle that turned out to be.

Twenty-Three

Katie

This time it was certain. I was pregnant for the first time at the age of 28 years old, and the gratitude and joy that filled my heart was indescribable. I couldn't wait to tell Thomas the news, so I left work at the hospital and caught a streetcar to his law office. The sun came out from behind the clouds, and the day glowed April warm.

When the streetcar stopped a very long Salt Lake block away from my destination, I exited, hoisted my skirts, and made a dash for it. I must have passed someone I knew because I heard a woman's voice call out, "Dr. Katie?" She sounded surprised, likely because I wasn't given to running through the streets. I waved over my shoulder but didn't stop to chat. A few moments later I arrived breathless, my hat askew.

Thomas was standing in the foyer with one of his law partners. He came to my side concerned, saying, "Katie, are you quite well?"

"Better than I've been in quite some time," I said, grinning from ear to ear. "Let's go to your office."

When I gave him the news, he danced a little jig the likes of which I hadn't seen before, and it made me laugh. He embraced me, our hearts beat as one, and somewhere inside another little heartbeat joined us.

Several weeks later, I read a full report of the Sixteenth Annual National Woman's Suffrage Convention in Washington March 1884. This was the first time the report had appeared in pamphlet form, and it included information on the hearings before Congress, legislative debates and action, along with suffrage reports from each state. It was interesting reading, though not the same as being present in the room when issues were debated and indignation ran high.

In a short opening address, Miss Anthony alluded to the progress made in the cause both in the Old World and the New. While abroad, she and Mrs. Stanton had attended several meetings in England and Scotland, and they reported the status of the question on that side of the water. Miss Anthony said that the right of suffrage was granted there in municipal and school matters which was only given to widows and spinsters. "A high premium," continued Miss Anthony, "do they offer to spinsterhood and widowhood."

I read on, pleased to learn of the women's latest victory in the Washington Territory granting women the right to suffrage. That victory had been heralded by every newspaper in America, England, and France.

Miss Anthony went on to remark that there had been "great progress in public sentiment within the year." As proof of it she had received a message from the New York Evening Telegram, asking for a hundred-and-fifty-word special by wire, giving the names of the noted women present. She was gratified, stating, "This is the first indication that a convention of women was of as much importance as a meeting of workingmen."

I applauded her words from the comfort of my sofa, alone in my house. I missed being in the company of these courageous and outspoken women, but I wouldn't trade it for being with child.

I checked the clock, noting that Thomas was due home for dinner soon. The pamphlet was 226 pages long and handsomely bound in a volume. I skipped to the report on the last day of the convention and read Miss Anthony's remarks to the Senate Select Committee on Woman Suffrage.

This is the sixteenth year that we have come before Congress in person, and the nineteenth by petitions. Ever since the war, from the winter of 1865-'66, we have regularly sent up petitions asking for the national protection of the citizen's right to vote when the citizen happens to be a woman. We are here again for the same purpose.

The pamphlet also reported her words to the House of Representatives, and she began her statement this way:

We appear before you this morning...to ask that you will, at your earliest convenience, report to the House in favor of the submission of a Sixteenth Amendment to the Legislatures of the several States, that shall prohibit the disfranchisement of citizens of the United States on account of sex.

I had always believed that the act of voting was a basic human right and not confined to men. *How much longer will an amendment take?* I wondered, knowing we had even greater cause for concern in Utah with the passage of the Edmunds Act two years ago.

I laid my reading aside when Thomas came through the door with a kiss and words of solicitation. He'd grown very protective since the news of my pregnancy, though I assured him all would be well. I was taking good care of myself despite working long hours at the hospital.

My stomach grumbled as we sat down to a simple meal of vegetables, fruit, cheeses, and breads. Growing up, I had left the task of cooking to Aunt Ada who considered the kitchen her domain and didn't welcome what she saw as interference from me. I didn't mind, finding debates with Father more engaging than whisking eggs.

Now that I was eating for two, Thomas and I wanted our meals to be as healthy as possible, and we took turns making them, typically dining late.

****

I'd been in bed in the Deseret Hospital for several days when the long-awaited moment finally arrived, and I gave birth to a baby boy on October 12, 1884. Martha Hughes Cannon delivered him, and I was pleased to have her attend me. She'd married Angus Cannon the week prior, becoming his fourth wife in a polygamous marriage. My birthing went without complication, thanks in large part to her skills and experience. The pain I endured gave me a new appreciation for the women whose babies I'd delivered. I'd never experienced such intense pain, but it was well worth it when I saw the face of my baby boy. For the first time, I understood the depth of my own mother's love for me and my brothers.

We named our boy Joshua Leavitt Forrest. Thomas and I lived by the scripture found in Joshua 24:15 in the Bible: 'Choose you this day whom ye will serve; but as for me and my house, we will serve the Lord.' That passage was one of Father's favorites as well, and I heard it quoted often growing up. I remained in the hospital a few days, taking my time recuperating before going home.

Father, Andrew, and Jacob came by to visit. My brothers were excited to be uncles, and Father was over the moon about being a grandfather again. Joseph and his wife had two children and still resided in Southern Utah and none of us saw them as often as we wanted.

Thomas brought his mother to see the baby. Rebecca was thrilled with her new grandchild, and 'oohed' and cooed over him, stroking his little face gently. I knew she'd help with the baby when I needed and counted it a blessing having her close.

After everyone left, I held Joshua in my arms, snuggled him under the covers, and the two of us slept soundly, side by side.

Emma

Emma was at home, reading Katie's letter telling about the birth of little Joshua. She grinned at Katie's words, anxious to go visit the two of them. *Perhaps Sunday,* she thought, setting Katie's letter aside and re-reading a letter she'd received a few weeks ago from Rosemary Shaw.

Emma had read in both Rosemary's letter and the newspapers that Alan Pinkerton had died July 1, 1884, and according to Rosemary, there appeared to be some question as to the cause of his death. She wrote that while he'd developed a case of malaria and had recently suffered a stroke, in the end he'd perished from gangrene of the tongue.

Such a strange way to die, Emma thought, *after escaping so many harrowing experiences with criminals.*

Rosemary wasn't certain how Alan had injured his tongue, but the most talked about story in town was that he tripped and fell to the concrete after his wife's poodle wrapped its leash around his legs. When he hit the ground, he severely bit his own tongue, and the gangrene set in.

Emma had always held Alan Pinkerton in high regard. It was he who had given her and many other women an opportunity when no one else was hiring females. Emma found Alan to be without prejudice when it came to hiring women and Negroes. *A pioneer in his own time,* Emma thought.

As she read on in Rosemary's letter, Emma was sadly not surprised to learn that after his father's death, Robert Pinkerton had finally gotten his way and closed the Women's Department. He had used his time-worn justification that the men's wives did not want their husbands working with women. Emma didn't believe that lame excuse for a moment. She'd worked with Robert and could sense his inherent disregard for women with brains whose capacities exceeded his own.

Alan would have been disappointed in his sons, Robert and Will. Will had worked with the first female Pinkerton, Kate Ware, and he seemed to admire her capabilities, just as his father had. But Will was obviously no match for Robert.

Now there were many women in Chicago with no visible means of support, and one of them was Rosemary. In her letter she'd asked Emma if she'd be willing to consult with her on cases, and Emma was happy to oblige, though she wasn't sure where she'd find the time.

Rosemary had included a confidential case she was investigating with her team and was seeking Emma's opinion. It involved George Westinghouse, who had this year opened a new plant in Pittsburgh, Pennsylvania, and hired 200 employees for the purpose of building an electric infrastructure across the country. Westinghouse advocated the use of Alternate Current, rather than the Direct Current that Thomas Edison was utilizing for the same purpose.

"I see the problem here," Emma said aloud. "We have two inventors who are also titans of industry whose money and reputations are both on the line." Westinghouse had hired Rosemary's firm to investigate Edison's claims that AC current was dangerous.

Would you be willing to come to Chicago and brainstorm with us? Rosemary asked. *I'd be happy to pay your ticket here, and you could stay with me. When we get paid for our work, I'll pay you a portion.*

Five-year-olds Joyce and little Wesley banged on the office door and burst into the room, making Emma smile. "Whatever is the matter?" she asked, laying Rosemary's request aside. It was always something with Emma's two little ones. Though they loved each other dearly, they were highly competitive.

"Wesley took my pencils and won't give them back," Joyce complained.

"Joyce won't share," little Wesley shot back.

"There are sufficient pencils to go around," Emma said, rummaging through the desk as Wesley came through the door.

"I have refreshments in the kitchen," he said, "for children who know how to behave themselves."

"I know how to behave," the twins said in unison, raising their hands.

"I said it first," Joyce said.

"No, you didn't," her brother retorted. "I did."

Wesley rolled his eyes and said, "Father has snacks in the kitchen. If you want some, each of you take hold of my hand and close your lips tightly," which they did. The three of them put fingers to their lips, making a hushing sound, looking in Emma's direction. It wasn't the first time they'd performed that little antic, nor would it be the last, but they knew it made Mommy laugh.

Before Emma could return to Rosemary's proposal, Burt Savage knocked at the door. It was time for his monthly update, and he was always prompt. "Come in, Burt," Emma said, motioning him inside and inviting him to sit in the chair across the desk. "May I get you something to eat or drink?"

"Nothing for me, thanks, Mrs. Emma."

After dispensing with a report on several petty criminals who'd been brought to justice, Burt returned to Jim Marshall's young protégé, Robert Leroy Parker. He seemed to have an intense interest in this budding new criminal.

"What's he up to now?" Emma asked.

"It seems that after the young fella reached the age of eighteen in June, he couldn't wait to leave home. Annie told me she'd tried to persuade her son to stay, but he claimed he wanted work that would bring him 'hard, solid gold.' The Parker family's real poor."

"Sounds as if young Parker is battling against his own greed."

"You'd be right about that, and I think he'd stop at nothin' to get him some gold."

"Did you ever meet Parker? Can you give me a description?" Emma always took notes when she met with Burt, and she'd started a small case file on 'Robert Parker from Circleville, Utah.'

"Just once. He's a good-looking fella, average height, sandy hair, blue eyes that can look right through a man, and a rapid-fire way of speakin'."

"Where's Parker going after he leaves home?"

"Him and a friend of his by the name of Eli Elder are gettin' themselves ready to head out fer what some see as the land of promise in the rough old mining town of Telluride, Colorado. Fella by the name of Matt Warner, a good old Utah cowboy, claims that Parker stole him a couple of horses from a neighbor, but I couldn't find no corroboration for that story. His mama don't believe it."

"Not that she's a reputable source when it comes to her son. Now we have two undocumented stories of thievery about Robert Parker. My belief is that where there's smoke, there's usually fire."

"A thief and a gambler too, I reckon, Mrs. Emma. Mike Cassidy taught Parker about horses, so I'm guessin' Robert knows enough to gamble on the horse racin' game in Telluride. He could take up ranch work of some sort or another to support himself, or maybe hire on with the mines, but I don't see his sort lasting as a miner."

"Well, if he leaves Utah, I suppose he becomes Colorado's problem," Emma said.

"Yes, Ma'am, but he still has family here, so I reckon he'll be back to the Utah area from time to time," Burt advised. "There's one other thing I got to tell you about him."

"Do go on, please."

"Makes me suspicious that he's takin' to usin' an alias. Heard tell he was planning on changing his name to Ed Cassidy, using Mike's last name, to save his family the embarrassment of using their last name."

"You're right to be suspicious, Burt, not a good sign." Emma was pleased with her protégé's work. He'd become an excellent detective.

"Parker has lately come by another alias with a different first name than Ed. There are those that now call him Butch cause he's said to be skilled at butcherin' hogs. Mark my words, Mrs. Emma, we've haven't heard the last of Mr. Butch Cassidy."

"Given his proclivity for crime, and his family connections in Utah, I think he remains our problem," Emma said. "Keep an eye on him and get in touch with the Colorado authorities."

"Will do, Mrs. Emma," he said, shaking her hand and walking out the door.

Twenty-Four

Katie

It had been a long and tiring day for me at the hospital. Rebecca was watching Joshua, and she'd offered to feed us all an early dinner at her home this evening. Our little monkey was two years old now, talking in complete sentences and as curious as they came. Thomas and I were proud of his little mind that sometimes worked so fast his words couldn't keep up. Every time I asked him to do something, the eternal question, was "Why, Mommy? Why?"

On my way to Rebecca's, I picked up a copy of the *Deseret Evening News*, March 2, 1886. I opened it on the streetcar, thumbed through the pages, and found that a mass protest meeting would be held four days hence in the Salt Lake City Theatre "for the purpose of making known the grievances of the women of Utah."

Federal officials were again threatening to undo our suffrage rights with the Edmunds-Tucker Bill now pending in Congress. The Congress was persistent in its efforts to halt the practice of polygamy, and if the bill became law next year, all Utah women would lose the right to vote. There was no doubt that I would participate in the protest.

Confident that Emma would want to attend as well, I got off the streetcar and walked to the telegraph office. I sent a telegram asking her to accompany me. She replied the next day in the affirmative, stating, "I'll meet you in front of the Salt Lake Theatre Saturday afternoon."

The following Saturday, Emma and I, along with a few thousand others, assembled for the protest meeting in the Salt Lake Theatre. We settled into our seats with a sense of anticipation. I looked around the huge theatre thinking that I typically came here to enjoy plays and be entertained, but today we were making a 'play' of another sort. I smiled at my own pun.

Isabella Horne, Stake Relief Society President in the Salt Lake Stake, delivered the opening address. She began by letting us know that Eliza Snow was absent from the city today but had sent a letter stating that "she was heart and soul in the movement of the hour."

President Horne began her address, saying, "It is with peculiar feelings that I stand before you this afternoon. To think that in this boasted land of liberty there is any need for a meeting of this kind to protest against insult and injury from those who have sworn to administer the law with justice and equity. It has been said by some: what good will it do to hold a mass meeting? If it does no other good, it will be a matter of history, to be handed down to our posterity, that their mothers rose up in the dignity of their womanhood to protest against insults and indignities heaped upon them."

I knew history mattered, believing that our deeds and written words were the best way to communicate our thoughts to subsequent generations. I wished my mother had left me with a journal of her life's story; there was so much I wanted to ask her about this stage in my own life and how best to manage its challenges.

At the close of the president's address, I was pleased to hear Romania make a motion that a committee on resolutions be appointed, and so it was. She was placed on the committee with several others.

Several speakers followed, though Mattie wasn't among them, having left for England a while ago with her first child, Elizabeth, in order to avoid a federal warrant requiring her to testify against polygamist women whose babies she'd delivered. If Mattie had been here, I had no doubt she would have been one of our most vocal and articulate speakers. She had earned a degree from the National School of Elocution and Oratory, and when she spoke, it showed.

Emma and I agreed at the conclusion of the meeting that Ellen Ferguson's speech was our favorite, and I noted that the female doctors were making themselves heard today. When I later read the entirety of Ellen's address, the words that mattered most to me were these:

> *Strange it is that while in New York Americans are erecting a statue to liberty that shall lift up the beacon light of freedom to all the nations of the earth, that here in one of the dependencies of this republic, women are led to prison and subjected to insult for no crime. Strange it is that here in Utah the purest, noblest and best of America's citizens should be compelled to make public protest against injury and injustice received from those who have sworn to uphold and maintain the laws—but no less strange than true.*
>
> *Sixteen years ago, the Legislative Assembly of Utah conferred upon the women of this Territory the right of franchise. Our own Legislature was the first to place the ballot in the hands of woman, feeling assured that she would use it in the cause of justice virtue, purity and truth. The women of Utah were enfranchised and have held the ballot as a sacred trust ever since.*
>
> *The ballot in the hand of woman is a mighty power, and our enemies know it, and this is why they seek to take it from us. Silent as it is, it voices to the whole world that women have never used it in the interest of vice. May the day never dawn that shall see the women of Utah without the ballot, but may that time speedily arrive when all the women of this nation will be alike blessed with us.*

When Ellen concluded her address, Emma looked at me and we both smiled. I had introduced Emma to Ellen two weeks ago when Emma stopped by the hospital. She leaned over and whispered, "Ellen's remarks stir my soul."

"Mine as well. Do you recall several years ago when women didn't speak over the lectern or at the pulpit?"

"See how far we've come."

Emma's comment about our progress brought to mind Miss Anthony's words regarding the women of Utah: "They remain vocal and articulate about their rights. Many sisters actively seek women's suffrage, or the right to vote. Their increasing ability to speak articulately is a blessing when they need to represent themselves as strong, dignified, and ennobled women."

Never was that statement more in evidence than it was here today, I thought, proud and pleased at the progress we'd made. At the end of the day, our committee came up with several resolutions, three of which related to suffrage.

Resolved, By the women of Utah in mass meeting assembled, that the suffrage originally conferred upon us as a political privilege, has become a vested right by possession and usage for fifteen years, and that we protest against being deprived of that right without process of law, and for no other reason than that we do not vote to suit our political opponents.

Resolved, That we emphatically deny the charge that we vote otherwise than according to our own free choice, and point to the fact that the ballot is absolutely secret in Utah as proof that we are protected in voting for whom and what we choose with perfect liberty.

Resolved, That we extend our heartfelt thanks to the ladies of the Woman Suffrage Association assembled in Boston and unite in praying that God may speed the day when both men and women shall shake from their shoulders the yoke of tyranny.

Emma and I and several of the others applauded as we listened to those words.

At the end of the meeting, a committee was formed to compose a memorial for Congress, and I was fortunate to be asked to participate. Our memorial included the resolutions adopted in the meeting, cited examples of officers infringing on citizens' rights in their zeal to enforce the Edmunds Act, and ended with an appeal: "We plead for suspension of all measures calculated to deprive us of our political rights and privileges, and to harass, annoy and bring our people into bondage and distress, until a commission, duly and specially authorized to make full inquiry into the affairs of this Territory, have been investigated and reported."

When the protest meeting ended, Emma and I made our way out of the theatre and walked down the streets of Salt Lake City arm in arm, having been together in our fight for suffrage since we were young women. "It was sixteen years ago that we traveled from Farmington to Salt Lake City by carriage," Emma said. "So much has changed since then."

"You're right, dear friend, and with all the progress that's been made in the intervening years, some beliefs remain stubbornly the same."

"Reminds me of an expression penned by a French writer," Emma said. "'The more things change, the more they remain the same.' Perhaps for the first time, I appreciate the meaning of his words."

****

Emmeline Wells and Ellen Ferguson invited me along with them to personally deliver our memorial in Washington DC to Congress and President Grover Cleveland. Emmeline described our experience that day in this way: "I walked into the White House, where we sat about an hour and a quarter waiting our turn to speak to the President of the United States. Shortly after twelve o'clock we presented to him our credentials and the Memorial of the women of Utah Territory, and had an opportunity of stating to him some facts and incidents relating to the abuses and outrages perpetrated in the name of law."

Senator Henry W. Blair, a Republican from New Hampshire, presented the memorial before the Senate on April 6, 1886, asking that it be printed in the Congressional Record.

That same month, the *Woman's Exponent* reprinted a January 1886 article from the Woman's Journal, the newspaper of the American Woman Suffrage Association, that urged its readers to oppose a bill then moving its way through Congress that proposed to deprive "the women of Utah of that suffrage which is theirs by long-settled law and practice."

We didn't stop there, publishing a ninety-one-page pamphlet with all the speeches prepared for the grievance meeting, including some that were not delivered because of lack of time. "The aim of this pamphlet," we compilers wrote, "is to preserve in convenient form, for present use and future reference, the record of the proceedings of that memorable day when the women, in mass meeting assembled, found it necessary for their own protection and the honor of their sex throughout the world, to memorialize Congress and the President of the United States for relief from insult and oppression at the hands of Federal officials."

Could things be made clearer? I thought not and found myself filled with a sense of optimism. We had presented our case well. *Surely, we will be heard!*

Emma

Emma learned that women's petition to Congress had been rejected when she read it in the newspaper. She growled, crumpled the paper into a heap, and threw it on the floor, exasperated. *After all that effort. How disappointing.*

To add insult to injury, the very source of the petition was brought into question by the *Washington Evening Star*. Their article falsely proclaimed, "It is understood that the petition was written by a well-known Mormon attorney, and is a device to gain sympathy for the Latter-day Saints."

Emma was outraged. She'd been in the meeting and she knew the women who had written the resolutions and who'd signed them. It wasn't some male attorney. *Don't they think we have brains in our heads? Or are they so imbued with prejudice against the female sex that they can't see beyond their own noses?*

Emma welcomed the protest letter Emmeline Wells shot off to the editor of the *Evening Star* which said, "The memorial was drafted by a committee of women whose signatures were attached to each copy."

That should do it, she thought. *That should lay the ridiculous and unfounded rumors to rest.*

And yet the Eastern press continued their attacks. A man by the name of Dalrymple, who was a cartoonist for the *New York Daily Herald*, penned a cartoon that showed male church members dressed in female garb delivering the women's petition.

Emma found his cartoon more highly repugnant than the article.

****

Emma wasn't all that surprised when the United States Congress passed the Edmunds-Tucker Act in March of 1887, taking away the right to vote from all the women in Utah. And just like that, Emma lost her right to the ballot.

Wesley brought home a copy of Section 20 of the new law from the sheriff's office and read it aloud to Emma, his hands shaking in anger: "It shall not be lawful for any female to vote at any election hereafter held in the Territory of Utah for any public purpose whatever—and any act of the Legislative Assembly of the Territory of Utah providing for or allowing the registration or voting by females is hereby annulled."

"It's even worse hearing the law read aloud," Emma said.

"On behalf of all the irresponsible men in Washington, I apologize to you, because I know they won't."

"I'm not without hope. While I've lost my right to vote, I've not lost my power to fight for the rights of women."

265

It gave Emma no small measure of comfort when the NWSA expressed their disapproval of the bill and called the action "a disregard of individual rights which is dangerous to the liberties of us all."

In return for their support of the Utah women, the NWSA was mocked in a color lithograph drawn by F. Victor Gilliam in *Judge Magazine* that depicted Susan B. Anthony, Belva Lockwood, and representatives of Mormonism and others as tailors trying to mend Uncle Sam's coat which represented the Constitution. The "Chorus of Tailors" in the cartoon asked, "Hadn't you better let us repair that coat? It's too old-fashioned for these go-ahead times." To which Uncle Sam replied, "The Coat is good enough for Me, and Will last at least Another Hundred Years."

How degrading. If the lampooners of suffrage in the East have their way, women won't get the right to the ballot before the year 1987. She balled her hands into fists and reminded herself of Miss Anthony's words, "Failure is not an option."

It wasn't only the women in the territory of Utah who lost their right to the ballot in 1887. The Supreme Court struck down the law that enfranchised women in the Washington Territory as well. Rhode Island, the first eastern state to vote on a women's suffrage referendum, didn't pass the bill.

"It's been a trying year for woman's suffrage," Emma said to Wesley.

He reminded her of the scripture, "Fools mock, but they shall mourn."

Twenty-Five

Katie

In November I missed my monthly cycle, which had never happened before except when I was pregnant with Joshua. Thomas and I were overjoyed at the likelihood of my pregnancy and this time we were praying for a little girl. I hadn't shared our potential good news with anyone, but Sophia would be here shortly, and I wanted to tell her. Thomas had taken Joshua out sledding for a few hours on an early December snowfall, and I would have her to myself until Joshua came home and insisted on playing tickle with Auntie Sophia.

I heard a knock at the door and opened it to an unusually downcast Sophia. Her mouth was slack, and she looked shocked.

"What is it?" I asked, inviting her in.

She took me in her arms and said, "Eliza Snow died today at the age of 83 years."

"No, no," I said, backing away from Sophia and shaking my head, a lump forming in my throat. "Not Aunt Eliza."

"I'm so sorry to be the bearer of bad news," Sophia said her eyes wet.

"Was she ill?"

"Her brother, Lorenzo Snow, told me she had felt for some time the probability of her passing to the sphere beyond. He was with her when she died."

"The two of them have always been close; I'm glad he was with her," I said, sitting on the couch, trying to absorb the magnitude of her passing.

"Lorenzo was by her side when she breathed her last and said she had 'that same resignation which characterized her course in all the dispensations of providence, even in relation to her approaching dissolution.' She told one of the friends by her bedside: 'I have no choice as to whether I shall die or live. I am perfectly willing to go or stay, as our Heavenly Father shall order. I am in His hands.'"

I said, "She was a pillar of faith who trusted in the Lord without question, even on her deathbed."

"Eliza took no thought for herself, sympathy for others being one of her defining characteristics. She believed that true religion best exhibited itself in loving others as Christ did," Sophia said. "She often sat by the side of the sick, administering comfort to those who were in need, and consoling those who were broken with grief."

"She also shared her private thoughts for the purpose of uplifting others through her poetry. Emmeline told me recently that she has 500 poems to her credit, some of which have been set to music. My favorite is, 'Oh, My Father,'" I said, thinking of the words to her song about passing to the other side.

"Katie, while we're alone here and have this now rare opportunity, would you mind if we speak about some of our own memories of Aunt Eliza?"

"I'd like that," I said. "It seems fitting to reminisce with you, the one who introduced me to her. I remember that day almost eighteen years ago. We were in the Relief Society meeting that Emma and I attended with you, and I was impressed with Aunt Eliza's grace and fortitude."

"After we won the ballot, Aunt Eliza sent a letter to then Governor Steve Mann, thanking him for supporting the suffrage proposal against his better judgment. Only she would do such a thing." Sophia smiled.

I handed Sophia a muffin from the table and said, "She encouraged us to be self-reliant and independent, to expand our domestic priorities to include social reform, home manufacture, and intellectual discussions. She put women in charge of the silk society, the grain society, and cooperative stores. Incredible."

"No one was putting women in charge of anything in those days. Even today most men in the East resist the expanding sphere of women."

"She helped us learn to speak publicly. Emily Richards recently told me Eliza had counseled her: When you are asked to speak again, try and have something to say." Sophia and I both laughed at that.

"Remember when Eliza called for equality and encouraged even our young ladies to participate in public service?"

"She started a physiology class for women, and I believe Eliza may have influenced Brigham Young's call for women to attend medical school."

"Which radically changed your life and improved the health of all the women in this city."

"If it weren't for her, there would be no Deseret Hospital."

"The list goes on and on."

"Through the ups and downs, a mother to us all." *There is no replacing Aunt Eliza, but the gifts she leaves behind are without parallel.*

Three days later, on December 7, 1887, Sophia, Emma and I attended Eliza Snow's funeral in the Assembly Hall. President Angus M. Cannon presided, and the hall was filled beyond capacity. The various stands were, in accordance with Eliza's wishes, draped in white. There was nothing black. There were white flowers everywhere, contributed by those who loved her, and not even the mourners wore black.

Stake President Cannon stood and called the congregation to order, and the choir sang 'I Know that My Redeemer Lives.' The opening prayer was offered by Bishop Alexander McRae, and this time the choir sang Eliza's song, 'Oh, my Father.' I wept.

Mormon Apostle John W. Taylor said, "We have the word 'mother' mentioned here. It is known among us that George Washington is called the 'Father of his country,' though he died without children. Yet through the devotion of the American people he has earned the name of Father.

"Inasmuch as the deceased was deprived of bearing children, she is entitled to be called Mother among this people, just as much as George Washington is to be called Father by the people of the United States. She has been a mother to this people. She has passed through trials and tribulations. She has made us joyful by her poetical effusions; we have sorrowed when she sorrowed, and we have rejoiced when she rejoiced. I pray that all who have seen her good works may endeavor to emulate them."

I adored his tender words.

There were many other speakers who paid glowing tributes that day, but true to form, Eliza had written her own epitaph, which was read to all assembled.

> *"Tis not the tribute of a sigh*
> *From sorrow's heaving bosom drawn:*
> *Nor tears that flow from pity's eye*
> *To weep for me when I am gone.*
> *No costly balm, no rich perfume — No vain sepulchral rite, I claim —*
> *No mournful knell—no marble tomb — No sculptur'd stone to tell my name.*
> *In friendship's memory let me live*
> *For friendship holds a secret cord. That with the fibers of my heart,*
> *Entwines so deep, so close, Tis hard for death's dissecting hand to part.*
> *I feel the low responses roll, Like the far-off echo of the night,*
> *And whisper softly though my soul, I would not be forgotten quite."*

I whispered to Sophia, "Eliza R. Snow will never be forgotten. Her legacy lives forever in the lives of all of us here."

After the benediction was offered, we passed in line around the casket and viewed the face of our beloved Aunt Eliza for the last time in this life. Then her body was taken to the private cemetery of the late President Brigham Young for burial.

After we left the Assembly Hall, Emma took a carriage to the train station, and Sophia and I went in search of something to eat. I had yet to tell her my good news about the baby, but as I did, it came to me that if our baby was a girl, I wanted her middle name to be Eliza. I shared my thoughts with Sophia, and she smiled. "Aunt Eliza would have loved that."

Emma

As Emma journeyed to Farmington, she knew she'd never forget Eliza Snow's funeral and the feelings she'd experienced there. After arriving home and greeting her family, she was still in a reflective mood and told Wesley she needed to take a walk and clear her head.

"I understand," he said. "We'll all be here when you return." The children seemed to sense her need for some alone time, and even their dog, Bandit, walked up and licked her hand as she prepared to leave the house.

When Emma stepped outside, the wind was blowing, and a light snow had begun to fall. On her walk through the streets of Farmington, she had death on her mind; Aunt Eliza's death, the death of her mother who perished giving birth to Emma, and the death of the baby she'd miscarried. It all made her feel so incredibly sad.

Sometimes the idea of her own death frightened her, though she was only thirty-three years old and looking forward to a long life. *But then, one never knows,* she thought. *Death is an inescapable part of life and one day, Grandmother Phoebe will pass on as well. What will I do without her?*

Emma stopped walking, sat on a bench in the park, and chided herself, *Aunt Eliza didn't fear death. She saw it as another step in the journey of life, the third act in a three-act play. What's wrong with you?*

Emma bowed her head and prayed. As she communed with Heavenly Father, the fear left, and her heart filled with the hope and joy of the resurrection. A passage from the Book of John she'd heard quoted came to her mind: "Peace I leave with you, my peace I give unto you; not as the world giveth, give I unto you. Let not your heart be troubled, neither let it be afraid."

You've been blessed with a deep and abiding faith, she reminded herself. *You know your family will live together forever together in the eternities. You don't need to fear death, so choose faith, not fear.* Emma took a cleansing breath and began the walk home.

When she came through the door, the twins rushed to her side and threw their arms about her waist, and Wesley joined them in a hug. Emma held her family close and savored the moment. Even Bandit got into the act, jumping up and down and barking alongside them as tears of joy coursed down Emma's cheeks. *God is in His heaven and all is right with the world.*

The following day, Emma and family sat in their usual pew, waiting for the Sunday meeting to begin. A baby wailed in front of her, two primary children were shoving each other down the aisle, and several of the women stood chatting about the latest Relief Society lesson. She knew each person by name, including the children—except for the family sitting in the back. *Are they new or just visiting?* Emma stood to introduce herself. She'd grown up in this ward congregation; these were her people now and for the rest of her days.

****

The children were at Christina's playing, Wesley was at the Sheriff's office, Bandit was asleep, and life for Emma had moved on to more earthly matters. *Too much introspection can be bad for the soul*, she thought, smiling, grateful to return to her work as a detective. She began looking through copies of the files she'd brought back from Chicago several months ago regarding the battle of the currents between Westinghouse and Edison.

It was an interesting argument the two men had going that had grown out of their different lighting systems. Westinghouse had an arc lamp street lighting system that ran on alternating current (AC), and Edison had developed a large-scale low-voltage direct current (DC) incandescent lighting system. Westinghouse was using transformers to adjust the high voltage so AC could be used for indoor lighting.

Rosemary had written last week that Edison and his team were escalating their efforts to present 'so-called evidence' to prove that the high voltages used in the Westinghouse company's alternating current were dangerous and should not be permitted. Westinghouse was her client and Rosemary was looking for someone she could plant in the Edison offices in Sunbury, Pennsylvania, to see what kind of shenanigans they were up to.

Since she could no longer rely on the Pinkerton network of agents in the East to provide her with contacts, Rosemary had written to ask Emma if she knew of anyone in Pennsylvania her new team might hire to work undercover in Edison's plant.

Emma didn't know of anyone in that area of the country, but Katie might. While Katie's contacts in Philadelphia were women in the field of medicine, Emma remembered Katie telling her about the brother of one of the students she'd known who had grown up in Harrisburg. According to his sister, the guy was bright, knew his way around an office, but was always in and out of jobs. Emma checked the maps and found that Sunbury was a little more than 50 miles from Harrisburg. The whole idea was so farfetched, and such a long shot, but it might be worth a try.

Emma went to the telegraph office and sent Katie a telegram. She replied the next day, giving Emma the name of her friend's brother in Harrisburg, AJ Herbert. First Emma needed to make certain Herbert was on the up and up and not a criminal himself, and that's where Rosemary came in.

Rosemary, through some of her male friends who still worked for the Pinkertons, had access to the 'Rogue's Gallery,' the collection of mug shots and case histories the agency used to research and keep track of criminals. The files contained notes with suspects' distinguishing marks and scars, and the agents had collected newspaper clippings and produced rap sheets that provided details of previous arrests, known associates of the wanted men, and their areas of expertise. Their system had revolutionized law enforcement. Emma sent Rosemary a telegram and asked her to run the name AJ Herbert through the system.

The guy came back clean, although he had once associated with a wanted man, so his name was in the files. Herbert had acted in the role of informant in that instance, taking a role in bringing the criminal to justice. He'd been on the right side of the law. The file indicated he was an experienced businessman, and he certainly didn't mind being a snitch. If he needed a job, Herbert had possibilities.

Emma asked Katie to talk with her friend to see if Herbert might be interested in a job as a corporate spy without providing her with details. Turned out he was. The next step was to determine his trustworthiness, and Emma would leave that in Rosemary's capable hands. If he hired on with Rosemary's team, Emma would get a generous finder's fee.

Twenty-Six

Katie

To celebrate the fortieth anniversary of the women's rights convention in Seneca Falls in 1848, Miss Anthony and Mrs. Stanton had invited women's associations from around the world to a March commemorative meeting in Washington DC.

Emmeline Wells informed me that the meeting would, for the first time, be marked by an International Council of Women. The Council would be organized to coordinate the efforts of all associations dedicated to advancing the status of women politically, economically, socially, and educationally. Following the International Council, a meeting had been called to unite our nation's women's suffrage organizations into one, the National American Woman Suffrage Association.

Combining the organizations had been a long time coming, and I was pleased they'd found a way to work to overcome their differences. This was an historic moment, and I wanted to be present.

Since attendance at the council was open to women from a wide range of institutions and offered the opportunity to report "the various phases of women's work and progress in all parts of the world," the women of Utah would be represented. We were again battling for the ballot and it was essential that we organize a Territorial Suffrage Association.

Emily Richards had been appointed as a representative along with Mrs. Arthur A. Brown, and it seemed a new generation of suffrage leaders was emerging. Emily's parents-in-law, Franklin D. and Jane S. Richards were avid supporters of woman suffrage and Jane had served on the Deseret Hospital Board. I knew her well.

Mrs. Jennie Froiseth, now editor of the *Anti-Polygamy Standard in Utah*, would also attend. I was aware from reading her writings that she didn't want Mormon women of any marital status to be part of the new Utah suffrage association. Jennie also opposed Mormon membership in the new National Council of women, and I could see a battle brewing.

Emily had asked me to accompany them in the role of recorder. She was not new to the Washington scene. Her attorney husband had been central to our legal battles for years. Because of her exposure to Washington and the best legal minds of our day, Emily was the best choice to lead our delegation.

I still had to convince Thomas that I could travel in my condition. I would be twenty weeks into my pregnancy in March, and home before I reached my twenty-sixth week. I spoke with Rebecca first, and she offered to watch Joshua. I'd never been away from him this long before and I was torn about leaving him, but I knew he'd be in capable hands.

When I talked with Thomas about the trip, he asked, "Is train travel advisable, Katie?"

"Ellis has checked me carefully and anticipates no complications. She has no real concerns about my attendance at the convention."

He looked worried.

"The second trimester is the safest time to travel when I will be in little danger of either having a miscarriage or going into premature labor. I'll be on a train with room to navigate easily, keeping my circulation going, and I'll drink plenty of water."

"I remain hesitant," he said.

"I'll book a premium ticket so that I have my own cabin and a berth to sleep in. Your mother will watch Joshua, and he'll be home with you each night. I'll send letters while I'm away and be back before you know it, safe and sound."

"What will your accommodations be in Washington?" he asked.

"We'll be staying at the Riggs House, and, as you know, lodging doesn't come any better."

"Very well," he said. "I agree, as you knew I would in the end." He smiled. "Is Emmeline Wells going?"

"No, but she's been organizing behind the scenes for the past several months to make certain our credentials for the International Council are in harmony with all the parties."

It was only days before the Council began that Emmeline and others attached the last ribbons and seals to the credentials and took them to the train depot. We were halfway across the country by then.

To complicate matters, shortly after we reached Washington, a huge and historic blizzard pummeled the city. Mrs. Stanton hadn't initially planned on attending the convention, then changed her mind at the last moment. She was caught in the blizzard. We were all grateful when she reached us safely.

Emily Richards had been given the opportunity to address the Council session and had chosen 'Philanthropy' as her topic. Because arrangements for us to attend were completed only several days before the Council convened, her name didn't appear on the printed program. When the session chair failed to announce her, Miss Anthony promptly met Emily in the wing and escorted her to the platform "with every demonstration of respect."

Emily spoke generally about our Relief Societies and the philanthropic work we were doing. There were now twenty-two thousand members of the Relief Society assisting the poor in more than four hundred wards and branches, some in other countries.

Emily told me she believed that attendance at this convention would be one of the "most interesting" meetings of her life.

I whispered, "I have no doubt, and I'm certain it will contribute to your success in the movement going forward."

Of the many speeches delivered that day, the one that best summarized the arguments for suffrage was delivered by Isabella Beecher Hooker. She was a grandmother of the movement, and a well-known leader, lecturer and activist from Connecticut. Mrs. Hooker's remarks were well received by the women, and I wanted a copy of her speech. The meeting organizers had one, so I borrowed it for the evening and used the new typewriter at the Riggs House.

The machine had improved exponentially since the first one I'd seen in Philadelphia and could save up to forty minutes out of an hour compared with the pen. In the last year I'd become proficient in its use, which helped immensely in keeping medical records.

It took me under an hour to type the sections of Mrs. Hooker's speech that most interested me, and the next morning I mailed my copy to Emma and returned the original to the convention organizers.

Following the International Council meeting, the National meeting began. Mrs. Froiseth vehemently opposed Mormon membership in both the National and Utah suffrage associations, and I kept my look of disdain and comments to myself. Cooler heads prevailed when Mrs. Harriet Robinson from Massachusetts offered a resolution that restated the National's commitment to retain in its membership, "women of all classes, all races, and all religions." Emily and I were pleased when the council accepted her resolution.

April 3, during the National Association's executive session, Emily presented the case for Utah's representation in the organized woman suffrage movement, and she was authorized to form an official woman suffrage association in the Utah Territory.

At dinner that night we were exuberant at our new prospects, and I remarked to Emily that she'd taken a most important step in reclaiming our standing in the national organization. "You were without doubt an inspired choice to represent us in Washington," I said, toasting her success with a glass of warm cider.

She smiled and thanked me.

Emma

When Emma went to the post office to collect the mail, she found a letter from Katie with a Washington, DC postmark. *Strange that she would write to me from the convention,* Emma thought. *It must be important.* She opened the envelope and found a speech that was several pages long. Putting it aside, she sat on the sofa next to Joyce, who was reading a book. Emma couldn't believe Joyce and Wesley would be nine years old in May.

"What's that you're reading?" Emma asked.

"It's Wesley's book, *Kidnapped*, by Robert Lewis Stevenson. "I love a good murder mystery."

Emma smiled. *The apple doesn't fall far from tree.*

"What did you get in the mail, Mother?" Joyce asked.

"It's a speech Auntie Katie sent me from Washington, D.C."

"Sounds important. May I read it?"

"Why don't we look at it together?"

"I'll go get it from the table," Joyce said, retrieving the paper and sitting next to Emma. "I see that a woman named Isabella Hooker gave this talk. Who is she?"

"A leader in the woman's suffrage movement from the state of Connecticut. She's been fighting for voting rights a long time and is a grandmother now."

"What does she say?"

"Mrs. Hooker begins by stating that there's not one line, nor one word in the United States Constitution that forbids women to vote. In fact, she says, when properly interpreted, the constitution guarantees women the right to vote."

"Is she right? Does the constitution say that?"

"Mrs. Hooker quotes the preamble to our constitution which will answer your question. Would you please read these lines from her speech aloud?"

Joyce read:

"We, The People of the United States, in order to form a more perfect union, establish justice, insure domestic tranquility, provide for the common defense, promote the general welfare, and secure the blessings of liberty to ourselves and our posterity, do ordain and establish this Constitution for the United States of America."

"The first three words again, Joyce."

"We, the People." Joyce handed the paper back to her mother.

"Mrs. Hooker makes the argument that women are people, too, and that the founding fathers surely did not mean that only men are people. She goes on to say this:

"Women are surely 'people,' and were when these words were written, and were as anxious as men to establish justice and promote the general welfare, and no one will have the hardihood to deny that our foremothers (have we not talked about our forefathers alone long enough?) did their full share in the work of establishing justice, providing for the common defense, and promoting the general welfare in all those early days."

"I agree with her," Joyce said.

"I do, too. No thinking person could make the case that women aren't people. The preamble makes that clear."

"What else does she say?"

"That for years and years, women have been petitioning Congress and the State Legislators to take down the political bars the men have put up and allow women to become active co-workers in promoting the general welfare of our nation."

"You and Father are active co-workers," Joyce said. "You own a business and work side-by-side."

"Yes, we do, my love, and we do a better job together than we do separately."

"I like this speech. Is there more?"

"Yes. Do you want me to go on?"

"Please. Someday I want the right to vote, too."

Emma put her arm around Joyce. "Mrs. Hooker says that back in 1871, a clerk in the Senate 'smiled at her with contempt' and asked her how many women really wanted to vote. She says the clerk was surprised when she got an order to search for the petitions on file in his office and found the names of 20,000 women." Emma laughed as she saw the next lines.

"What's so funny?"

"Mrs. Hooker says those names had been 'slumbering in the dusty pigeonholes' in his office."

Joyce giggled, saying, "I like that."

"I do, too. She declares that even back in 1871, the 20,000 names were: *not a tenth part of the number who had been wearily petitioning our legislative bodies year after year since 1848.*"

"I know math," Joyce said with pride. "That was forty years ago, Mother."

"It was."

"When do you think Utah women will get the vote back?"

"I wish I knew the answer to that, my dear daughter. Auntie Katie told me in her letter that Emily Richards has been authorized by the national women's movement to form a Utah Territorial Suffrage Association, which is an important step. There will be many of us fighting to make sure women get the vote back."

"What else does Mrs. Hooker think?"

"Please read this part aloud about voting qualifications," Emma said handing her the paper.

Joyce read:

> "*The constitution of Connecticut, for instance, declares in Article VI, Section 2, that, Every white male citizen of the United States, who shall have attained the age of twenty-one years and resided in this state one year and in the town six months, and shall be able to read any article of the constitution, shall, on his taking such oath as may be prescribed by law, be an elector of the state.*

"What's an elector, Mother?"

"It means a voter."

Joyce nodded and handed the paper back to her mother.

"Mrs. Hooker is making the point that using a person's gender as a qualification to vote is ridiculous because being born male or female is something we can't change, such as whether or not we know how to read. Learning to read is an important qualification that can be changed."

Wesley came into the room at that point and removed his Stetson.

"Hello, Father," Joyce said.

"Hi, Princess. I heard what your mother said, and I agree. Who on God's green earth would insist that someone's gender be a voting qualification, a skill, or a requirement? It's outrageous."

"Joyce and I were finishing a speech Katie sent from Washington D.C."

"May I join you and listen to the end?"

"Of course," Emma said.

"Sit here by me, Father."

"This is one of her final paragraphs" Emma said, "and provides a good summary of why women should vote:

And herein is the degradation of woman today, not only that she cannot have a voice in making the laws and choosing officers to execute the laws, but she is compelled to be taxed, fined, imprisoned, hung even, by the verdict always of her political superiors—her male sovereigns, every one of whom is considered competent to legislate for her and to sit in judgment upon her by court and jury now and for evermore."

"What does she mean, Mother?"

"She means that women can be taxed, fined, or even put in prison, but we do not have a voice in voting for the men who make the laws that we must follow."

"That doesn't seem fair," Joyce said.

"It's not," Wesley agreed.

"She concludes her speech by proclaiming that the Constitution of the United States of America is the grandest charter of human rights that the world has yet conceived," Emma said. "Her words give me hope that one day all women in our nation will have the right to vote."

"Mrs. Hooker is an experienced writer and speaker and a grandmother to boot. I like that," Wesley said.

"She may be growing older, but she's still relevant," Emma observed. "Just like Grandmother Phoebe. I've always believed that with age comes wisdom."

"Always remember, Joyce," Wesley said, "that while the body may grow weaker, the experience of our older people is without price. We would do well to listen to their words."

"Yes, Father," she said and turned to Emma. "I've learned things about suffrage, Mother, but there's something I still don't understand."

"What is it?"

"In school, my teacher told us that in England, they call women suffragettes. Why do we call them suffragists in our country?"

"That's an excellent question, Joyce. A suffragist is a woman, or a man, who believes in extending the right to vote to women. A suffragist supports peaceful campaigning for the vote and belongs to a national organization that allows men to join as well. The word suffragette is used to describe the type of women who spit on policemen, get arrested, and go on hunger strikes."

"I'm a suffragist, mother."

"I am as well, Joyce. The women in America prefer the more serious and respected term suffragist over the word suffragette."

Twenty-Seven

Katie

On July fourth, our little girl was born, and we had our own female Yankee Doodle Dandy. We named her Elizabeth Eliza; Elizabeth after my mother, and Eliza after Aunt Eliza. Mattie was living in Utah again and birthed my baby in the hospital. I always felt secure in Mattie's care. She'd come back to the Utah Territory from England last year after the warrant compelling her to testify against polygamous women whose babies she delivered had expired.

She sat by my bedside the next day while the baby was sleeping, and we talked for the first time in a long time. "What did you do while you were away?" I asked.

"While in Europe I visited hospitals in Britain, France, and Switzerland, obtaining textbooks that I can use in the nursing school I'm establishing."

"Your many skills now include touch points with international medicine. I hadn't heard about your new nursing school."

"My patient load is growing heavy, Katie, and I've acquired a pair of fast horses from my husband's stable so that I may drive my carriage from house to house quickly. I suspect there are days when I'm quite a sight tearing through the streets of the city." She laughed.

I laughed. "Yet you are well groomed, beautiful, and always beloved by your patients."

"Thank you, Katie," she said. "It's nice to speak with you again and renew our friendship."

"I'm grateful as well, and happy to have you back. I only wish I'd been more supportive of what you must have been going through while you were away."

"There were some very difficult moments, but you're here for me now." She smiled. "Please catch me up on suffrage activities."

"One of my favorite topics, and you'll find this of interest. In January, Emily Richards and Martha Caine will create a Utah Suffrage Association."

"How wonderful. Is Emmeline involved?"

"Not much gets done around here without her."

"She's been a great friend and mentor to us both."

"An amazing woman, and she's been made a member of the Advisory Committee for the National Suffrage Association. I believe Emily plans to submit Emmeline's name as Vice-President for the Territory."

"Will there be local suffrage associations as well?"

"In association with the local Relief Societies. I remember what Miss Anthony said about our Relief Society: that through such an organization, it is always comparatively easy to promote any work."

"She's right about that."

Elizabeth Eliza woke and began to cry.

"Your daughter is beginning to make her voice heard, just as her mother does."

I smiled, looking at my new baby girl.

When Elizabeth Eliza was eight months old, I began helping some of the local Relief Societies create their own nursing classes. Rebecca was happy to come by and watch the children for several hours. Zina D. Young had been sustained as the new General President of all the Relief Societies, and she was the one who'd asked me to help with the classes. I hadn't known how much I enjoyed teaching until I taught those classes.

****

Emma

Emma was finishing the last of her eggs and toast, waiting for Burt. The twins had already left for school, blowing her a kiss as they left with the lunches she'd packed.

When Burt came in, he carried a newspaper in his hand. After the usual pleasantries, he gave Emma the paper, and said, "Take a look at this."

The newspaper had come from Colorado, and Emma read: "On June 24th, 1889, three men robbed the San Miguel Bank in Telluride of some $21,000.

"Our Mr. Parker lives in Telluride. Do you suppose he had anything to do with it?"

"I sure do, though a witness identified him just as 'Butch.' It was Parker and his friend, Matt Warner, along with another fella name of Tom McCarthy that done the deed."

"I recall you predicting we hadn't heard the last of him. Is he still in Colorado?"

"Last anyone heard of him, he was back here in Utah."

"Was this his first attempt at robbing a bank?"

"Yep, and he was dern smart about it."

Emma leaned forward in her chair and asked, "How did he pull it off?"

"The three of 'em went into Telluride a few days earlier to case the bank, and I hear tell they visited the local saloons as well. On the day of the robbery, a witness to the crime said that at about 11:00 on the forenoon, 'they quietly rode their horses up to the bank, and one of em stayed outside, while the other two went in.'"

"How many others were inside the bank?"

"There was only one cashier on hand, a Mr. C. Hyde, who reported the event like this," Burt said, removing notes from his pocket. "Mr. Hyde claimed: 'One of 'em shoved his gun in my face, and the good-lookin' guy with the sandy hair jumped behind the cage and started filling sacks with money and gold from the counter and the vault. Then they told me to keep quiet and stay inside, or they'd kill me.' He was pretty shook up."

"I'm guessing he did as he was told."

Burt nodded. "The first witness said that after the robbers left the bank, they 'fired their pistols in different directions' to intimidate people on the street. Then, they jumped on their horses and skedaddled out of town."

"Where was the Marshall while all this was going down?"

"That's a good question. Turns out our trio of bandits cut a deal with Marshall Jim Clark, so's he'd be out of town during the robbery. Another sheriff found his cut of the loot later in a hollow log outside town."

"Who identified the men?" Emma asked.

"As they hightailed it out of town, they were recognized by a man who was comin' into town, by the name of Harry Adsit. He's friends with Butch and even gave him one of his horses after Butch claimed he wanted to leave town and visit his family in Utah.

"Adsit told the sheriff: As they neared me, I recognized my two boys. I shouted, 'What's up?' They replied, 'Haven't got time to talk. Adios.' Butch's hat was missing."

"So, he called him Butch?"

"Yep. Then Adsit said: I continued on my way, wondering at their delay in going home, and I looked up and saw a mile away, a posse approaching.

"When Adsit asked the sheriff what the men had done, he said they'd robbed the bank in San Miguel. The sheriff summoned Adsit to become a member of the posse, telling him that he had a fresh horse and a Winchester, and ordered him to lead out. Adsit did what the sheriff asked, but the posse was made up of clerks and other types who didn't know the first thing about ridin' in a covered wagon. Most of em was far behind him when Adsit and two men who were with him crossed the San Miguel on the trail of the thieves. Turns out they stopped there when Adsit told the other men they'd likely be killed."

"I suspect Adsit didn't want his friend caught, either."

"Yep. I think the way he saw it, no one had been hurt nor killed, so it wasn't that bad. Butch had also arranged for relays of fresh horses along the way, so the gang just kept right on goin.' Ten days later, Adsit received a letter from Cassidy, and I got me a copy here. Let me read it to you.

> "Dear Harry: I understand the sheriff of San Miguel county is riding the dapple brown colt you gave me. I want you to tell Mr. Sheriff that his horse packed me one hundred and ten miles across that broken country and declared a dividend of $22,500, and this will be your order for the horse. Please send him over to me at Moab, Utah, on the first opportunity."

"He's a brash man who likes to stick it to others," Emma said.

"When Adsit presented him with the letter, he asked the sheriff for his horse back, sayin' it carried his brand, the Circle Dot. The sheriff refused and said Adsit had given his horse to Butch, so the horse no longer belonged to him, and the sheriff kept it."

"So Butch, or Bud, or Robert, or whatever he calls himself at the moment, is back in the Utah Territory."

"Yep, down south in Moab, least ways he was. Don't know where he might be now."

"The man executed a textbook bank robbery on his first try."

"Yes, ma'am, he did."

"Robbing banks is a cut above the other the kinds of petty thievery he's been practicing."

"Yep. He's hit the big time as a full-fledged outlaw."

"There's no going back now. I predict he'll be robbing banks and trains and stealing all the money he can get his hands on."

"Yep, and it'll all come to no good in the end. I'm sorry for his family, Miss Emma. His mama is a real good sort."

"It must be difficult for her to watch her child going down the wrong path."

"His brother Dan ain't up to no good neither. The telegraph wires were cut afore the robbery and someone had to wait with the relay horses. My money's on Dan."

288

"Do what you can to keep eye on both of them, and I'll get a telegram off to the law in Moab."

Burt left, and Emma thought, *In the West we have dusty streets and bank robbers to contend with. Back East they have inventors engaged in current wars, and in London, they're sipping tea with the Queen. It's an interesting time in which we live.*

AJ Herbert had taken the job Rosemary offered him and was working as a corporate spy at the Edison plant. She was keeping Emma apprised, and the whole thing wasn't over yet, not by a long shot. Edison's men were using Westinghouse's AC current on animals to demonstrate how quickly they died when they came in touch with the current.

Part Three

"All men and women are created free and equal."

Martha Hughes Cannon

Twenty-Eight

Katie

July 10, 1890 was a day for celebration as the Wyoming Territory was admitted as the forty-fourth state in the Union. The leaders of the Utah Suffrage Association sent a congratulatory telegram to Mrs. Amalia Post at Cheyenne, and a few weeks later convened a gathering in Liberty Park 'to rejoice in the good fortune of Wyoming women.'

Thomas and the children had come with me to join in the festivities, and they loved seeing the trees filled with flags. The music of several bands resonated throughout the park, and little Elizabeth Eliza fidgeted through a few speeches. Many of us sang from the Utah Suffrage songbook, 'Woman Arise.'

> Woman, 'rise, thy penance o'er.
> Sit thou in the dust no more;
> Seize the scepter, hold the van,
> equal with thy brother, man.'

That song is my favorite, and even though my little two-year-old daughter didn't understand the words, she hummed along and clapped at the end which made me smile. I looked forward to the day when Utah women would again have the right to vote, and I wanted my daughter to have that right when she came of age.

A few months later, President Wilford Woodruff issued the 'Manifesto,' a written declaration to both Church members and the public at large stating that 'the Church was no longer teaching plural marriage, nor permitting any member of the church to enter into it.' While the declaration surprised some, it didn't surprise others, and I was in the latter category. Mother taught me some twenty years ago that the standard doctrine of our church was monogamy, and polygamy was an exception, for whatever the reason. The President of our Church had declared that the time for practicing polygamy was over.

Thomas and I were present in the Tabernacle for the October session of General Conference when the matter was brought to a vote. President Lorenzo Snow, counselor to President Woodruff, proposed that because the members recognized Wilford Woodruff as the President of The Church of Jesus Christ of Latter-day Saints and the one who held the sealing keys, that they support the Manifesto as it had been issued by him. A vote was called, and the vote was unanimous in favor of the accepting the Manifesto as written.

President Wilford Woodruff closed the conference bearing testimony of the revelation that had come to him, saying, "I want to say to all Israel that the step which I have taken in issuing this manifesto has not been done without earnest prayer before the Lord."

Thomas turned to me and whispered during the closing song that issuing the Manifesto would be an important step in achieving reconciliation between our church and the United States government, who was threatening to confiscate all church-held property.

"It will also help the women find greater acceptance in the national women's movement," I said.

****

The following January, a few weeks before the first triennial convention of the National Council of Women was scheduled to begin, President Zina Young sent letters to Relief Society presidents, asking them to collect donations to help cover the costs of sending delegates. Emmeline Wells was now corresponding secretary for the Relief Society General Presidency that was over all the local congregations. Emmeline thought first counselor Jane Richards the best-qualified woman to speak at the convention. Emmeline would attend as a delegate and asked me to go along once again as recorder.

We left by train and arrived in Washington, February 19. Franklin S. Richards, Jane's son, and his wife, Emily Richards, met us at the depot and accompanied us to the Riggs House. We hadn't been in the house long before we met Miss Anthony in the hallway, and she was so pleased to see us. *What a champion she continues to be for the women of Utah.*

On Saturday morning the Utah Delegation presented our credentials. The Executive Committee met in the afternoon, and after the meeting ended, we were told that the Relief Society and Young Ladies' Mutual Improvement Associations were admitted to the Woman's National Council and the delegates were entitled to representation. This was a big step for us, and we were gratified by the decision.

Later, Mrs. Jane Spofford gave a reception for the ladies of the Woman's Council and Convention. The dining room was large and beautifully decorated with stars and stripes, and at one end of the room, there was a raised platform for the musicians. At the other end, a group of ladies stood who were receiving guests with Mrs. Spofford. After we greeted Miss Anthony, now Vice-President at large of the combined National American Woman's Suffrage Association, Emmeline said to me, "Large she is in every way as well as liberal. She is certainly one of the grandest women of her time, or any other time."

The reception was lovely, and we enjoyed it immensely. There were women lawyers, doctors, ministers, artists, editors, correspondents, and reporters – accomplished women from so many professions. It was a joy to be in their company.

The ladies gathered in groups chatting about one thing or another. There were very few men in attendance. After some of the others left, we went up to Mrs. Spofford's apartment where we were shown to a room filled with flowers. We had ice cream, cakes, and salads, but the best thing of all was being in the presence of Susan B. Anthony, Isabella Beecher Hooker, and Clara Barton, who founded the American Red Cross.

Sunday, we attended services in Albaugh's Opera House, and in the evening, entertainment was offered for the purpose of raising funds for a Mary Washington monument. Although, as Miss Anthony said more than once, "They never even mentioned that Washington had a mother."

Monday morning the Woman's National Council opened with the President's address, which began with Elizabeth Cady Stanton's words, "A difference of opinion on one question must not prevent us from working unitedly on those on which we can agree." *How beautifully stated, and what a better place this world would be, if we began our conversations with what we agreed on, rather than wandering into topics on which we disagreed.*

An article in the *New York Woman's Tribune* of Feb. 28 stated, in the report of the Council, concerning the Utah delegation:

> *"The National Improvement Society, was represented by Mrs. Thomas, who spoke briefly on and told in an interesting manner of the benefit young ladies were deriving from it. The next speaker introduced to the audience was Mrs. Richards, of the National Woman's Relief Society, who began her brief address by saying: "I have the honor to represent Utah. The 25,000 women whom I represent are seeking to have love and peace and goodwill extended to all. On account of the length of the program, I will not speak longer, except to say that I am stopping at the Riggs House and will be pleased to answer questions."*

The article concluded with well-deserved praise for Emmeline.

> *"Mrs. Wells is editor of the* Woman's Exponent, *of Salt Lake City, and one of the most interesting women at the Council. She has been chastened and spiritualized by suffering into a sympathy with woman that truly represents the spirit of Him whom those of her faith call Master, as well as those of Christian denominations. Mrs. Wells gave a short account of the Relief Society [and the headquarters here] in New York; and it has branch societies all over the country, a hospital managed entirely by women, and has its own organ—*The Woman's Exponent."

We had come so far since the early days when the Eastern papers referred to us as 'degraded' women. This was our most fruitful convention yet.

I was tired but exhilarated when we returned to Salt Lake, and I was so anxious to see my babies—though they weren't babies anymore. *When I'm with them, I often find myself wishing I could do something to stop the march of time.* Joshua was seven, and Elizabeth Eliza was three, and they were quite the pair. Joshua was serious, determined, an excellent student in school, and always protective of his little sister.

Elizabeth Eliza, as we always call her, using both names, was playful, loved to dance, and the look of surprise on her face was always worth the price we paid to see it. In primary, she sang the songs with gusto, loved to draw pictures, and she didn't hesitate to take charge of the other children in her class. She was a beautiful little handful who had her father wrapped around her little finger.

Emma

In January of 1892, Susan B. Anthony became the president of the National American Woman's Suffrage Association, and no one could imagine anyone better suited than she to run the organization. When her seventy-second birthday came around February 15, the women of the Utah Territorial Suffrage Association celebrated it with a meeting dedicated solely to suffrage. Emma attended the gathering in Salt Lake City, and Grandmother Phoebe joined her. Katie was there with her mother-in-law, Rebecca.

The hall was beautifully decorated in Miss Anthony's honor, and the Stars and Stripes hung over pictures of Miss Anthony and Mrs. Stanton. Several members of the legislature were in attendance.

Emma and Katie were gratified when the Utah women later received a telegram from Miss Anthony, expressing her love and appreciation for the celebration. She said: "Greetings, dear friends, that your citizens' right to vote may soon be secured is the prayer of your co-worker."

It's remarkable that Miss Anthony has the humility to speak of herself as a co-worker, Emma thought as she attempted to get the twins to go to bed. They loved staying up late, so it typically took both parents to get them there. Emma read something fanciful to them each night, hoping to spark their imaginations. Then Wesley packed them off to bed and tucked them in, kissing them on both cheeks. Emma and Wesley adored their children.

When Wesley came into the parlor after telling the twins good night for the third time, he joined Emma on the sofa. She was reading as usual and informed him, "It says here in the *Exponent* that the Relief Society is organizing a Jubilee celebration March 17, which falls on Thursday and is the same day of the week when the Relief Society was first organized in 1842, fifty years ago. Can you believe it's been fifty years?"

"What astonishes me is how much change we've experienced during that time."

"From pioneers to industrialists," Emma said. returning to her reading. "The paper is predicting: The Jubilee to be celebrated this year will crystalize the works and efforts of the women of Zion into something of greater magnitude and more extensive proportions than the Society has hitherto assumed," Emma finished. "I want to attend and take Grandmother Phoebe with me."

298

"I think you should. It would be a watershed moment for both of you."

Grandmother had celebrated her 70th birthday the October prior and had been present fifty years ago when the first Relief Society was organized, as had many other women in the territory.

President Zina Young, her officers, and the Central Board of the Relief Society were planning the event that was intended 'to acknowledge the accomplishments of the society in the past and herald the possibilities of its future.' She sent a letter of greeting to 'The Relief Society Sisters Throughout the World,' informing us of the upcoming Jubilee, with the following instructions: 'First, to notify all members of the celebration of the Jubilee; second, to send a cordial invitation to their members to attend, third; to appoint committees to assist in making preparations for the day that 'none may be neglected or forgotten; fourth to meet promptly at ten o'clock the morning that day and select someone to read a brief sketch of the history of the Relief Society; and fifth, at 12 o'clock pm (high noon) 'let all join in a universal prayer of praise and thanksgiving to God; after which 'let each branch manage an entertainment according to their circumstances, that it may be a time of rejoicing never to be forgotten.'

Grandmother and Emma were together in the Farmington Relief Society meeting the day the letter was read to the women. "Grandmother," she whispered, "rather than celebrating here, I'd like us to travel to Salt Lake City and observe the proceedings in the Tabernacle. Are you willing to do that?"

"I would be so pleased to attend that celebration with my granddaughter. It would be another memory we share."

****

When Emma and her grandmother entered the tabernacle the day of the Jubilee, they saw a beautiful floral representation of the key "turned to women" in Nauvoo by Joseph Smith, when he had first established the Relief Society organization. A life-size portrait of him, Eliza R. Snow, and Zina D. H. Young, hung on the pipes of the tabernacle organ. A life size portrait of the first Relief Society President, Emma Smith, hung there as well.

"Look at all the flags, bunting, and flowers," Grandmother said. "It's a stunning display."

"I believe the music will be especially fine today, Grandmother," Emma said as the choir opened by again singing Eliza Snow's beloved melody, 'O, My Father.'

The opening prayer was offered by President Angus M Cannon, and the choir and congregation joined in singing the hymn, 'How Firm a Foundation.' President Zina Young stood, welcomed everyone, and began her instruction, saying, "A word as to the duties and labors of the members of these organizations, of the Relief Society is appropriate at this time; as sisters of this organization we have been set apart for the purpose of comforting and consoling the sick and afflicted the poor and distressed, particularly those who love and fear God; to comfort one another in every trial of life, and cheer the depressed in spirit, on all occasions; this is our special mission, therefore keep this in remembrance. If we continue to do these things in the spirit thereof, the Lord Jesus Christ, at the time when He comes to make up His jewels, will approve of us."

When she began speaking of suffrage, Emma's ears perked up.

"We are blessed with glorious privileges and have been. The franchise so gloriously given us, and enjoyed so long, has been taken from us without cause. It may be restored to us again; let us hope for this. Let us be pure and upright in our lives and do good continually; be true and humble all our days; may we be guided by the spirit of the Lord day by day."

She also encouraged home productions of every kind and urged us to support our paper the *Woman's Exponent* by subscribing to it, saying "This paper should be in the family of every Latter-day Saint."

At high noon, in order to unify the celebration between the events in Salt Lake City and Relief Society branches throughout the church, each participating group offered their own commemorative prayer.

After the services ended, Emma and her grandmother walked a few blocks downtown to ZCMI to do a little shopping. Grandmother still loved looking at the display of electric lights and riding up and down the hydraulic elevators.

When they went inside the huge iron façade and into the department store, Grandmother looked around and said, "This building compares well with almost any other mercantile building of its kind in our country. Did you know that ZCMI opened its doors before R.H. Macy and Company in New York City even became a department store?"

"I didn't know that, Grandmother," Emma said. "It meant a great deal to celebrate the Jubilee with you, and if you'll permit me, I'd like to purchase a small gold ring as a memento of this historic event," Emma said as they walked past a display of rings.

"Emma, that would be lovely, thank you," she said placing one on her finger. "Someday when I pass from this world to the next, the ring will belong to you."

"I love you, Grandmother. Don't ever leave me."

In July, Emma and Wesley spent a few days with friends in American Fork, where they attended a large suffrage rally. Suffrage leaders from Salt Lake City and other parts of the territory were also in attendance. When the couple arrived, they found crowds of people already assembled, and the ladies all wore a yellow ribbon. Most of the men, including Wesley, had pinned sunflowers to their lapels. Even the carriages and horses were decorated in the yellow suffrage colors.

There were several bands playing as Emma and Wesley sat down to a delicious banquet that Mrs. Hannah Lapish, the local suffrage president, had organized for all the attendees. Their orator for the day was Charles W. Penrose, a prominent public speaker who had emigrated to Utah from London at the age of eighteen. Emma always enjoyed listening to his stirring words spoken in an English accent. It was a full day of feasting and suffrage. The couple stayed the night with their friends, making the trip back to Farmington the following day.

Twenty-Nine

Katie

Thomas and I were traveling by train to the Chicago World's Fair, also called the 'Colombian Exposition' in honor of Christopher Columbus. The opening day was supposed to take place sometime in 1892 four hundred years after he landed. But since the building construction had gone on longer than anticipated, the opening day was scheduled for May 1, 1893. We wanted to be in attendance, and we were on our way!

We had invited Rebecca to come along, but she detested crowds and said she much preferred to stay home with the children since it was anticipated that there would be as many as 700,000 attendees on any given day.

Thomas read to me from the *Tribune* that the White City at the Exposition had been so named because the Fair buildings were all covered in white stucco. "It says here," he said, "that the cost to drain the swamplands on Lake Michigan, and build 200 structures, was a hefty 21 million dollars. I hope Chicago makes a small profit."

The day we finally got off the train and reached the Exposition, Thomas purchased two tickets at 50 cents each, and we proceeded to the southeast corner of the Fair to the 'Inside Inn,' our accommodations for the next several days. It was the only hotel located

302

on the fairgrounds, and it was a temporary building built of yellow pine, stucco and fire-proof burlap. Our brochure informed us it could house up to 5,000 guests in its 2,257 rooms.

When we went inside the main entrance, we found two restaurants, a drug store, a haberdashery, shoeshine parlor, barbershop, and a newsstand. "I'm delighted we're staying inside the fair," I said. "Most of what we need is onsite."

The opening day began cloudy and gray for the hundreds of thousands of us who had gathered for the ceremony. We women were all clad in our finest attire, long dresses with high necks, bustles and petticoats underneath, and even the men wore topcoats and cravats.

To say the White City is massive would be an understatement, I thought while standing in the center square and looking around. I'd never traveled to Rome or Venice, but the square resembled pictures I'd seen of those places. I turned to Thomas and said, "If Elizabeth Eliza were here, she'd say it was 'ginormous.'"

Thomas laughed and said, "And that's putting it mildly. I understand that a single exhibit hall has enough interior volume to house the U.S. Capitol, the Great Pyramid, Winchester Cathedral, Madison Square Garden, and St. Paul's Cathedral, all at the same time."

"That's hard to imagine," I said.

The sun came from behind the clouds and warmed the day as President Cleveland began the opening address. He concluded his remarks with: "Let us hold fast to the meaning which underlies this ceremony and let us not lose the impressiveness of this moment. As by a touch the machinery that gives life to this vast Exposition is now set in motion, so at the same instant let our hopes and aspirations awaken forces which in all time to come shall influence the welfare, the dignity, and the freedom of mankind."

Then he pressed his finger on a telegraph key, and all over the fairgrounds electric lights and huge engines came on simultaneously, as colored fountains powered by electricity shot high into in air. More than a few wept at the beauty of it all, and I was among them.

While we'd never be able to see all the exhibits, we wanted to see everything we could. Thomas had an important court trial coming up soon, so he'd go home in a few days, and I'd stay for the World's Congress of Women.

Until then, Thomas and I marveled at the sights, sounds, and tastes of the fair. We tried a new snack called Cracker Jack and a new breakfast food called Shredded Wheat. We saw whole villages that had been brought here from Egypt, Algeria, Dahomey, and other far-flung areas of the world, and we found it all quite exotic.

We spent no small amount of time in the Agriculture Building, which had a structure inside constructed from dried corn on the cob. "How creative," I said, running my hand along the cobs.

While Utah had exhibits in this building, it also had its own building that was open all day to visitors. "Let's leave here and go to the Utah building," Thomas said.

"You read my mind." I smiled.

The exterior of the stately Utah building was also white with a round columned portico leading into the entryway. "Look, Thomas," I said as we approached, "a statue of a seagull is poised in flight on the top of four columns."

"How appropriate," he said. "Seagulls saved Utah's crops in 1848."

I paused and thought about the miracle of thousands of seagulls that had flown into the Salt Lake Valley coming every day over the course of several weeks. The birds ate, then regurgitated, an infestation of crickets, saving the crops.

When we walked inside the Utah building, I told Thomas that our Territorial Board of Lady Managers had selected noteworthy pieces—made entirely by Utah women to display in our building and at other locales at the Exposition.

Thomas thought that the most beautiful displays were sets of embroidered silk curtains that had been both sourced and manufactured in Utah. "This is amazing," he said, touching the silk.

"It's lovely, and just look at this quilt."

We later enjoyed the first national performance of the Mormon Tabernacle Choir at the installation of the Liberty Bell which had

304

been brought here from Philadelphia. An article I read observed, 'Mormons have shaped an image of themselves and of their faith that blunted a half-century of sometimes vicious stereotypes and paved the way for acceptance of Utah into the Union.' *Our world is changing,* I thought, *and the Utah women will again claim the right to the ballot.*

Thomas and I visited most of the other state buildings. The California building was huge, and people of the state gave away fresh fruit every day. I had to admit we went there more than once to sample the tasty produce. The Missouri building had a replica of the St. Louis Bridge built entirely out of sugar cane, and the New York building had a replica of the Brooklyn Bridge made from soap. "This is all so festive and fun," I said as we walked. "What's next?"

"Let's view the whole of the city from above the buildings," Thomas said. We took the new Otis Hale Company elevator to the observation deck, and it was worth the 25 cents each it cost to take a fast ride straight to the top. We found a wonderful spot to view the fair from behind the waist high chain link fence. It was a bit daunting looking down, and several people soon made their way quickly back to the elevator, but we lingered and enjoyed the view. Thomas and I rode the elevator more than once and found that the best time to be on the observation deck was at night when the whole city was illuminated.

When our time at the fair ended several days later, I was sorry to see him go. "It's been a wonderful trip, and I've loved our time together," I said as he packed his valise. "Part of me wishes I were traveling home with you."

"But only a small part, I'll wager." He grinned. "I know you're looking forward to the Woman's Congress. When do the rest of the ladies arrive?"

"They're already here. After you leave this morning, I'll join them."

"Enjoy yourselves," he said. "Good-bye, my love."

"Please give the children a big hug and kisses from me."

Later that day, Mattie, Emily Richards, and I went to the Woman's building and saw a variety of arts and handicrafts. The emphasis of the displays was on domestic roles and activities, which was fine, but didn't yet represent the roles of female lawyers, doctors, educators, and orators.

Our week-long woman's convention was held at the fair in the World's Congress Auxiliary Building. Meetings had been organized by women from each of the United States and her territories, and Martha Cannon was our featured speaker from Utah.

Miss Anthony addressed us several times without the use of notes. Some of the women craned their necks and gawked, anxious to see and hear this well-known icon of the suffrage movement.

When Mattie spoke, her words were well received and applauded. The *Chicago Record* noted that "Dr. Martha Hughes Cannon ... is considered one of the brightest exponents of the women's cause in the United States." *High praise indeed and well deserved*, I thought.

After the Woman's Congress ended, I left for home, and Mattie went on to appear before a congressional committee in Washington to give a status report on our suffrage work in Utah. I heard later that she debated with others that a 'woman involved' was a better mother and created a happier home.

That was our Martha Hughes Cannon, and I was proud to call her friend.

Emma

Emma received a letter from Rosemary asking her to come to Chicago to discuss the wrap up of the Edison and Westinghouse case, indicating there were some things she preferred to talk about face to face. She also invited Emma to come see the Columbian Exposition. She wrote,

We will, of course, pay your fare to Chicago, and I would be pleased if you'd stay here with me for a few days. While you're in town, we simply must see the Fair; it's a delight. And while you're here, I'll pay you both for the referral and the ongoing consultation you've offered.

Wesley agreed with the arrangements, and Christina offered to take care of the twins, who always enjoyed staying the night with their cousins.

When Emma reached the heart of Chicago and stepped outside into the chilly October weather, she smelled the familiar scent of the stockyards, and knew there was a reason the Fair had been built seven miles outside the city. Emma smiled as she recalled that Chicago had been called 'The Windy City' for years, ever since journalists declared the city full of 'windbags.' She loved the City nonetheless and had many fond memories here.

"I'm so pleased you've come," Rosemary said when Emma reached her home. "Allow me to take your things." She reached for Emma's case. "How was the train trip?"

"It's energized me, and I'm looking forward to my visit with you."

"Let's retire for a good night's sleep, and tomorrow I'll take you to the fair and show you around the Electricity Building which will provide you context for our conversation."

The next day, when the two women reached the Fair, Rosemary took Emma first to the spot where the Cold Storage Building had once stood, and Emma wondered why they had come here.

"I hope you don't mind," Rosemary said, "I can't attend the Fair without stopping to pay my respects. I don't believe I told you that my brother Dan lost his life here in July."

"Rosemary, I am so sorry," Emma said, holding her hand. "I read about the tragic fire and didn't know how it much it had touched you personally."

"Do you mind if we sit on this bench for a moment?" she asked, sitting down. "As awful as the story is, may I share it with you?"

"Of course," Emma said, sitting next to her friend.

"When the small fire started in the large smokestack, my brother was one of the firefighters who climbed the tower to extinguish the flames. As they fought the blaze, another fire broke out below them. Some of the men slid down fire hoses to the ground, and ropes were tossed to save the stranded others, but as they grabbed the ropes, the ends burned, and they plunged into the fire below them. There was no way out."

As Rosemary's tears flowed freely, Emma offered a handkerchief.

She wiped her eyes and said, "As Dan and one of the other firefighters stood on the narrow ledge, they determined to meet their fate with bravery. So, they took each other's hand, said their good-byes, and leaped into the flames."

"I can't conceive of such bravery," Emma said. "What a wonderful man your brother was." She paused and waited until Rosemary was prepared to speak again.

After a time, Rosemary took a shuddering breath and said, "Just look at me, a hardened detective who's been bawling like a baby." She stood and said, "I'm ready to go now."

"Are you certain?" Emma asked. "We can stay a little longer if you like."

"I am. Thank you for listening and caring deeply."

"I do, you know."

"You're a good friend," Rosemary said.

As the two women made their way to the Electricity Building, Rosemary assumed her business face and said, "You may know that the exhibits in this building belong to General Electric, Western Electric, and Westinghouse."

"General Electric is the company that bought out Edison, right?" Emma asked.

"Correct, and they offered a bid of $1,800,000 to illuminate the Exposition which the City deemed exorbitant, so they dropped their costs to $554,000. But George Westinghouse came back with a counter-offer of $399,000 and, armed with the help of a system Tesla created, was awarded the contract."

"I'm guessing he's losing money at that price point," Emma said.

"His goal is to have the public observe the power and safety of alternating current firsthand."

When they reached the large Electric Building, Rosemary suggested they begin in the center of the room.

"See this huge tower of lights," Emma said, noting that its shaft was enclosed by thousands of miniature lamps arranged in different pieces of crystal, with a large pavilion at its base. "What does it do?"

"Wait one moment," Rosemary said, "and you will see the full effect."

Emma watched as the tower draped itself in dazzling lights from top to bottom. "This is marvelous. Who created it?"

"Edison, and it's the highlight of the building which I suspect is just what he intended. Edison has a rather large ego."

"So I've heard," Emma said.

"It was your man AJ who first informed us that Edison had decided the only way to beat Westinghouse was to prove that the Westinghouse generators were more dangerous than his. That's when Edison began electrocuting animals with AC current. He held public executions of dogs and horses, often in front of reporters."

"Such a display of animal cruelty. The stories reached our papers as well. The worst was the demonstration Edison held at Coney Island when he electrocuted and killed Topsy, the circus elephant."

Rosemary nodded. "It's hard to believe he would stoop so low, but his fortune was on the line. That's when we pulled AJ out of Edison's plant. While Westinghouse could do little to stop Edison, we were able to forewarn him before the events occurred. He and his men then mapped out a strategy to show the safety and efficiency of AC current."

That night as Rosemary and Emma ate a late dinner in downtown Chicago at Rosemary's favorite restaurant, one of her agents came through the door as they were finishing dessert. He was clearly flustered. "Thought I might find you here," he panted.

"Whatever is the matter?" Rosemary asked.

"It's Mayor Harrison—he was murdered tonight."

"What happened?" Rosemary asked, looking stunned.

"Fella by the name of Prendergast pulled out a revolver and shot Harrison three times. He bled to death in a matter of minutes."

"How'd they discover the identity of the killer so quickly?" Emma asked.

"He didn't even attempt to get away from the police, just sat there and let them arrest him."

"I've heard of Prendergast," Rosemary said. "He's an office-seeker who supported Harrison's re-election."

"That's the guy," the agent said. "Turns out he thought the mayor would award him a post in his administration, and it never happened. So he killed him."

"Where was Harrison murdered?" Rosemary asked.

"In his own home. When Prendergast knocked on the door, Harrison let him in. After all, he knew who he was. Mayor never suspected he'd be shot and killed that night."

"Harrison murdered in his own home. This is rough even by Chicago standards," Rosemary said.

"The police want you to come down to the station and talk with Prendergast," the agent said. "He's already claiming insanity and they'd like the benefit of your skills in questioning him."

Rosemary looked at Emma.

"Don't worry about me," Emma said. "You go; I'll be fine."

"Here's a key to my home. I'm not sure when I'll get there," she said, standing. "Tomorrow likely won't be a good day for the fair. I'm sorry, Emma. I wanted to show you the grand basin and take a gondola ride around the Lagoon."

"You have far more important things on your mind. I'll see about taking a train home tomorrow instead of waiting another day."

The next day, Emma took a carriage to the train station and left for Utah. Rosemary, an active suffragist in Chicago, had given Emma a full pamphlet from the Woman's Congress to take along with her. Emma read the speeches as she traveled. She learned that nearly 200 prominent women, including Miss Anthony, Miss Stanton, and Jane Adams had spoken on public health, women's suffrage, industry, history, and religion. She treasured reading some of their inspiring words.

With Utah statehood approaching, Emma decided now was the time to dedicate all her time and effort to the woman's cause. *I'm going to ask Wesley and Burt to assume the reins of the detective agency until we women have won the right to the franchise again.* Emma was incensed that after voting for several years, she no longer had the right to exercise that liberty.

Thirty

Katie

When the New Year began, the women's attention was focused solely on preparing for next year's Utah constitutional convention. We would work to ensure woman's suffrage was placed into the constitution. "This is likely to be a long and protracted battle," I said to Thomas as we dressed for today's meeting.

"If anyone's up the challenge, it's the women of Utah," he said.

"Now if we can just get the men up to the challenge as well." I smiled.

"I promise to play my part," he said, adjusting his cravat.

"Here, let me help you with that," I said. "Can you believe the national woman's movement has struggled for over 45 years to get a suffrage amendment into our nation's constitution to no avail?"

"The women must not lose the battle in Utah," Thomas exclaimed as we left the house.

Emmeline Wells had called an assembly of citizens 'for the purpose of arousing a greater interest in a Statehood which should include equal rights for women as well as men.' Thomas and I were attending, and we anticipated listening to several notable speakers.

Emmeline had been elected president of the Utah Territorial Suffrage Association last October, replacing Sarah Kimball, and this was her time to shine. The meeting she'd organized promised not only to be rousing, but patriotic. I was delighted when we sang Julia Ward Howe's 'Battle Hymn of the Republic' and 'America.'

Splendid addresses were made by the Hon. John E. Booth, the Hon. Samuel W. Richards, Dr. Richard A. Hasbrouck, a famous orator formerly of Ohio, and Martha Hughes Cannon, as well as Zina Young. This gathering was intended to launch subsequent parlor meetings in various parts of the city. Serious discussions were stirring everywhere about what our state constitution might look like.

A week later, I dropped by the *Exponent* offices to speak with Emmeline and thank her for the tremendous effort she was making on behalf of the women of Utah. When I came through the doors a whiff of nostalgia greeted me, and I recalled laboring here long ago as a typesetter with Mattie. We were so young then and couldn't ever have imagined what adventures and challenges lay in store for us. *The office hasn't changed much over the years*, I thought, looking around.

I knocked on Emmeline's door, and she invited me in. We embraced and she said, "It's good to see you, Katie. Will you stay a while and visit?"

"I was hoping you'd have the time."

"How's your work coming along at the hospital?" she asked as I sat next to her.

"I've taken a leave of absence for two years in order to devote myself to the suffrage cause."

"Your contributions will be valued and most welcome. You're respected and admired for your work as a physician and a woman's advocate, Katie."

"That's kind of you to say, Emmeline. I had a wonderful mentor." I smiled, nodding in her direction. "But, please tell me how you are? You must be terribly busy with all that's going on."

"To be truthful, Katie, I'm often exhausted from the demands I face daily. But I must admit that I enjoy working in the political arena," she said, eyes brightening. "May I share something that occurred recently? It's brought me great joy."

"Please do. Your happiness is mine as well."

"I received word that I've been made a patron of the National Council of Women, which is an honor I should never have anticipated. If anyone had given me a quantity of gold, I could not have been much more astonished."

"It doesn't surprise me, Emmeline. No one is more deserving of that honor than you."

"Being a patron doesn't make me a voting member of the Council, but it does confer a lifetime membership."

"Which I know you'll use to the full advantage on behalf of the women of Utah." I smiled. "Emmeline, I wanted to tell you that the words you wrote in a recent editorial stirred me to action."

"Which editorial was it?"

"It was the issue where you observed that the women of Utah had the ballot wrested from them without adjudication, giving us no benefit of the law."

"It's true, and I see it as a simple act of justice for that wrong done to restore the right to the franchise."

"Eloquently put," I said. "Do you expect we'll encounter great difficulty getting the right to suffrage into the state constitution?"

"More than I imagined several months ago. There are both men and women in the territory who oppose it."

"I find that disheartening after all we've been through."

****

In early July, Congress passed the Enabling Act for Utah which authorized that a constitutional convention be held the following year. While we were jubilant at the prospects, Miss Anthony sent a message that same month to the officers and members of the Utah Suffrage Association, saying:

"My dear friends, I am delighted that you are now to be in the United States, as you have been for many years in the union of the

314

dear old National Woman Suffrage Association! I congratulate you not only because Utah is to be a state, but because I hope and trust that her men, in the Constitutional Convention assembled, will, like the noble men of Wyoming, ordain political equality to her women."

At this point in our nation's history, only Wyoming and Colorado had granted full political rights to women, and we all wanted Utah to be next. Miss Anthony had always been politically astute and foresaw a struggle ahead. Her letter wisely advised us to get the right to vote now and not leave it to future legislation or a separate vote of the electorate, warning: "the adjective 'male' once admitted into your organic law will remain there. Don't be cajoled into believing otherwise."

On July 16, President Grover Cleveland signed the enabling act that began the process of establishing the Utah Constitution. The *Woman's Exponent* reported the event with words of patriotic zeal, 'urging the women to stand by their guns and not allow the framers of the constitution to take any action whereby they might be defrauded of their sacred rights to equality.'

Miss Anthony had again written a message in support that was also printed in the *Exponent*, saying, "Let it be the best basis for a State ever embossed on parchment." Never for a moment did Emmeline's faith waver in the belief that we could accomplish such a task.

We worked incessantly in all directions to make our dream a reality. As women of Utah, we worked side by side, our past differences forgotten. We made every effort possible to support men who would frame a constitution without sex distinction to ensure that the woman suffrage article would be included in our new document, knowing the argument would be made that it be proposed separately.

In September, both political parties, now the Democrats and Republicans, held territorial conventions, and the women set about lobbying the leaders of both parties. The Republicans met first at the Opera House in Provo. The party platform contained a list of twenty-one items, starting first with the essential nature of a protective tariff and the 'free coinage of silver.' It wasn't until they reached the eighteenth item, that they addressed female suffrage, merely stating: "We favor the granting of equal suffrage to women." I found it a rather weak pronouncement at best and could see problems ahead.

When I read an account of the meeting in the *Tribune*, I saw no mention of debate over the provision. I learned later that it had been placed on the platform by a minority of the delegates, which I did not believe would bode well once the debate ensued.

The Democrats met days later in Salt Lake City, and once again, female suffrage was put near the end of the platform. Emily Richards and I were present in the meeting when the endorsement was read:

> *The Democrats of Utah are unequivocally in favor of woman suffrage, and the political rights and privileges of women equal with those of men, including eligibility to office, and we demand that such guarantees.*

Emily Richards rose to thank the convention for the actions taken on behalf of the women's political rights, pointed out the difference between the platforms of the two political parties, and promised that the women would never abuse our political privileges.

Those words need to be said for the benefit of some, I thought, *even though women voted for seventeen years before they lost the ballot. Abusing our political privileges was never a concern during that period.*

Over the course of the next several weeks, the political parties held precinct and county conventions, during which candidates were selected to run for seats in the constitution. The work ahead of us heated up as we worked hard to support delegates who would place equal voting rights in the Utah constitution.

Following the November election, Ellen Ferguson, who was president of our local Woman Suffrage Association of Salt Lake County, implored us to visit the newly elected delegates to determine whether they planned to put woman suffrage in the constitution. She warned us that some of the delegates were wavering, saying, "many are inclined to hang back, saying wait till we are a State, then we will give to women the right to suffrage."

I recalled Miss Anthony's alert earlier that year: "The adjective 'male' once admitted into your organic law will remain there. Don't be cajoled into believing otherwise."

As if the men's lack of constancy weren't bad enough, there were women who argued against having the right to vote. The very notion raised Emmeline's hackles, and in November issues of the *Exponent*, she wrote that some women in the territory felt no need of extending the political rights to members of their sex because they were sitting in "luxury and ease." These same women, she wrote, might one day need political rights "for their own defence and protection, or mayhap for their little ones."

The Utah Woman's Suffrage Association used every means possible to educate and convert the general public to the need to include female suffrage in the new constitution. Emma and I and so many others circulated suffrage literature among our neighbors and friends, as did our sister suffragists in the more remote corners of the territory. We were aware that even after the men met in March to adopt a constitution, the men in the territory would still need to vote on it.

Emma

In January of 1895, the National Suffrage Association had planned a gathering in Atlanta, and Aurelia Rogers was invited to attend as a delegate. She asked Emma if she would like to accompany her, and Emma was pleased and astonished at Sister Rogers's generous invitation. Emma had never attended a national suffrage meeting and relished the opportunity. *But what about the twins?*

When Wesley and Christina learned of Emma's concern, they insisted she accompany Aurelia. "You won't be away long, and I'm happy to have the twins stay with us," Christina said. "You've made them so proud of your work with the women."

"I agree with your sister," Wesley said. "I'm certain a national meeting will reenergize your efforts, so go and join your sister suffragists in the South."

Emma told Aurelia the next day that she'd be pleased to accompany her to Atlanta. As they spoke about their upcoming journey, Aurelia said that the Georgia suffragists were rejoicing that a movement 'that had originated in the North and achieved great successes in the West was finally coming to the South.'

"It's high time," Emma said.

"Just think of it, Emma, two ladies from Farmington visiting the grand old city of Atlanta." She smiled and patted Emma's hand. "This will be an adventure of the highest order."

Emmeline Wells, Marilla Daniels, Aurelia Rogers, and Emma later took the train across country to Atlanta and found the city every bit as lovely and welcoming as they expected it would be.

On January 31, the women made their way to Peachtree Street and walked into a packed house at Atlanta's De Give's Grand Opera House. The building had been completed only a few years ago. A few of the ladies at the entrance said proudly that this site was the "first Atlanta stage to boast incandescent lighting, and it stood as one of the city's more popular attractions."

When the women from Utah walked inside, they marveled that all the entrances to the large opera house were heavily draped with gold velvet curtains and noted that the carpets were trimmed in a beautiful maroon and gold color. As they moved into the lobby, Emma commented on the ornate inlaid marble, and the spacious vestibule that was decorated with such a lovely tile.

In the auditorium, Emma saw a banner hanging over the speaker's platform. "See," Aurelia said, "the banner has been designed to portray the suffrage standing in states across the nation with the different colored stars representing the status of each state."

As the only two states that had granted women complete rights to suffrage, the stars for Wyoming and Colorado gleamed the most brightly of all. Emma crossed her fingers, hoping that Utah would be added to the company of those two states later this year.

The Woman's National Association flag also hung over the platform, along with portraits of suffrage pioneers, Lucy Stone and Elizabeth Cady Stanton. "It's all quite grand," Emma whispered to Aurelia.

"Indeed, it is," she said. "And haven't you appreciated the Southern hospitality of the women here? They're so warm and gracious."

Emma agreed wholeheartedly.

The convention began with speakers praising the reforms women had made in suffrage states. Miss Anthony, presiding as the NAWSA's president, called Alberta C. Taylor to the platform, where she spoke on the successes Colorado had made in the area of legal consent.

Emmeline Wells spoke about the progress of Utah women in claiming their place in the new Utah State Constitution and informed the audience that the constitutional convention was coming up in March of this year. In her report, she also stated that the women of Utah had not allied themselves with either party but had 'labored assiduously' with both Republicans and Democrats.

In closing she said, "There are two good reasons why our women should have the ballot apart from the general reasons why all women should have it—first, because the franchise was given to them by the Territorial Legislature and they exercised it seventeen years, never abusing the privilege, and it was taken away from them by the Congress without any cause assigned, except that it was a political measure. Second, there are undoubtedly more women in Utah who own their homes and pay taxes than in any other State with the same number of inhabitants, and Congress has, by its enactments in the past, virtually made many of these women heads of families."

Emma had long admired her facility with words.

At the conclusion of Emmeline's report to the Atlanta Convention, Miss Anthony came forward and put her arms around her. The rest of us were pleased to witness the strong support Emmeline received from a notable sister suffrage worker.

As Emma observed the two women together, she thought about what a lengthy history they'd enjoyed. It was twenty-four years ago when Miss Anthony had come to Utah to congratulate the women on winning the ballot, and that still great lady of suffrage and Emmeline were now fast friends. They shared correspondences, met and conversed at countless meetings, and Miss Anthony was an avid reader of the *Woman's Exponent.*

When the NAWSA convention in Atlanta ended, the Utah women went on to Washington, DC, to wait for the triennial meeting of the National Council of Women. Marilla, Aurelia, and Emma spent time seeing the nation's capital, while Emmeline prepared for council meetings. Seven days later, Elmina Taylor, Ellis Shipp, Minnie Snow, and Susa Young Gates joined them.

For Emma, the highlight of the council occurred the evening of February 15, when she and some fifty other women attended a banquet at the Ebbitt House in honor of Miss Anthony's seventy-fifth birthday. It was a lovely affair, and several speeches were made. One of the women rose and said that the friends of Miss Anthony from 'ocean to ocean, and the lakes to the gulf' had placed in her hands the sum of $5,000, which she presented to Miss Anthony in the form of an annuity.

All this came as a surprise to Miss Anthony, and it was obvious that she was overcome. Aurelia whispered to Emma that for the past 45 years Miss Anthony had spent almost everything she earned in support of woman suffrage, and since she was getting on in years, this sum would allow her to cut back on her lecturing and focus on writing her book, *History of Woman Suffrage.*

Thirty-One

Katie

Spring had arrived in Salt Lake City in time for the Utah Constitutional Convention. The delegates were convening in the new City County building completed this past December, and while women were not eligible for a seat at the convention, they were permitted to attend. Emma and I planned to be present for every discussion on woman suffrage.

Thomas had brought me by carriage to today's session, and as he dropped me off, he looked at the tall spires of the new building and commented on what a fine example of Romanesque architecture it was. "It does our city proud," he said, as I stepped out of the carriage. "Enjoy your day at the convention, and I'll come for you and Emma later," he said.

"Thank you, my dear."

Emma had come by train from Farmington, and she was already inside when I walked through the doors. We embraced, and she said, "I've decided this place looks like pictures I've seen of European palaces. I'm still amazed at its sheer size and volume."

"It's so much grander than the old city hall."

Emma and I went inside and found chairs just as the meeting was called to order. Since we had received a positive report on suffrage during the prior year's political conventions, we were surprised when some of the delegates from both parties began arguing against including woman's suffrage in the new constitution.

321

Delegate Brigham H. Roberts represented Davis County which included Farmington. I knew him as a leader, politician, and respected historian, but as the debates continued, he turned out to be the key voice opposing the inclusion of woman's suffrage in the state constitution. He said its insertion would make Utah a 'freak state' in the minds of most states who opposed giving women the franchise.

Emma and I were shocked as we listened to Roberts's ongoing anti-suffrage rhetoric.

He said, "The elective franchise ought to be granted only to those individuals in a position to act independently, free from dictation."

It was clear that he meant the women. I became so incensed, I rose from my chair and stood in the back of the room to calm down. *How dare he insult the women in such a manner!* I fumed. *Maybe the women of in his household aren't capable of acting independently without him telling them what to do, but that hardly applies to the rest of us. Has he met Emmeline Wells? Or Martha Hughes Cannon? Or Emily Richards?* I took a few deep breaths and sat down again.

The debates on suffrage went on over several days, and Roberts continued his attacks. "Let me say that the influence of woman as it operates upon me never came from the rostrum, it never came from the pulpit... it never came from the lecturer's platform, with woman speaking; it came from the fireside, it comes from the blessed association with mothers, of sisters, of wives, of daughters, not as democrats or republicans."

I wrote a note to Emma, saying, "I wonder if he's ever read the *Woman's Exponent* or heard Zina Young or Emily Richards speak from the pulpit? Perhaps if he had, he'd be a more informed man today."

Emma took the pen from me and wrote across the bottom of the page, "I agree, and I can tell you his views don't represent those of us in Farmington, nor the majority of his constituents in the remainder of Davis County."

One of the male delegates stood and made a similar observation, saying, "As you are all aware, gentlemen, the honorable Mr. Roberts gave no heed whatever to this advice from his friends, from his constituents, but has utterly disregarded it. They not being here to listen to his argument know only what they get through the press as to what is going on here, and it is very evident from what the gentlemen have said that their feelings are worked up to that pitch that they feel that they can no longer endure it."

While Roberts did concede that a majority of the people of the Utah Territory were in favor of woman suffrage, he said, "There is nevertheless a large number who are not in favor of it, and are bitterly opposed to it, and will vote against this Constitution if it contains a provision granting it, and you may set it down and mark it, because it is true."

I couldn't help but compare Roberts to Hector C. Haight, who had represented Davis County 25 years ago. He was a staunch supporter of suffrage who voted in favor of giving the women the ballot, along with every other man in the territorial legislature. *While we have moved 25 years forward, some of the men have stepped backward the same number of years.*

The discussion among the delegates returned to the fact that Wyoming and Colorado had already granted women the franchise. Emily Richards's husband, Franklin S. Richards, an attorney for the Church and a true male suffragist, spoke one day about the two states.

He reported that Colorado's United States senators Teller and Wolcott had this to say about woman suffrage:

"Women bring to the exercise of the right of equal suffrage an intelligence fully equal to that of the male voter. One of the apparent results of the presence of women as participators in political matters is that political parties must exercise greater care than before as to the character and standing of nominees for office. The presence of women at the polls is looked upon as an undisguised blessing, and if the question as to whether the right of suffrage should be bestowed on women should be again submitted to the voters of Colorado, it would be carried in the affirmative by a far greater majority than it received a year ago."

I applaud the comments from the Colorado senators and wonder if some of the men here have forgotten that the Utah women voted for seventeen years with no ill effects.

Richards turned his attention next to Wyoming, declaring, "On the eve of statehood, the governor gave public testimonials of the highest character in behalf of the efficiency and value of woman's enfranchisement. He predicted that it would be incorporated into the state government. His constituents replied that unless women were admitted to equal suffrage, they preferred to remain a territory."

But did the logic and experience of Colorado and Wyoming change Roberts's views? Sadly, they did not.

I found Roberts's response insulting when he said, "We are told that Wyoming has had woman suffrage for twenty-five years, and it has worked admirably. However, upon this model state there is a dark blot of shame—the evidence of the savagery of the men who inhabit that state, and that the influence of woman was not able to restrain them."

"What's that he said?" I whispered, turning to Emma. "Roberts is attacking all the Wyoming men as being savages and declaring that it's up to the women in the state to restrain them? Such inflammatory language. I hope we have no one from Wyoming in the room today."

Emma shook her head and said, "Roberts continues to reach up, only to touch bottom."

The Salt Lake and Utah County suffrage associations had written a memorial stating why we should have equality with men. The day the memorial was read to the men, the room overflowed with more than 75 women. Our memorial stated in part:

"The undersigned delegates to the Woman's Suffrage Association of Utah County, appointed to represent said association in presenting this memorial to your honorable body, respectfully represent that the women of said association, in common with their sisters throughout the Territory of Utah, are at present deprived of the privileges of American citizenship, notwithstanding the great majority of them are native born citizens of the United States. We further represent that notwithstanding that we are taxed and are amenable to the laws equally with men, still we have no voice or vote upon the justice or propriety of such taxation or expediency of the laws to which we are equally amenable with men.

"We recognize with feelings of gratitude that both the great political parties in Utah have declared in favor of equal suffrage. We have no doubt that you will keep the pledge and confer upon the women of Utah that political freedom and equality which justly and logically belongs to them as citizens of the most enlightened, just, and progressive nation on the earth."

After the memorial was read, Richards reminded the delegates that both parties had pledged their support to include woman suffrage in the new constitution. I was grateful that he stood squarely with the women.

Roberts then made jokes about the women's presence in the room which outraged us, and to which Richards responded.

"And now a word, which I do not mean to be offensive, in relation to a remark made by my friend [Roberts] which I was somewhat shocked to hear. It shows to what desperate straits he was reduced, that he must use an argument which he himself was compelled to discredit and cast into the wastebasket. He only gave it time to be noted down in the hearts and minds of those whom he wished to convert, then he discarded it, for he felt ashamed of it; and I must add that his shame did him more credit than his argument.

"He said, in reference to what he termed an 'invasion' of ladies, who came into the Convention in response to the hearty and whole souled invitation of its members, extending to them that courtesy; that if they could have heard the gibes and jeers that he had heard concerning them, they would have hung their heads in shame.

"Who are these ladies that have presented their petitions here, who have listened with the greatest respect to the remarks made by the honorable gentleman and by others who have spoken? They are intelligent, high-minded women, among the purest, noblest and best of the land."

With that, the room erupted in applause, and I may have clapped the loudest.

Richards continued, "It is my purpose in this discussion to deal with the suffrage question in its broadest and most comprehensive form. The first section of the article reported by the committee on elections and suffrage is elementary and primary. It is as broad as human nature and it responds to every possible demand of men and women in the complex relations of human society. It reads as follows:

"'The rights of citizens of the State of Utah to vote and hold office shall not be denied or abridged on account of sex. Both male and female citizens of this State shall equally enjoy all civil, political and religious rights and privileges.'

"It means that the narrowness, the selfishness, the passion and the prejudice of the long, dark past, shall no longer dominate our civilization. It means that men and women, equally members of society, equally answerable to law, equally responsible in taxes for the support of the State, equally creators and consumers of wealth, shall no longer find themselves subjected to discriminating legislation degrading to one-half the population and dishonoring to the other half, while the foundation of all legislation, the source and ground of all obligation and all right, is the same in both classes, all being created equal, all being endowed with the same inalienable rights of life, liberty and the pursuit of happiness."

Richards was a fine orator, and I was thankful he was on our side.

As the debates resumed the following day, another male champion emerged in the person of Orson F. Whitney, a politician, journalist, and academic. Emma and I agreed that he was a persuasive delegate when he pled for our equal rights, saying:

"All the arguments against woman suffrage, however plausible, however sincere they may be, are simply pleas for non-progression. The eloquent notes that have been sounded here, while they please

326

the ear and charm the senses, are not harmonious with the morning stars. They are not in tune with the march of human advancement. I stand for progress and not for stagnation. And I believe in a future for woman, commensurate with the progress thereby indicated. I do not believe that she was made merely for a wife, a mother, a cook, and a housekeeper. These callings, however honorable, and no one doubts that they are, are not the sum of her capabilities."

Emma whispered, "You're a physician, I own a detective agency, and we're both wives and mothers who cook for our families. Why must we be one or the other?"

"I have no idea. It makes no sense to me either."

On the morning of April 8, the section on equal suffrage which had passed a third reading was brought up again for consideration. "The hall is crowded to suffocation," Emmeline observed. But since the debate was limited to fifteen minutes, the question was soon dispensed of without much argument from either side.

The vote was then called on the new constitution: 75 voted aye, 6 voted no, and 12 were absent. Every delegate signed the document.

"A great victory to be sure," I said to the ladies as we left the building, "but the rest of the men in the territory still have to vote come November."

Emma

In May, Miss Anthony and the Reverend Anna Howard Shaw, president and vice-president-at-large of the National Association, arrived as promised to hold the first ever Rocky Mountain Suffrage Conference. They would be joined by Mrs. Mary C. C. Bradford and Mrs. Ellis Meredith of Colorado.

Early on the morning of May 12, Emma, Katie, and more than 75 women, most of them wearing the yellow suffrage colors, gathered at the train depot to pick up Miss Anthony and Miss Shaw. They took the ladies first to breakfast at the Templeton Hotel, then escorted them on a tour of Salt Lake City. Heading the caravan was a large omnibus that seated about thirty people, and Emma and Katie, along with some of the other women, rode behind the bus in carriages.

After lunch, the ladies progressed to Temple Square where a special meeting was held in the Tabernacle. Both Reverend Shaw and Miss Anthony spoke from the pulpit to an audience of more than 6,000 people. In her speech, Miss Anthony said,

"Justice is what every human being longs for, and therefore I today congratulate you upon this auspicious moment when the Territory of Utah is about to become a state, and the women who for the last few years have been disfranchised—not by the law of the territory, but by national legislation—will be restored to their just right."

The audience cheered her words.

The following day, the women met in the City County building to begin the Rocky Mountain Suffrage Convention that would last for the next two days. Gov. Caleb W. West introduced Miss Anthony, 'assuring everyone that it was a distinguished honor, and predicting that the new State constitution which included woman suffrage would be carried at the coming election by an overwhelming majority.'

What a welcome statement, Emma thought, looking at Katie, reminding herself that this was the first time the two of them had attended a suffrage convention together. *It's here in Salt Lake City, not in Washington, DC, which seems almost surreal.*

That afternoon a reception was given in honor of the ladies from out of town at the lovely home of Emily and Franklin Richards. Emma and Katie were pleased to be included in the gathering which was attended by over three hundred guests.

Later, Miss Anthony and her party held meetings in Ogden and Emma attended those as well. The ladies were honored in every possible way and met with the Hon. Franklin D. Richards and his wife, Jane, parents of Franklin S. Richards, one of the outspoken delegates at the convention.

The question came up one day whether women should vote on the adoption of the constitution at the coming November election. At this point, there was no indication that the women would be able to vote on the constitution, and Emma doubted that at the end of the day, it would be permitted.

A test case was brought before the District Court in Ogden, and the courtroom was 'crowded with attorneys and prominent citizens' to hear the decision of Judge H. W. Smith, which was that women should register and vote.

But when the case was carried to the Supreme Court of the Territory, and a decision rendered, Chief Justice Samuel A. Merritt stated that 'the Edmunds-Tucker Law had not been repealed and would remain effective until Statehood was achieved,' saying that he would 'file a written opinion reversing the judgment of the lower court.'

"The women must now, I suppose," Emma said to Wesley that night, "acquiesce with grace and wait to vote until next November's election."

Following that ruling, the tireless members of the suffrage associations sprang into action once again, as they urged the women to see that the men voted in support of the constitution. Emma and Katie did their part along with the others, going from door to door, canvassing their neighborhoods.

One night, after the children were in bed, Wesley and Emma sat on the sofa, reading. Emma put her book down, still puzzled by the debates at the convention.

"What's troubling you?" he asked.

"It's nothing really," Emma answered.

"I've loved you more than twenty years, and I can see the concern in your face."

"I was thinking about B.H. Roberts. The vote to include suffrage in the Utah Constitution was carried by a large majority of the delegates, and I continue to wonder why a man of his standing chose to wound his reputation on the hill of suffrage."

"We may never know the answer to that question," Wesley said. "For my part, I try to live by the words of Proverbs: He that hath knowledge spares his words: and a man of understanding is of an excellent spirit."

"Sound advice for us all," Emma said.

On November 5, 1895, the women's hard-fought efforts were rewarded when some eighty percent of Utah's voters, all of them still male, adopted the new constitution. Full suffrage rights had been conferred on the women!

Thirty-Two

Katie

January 4, 1896, President Cleveland signed the Utah constitution, making Utah the 45th state in the Union. The women officially have the right to vote!

When I read the telegram from a friend in the East, I danced happily around the room as Thomas walked in. "What's this?" he asked, smiling. He picked up the telegram and said, "So, it's official at last." He folded me in his arms and danced me about the room.

The children heard us from the kitchen and came in puzzled. "Mother?" Joshua asked. "Father?"

"The Utah women have the right to vote," I said, waving the telegram.

"It's no wonder you're celebrating." Joshua grinned. "May Elizabeth Eliza and I join you?"

"Four-way dance and hug," I said, motioning to the children.

"I think we should call this the 'Forrest Family Dance,'" Thomas said, breathless.

"Or," I said, "we could call it dancing in the Forrest." We all laughed.

"Let's go into the dining room and have supper," I said. When we sat down, I heard sounds of construction on the other end of the house. Thomas and I were adding two rooms with an outside addition that would serve as my new medical offices, and the work was scheduled to be completed in the spring. I had decided to open my own practice and work from home.

Thomas raised a glass of apple juice and offered a toast. "To your mother and her devoted work in the cause of woman suffrage."

"Hear, hear," the children chimed in.

"Thank you," I said. "It took a territory full of dedicated women to make it happen, but we did it."

Twelve-year-old Joshua piped up and said, "Someday, I want to be a doctor like Mother."

I looked at him, surprised and pleased.

"I love you, Mother." He stood and placed his arms around me.

Not to be outdone, seven-year-old Elizabeth Eliza said, "I'm going to be an attorney like Father."

Thomas smiled and said, "I'd be honored if that were your decision."

As the others finished their pork chops and potatoes, I thought, there's no time like the present, so I asked, "What would you think about adding another person to our family?"

"Are you talking about Grandma Rebecca?" Joshua asked.

"No, not yet. Your father and I have news. I'm with child."

It was impossible to misinterpret the look of surprise on Joshua's face. I was, after all, forty years old.

"Mother," he began, concern in his voice.

Thomas interrupted. "If anyone can make a success of this, it's your mother." Turing to Elizabeth Eliza, he said, "You're going to be a big sister."

"I'll be such a good one, Father," she said, excited. "Mother, I'll watch the baby and be a wonderful helper."

"Thank you," I said, reaching over and patting her hand. "I have no doubt of it."

"When's the baby coming?" she asked.

"Sometime in early July."

"Maybe she'll be born on my birthday!" Elizabeth Eliza exclaimed.

"What if it's a boy?" Joshua asked.

"It won't be," Elizabeth Eliza said with certainty.

"Why don't you and I clear away the dishes," Joshua said.

"It's my turn to dry, so you'll have to wash."

Joshua rolled his eyes, took her hand in his, and they left for the kitchen.

"What lovely children we're raising," Thomas said.

"We're fortunate they're doing so well."

"Are you looking forward to the inaugural ceremony January 6th?" he asked

"Very much so," I said. Inaugural ceremonies were scheduled to be held in the Tabernacle. Thomas, along with two of his law partners and their wives, would attend with us.

When the red-letter day arrived, we watched as Governor Heber M. Wells took the oath of office, to the sounds of artillery being fired from the hills. "It's glorious," I breathed to Thomas. After the ceremony ended, we walked to the Alta Club and dined on a delicious lunch of steak and vegetables, discussing our prospects as a new state.

A little after two p.m., we proceeded to the City County building to sit in on a meeting with our new state legislature. Mrs. Pardee was elected clerk of the Senate and assumed the duties of her office on the spot. It was she who signed the credentials of our new senators and congressman with pride and awe. I whispered to Thomas, "This is the first time in our nation's history a woman has signed the credentials of government representatives."

C. E. Allen had been elected as a representative to Congress, and the Legislature now selected Arthur Brown and Frank J. Cannon to serve as United States Senators.

As I listened to the names of the Senators being called, I thought, *Why not elect another 'Cannon' to the senate? Martha Hughes Cannon would be an ideal candidate for next November's election.*

333

When I broached the subject with Mattie a few days later, she'd already reached a similar conclusion. "Great minds think alike." She laughed. "Would you be willing to assist with my campaign?"

"I'd be honored."

"We're off to the races." She laughed.

Later that month, Mattie, Emily Richards, and Thomas and I attended the National Suffrage Convention in Washington, D.C. The evening of January 27th was devoted to welcoming Utah into the confederation of states, and Representative Allen and wife were sitting on the platform. The Reverend Miss Shaw welcomed us on behalf of the association.

Senator Frank Cannon spoke saying, "Woman is the power needed to reform politics." His words much pleased the ladies.

I whispered to Mattie, "You're the right one to make that happen."

Emily Richards also spoke, giving a detailed account of the hard work the Utah Suffrage Association had done to ensure our voting privileges would be restored.

"This is an evening not to be missed," I said to Thomas. "I'm so pleased you're here with me."

"I am as well. I didn't know what I'd been missing," he said.

****

By the time we returned home, national issues were becoming a hot topic for both the Utah Democrats and Republicans. Romania Pratt, Ellen Ferguson, Martha Cannon, and I became active in the Democratic party, while Emmeline Wells joined the Republicans, along with Jennie Froiseth and many others. It was a testament to change to see the two women working side by side in the newly founded Republican party; Jennie a long-time advocate of woman's suffrage and anti-polygamist, and Emmeline, a long-time advocate of women's suffrage and supporter of polygamy before the practice ceased.

One evening as I was speaking with Thomas, he said, "I understand that this November, women will not only vote, but several of them will run for office."

"I hope we will have several winners. The unreal thing for me is that Mattie will be running as a Democrat against her husband, Angus Cannon, a Republican."

"That promises to be an interesting race."

"The *Salt Lake Tribune* agrees with you. Did you see where the editor of the paper proposed a public debate between the two of them? They declined, of course."

"Of course. What a daft suggestion," Thomas said. "Technically speaking, as you know, Mattie is not running directly against Angus. There are five Republicans and five Democrats running for five-at-large seats in the senate, with Angus on the Republican ticket, and Mattie on the Democratic ticket."

"I hope we can count on the popularity of William Jennings Bryan during this election to win the day for the Democrats."

"He might help make that happen. He's very influential among the Democrats."

The following month, Mattie came by my office and we discussed her platform. "What is it you want to accomplish when you're elected?" I asked.

"I appreciate your use of the word when and not if."

"As far I'm concerned, your election is a certainty." I smiled. "Allow me to take my place at the typewriter and take notes." After I sat down, I said, "Please proceed," placing my hands on the keys.

"First and foremost, I want an opportunity to make a difference in the public health conditions of the people of Utah. I'd like to begin by creating a State Board of Health, outlining its duties."

"Something sorely needed," I said, typing.

"There are lobbyists who wish to abolish the State Board of Public Examiners, Katie, and we need that board to certify the qualifications of our doctors and prevent quacks from practicing medicine."

"Amen to that. I'm certain you'll have the support of the Utah Medical Association."

"I'm concerned about our deaf, dumb, and blind children, many of whom don't have the opportunity to attend school. I wish to sponsor legislation that provides them with a compulsory education, so they're not left behind their peers."

"That one is long overdue."

"I also want to get an act passed that will protect our girl and women employees throughout the state and require employers to provide chairs, stools, or other contrivances, where they may rest when not working."

"Which contributes to leg pain," I said.

"Exactly. I believe that's all for now," Mattie said.

"It's an excellent platform on which to campaign. Here, I've made notes of all your words," I said, pulling the paper from my typewriter.

"Thank you, Katie. While I'm here, would you mind having a look at something I've written?" She removed a slip of paper from her bag and handed it to me.

I read her words aloud. "Let us not waste our talents in the cauldron of modern nothingness, but strive to become women of intellect, and endeavor to do some little good while we live in this protracted gleam called life."

"What do you think?" she asked.

"It's beautiful sentiment," I said. "I admire your advice to the women, and I love your poetic words describing life as a protracted gleam."

Emma

Emma was reading another article in the paper about Martha Hughes Cannon running against her husband for a senate seat. *It seems that the novelty of the situation is beginning to garner national attention*, Emma thought, when Burt Savage came to the door. As it was a warm day in early August, Burt was sweating profusely and short of breath.

Emma offered water and asked, "What is it, Burt?"

"It's Butch Cassidy," he puffed.

"What's our friend up to now? Last I heard he was sitting in prison in Wyoming."

"The Governor gave Cassidy a pardon, and Butch repaid him by stealin' a herd of cattle six months later. Local paper reported that the Governor was 'not pleased' and the authorities of Sweetwater County want him bad."

"I believe Cassidy could talk his way out of a brown paper bag," Emma said. "Looks like he pulled the wool over the Governor's eyes. Where do we come in?"

"You might recall a fella by the name of Matt Warner, one of Butch's friends? He's right now sittin' in jail in Ogden."

"Did Warner commit a crime in there? I don't recall reading anything about that."

"Nope, Warner got himself into a gunfight near Vernal and killed two men he claimed ambushed him. After Butch come to visit him in jail, Sheriff Pope decided to move Warner to a more secure location in Ogden. Heard tell the sheriff took him and two others in the dead of night 'cause he was scared Butch might come for Warner."

"A prudent move on Pope's part."

"Yep, he didn't take no chances. Story is that the sheriff tied Warner's feet together under his mule and wouldn't let even him down even to relieve hisself. Warner figured he needed help, so he sent a letter to Butch, that his family got hold of, and showed it to me. Warner warned, 'Butch, we're goners if we don't get some money quick to hire lawyers.'"

"Does Butch have money?"

"Not that I'm aware of. He's too lately out of prison."

"Any ideas what he might try next?"

"Warner will be put on trial soon, and it will take a lot of money to pay lawyers to get him a reduced sentence. Wouldn't surprise me none if he were to rob a bank."

****

On August 13, Butch Cassidy and his gang robbed the Bank of Montpelier, Idaho. Within a few hours, Emma received a telegram from the Pinkertons stating that Cassidy was a person of interest, and they wanted to hire her as an independent contractor to go to Montpelier and investigate, saying they were prepared to pay her handsomely. *Guess they don't mind working with a woman.* Emma smiled. *I can take the first train out in the morning and be in Montpelier in a little over three hours.*

When she consulted with Wesley, he said he wanted to go along. "What about the twins?" Emma asked.

"The twins are seventeen and they can take care of themselves for the night."

Emma hesitated.

Wesley put his arms around her and said, "They'll be fine, and we'll alert your sister."

When they told the twins, they were delighted.

"When we return," Emma said, "why don't we all spend a day at Lagoon?"

"Let's go roller-skating there," Joyce said.

"And ride the mule-drawn merry-go-round," Wesley added. "And no, I'm not too old for that." He laughed.

"We'll do all that and take a rowboat out onto the Great Salt Lake," Emma said, closing her valise. "And remember, while we're gone for the night, if you need anything, Christina's only a few blocks away."

"Mother, we're not babies," Joyce said. "We'll be fine."

The next morning around 8, Emma and Wesley took the train from Ogden to North Logan, changed trains and went on to Montpelier, arriving just after eleven. They walked to the Bank of Montpelier to conduct their interviews, speaking first with G.C. Gray, advising him they were there on behalf of the Pinkertons.

Gray told them, "I was standing on the steps of the bank, talking with my friend Ed Hoover, when I saw three men ride up just before closing time. They tied their horses to the hitching track, but I paid them no mind. There were three of them, and one tended the horses, and the other two stepped across the street."

"What happened next?" Emma asked, taking notes.

"The pay teller, A. N. Mackintosh can take it from here. This part of the story is his. Mack, can you come over here and join us?"

His black and badly bruised eye is a standout, Emma thought.

Mackintosh began telling his part of the story. "After the two men came in the bank, they pushed me and a girl stenographer up against the wall and trained their guns on us. Even with my face against the wall, I could look out the window, so I made a mental note of the third gang member holding the horses."

"That's quick thinking," Wesley said.

Mackintosh nodded and said, "Cassidy entered the vault and gathered up all the gold and silver. There wasn't any currency in there, so I told him we didn't have any on hand. He hit me in the eye and called me a liar. I was scared what he might do next and told him where we kept the currency. He put all the loot in bag he'd hidden under his chest. It was over $7,000."

Then Gray said, "About that time, the desperado standing watch tried to order me and Hoover into the bank. When we resisted, he was ordered to hit us over the head if we didn't cooperate. We did as we were told and entered the bank. They forced us against the wall, and the three of them rode east out of town."

"Thank you for your cooperation," Emma said, "and your detailed recounting of events." Having dealt with countless witnesses over time, she determined that these two were credible.

"Is the sheriff around?" Wesley asked.

"He and his posse are still out of town," Gray said, "chasing after the gang."

Emma turned to Wesley and said, "If Butch follows his usual pattern, he'll have relays of fresh horses waiting, and the posse won't catch them."

Wesley and Emma returned home the next day, and she reported her findings to the Pinkertons by mail.

On September 9, Emma read an article from the *Salt Lake Herald* that correctly identified the robbers as Cassidy, Lay, and Meeks, reporting that the three men were camping in the mountains outside Ogden, ready to spring Warner from jail. The article also claimed that recently uncovered evidence showed the robbery had been committed to pay for Warner's legal defense, saying that the money was being used to pay attorney D.V. Preston from Rock Springs and his team that had defended Cassidy on prior occasions.

Preston denied the accusations, calling the article a "gigantic lie" and threatening to sue the *Herald*. The story was then dubbed "The Fake of the Century," and the trial continued.

My money is on the Herald *article*, Emma thought.

In the fall, Burt came back to report that Butch had been visiting the Allen and Matilda Davis family in Vernal. "Sheriff Pope had a warrant for Butch's arrest, and when he heard Butch was out at the Davis ranch, he got a posse together and spoke with Allen, who said that while the outlaws had been there earlier, they'd left," Burt said.

"Do you think they were telling the truth?" Emma asked.

"Partial truth, maybe. When the posse reached town, one of the men spotted Allen's son, Albert, sitting on the steps of the Antler Saloon. As the posse passed, he run inside lickety split, and Butch high tailed it out the back, jumped on his horse, and rode away."

"He's a slippery one," Emma said, shaking her head.

"Wait until you hear what Butch did next, Mrs. Emma. Three weeks later, Sheriff Pope got a postcard from Cassidy, now in Arizona. He warned Pope to lay off him, writing, 'I don't want to kill you.' It was signed, Butch. So, he's up and gone again."

"And out of our jurisdiction. But I suspect Utah's connection with Mr. Cassidy will persist for years to come." Emma paid Burt a bonus for his work, and after he left, sent an update to the Pinkertons.

****

Emma waited with anticipation for the November election and for the first time in a very long time, voted in the state-wide election.

340

Emma was exuberant as she slipped her ballot into the box, voting for the five Democratic candidates at large.

Early the following morning, Emma received a telegram from Katie: "All five Democratic candidates elected, including Dr. Martha Hughes Cannon!"

"We have our nation's first woman senator!" Emma cheered aloud.

In addition to Mattie's senate win, two other female Democrats, Eurithe LaBarthe and Sarah Anderson, were elected to the lower house, and eleven other women were elected to county offices throughout the state.

An incredible victory, Emma thought. *Not only is Utah the first place in the nation where a woman cast a ballot in 1870, but we've now elected the first female state senator.*

The state of Utah stands proud.

Thirty-Three

Katie
1897

Mattie was coming by and had advised me in advance that she needed to 'take a deep breath in a safe space.' Since she'd defeated her husband Angus for a state senate seat, she'd gained a great deal of national attention. Newspapers such as the *San Francisco Examiner* had requested interviews following her election. In the article, she'd called for a wider sphere for women. I was proud of my friend.

I gazed around my newly completed home medical office and thought about Doctor Axel who had now reached sixty years of age. He'd been so pleased when we'd named our child after him. He's "Uncle Axel" now and comes once a month from Farmington to visit.

I heard a knock coming from the outside entrance. *Must be Mattie.* I went to the door and invited her inside, giving her a warm hug. "Help yourself to pumpkin pie and apple cider."

"Thank you. The pie looks scrumptious. Is it your mother's recipe?"

"It is." I smiled. "Although I can never get the crust to be as flaky as hers was."

"Tastes perfect to me," she said, taking another forkful.

"How are you, Mattie? I mean, really. I'm not looking for the traditional 'fine' response."

"The last few weeks following the election have been a circus—although I do enjoy a good political circus." She laughed.

"I saw your interview in the *Examiner* and loved it." I picked up my copy from the table and read her words aloud. "'You give me a woman who thinks about something besides cook stoves and wash tubs and baby flannels, and I'll show you, nine times out of ten, a successful mother.' Nicely put."

"Thank you, Katie. I appreciated your help in the early days of the campaign and it was kind of Emma to assist as well."

"We enjoyed it. How's Angus taking defeat at the hands of his wife?"

"He laughs and claims it doesn't matter, but I think it's difficult for him."

"Mattie, I've been wondering what it's like to be the only woman in an all-male Senate."

"It's peculiar to look around the chamber and know I'm the odd one out, but that won't stop me from speaking up and introducing new legislation. You know my philosophy is that all men and women are created free and equal."

"I remember you proclaiming that very sentiment at the *Columbian Exposition*. What's your first legislative priority, Senator Cannon?"

Mattie laughed. "It still sounds strange to be addressed that way."

"It's wonderful, and incredible, and you can be proud of your victory: 'The first female state senator in the nation.' I never tire of using that phrase when I speak with others."

Mattie smiled. "It seems surreal, as if it happened to someone else," she said. "May I have more apple cider?"

"Absolutely. Here, let me get you some," I said, picking up the jug.

"The first item on my legislative agenda is to champion a measure creating a State Board of Health. I have my work cut out for me, Katie, balancing the demands of mothering my three children, my passion for public service, and maintaining my medical practice."

"Your plate is overflowing. Is there anything I may do?"

"I appreciate your offer, but you're busy practicing medicine and raising your own three children. How's the new baby?"

"Axel is almost five months and as healthy as they come. I had difficulty nursing him after four months, so we put him on goat's milk. You may have seen 'Gus the Goat' in the side yard."

"I did, and he looked quite vigorous." She smiled.

"Elizabeth Eliza adores the baby and misses him when he goes down for a nap."

"An excellent big sister who takes her responsibilities seriously. How are Emma's twins?"

"They begin classes at the University of Utah in the spring."

"They grow up and go away so fast. I'm only now getting used to the school changing its name from the University of Deseret to the University of Utah. My how our alma mater has grown."

"Twenty-five years since we began our classes."

"Stop, please, you're making me feel old," she said, eyes twinkling.

"No matter how old you are, you'll always be two years younger than I am."

She laughed. "I must be on my way," she said looking at the clock on the wall.

"Good luck, dear Mattie, in all your endeavors." We embraced again, and she left.

Now that we'd won the vote, and our goal had been met, the focus of the Utah Suffrage Association was on continuing education in the political process. Emmeline was busy speaking to local clubs and Relief Societies. Lately she'd been looking for delegates to attend the January meeting of the National American Woman's Suffrage Association. The meeting was to be held in Des Moines, and if I had to pick an heir apparent to one day succeed Miss Anthony, it would be Carrie Chapman Catt from Iowa. In 1892, she had addressed Congress on the proposed woman's suffrage amendment.

I had no interest in traveling to Iowa in the winter, leaving a young baby at home. Many others lacked the funding, so Emmeline went alone. On the day she arrived, the January weather in Des Moines fell to minus 24 degrees Fahrenheit, making our low of 27 degrees in Utah seem almost balmy by comparison. I didn't hear much about the convention until early February when I read an article in the *Deseret Evening News*.

The article reported that Emmeline had unexpectedly met her daughter Melvina at the convention, who was in Des Moines representing the state of Idaho. Neither of them had thought to mention their attendance to the other. *What a welcome surprise that must have been.* Idaho had recently become the fourth suffrage state in the Union which pleased the NAWSA no end.

Miss Anthony heard about the mother-daughter suffrage pair and invited them to sit on the stand, asking that they address the convention. *Two generations of suffragists. Emmeline must be thrilled.* As I read on, I learned that she'd been hailed at the convention as the woman "who has done more than any other person to secure woman suffrage in Utah." *There's no doubt of that. What a wonderful friend and mentor she's been to me across the years. I'll miss working closely with her now that our rights are secure.*

Thomas walked into the room and found me lost in thought. "Katie," he said, waiting until he had my full attention. "I have here in my hands an advance copy of the Utah Semi-Centennial Celebration program in July. Have a look."

"What a colorful cover, a nice sketch of the buildings and piers of Saltair in the background, with the beach in the foreground. I understand the commission has planned five full days of festivities and raised over $60,000 in both public and private funds."

"Some of those monies were donated by ten other states. The celebration is being promoted on a national level. The organizers are saying they want this to be the biggest celebration in the country since the 1893 World's Fair, and the largest ever seen west of the Mississippi."

"That's a tall order. I'm assuming the goal is to highlight the advancements of Utah and neighboring states over the past fifty years?"

"You are correct, as well as to emphasize that Utah was founded in 1847 with the arrival of the pioneers. There will be several events honoring the surviving Pioneers."

I leafed through the official five-page program. "So many experiences not to be missed. I'm certain Emma, Wesley, and the twins will want to participate, and I see that a portion of July 22nd will be at Calder's Amusement Park."

"Where we'll find several activities that will appeal to Emma's grown children, including trick bicycle riding and boating on the lake."

"Let's invite Emma and Wesley to join us for a picnic."

"Capital idea. I'm certain my mother will be happy to come here and watch baby Axel for the day," Thomas said. "I believe she'll be most interested in the first day of the celebration, particularly the public reception in the tabernacle dedicated to the pioneers."

"It says in the program that the reception will include a presentation of a pioneer badge to the 650 remaining pioneers from the original companies, saying the badge will be made of gold, the work of Messrs. Tiffany& Co., New York."

"That's impressive. The organizers are not skimping on quality."

"Nor should they. The badge is, and I quote from the program: 'to be given as an insignia of honor to the Pioneers, something to be handed down as a perpetual reminder of the achievements of their ancestors.' Emma will want to take her grandmother Phoebe to the reception."

"Mr. and Mrs. William Jennings Bryan will be present as guests of honor, and I'd like the two of us to attend as well."

"I'd be pleased to accompany you. The last day of the Jubilee will be Saturday, July 24th, beginning with a state salute at sunrise and a huge parade, the likes of which we've never before experienced."

"The day ends on Capitol Hill with a free exhibition of fireworks that promise to be 'the largest pyrotechnic displays ever seen in the United States, consisting of brilliant illuminations, thousands of Roman candles, rockets, bombshells, tourbillions, and whirlwinds."

"Imagine that," I said.

Joshua and Elizabeth Eliza walked into our conversation with their crying baby brother. "Mother, I can't find a clean shirt for Axel," Joshua said.

"There should be a few of them hanging on a line in the washroom. By the way, Uncle Axel is coming this afternoon for a visit."

"Hooray," Elizabeth Eliza said. "I want peppermint candy!"

"He never forgets to bring sweets," Thomas said.

Katie and Emma

The spring months crawled by as the City prepared for the upcoming Jubilee. At last the day arrived when our families planned to gather at Calder's Park. Thomas had purchased a new summer suit from J. P Gardner, and he looked positively nobby, though I hoped he wouldn't be too warm. The day promised to be a scorcher.

"Time to go," I called up the stairs.

"Coming, Mother," Joshua said, clattering down the steps, his sister on his heels.

The four of us boarded a streetcar, picnic baskets in hand, bound for Calder's Park.

"Let's set up over there in the shade," I said after we reached our destination. "Emma and Wesley should be along soon."

"This is one of the best amusement parks between the Missouri River and the Golden Gate," Thomas said, local pride in his voice.

"I see the Hatches by the merry-go-round," Joshua said. "I'll go let them know where we are."

Emma, Wesley, and the twins joined us for a delicious picnic lunch of cold fried chicken, potato salad, and watermelon. Emma had brought cake for dessert. When we finished, our children were anxious to go roller-skating and see the trick bicycle rider.

"Wesley, what say you and I go along with the children, and perhaps Katie and Emma could remain here, so we don't lose our spot. The park is crawling with people," Thomas said.

"I'm game," Wesley answered.

It was fine with me because I wanted to chat with my friend, our opportunity for time alone having become far too rare.

As we watched them walk away, Emma said, "Our children are grown."

"Where has the time gone? It's hard to believe I'll be forty-two years old next October."

"Neither of us looks a day over forty," she said, and we both laughed.

"I was fifteen when we attended our first suffrage meeting in Salt Lake, riding in your grandmother's carriage."

"Ada was so angry when she discovered your absence."

"She was opposed to suffrage—that is until she voted last November." I smiled. "That's one change I wasn't certain I'd ever witness."

"Do you recall when Ada claimed you shouldn't become a doctor and suggested you try being a midwife instead?"

"I do, and now she couldn't be prouder of my accomplishments in the medical field. What about you? Remember the day you executed your first eavesdropping caper, using a glass pressed against a wall?"

Emma laughed. "That's when I first laid eyes on Wesley. It's been an up and down ride for the two of us through my miscarriage and his leg amputation. But you know what? At the end of the day, I'm happy with where we find ourselves today."

"You have two wonderful children, and you're a respected detective with your own agency. Not bad, my friend. Do you ever miss being in Chicago?"

"There are days when I do. Rosemary's retired, but we continue to keep in touch. I'm willing to wager you miss Philadelphia and your time in medical school."

"As busy as it was, I see now those were the halcyon days of my youth," I sighed, wistful. "You and I had so much fun together at the 1876 Convention."

"It was the best. I also enjoyed doing battle for the ballot with you here in Utah. But sadly, there are still only four states where women have the right to vote, and they're all in the West."

"I'd hoped Miss Anthony might live to see a constitutional amendment passed, but she's seventy-seven now, and there's still nothing promising on the horizon. She's fought long and hard all her life for the women of our country, and I fear she may never see her efforts come to full fruition."

"You may be right, but Miss Anthony is a courageous woman who is much admired. She leaves a lasting legacy."

"I was reminiscing the other day about her first trip to Salt Lake with Mrs. Stanton back in 1871. I was star-struck when I found myself on the same train with the two of them."

"So much has changed, even our mode of travel. Remember when the train was a novelty? I delighted in my first ride across the country to Boston with Grandmother Phoebe."

"That was a grand trip compared with my first train ride from Farmington to Salt Lake." I smiled.

"Short though your trip was, the purpose of your travel was beyond compare. You witnessed the legislature grant women suffrage the first time."

"That was a thrilling moment that I'll never forget. You know I've never had a sister, but I have you, and I cherish our life-long friendship."

"Sometimes best friends are better than sisters because friendship doesn't come with family baggage." She smiled. "You've been a support since we were children, through the good and the bad."

"We've mourned our losses and celebrated our triumphs together," I said. "What a journey."

"One day, we'll be grandmothers as well." Emma laughed.

"Let's not rush that part of the voyage." I grinned. "I see Joshua approaching at a fast clip."

"Mother," Joshua said, out of breath by the time he reached us. "Father wants us to change our location; he and Mr. Hatch are holding a spot with the others. There's to be an illuminated balloon ascension this evening, and we want to be right up front."

"Sounds delightful," I said, gathering our things.

"Here, I'll take the picnic basket," he offered. "Just follow this line of people and you'll see us up over the hill."

The crowds were thick with those seeking a spot to view the balloon ascension. "I know another way to get where we're going," I said. "The terrain's more challenging, but the flowers along the way are lovely, and we should arrive ahead of the throngs. What do you say?"

"Let's step out of line," Emma said, smiling, "and take a different path."

*****

Historical Note

Sister Suffragists is not intended to be history. It is a mixture of fiction and fact, with events and characters that are both imagined and real.

The story was inspired by my great-great grandfather Haight, a legislator from Davis County, who voted to pass the Utah woman suffrage act of 1870. What was it about the women of Utah that made them suffrage pioneers?

As I began my research, I found the women determined and courageous. These champions won the vote, then lost it seventeen years later, throwing them into a new battle for their rights.

It's impossible to tell the suffrage story of the women of Utah without including national leaders of the time, Susan B. Anthony, Elizabeth Cady Stanton, and Belva Lockwood. They supported their Utah sisters and fought alongside them.

Thanks to the Utah archives, the Marriott Library Special Collections at the University of Utah, the Library of Congress, and The New England Historical Society.

A special note of appreciation goes to Better Days 2020 for their meticulous research on Utah suffrage, to Anette Tidwell and the Farmington Utah Museum, and to the Daughters of the Utah Pioneers.

I knew I'd found my first fictional narrator, Katie Leavitt, when I discovered several Utah women who were doctors and also championed suffrage. I was gratified to find that one of them, Martha Hughes Cannon, eventually became the first female state senator in the nation. Thanks goes to the National Women's History Museum, and Jennifer Baker for "Martha Hughes Cannon," and to *The Contributions of Medical Women During the First Fifty Years in Utah*, Keith Calvin Terry

The second fictional narrator, Emma Gregory, is both an avowed suffragist and a Pinkerton detective in the Utah Territory. The Pinkertons were one of the few organizations at the time who employed both women and male minorities. I enjoyed researching the history of the agency and reading related books such as *Pinkerton's Women* by C.A. Asbrey.

Select Sources

History of Woman Suffrage by Susan B Anthony, Chapter 66 Utah

Champions for Change, Naomi Watts, Katherine Kitterman

Various issues of the *Woman's Exponent* newspaper that was written, edited and published entirely by women, beginning in 1872

Battle for the Ballot, Carol Cornwall Madsen

The First Fifty Years of Relief Society, multiple authors

Heart Throbs of the West, Volume 5, Kate B Carter

Tales of Triumph, Daughters of the Utah Pioneers, 2019

"Lula Greene Richards: Utah's First Woman Editor," BYU studies quarterly, Vol. 21

An Advocate for Women, Emmeline B Wells, by Carol Cornwall Madsen

Emmeline B. Wells diary

The Life and Labors of Eliza R. Snow

Patty Sessions journal

Philadelphia's 1876 Centennial Exhibition, Linda P Gross, Theresa R. Snyder

Lucretia Mott Speaks, The Essential Speeches and Sermons, edited by the University of Illinois Church Historian's Press

"The Constitutional Rights of The Women of The United States." Address Before The International Council Of Women, Washington, D. C., March 30, 1888, Isabella Beecher Hooker

"The Northampton National Bank Heist"

Butch Cassidy My Uncle, A Family Portrait, Bill Betenson

"1893 Expo: Magic of the White City" (television documentary)

The Women's Suffrage Movement in Georgia, Elizabeth Stephens Summerlin

Utah, Constitutional Convention, 1895, "Official Report of the Proceedings and Debates"

My Farmington: A history of Farmington, Utah, 1847-1976, Margaret Steed Hess

The Book of the Pioneers, volume 2

"A Place to Sing and Pray: A Story of Faith" by Shauna Gibby

Key Historical Figures

The Women

Sarah M. Kimball,
strong-willed President

Eliza R. Snow,
General President of the Relief Societies

Seraph Young,
the first woman in the nation to vote

Susan B. Anthony,
national champion for women's rights

Elizabeth Cady Stanton,
American suffragist and social activist

Emeline B. Wells,
newspaper editor and suffrage leader

Belva Lockwood,
American attorney and suffrage advocate

Fanny Brooks,
determined businesswoman

Aurelia Rogers,
active suffragist and founder of the Primary

Dr. Ellen B. Ferguson,
mass protest speaker and delegate

Jennie Froiseth,
organizer of the Anti-Polygamy Society

Isabella Beecher Hooker,
national suffrage leader and lecturer

Dr. Romania Pratt,
first Utah woman doctor and suffragist

Mary Isabella Horne,
organizer and speaker

Dr. Ellis Shipp,
early doctor and bold suffrage speaker

Emily S. Richards,
organizer of the Utah Suffrage Association

Zina D. H. Young
Suffrage advocate and religious leader

Dr. Martha Hughes Cannon,
first female state senator in the nation

Male Suffrage Champions

Hector C. Haight,
legislator and founder of Farmington, Utah

Abram Hatch,
legislator who sponsored the 1870 suffrage bill

Franklin S. Richards,
attorney and legislator

Orson F. Whitney,
Salt Lake City Council and Utah state legislator

Acknowledgements

I'm grateful to Soni Rice, an extraordinary editor and friend who believed in the project even before I did.

Deep appreciaion goes to my sister-in-law Marcia Nielson for assisting with the research, reading countless drafts, and supporting me from beginning to end.

To Dana Tolbert for the beautiful cover she created after patiently brainstorming ideas for months. You are a talent.

To my niece Amelia Nielson-Stowell for her invaluable editorial polish.

To my amazing beta readers: Lori Wynne, Lori Nebeker, Susan Gant, Barbara Thompson, and Toni Bellon. I couldn't have done it without you ladies.

Thanks to Will Robertson for final edits, website creation, and design advice.

To Dodie Truman Stallcup for walking me through post-production steps.

To family members: Shirley Carmack, Norm Nielson, and Brent Nielson for their support. Last, but not least, to my daughter Alicia who listened to me talk aloud about my characters even when she didn't want to.

It takes a village to write a book.

CPSIA information can be obtained
at www.ICGtesting.com
Printed in the USA
FSHW011629200220

9 780984 864539